BLOOD AND SHADOWS

JP ROTH

Black Rose Writing | Texas

©2021 by JP Roth
All rights reserved. No part of this book may be reproduced, stored in a retrieval system or transmitted in any form or by any means without the prior written permission of the publishers, except by a reviewer who may quote brief passages in a review to be printed in a newspaper, magazine or journal.

The author grants the final approval for this literary material.

First printing

This is a work of fiction. Names, characters, businesses, places, events, and incidents are either the products of the author's imagination or used in a fictitious manner. Any resemblance to actual persons, living or dead, or actual events is purely coincidental.

ISBN: 978-1-68433-778-1
PUBLISHED BY BLACK ROSE WRITING
www.blackrosewriting.com

Printed in the United States of America
Suggested Retail Price (SRP) $19.95

Blood and Shadows is printed in Baskerville

*As a planet-friendly publisher, Black Rose Writing does its best to eliminate unnecessary waste to reduce paper usage and energy costs, while never compromising the reading experience. As a result, the final word count vs. page count may not meet common expectations.

This book is dedicated to my wonderful lover, husband and friend. I have loved you through all my lives, you are the prince in all my tales.

Special thanks to Stephanie Hansen for the time and effort she put into this manuscript. Thank you for putting up with all my crazy questions, and always being there to help. As always none of this would be anything without you.

Special thanks to Regan Rothe, David King, and the wonderful souls at Black Rose Writing for going another round with all my make believe.

BLOOD AND SHADOWS

DIARY ENTRY — HANAKA OF TRANSYLVANIA

*Fair*haven *is a strange, magical land. I find myself enthralled by the constant rain. Always in my dreams, I hear the persistent patter. We found a house yesterday. Lillianna hates it. She told me it's a cold place filled with crying spirits. I see it as a sanctuary. Our need for immediate shelter was great—my options limited. Lillianna will come to love it; I know she will. There is peace here. The folk in this place are not kind, we must mind our actions—or I fear we will taste the flames yet again. I am tired of burning at the stake. I will try to blend in. I do not know if I can—but I will try for— the twins. Today they were born, beautiful, perfect girls, my precious priestess, and her fiery protector.*

I brought them into this world, on a stone altar in the center of a dozen long-stemmed candles—in the middle of a graveyard. The spot, like the house, was not my choice. Lillianna refused to move once she went into labor, any cajoling on my part was rejected. I did what I must. Today was darker than usual. I smelled the dripping turquoise wax falling on the black soil. I stood in the center of the candles, spread my arms, and lifted my head to the blue cratered moon. I recited the chant I learned so many millennia ago: 'Inciatashmum mes vector calla.'

Lillianna climbed up on the altar. Her screams drowned out my voice. I took my knife and used it to slice my wrist. The skin peeled back; blood poured onto Lillianna's lips. Lillianna grabbed my hand; her face was twisted in pain.

"You swear this will not harm my girls?" she asked me. I could not swear, not really. Even after all this time, I do not know the full repercussions of my actions.

"It will not harm them, I swear it." I said this, hoping I did not lie. "I must place this soul inside of Cara's body, or she will die, and it will all be for naught."

"You wouldn't lie to me, would you?" Lillianna asked me, I had to struggle not to drop my eyes.

"I would not lie to you, sister," I promised her.

"If the soul of this Arias is truly cursed, you will in essence be condemning my daughter to death," screamed Lillianna over a contracted gasp.

"I am giving her everything she needs to stay alive. If she is brave and true, she will live," I said. It was not good enough for Lillianna.

"What if she isn't?" asked Lillianna, I had no more broken answers.

I had to tell her the whole truth. "Arias will return, because Aphrodite ordered her to do so, by her own will, by her own promise, Arias is bound to her word. Merging Arias with the soul of your daughter, Cara, is her best and only protection. If I don't save her life, the world—as the humans know it—will be forever changed."

I finished speaking and begged her to lie back and close her eyes. Transferring Arias's soul posed little difficulty. I have carried her essence near my heart these many years. If I do not do this, then they will return. If they return—Ares, and his golden goddess of love—their revenge will break the world.

CHAPTER I

SPARTA, MARCH 14TH, 1202 BCE
SPLIT SOULS

My name is Cara Wynter, and I am lost in the past as Andi's spell continues.

The golden room where I died was far beneath me, even the goddess who had killed me seemed to fade away. For a little while I floated, free of the world and all its strange pain. It was difficult to stay alert to Draken's present because time now moved quite differently for me. It was the raindrops falling through my opaque body that snapped me back to whatever fresh reality imprisoned me. Pluto nickered at the space in the air that held a shimmer of me. I lifted my hand and little white wisps of air followed it. I meant to stroke his glossy nose, but it was useless—my hand passed through the horse like I was made of water and light.

If souls could sigh, mine did. Colors dimmed and it grew increasingly difficult to stay close to my body. Pluto screamed, I did not start—just floated alongside him, listless and lost. His hooves broke through the base of the clouds, smacking audibly against the unshed raindrops. To the east, just a little below where the sun would rise, an enormous, hazy forest slumbered fitfully, the tree line wavering dizzily under its cloak of night. I saw exactly where the white owl—still circling our heads with long, fluid strokes of its effervescent wings—had taken us. Arias knew everything there was to know about Dengora—now so did I. In a way we were still one, I was part of her, and she was a part of me, yet we were also divided. I was Cara— separated from the soul of the dying girl on the ground, and through my own misty eyes— I saw it all. Her perspective and mine, even at times—Draken, my Drake, who still held Arias and that piece of me in his arms. I felt it all too, as if I were holding each of their hands, rather than floating beside them, lost and listless as a misplaced sigh.

Dengora was a place of old magic, where creatures of myth might walk but no ruling gods could enter. A faraway place referred to in children's bedtime stories, a world of pure fantasy said to have once sheltered the body of Megara while Hercules went down to the depths of Hades to battle for her soul.

Pluto landed with graceful speed in a small clearing of white daisies, boarding the dense tree line like an old lace fringe. In the center of the clearing stood a lone woman, pale and luminous. She held her back ramrod straight, and cut a dramatic figure, head high, crushed silk skirts swaying in the wind. Moonlight touched her rain-washed face and form, gently highlighting the curls in her flowing hair. Her look differed vastly from the one she sported in my world, yet I would have known those silver eyes anywhere. The nettling questions that plagued me during the thirteen days of dreams dissipated into vapor and floated away. Standing here, outside myself wreathed in threads of another era, I recognized her instantly. Androsia is a beauty queen in any century, any world.

Pluto came to a skidding halt a few feet shy of her, sending up wild sprays of broken earth. Androsia yelled and threw up her arms. "Pluto! Down, you silly boy!"

"What in Hades are you doing here, Androsia?" bellowed Draken. He dismounted in a fluid movement that barely stirred Arias's dead body. He laid her down with epic gentleness on the wet grass and swept a wild clump of curls off her face.

Andi broke free of her shock and knelt beside us. "Oh, Draken," she cried. "Is that the girl you love? Is she dead?"

"Yes," he said, his toneless voice drenched in unshed tears. "What in Zeus's name are you doing here Androsia?"

"I don't know," she wailed. "Ares came to my chambers not an hour ago. Told me, in an extremely agitated fashion that it was imperative I ride with him, he told me you would need me. Do you?" She sniffed and used a dainty hand to wipe at her nose. "Do you need me?"

Draken said nothing. I felt his desire to respond, yet knew he found no words. He did not know all of what he needed, only that he needed me to breathe, to open my eyes and breathe. Androsia threw her arms around his shaking shoulders and pressed her cheek to his neck. The hand not touching me went to her back, he held her, and they rocked for a time.

I looked at him, really looked, perhaps for the first time since I died, on that terrible, beautiful altar. The falling rain made little rivers out of the blood coating his cheeks and bare chest. The golden paint that had been my shroud still covered him from head to toe. His wind raped hair hung past his shoulders, cluttered with leaves and chunks of rock. From the swollen rims of his red eyes, it looked like he could have wept blood. Insanity—a byproduct of mindless rage—stamped a tattoo of horror on his face.

"I feel her," he choked out finally, lifting his head to swipe at his eyes, leaving a streak of teary gold. I thought it looked like war paint.

My very own trail of tears, my mind whispered, suddenly I felt very lonely. I wanted to be home, with Lily, nestled safely between my sheets, or cuddled under my purple throw in front of the library fire, even walking through Wynter haunt, listening to the hoots and shrieks in the wind. I wanted to be anywhere but here, not because I ever wished to leave his side, but because I knew something had happened—was happening now… something terrible my heart had no wish to remember.

Draken let go of his sister and sat back on his heels, swiping once more at his face. "She is still here with me," he said. "Hovering somewhere in the in-between, I feel her, she's fading." He looked down at his hands, balled into powerful fists. A small sound escaped him, I heard a gasp, then his shoulder shook miserably.

I wanted to say something, tell him I was here, touching him, seeing him, but couldn't, so I did nothing.

"The mists!" whispered Androsia, horrified. "That's where Aphrodite sends the women after they die… I've heard the stories."

"I know the damn stories!" Draken's raw voice broke. "If ever I see that goddess again, I will kill her where she stands. Zeus may do his worst." He turned and grabbed Androsia's shoulders, a ferocious snarl twisting his handsome mouth.

"What happened to you, Draken? You look…" Androsia stopped talking, utterly lost.

"Never mind that now," he said, his voice tearing over each word. "You stay here and guard her. Don't let her out of your sight, not for one instant!"

"You're leaving me here? With her? No, Draken—please," her voice quivered, then broke. "I'm afraid."

"I know, Androsia, so am I. I would never ask this of you, but Ares is right. I think he knew what tonight would bring. I could kill him too. Kill them all!"

"Draken hush," cried Androsia. "You don't mean that. Ares loves you and you him. Don't cast this at his feet. He came to me in the middle of the night just to tell me the girl you loved was dying." Her recalled memories seemed to return a portion of sense, her rosy lips parted to pull in a gasp and her painted lids snapped apart, her silver eyes bulging like, bulbous, snow spattered ornaments. "He told me to tell you to be careful, this one means more to Aphrodite than all the others combined."

Draken's dark brows arched as she finally gained his attention. "What else did he say?" he asked.

"I don't know, I was so altered. He went on about Persephone, Gaia, and Athena, I didn't understand half of his prattle. He said you were under some hideous love spell, like the kind cast on Mother?" She threw her hands in the air. "Oh, I hate spells! Evil, grasping things, don't you think, if it's just a spell that it might fade in time?"

"It's not just a spell," Draken said, his attention focused once again on my pale, dead shell. His voice was flat as sheeted ice. "My soul died inside this girl's body tonight."

Androsia sat back on her heels and buried her head in her hands. "I hate magic," she said. "Hate it. Hate it." Her voice faded into the thud of something striking the wet earth. The sound made me turn and search the shadows wavering between the knitted line of trees. Willow branches thick in foliage blew through the air. They fluttered back and forth, caught up in the rainy breeze, I thought the snapping vines looked like jade butterflies on a string. As I watched the restless dance of the trees a

Centaur broke through the forest line and galloped directly toward our sad, strange little company. His head and shoulders were large, jutting out in a prominent way, regally framed by a mop of chestnut hair that flared around him like an aura of fire. The thick braids dreading the hair by his temples was woven through with crisp green leaves and thorny vines. His face had the features of a man, all except for the eyes. Those were too far apart and deeply slanted in a feline fashion. The pupils were a cold black and, in the irises, swirled a dark fusion of russet and amber. Across his chest and arms the skin was such a deep ebony it held a midnight-blue sheen. He came to a commanding halt; a few feet shy of my wavering form. His hooves dug deep grooves into the earth, and little chunks of dirt flew through my stomach. He stared directly at me and took a step forward.

Androsia gave a shattered screech and skittered back a pace, throwing up a hand to shadow her eyes, though the night itself was dark as pitch.

"I am Vasilios," the centaur boomed, in a voice that sounded like rushing waves, or kissing thunder. "King of these lands." His eyes looked into the eyes of my ghost, but his words were for Draken.

"What is your business here?" Vasilios cleared his throat and reached out to touch my hair. The hand passed straight through me. He seemed unsurprised by this result, around his grasping fingers my form wavered, smoky in the changing wind. The leathered skin between his eyes wrinkled in confusion. Somewhere above me the snowy owl hooted.

Finally, Draken lifted his eyes to meet the centaur's big face, but he did not rise. "I am Draken, son of King Menelaus, and Queen Helen, prince of Sparta. I humbly beg sanctuary."

"We do not offer sanctuary to the gods," was Vasilios's harsh reply.

"I am no god," spat Draken.

"HA!" Vasilios's shout moved the air around me, it rippled like a disturbed pond. "You are nephew to the lightning thrower," he continued, and the shadow of his dark shape drooped over Draken's shoulders changing him from young golden god to a creature who belonged in this place, one of mysterious blood and shadow. "His father caused the near death of my world, you carry his toxic blood, I can smell it."

"It is not my blood that needs sanctuary," Draken shot back. "Arias is the one I ask for, she is human and innocent," his quaking voice dropped until it was nearly inaudible. "Her soul is pure. I swear it."

"Aphrodite killed her," Androsia put in unhelpfully. "She is Leisha."

"I see," said Vasilios, his eyes said he saw much. Looking only at me, he walked to Arias and placed a dagger-sized finger in the center of her forehead, the wisps of smoke swirling through my ghostly form wrapped his hand. Hair rustling like a lion's mane, he tilted his head to the side in a quizzical fashion, and his eyes seized mine with renewed vigor. "What blood remains in her veins is thick with poison, and there is a knife in her heart," he said these words to Draken, but told them to me. His hand fell away from her corpse. "She is dead." He released a long sigh that spoke of deep exhaustion, as he straightened to his towering height. "We can only preserve a soul which still clings to life, this one means to leave. What do you expect I can do?" His liquid eyes passed briefly over Draken, his question—I knew—was directed at me.

Draken's hot lips fell on my forehead, he kissed me while his fingers wiped the raindrops off my still face. His lips traveled to mine and I felt all Dengora hold its breath. "My tutor, Leandros, often speaks of this place," said Draken, his broken voice rasping over my cold skin. "He preaches that magic living here can preserve a body and stay the full departure of a soul." Draken released me with one last kiss and stood up, his movements shaky, aged. He turned to Vasilios and dropped back to his knees. Respectfully he bowed his head and folded his hands over his heart. "Please do this for me, great king, keep her body safe while I go to my father and barter for her soul. Do this for me, and I will be in your debt. No matter the service you require, you may ask it of me. In any place, no matter the time, I will do it. Please," his voice dropped to the barest whisper. "She's precious, without her, my soul is blood and ashes."

Vasilios turned heavy-lidded eyes away from me and cast them on the kneeling prince. "Very well," he said. "I will keep her soul tethered to her body for as long as centaur magic is able. She is beautiful," he told Draken, still looking at my ghost, rather than her corpse. "Why do the gods always insist on destroying beauty? They never want the plain ones; only the best will do for them." Vasilios shook his lion's mane while something akin to the growl of a starving bear, rumbled ominously in his barrel chest.

"I will care for her myself," Vasilios promised, and bent to lift my lax body into his arms. He placed me gently on his back, careful not to jostle me. "I swear no harm will come, save that which is already done." His coat was smooth and slick as oil, my white arms slid down his sides like silly putty. Muttering a stream of soothing sounds which may have been words, but had no meaning to me, he settled my limbs, cradling my torso in his luxurious tail. When it was done, he bellowed out a shattered sigh, then turned and spoke directly to Pluto. "Take your rider North across the caves of Mur," he said. "The river Kokytos runs along our borders, follow it south. You will reach River Styx and the boatman," his dark, swimming eyes met my own. *"You should not be here,"* the thought echoing in my mind was for me alone, I answered him in kind. *"I am where I belong."* I don't know why I said that, but it felt true. No matter how we tumbled or broke on time's wheel, I had always, would always live this death, even if a spell had to pull me from my own time to deposit me in another. At the moment I knew I looked more like a drowned rat than a child of destiny, yet a thing in my eyes sparked belief in his.

"Perhaps, my powers are strong with humankind," said Vasilios in the same voice that rushed through the halls of my mind like wildfire. *"You time walker are something else."*

"Yep," I thought, *"that's me, always something else."*

Vasilios's lips parted in another deep sigh, I heard wind rushing through the bordering trees and looked up to see a beam of moonlight illuminate the soaring owl's pearl white wing.

Vasilios stomped his hooves and pivoted toward Draken. "Stand, half-blood," he commanded, the toss of his head sprayed glittering drops in all directions disrupting sheets of pouring rain. "Charon—the creature who meets the souls of the dead at the bank of Styx, will not let you pass easily into the realm of Hades."

"That is my concern alone," said Draken.

"Are you planning to go into the underworld naked and unarmed?"

Draken looked down at his tattered loincloth, dripping golden skin and bloody palms. He shrugged woodenly. "What do I need with a weapon? Charon will ferry me across the River Styx, or I will kill him with his oar." He ran trembling hands through his dark hair, making a couple wayward curls stand up. "And the soulless wear no clothes," continued Draken. "Tonight, I am one of them."

Vasilios rocked back on his heels and folded his arms genie style across his rumbling chest. The sky belched out a flash of blue lightning, and slate gray clouds scurried along its blackened face. Movements stiff from sorrow, face twisted in an expression so broken I knew it would haunt my waking—Draken mounted Pluto, barely flinching when the stallion reared up, screaming his own rage.

"Let the goddess find her power somewhere else," said Draken, grabbing a handful of Pluto's mane. "The needs of the immortals mean nothing to me. This one is mine." Together, Pegasus, and his rider turned away and disappeared into the dark night. One final, searching look in Vasilios's knowing eyes, then, I turned and followed my broken god into the unknown. If a soul could sigh…mine did.

CHAPTER II

ALL THE WATERLOGGED VARIETIES OF DEATH

Pluto lifted above the dusky rain clouds, and Draken felt a sharp pain spreading like acid in his brain. He was sick with dread and running mad with fright. In his mind he still saw my lips, lying slack and blue from lack of breath. In front of his eyes, he saw my own, milky from poison that slowly sapped their light. He remembered the way he had counted off the final beats of my heart. There was nothing in his mind that was not Arias—me. My taste…my touch…my words.

Draken had to bite back the urge to shout at Pluto, he knew the Pegasus employed each ounce of his speed. To him, it felt like we were going backward in time.

Finally, we broke free of the low, bloated clouds. The sky beyond was overrun with stars, color-soaked shooters streaking brilliance everywhere. The beautiful kaleidoscope only fed Draken's rage as Pluto bore down towards desolate grey cliffs sheltering river Styx. For an interminable length of time, the stallion cantered in the sky. The deeper we flew the faster the light disappeared, until the darkness was so intense, Draken could see nothing of the hand he held out in front of him. Beside him, my soul disintegrated, fast as the shadows at dusk.

Pluto brayed loudly, the sound echoed around us like the dark had substance to repel it; he blew out a long stream of air, it lit the world momentarily in a misty blue light, electrifying a small patch of sand. Pluto flew toward it, bracing his front legs for landing. In the shifting distance, I could make out a light green glow, throbbing vividly as a paper cut. River Styx, I assumed, and its collection of swimming souls.

"This is where you leave me, Pluto," said Draken, his muted voice layered by painful, unshed tears. "This is no place for you. You're too rare, my friend. I won't let what I meant to do pollute your magic." Pluto brayed out a snorted reply. Draken dismounted.

He has nothing to do with this. Draken thought, absently stroking Pluto's heaving nostrils, liberally stained with blood and gold. "It won't be the same," swore Draken. "You know I am only half the warrior without you."

Pluto objected in a long whine and stomped his front hooves. "I don't want to leave you," argued Draken. Pluto nudged his back, and Draken turned to press his forehead against the stallion's silky nose. "Go now, Pluto. Guard Arias's body for me. I will come back with her soul."

Pluto let loose a long, miserable noise and flapped his wings in denial, caution, or farewell, Draken could not say. He turned and ran in the direction of the smoky green light. Every stride he took, the restless sounds surrounding him morphed into tortured moans and blood chilling screams.

"Are you with me, Arias?" he panted, stopped near the water, hands resting on his knees. I nodded my head, not bothering with the formalities of a useless reply. "I feel you, in the air—I'm coming for you. Know that."

"I know," I whispered, wishing he could hear me.

Slimy, green reels of steam lifted from the banks of the river, and the surrounding air shimmered in the same slippery light. The sight of the naked, grasping souls chilled me to the bone, in a way they had not done in Wynter haunt. Soon, I would be one of them, forever destined to swim and burn. It was an awful thought and my whole soul shied away from it.

When Draken was close enough to put his feet in the water he looked down at the lake, I heard him catch his breath in horror. His white teeth clashed together, his lips twisting in a snarl as he cringed back in revulsion. The stories were true, I noted. The river contained no water at all. What rippled there were the stringent souls of countless floating bodies. They leaked the fluid from their mouths and ears, and its color was that rare turquoise light found in the very center of a flame. I knew these souls; they had come to me on the hallowed grounds of Wynter haunt and begged me to follow them down. Here, like there, the dead were screaming songs of endless pain. Green swirls of thick liquid goo gushing from gaping holes in their tortured faces splashed up against the shore.

Draken took another stumbling step back. He would be no good to me if he placed even one toe inside that water. Bastard god, or not the human part of him would be sucked down in all the eternal, waterlogged varieties of death.

I heard muted shouts and saw stone arches towering in the distance, their curved, rocky bodies wreathed in fluffy mists, coloring the horizon in the muted hues of a stormy rainbow. I felt myself sink in the spell of the place. Draken could see the lonely Elysian fields of death stretching out in the distance, wide, empty spaces full of grey, limping souls destined to wander forever under the shadow of Hades's lair.

"I swear I won't leave you in this place," whispered Draken, and I knew he told the truth, the boy Arias had met thirteen days ago, the boy who cared about nothing, now walked into hell as a man who would gladly die for me. For us. It was a strange and powerful knowledge.

A threadbare, keening voice seeped through the air like a dark virus injected in a swollen vein. "I am Charon, guardian of the gate. Who summons me?"

Draken pulled himself to his full height. *"I am Draken, Son of Hades!"* he shouted. His voice made ripples in the moving light.

Charon looked at him curiously, tilting his head like a confused bird.

"You are yet alive, Draken son of Hades," replied Charon. In the middle of the churning mist Draken could make out the shape of a boat moving over the waters. The base of the thing was streaked by the same pale green slime flowing from the writhing souls. This small detail stood out to Draken as the boat appeared to make no contact with the churning surface; rather it floated through the air, light as restless leaves on a winter wind. Violet mists wrapped the dilapidated sides of the old boat, it seemed the mists alone pushed the vessel forward. Charon stood at the boat's helm. He wore a dark cloak that made me think of drug fueled raves and post-apocalyptic wardrobes. I smelled the tang of cold blood, saw the shadows that rode the wind behind him. The tattered edges of the dusky cloth flapped limply against his hollow face. The creature stroked his oar in and out of the river, when the oar entered the writhing slime of green souls, the stuff splashed up, mimicking boiling mud.

"Where is your payment for passage, living creature?" Charon called out, his voice bore only the palest resemblance to human sound, more like colliding boulders, or screeching tires.

"I have no payment. I seek an audience with my father."

The mists placed the boat against the shore. The shattered pieces of wood holding the thing together looked like they had been attached with spindle thread, either that, or a giant spider had aided in its construction. Large, splintered planks swayed against each other, clanking noisily in the night. Draken walked forward, stopping when he was two inches from the decrepit hull.

"Give me passage, I will see you paid on my return," Draken swore.

"That's not how it works, oh unfortunate son of Hades," cawed Charon. "You must place a coin in my hand, or my oar does not move…the lake must feel the oar, and the oar must feel my bones. There's no crossing without me."

Charon glided toward, the wind whipped around us, and my soul gagged. Draken had several choice remarks for the stench flowing off the creature—to me the smell was worse than all the rot in the world combined.

Charon lifted his trembling hand. The skin coating the fingers had melted away leaving the bones looking parched and charred. A black fluid dripped from where the tattered joints gaped through raw tissue and muscles. Charon pushed back his hood. Draken jumped reflexively, snarling at the leering face. He couldn't help it. Where the face should have been, was a gaping skeletal wreck. The white bone around the left eye was so shattered that the jaw and nose on that side of the face had also been chiseled away. There were no lips, only open wounds to frame his mouth. That putrid thing was home to a few small, black rotting teeth that clung by threads to blister ridden gums. The one remaining eye was black all the way through, and it oozed the same muck gracing the joints.

Draken had seen ugly creatures in his life, they had nothing on Charon—he was death personified. Charon leered down into Draken's face and opened his jaw. The oily scent of disease wafted through the air as the creature breathed out a cloud of brown smog.

"If you cannot pay my fee, oh poverty-stricken prince," whispered Charon gleefully. "Then you cannot have her. There is no other way to Hades's throne save to cross this river. I know she is coming to me. I see her beside you, soon her soul takes its last breath." Charon pressed the remains of his nose against Draken's and howled like a hyena.

Draken looked at Charon's filthy, threadbare sleeves and the long bony arms springing from them. His right fingers were clenched around the thick wooden handle of his oar. It had a sharp column of slashes running down its splintered spine, and the end of the twisted staff curled upwards like an arrowhead. "My body must touch the oar…" said Charon in his dying squall, waving the strange looking thing before Draken's eyes. "And the oar must touch the water…"

"Or there is no crossing," said Draken murderously, and Charon laughed. Draken contemplated the creature, and I felt him smile. He continued smiling as he reached down and broke off Charon's oar-holding hand at the wrist. Charon looked down at his severed limb, then twisted his head up to the sky and wailed in agonized shock. Of its own accord the oar spun in the air, the broken hand still clinging precariously to it. Draken reached out and caught the severed wrist, he let go of the broken bones for a second and grabbed the oar before it fell, then swung it above his head and stabbed downward in one fluid motion. The oar's tip shattered Charon's few jagged teeth and exploded through the tissue of his throat. With a twist of his arm Draken pressed the stick further until he felt it bore its way through the creatures rotting stomach wall. Still smiling, Draken lifted the oar—where writhed the impaled Charon—and stepped onto the boat. It rocked sharply beneath his braced feet, Draken scarcely noticed, he was a man possessed, he had only one focus.

Draken twirled the oar between thumb and forefinger, looking at the twitching creature—arms and legs hanging exactly like a skewered chicken—listening to his delicious wail of misery. Then, Draken knelt at the boat's helm, and shoved Charon headfirst into the mass of teeming souls.

"You cannot do this!" screamed Charon, panicking as the bones of his head filled with liquid. Grasping hands jutted out of the water to pull and scratch at his face.

"You said you needed to be touching the oar and the water simultaneously…" mused Draken. "This is the perfect solution. Think of it this way, Charon," he continued cheerfully furious, "at least you cannot die. Otherwise, it is certain you would be down there rotting with the rest of them. I would kill you and maim your ashes if I could."

The moment he finished speaking, Draken forgot Charon completely. He swept the oar though the bodies, using all his strength and begged the mists for speed.

If Charon said anything of worth, it was that Arias's soul was dying… Draken knew it. A true death, or as Leandros called it, the final separation of soul from flesh. The death cries were in everything around him now, they poured off the fields as if cries were what the wandering souls harvested. Looming in the sky and spreading its twin shadows across the whole land were the fiery caves of the suspended Tartarean pit, where his father and the goddess Persephone slept—and the hellhound. Draken glared up at the slowly rotating rock formation. From his underside perspective it looked like nothing more spectacular than a giant stone slab with a string of thirty-three flat white stones, leading from the ground, into its cratered face. The stones were spaced a perfect foot apart, supported by air alone. To me, the stone staircase appeared too balanced to exist in such a contradictory place.

When the mists finally pulled the boat to a stop, Draken glanced at Charon—quite the worse for the boat ride. The rest of his face had been chewed away so the only thing left was the oar-smashed gums attached to a small white bone desperately trying to hold on to the remainders of the cranium.

"Sorry if it takes time to find your way back to the boat," said Draken conversationally. "I can't have you waiting on the other side to meet her, now can I? Oh, don't bother to answer Charon…the question was rhetorical." Draken pressed the oar down in the transparent sea of bodies, until only Charon's feet were visible, kicking uselessly at the stringy air. Draken watched in horrific fascination as the fluorescent souls pulled the madly struggling Charon ever downward into screaming silence.

CHAPTER III

They say it is a throne of corpses he sits upon
But I know for certain it is not.
Corpses are bodies that held a soul now gone.
These are blood ridden stallions of men, forgot.

It's a very strange feeling, being dead. You're everywhere and nowhere at once. You're in a place where every question is answered, yet oddly, nothing makes sense. I left Draken on the shore of Tartarus, though not at my command. A short time ago I was floating beside him, swaying in the wind like a slowly deflating balloon. For a single second, I thought of my body lying on Vasilios's back, and the next I was there, walking beside him into the moving sphere of Dengora, and the oasis of Mur.

While leafy branches coasted through my body, I realized I was in a world humanity only whispered of, barely even dared to imagine. I knew too, I was one of the few humans in existence ever to step on this fragrant ground.

You're not really human, though, I told myself. *Just a fading thought, a forming memory.* I studiously ignored my own negativity; the surrounding beauty was stunning enough to swallow my depressing thoughts. Every branch, twig, and creature had its own glow, like the underwater life in Wing Lake, the night Drake swam with me. At first, I noticed it in the wildly swaying grass, each blade a million strands of green, then it was pulsing in the hills who threw their faces back into the break between earth and sky. It poured from the trees floating at least six feet off the ground, hanging from the roots climbing down from tumescent trunks, swung vines fatter than a child's arm. The vines crawled from their upside-down perch, all the way up the rocky face of the trees, dancing to a silent music.

The sky too was different. Nothing simple as our solar system existed here. Six multi-colored moons spun through a swirling mass of tiny drifting planets, linked by roaring halos of stars. In the center of each moon throbbed a mixture, similar in form, to a burning compression of lava and oil.

Arias and I knew we had left the known world. We were on Centaur grounds now. Moving through the place mystics of our time called *the old world*—the land before the gods.

Vasilios walked through the long grass, alive with fairies and sprites. I could see lights shooting from their pores as they flew past my face with a speed that was almost comical. Androsia ghosted alongside him, her eyes wide, and mouth parted, hand clinging tightly to his mane.

"Vasilios?" I heard her whisper as she tried to bat away the fluttering fairies, without offending them. "Is she still alive?"

"What is that to you, princess? I don't believe you care if she lives or dies."

"I do care," said Androsia harshly.

Vasilios sighed, long and loudly. "In a way, yes, her soul is drifting. It will settle soon."

"Fine," she said. "Of my own, I don't care either way about this girl; she's nothing to me but another dead priestess of Enisis. I know I sound hard, cold even. But that is my world. I do however, care about my brother, this seems to be hurting him more than anything. My brother is the only thing I have worth loving. So, you're wrong Vasilios. Quite wrong."

At the end of her statement, the hard skin wrinkling Vasilios's forehead softened. Now that I saw him here, in this impossible place, he didn't seem so very fearsome at all. He belonged, same as the wild sky or flying trees.

"Yours is a terribly turbulent world, Androsia," Vasilios finally said. "You are ruled by creatures propelled into orgasmic action at the mere thought of mayhem."

Vasilios looked up at a tree suspended so far off the ground, the waterfall gushing out of its center evaporated before it touched earth. The distance between myself and the tree was great, still, the breathing Ent filled the sky—I couldn't begin to comprehend its enormity. "The priestesses of Enisis are some of the most beautiful, wise and innocent women in our world, each of their deaths is a travesty, and" he said almost kindly, "she is standing right beside you."

Androsia jumped. "Why would you tell me such a thing?" she shrieked, spinning around, searching the sparkling air for a sign of me.

"Because it's true," Vasilios told her.

"Sweet Cronos," Androsia shivered.

Vasilios growled. "Do not speak that name here."

Androsia, still searching the empty air rubbed chills off her upper arms. "Fine," she said peevishly. Then, "is she really here? I mean how can she be? She looks worse than when we brought her here, don't you think? Terrifyingly pale, she always was."

I gave my limp body a once over. Did I look worse? It was difficult to tell, was there a state worse than cold, grey death?

Vasilios reached down to touch my corpse's thick red hair. "I'm giving her my magic," he said, in his resonating baritone. "There is no greater healing than what rides on the winds of Mur. Here we are life."

"May I ask a question?" posed Androsia.

Vasilios grunted over a nod.

"How is it that you exist? I mean, there's no relation between this place and the one I know, is there? How were you created? Or have you always been?"

"That is more than one question child."

Androsia stomped her golden, sandaled foot. For a second I saw a glimpse of the girl I would meet in the modern world, thousands of years later. "Why does everyone persist in calling me that? In this place I am not a child," she spread her arms wide and inhaled the air that tasted like magic.

Vasilios said nothing. We walked together in silence for a time, listening to the sound of laughing nymphs swimming in streams running into babbling brooks. I focused on the grass ghosting through my invisible feet, it ran into a wall of purple wildflowers that crawled up the face of the nearest rock formation, like a weird growth of velvet. The fragrance in the air was unlike anything, rich and flush with colors I have no name for, making music I can never describe. I threw my ghostly body down into the flowers, breathed like it was my last taste of air. I was dead in a world of gods, lying in a place where my every imagining was true. Vasilios lifted my shell from his back and cradled it in his arms.

"I will explain it to you," Vasilios told Androsia. "Though you will not understand."

"I will." I said. "At least I will try," he heard me and nodded. He lay my body on the ground and brushed the clinging hair off my cheeks. Instantly, the glowing vines running over the ground wrapped my limbs, they drew my body down, anchoring it to the earth. Leaves fell from the trees to land on my face. My skin sparkled where they touched.

"If you only see it from the outside," said Vasilios, arranging the vines around my waist. "Our world consists of a single dimension; you must slice it open if you wish to see the layers. If you were to cut this world, you would find many layers, cut the universe, it would bleed dimensions. The ruling gods came from one of those dimensions, bored with their turbulent existence in the skies. They found this planet you call Earth and took it. They were strong and we—the creatures of this earth—did not understand the concept of cold-hearted evil. We were unprepared. We, the centaurs, elves, fairies, nymphs, unicorns, and sprites, lived in a world which fed off magic so pure, it gave whatever it touched unending life. There are others here too, the true children of Gaia born from the heart of the earth. Elementals. *Old souls*—the real powers of this earth. They are timeless; living without fear of death, for such a thing does not exist to them. They know the planets and their meanings, they can decipher past, present, and future in the stars. They fell to sleep a long time ago, having exhausted their powers and dreams. Man is dying now; they do not care enough to wake and help him. I believe they hope he destroys himself."

"You hate humans too?" asked Androsia, sounding like she might cry. "What did we ever do, except try to survive?"

"No," said Vasilios sadly. "I do not hate you. I do not agree with the ways of man. The selfishness, greed, their lust for blood."

"You could say the same of the gods," I snapped.

Vasilios smiled at my tone. "I do. I forgive humans for their flaws more than I pardon gods."

"Are you...?" Androsia glanced around again. "Are you speaking to her? Arias?"

Vasilios looked at me in askance. I shrugged, Arias, Cara, potato, potato.

"Yes," said Vasilios.

Androsia groaned again, rubbing away her chills.

"How did it happen?" I blurted. "I mean... how did Zeus win?"

"Zeus did not win," said Vasilios. "He could not have won because he is not like his father. Zeus has good in his heart—if you were to judge from a human perspective—even though he struggles to bury it. He has no love for death but loves to fight. He would never set out to conquer us, because he would not wish such beauty to die. Cronus, his father, and the rampaging Titans cared nothing for what they destroyed. They ravaged our world with winds traveling hundreds of miles a second, hailstorms and harsh years of frost. You see, we could not control them because they did not come from our ground," he shook his wild head, "not even the strongest of our magic could prevent what the Titans did to fragile life. Our world...it was not ours anymore, nearly everything we treasure was destroyed." He looked up at the swirling vortex of the sky with wide swimming eyes. "My kingdom, the kingdom of Mur, land of the Centaurs and Moon Elves, yet survived.

We could have fought back. Our magic is stronger, yet battle is abhorrent to us. So, only one choice remained. Lose our souls or lose our world. We were on the brink of extinction when the running thread of destiny split, Zeus destroyed his father. I would venture a guess our elementals had something to do with the split."

Vasilios turned to face Androsia. "The first time I met your grandfather he was covered in the blood of his cousins, hands charred black from his lightning. He had won the battle for Earth. I swore my kind would take no revenge on him for his father's crimes, if he gave me his promise that he and his Olympians would not spread their evil into the lands of Mur. He swore me an oath in blood and it was done. We saved who we could."

Vasilios leaned over Arias's body to touch her cheek; my ghost felt it. "I did not make the right pact," he said. "They still destroy beauty." He stroked his hand through my long strands of silky hair. "She will go to Hades," he whispered. "A whole world built to house the dead. Why would anyone come to a world of life and create a place of death?" He leaned his face down until it completely obscured the upper half of Arias's body. I heard him expel a great stream of air and realized the centaur god was breathing into her mouth. "Stay, child," he whispered. "Daughter of Gaia stay a while longer," he exhaled another stream of life. "Stay priestess. He comes for you. Take my breath and stay just a while longer."

I felt the contents of my soul shudder. Wanting to obey his command. Arias was too far gone, and my soul was passing. There was no more holding on for either of us.

Somewhere in the distance a Phoenix trilled out a long depressive note and held it powerfully. "I can't," I whispered. "Death is calling." I don't know why I said those words, except they felt true. He breathed another strong stream of air into Arias's lungs, her chest lifted and fell. His eyes found my disintegrating ghost. "Stay," Vasilios commanded. I almost did. There was something in his voice that touched me. Compelled me to do what the dead girl could not.

CHAPTER IV

Draken paused to catch his breath, the climb up the thirty-three swinging stones was surprisingly hard. The stones rejected being scaled, bucking, and swiveling when he tried to grab hold. His progress was further impeded by the irate dead who struggled to reach him, begging him to fight in one of their games and give them some sport. Uselessly, Draken tried to shake off their slimy, grasping hands. Men with more honor, sat on the sidelines taking bets against the shaky outcome of his mission. Among them he saw Achilles, Hector, and Ajax. They saluted him as a brother.

Keening fog poured off the Elysian fields obscuring his vision as he reached the last step. It hovered before the small mouth of a crumbling cave. Its curved, rocky face sunk deep into the iron and lava surrounding it.

I was back. Standing beside Draken, staring in wonder at Hades' rock—a floating world existing in its own atmosphere. The air was cleaner here, the screams distant now, blending in the moaning wind.

Draken ducked through the mouth of the cave. All around us golden pillars reached into an agitated sky, sunk into foaming black clouds rushing past a net of stars. Draken walked forward, no substance under his feet, only the same violet mists that ferried him across the river Styx.

The drama of my past life and violent death was almost worth this sight. I saw myself suddenly, a quiet, sixteen-year-old girl, red hair hanging in her eyes and a perpetual frown marring her face. She sat on the floor of Fairhaven library with a compilation of Homer's Iliad and

Odyssey open in her hands. I clearly remember how that girl felt reading those wild, unbelievable stories for the first time. Something had sparked in me that day, unwanted yet necessary. Looking back now, I suppose reading those words was what started it all. The strange feelings, the Deja Vu's, the memories and eventually, the dreams.

We continued to walk down the hallway to nowhere. I could hear each beat of Draken's heart, feel his pounding fear for Arias congealing into numbness. A strange sense of inevitability came to walk with me, and the walk was long. The distance of the hall could never be contained in the floating boulder I had seen from the outside.

After what felt like several lifetimes, and no time at all, we reached the end of the hall, where we came face to face with the god, I suspected was Hermes. I recognized his shoes and bowl hat, with their falcon wings. He carried a golden stick resembling some weird version of Merlin's staff, only with a rooster head instead of a blue diamond gracing its tip. Hermes looked exactly how I imagined him, a boy just entering the first draft of manhood. He stared at Draken through piercing violet eyes, leaning his tall body against the marble base of a huge stairwell that swung up from the ground in a wide loop, curling ever upwards until it disappeared into the strange sky.

Hermes gave Draken a jaunty wave and sauntered forward. He had sleek brown hair swishing over high cheekbones, and framing pink, full lips. He wore a long black cloak over a short toga ending just above his knees. He would be handsome—in his own way—if the whites of his eyes were not crisscrossed by breaking blood vessels if his skin were not sickly grey as my own.

"Welcome, prince," he said, in a high, cultured voice. He reached out his long fingers and slapped them against Draken's shoulder.

Draken stiffened. "I'm not here for conversation or welcome, Hermes," he said stoically. "Take me to Hades."

Hermes rocked back on his heels; his lips contorted in a smile gaining increasing resemblance to the snarl of a rat. "In the throes of death, they are greeted with all of this, beauty," he tossed around his hand to encompass the room at large, Draken wanted to punch him in the mouth. "Still," he sighed dramatically. "They yell at me. Everyone always just bursts in here in such discourtesy. Why, you ask?"

"I did not ask," spat Draken.

Hermes continued undaunted. "I do the dead a service. It is not *I* who killed them." Hermes raised an eyebrow, still rocking from heel to toe, his arms held across his chest, his chin tilted at a cocky angle. "I have carried many bodies up those stairs, a number of which died at your hands. Recently, a few holy men hailing from Aphrodite's temple found their way to these hallowed halls."

"You should have left them where they fell," spat Draken.

"Ah, that is not part of my contract. I take the dead to Hades for their audience, and escort them away when it is finished. In this task my immortality is assured."

"Eternal death," said Draken.

Hermes tapped his chin and looked down at Draken's paint smeared body. "You, great prince, are not dead, and I... do not think I will lead you up those stairs."

Draken barely resisted the urge to shout. "Then, I don't believe I find myself in need of your assistance." He gave a little bow and turned away, but Hermes called out after him.

"You will never make it past Cerberus without me. That monstrous canine bows his heads to none but his master." Hermes returned a replica of Draken's bow. "And my humble self of course, however," he said, clapping his hands loudly. "'Eternal death', as you called it, tends to have its dull moments. You are welcome to stay here and keep me company."

"I have the perfect company for you, Hermes. He is presently warming the bottom of river Styx... or what is left of him anyway."

Hermes's eyes widened and he took a step back. "You could not have harmed Charon. You are not an Olympian; you are not one of us."

Draken shrugged. "Go and see for yourself," he paused, shaking his head. "Poor soul, I never knew bone could disintegrate that quickly."

I watched Hermes tremble, his blood smeared eyes spastically alternating from glaring down the long hall to peering up the golden stairwell.

"Hermes," said Draken dangerously. "I am rather pressed for time."

"But..." stuttered Hermes.

"Now!" roared Draken.

Hermes spread his arms wide and stepped back. "Very well, very well." He stuck a long finger in his ear and moved it around in a mock show of pain. "I can't quite see the need for all that volume, she's standing right beside you."

Draken froze, I saw tears of rage rush to his eyes. "You can see her?" He spun in a circle, grabbing at the air near my heart.

"Say goodbye," chimed Hermes, waving happily at the empty air. "She is soon to fall." The moment Hermes spoke his words I saw the soul of Arias's come crashing through the break between earth and sky, in the same instant, my own soul took form, and the ghost I was, shot toward the ceiling of stars with shocking speed. I heard Draken's choked cry. Saw him fall to his knees. I began to plummet. Seconds before I hit the stone floor, my wispy body encountered Arias's falling form and we merged with a sigh, and together, as one, her and I fell into the net of glittering stars. It caught us, sagging slightly under the weight of our combined souls. Draken reached for me and the net drew me away from his hands. I flew back in the dizzy sky, then fell again. This time when my soul touched the net of stars I flowed through the gaps—the texture of my soul fluid as melting ice—slid down to the waiting darkness.

My heart bled for Draken as he watched my fall in the world of the dead. Even like this—no more substance than the green-grey mesh of my soul—Arias, I was beautiful to him.

My body drifted down, nearing Draken's bowed head. The second I was in reach, he caught me. I dripped through his skin. In agony he was forced to watch as his hands busted through my face and stomach. Hermes stepped in front of Draken, chuckling quietly, he took my soul in his arms. Against my will the wispy energy of it folded over his body, curled against his chest.

Draken stared at the shadows of my long lashes against my cheek, my dry hair swaying in the invisible wind. Save that small movement, there was nothing. No heartbeat, not even the barest hint of breath rising from my chest. My soul was a sleeping shadow, a faulty reflection of what I— what we had once been.

"You cannot have her, Draken," said Hermes, drawing me close. "Hades will decide her fate. Until it is settled, she is untouchable in death as she was in life."

"She was not untouchable in life," said Draken haltingly. "I touched her. She is mine!"

Hermes turned and sauntered off toward the staircase, he placed his sandaled foot on the first step, under his foot the stone rippled like water. "That," he called over his shoulder, "is presently up for extensive debate."

Draken laid a hard hand on Hermes's arm, firmly preventing his progress. "You will take me Hermes, the same way you do the others."

"Or what?" Hermes scoffed, tossing his pretty head in the air. "You can do nothing to hurt me, Prince of Sparta. I am a true immortal. I would be impervious to the weight of your… umm," he gave Draken's naked body a look. "Fists, I suppose, since you carry no other weapon."

"We could give it a try," said Draken softly.

Hermes sniffed, offended. "You know what, I've changed my mind. And not because of your monosyllabic threats."

"Why then?" asked Draken.

"Because" Hermes stroked my hair, I could hear the grind of Draken's back teeth. "I think this will divert me greatly." Hermes released a squeaking giggle. "Yes, I think it will be very diverting indeed."

Draken snorted. "Whatever it takes," his voice mocked. "True immortal."

Hermes fell into a pouting silence, his footfalls heavy on each step. Draken followed close behind. I watched him walk the long stairway like a sleepwalker, moving in dreamlike concentration; now he was not battling some new horror, or racing about like a wild man, he could feel the exhaustion of the drug throbbing in his veins. Draken knew Hermes would take his time on the climb, just to spite him. It did not matter; he would bear it so long as the smiling demon held our fused souls in his arms.

CHAPTER V

My rose I hold whispers to me like raindrops.
Gold brilliance in her face, and light in her eyes
I borrowed back from death what I could not stop,
But she tells me destiny has a motive, and again she dies.

Before we crested the top of the staircase, I heard the deep howls of Cerberus. Face downturned, Hermes threw my ghost a secret smile, then stepped proudly through the entrance of his master's den. Stalactites twice my height hung from the vaulted cave roof, their texture black and glassy, mirroring the rocks underfoot. I heard Draken take a deep breath, he coughed, inhaling sulfur, and wet dog, emanating, I assume, from the infamous monster lurking around the corner. His multi-layered heartbeat echoed off every wall.

Draken wrung his hands, then dropped them when he realized what he did. I could hear his thoughts loudly in my own mind. What if Hades refused to return my soul to him? The thought hit him hard. Now that he was here, surrounded by watery souls and rabid monsters, the possibility was far more tangible. Could he kill them all? Of course not, the gods possessed unconceivable powers. For the first time he considered the possibility of what would truly become of him if he were forced to let Arias go.

In the middle of Draken's dark reverie, Hermes appeared to buckle at the knee and stumble. Distracted, Draken missed his step, glass rocks crumbled under his feet.

Instantly, Hermes vanished from the spot where he stood. Arms flailing for salvation, Draken's body hit the ground. His face slammed against the hot rocks, they hissed scorching his cheek. Draken rolled to his feet, I felt the pain dancing across his stomach and chest from where the rocks burned him. Hermes was standing ten feet in front of him, wearing the same ridiculous smile. At his right side stood Cerberus.

I believe Draken had come prepared to battle a monster, but the sight of his father's dog was a jarring shock. The beast stood an easy twenty feet on four legs, thicker than Ent trunks. Resting on top of three imposing necks, three hoary heads focused their six yellow eyes on Draken. Cerberus's looked like a battle mastiff—wide sunken eyes, and a short, iron jaw—the sets of bared teeth were long as swords, grinding together in rhythm to the wet growls issuing from the three throats.

Hissing cobras jutted from his foreheads, just like the legends told. The forked tail was in existence as well, only the fork looked more like a mouth sporting small razor teeth, snapping when it hissed at the singed air. Huge fountains of saliva dripped from the sagging corners of the mouths, it splashed down against the creature's paws.

Draken took it all in with a sigh of resignation. In the way of the Igori, he closed his mind one door at a time. His breath turned shallow, his heartbeat steadied, and he reached the room where stood the warrior, hands folded over his chest, preparing himself to become one with the pain.

Besides Draken, Hermes and myself, a couple souls milled about the chamber, flowing in sparkling transparency, or chalky grey and rain-washed. On either side of the entrance to Hades' den two bodies stood tethered to the hot wall crying piteously. Colorful snakes wound their legs locking them in place. I could see the exposed fangs of the serpents when they sunk their teeth into the flesh of the two unfortunate souls again and again. Draken saw them and shuddered. He took a tentative step. Hermes stroked my hair, he lifted a lock of it to his face, and smiled into Draken's livid eyes.

"He is not among the dead, Cerberus," said Hermes, his voice a soothing sonnet. "You cannot let him leave this place alive." Hermes raised his voice, as if the ravenous beast needed clarification to do what he was craving. "Cerberus, kill him!"

I was with him then, linked to his thoughts, as if some part of me touched the surrounding air, and the molecules constructing it told me all. Draken had no time to react. My eyes barely followed the movement of the dark paw that seemed to come from nowhere. It connected to Draken's ribs, punching the breath from his lungs. In his tired mind, he thought it was almost funny, how the blow lifted him off the ground, and sent him hurtling into a burning glass wall. Sharp pain lashed his face and back. His body stuck momentarily to the rock as it sank hot teeth in the fibers of his skin. A second later, he hit the ground with enough inertia to send him flailing back in the air. Funny again. In my mind's eye—so connected to his—I saw him replay my body falling in through the net of stars, flowing through the small squares, that was pretty funny too…and the oar down the throat…? Priceless. Pure art.

Struggling to his feet, bleeding and battered, Draken was laughing. I wondered if he was in some sort of stress related shock. Draken watched Cerberus lumber toward him and could not stop laughing. Even this creature was hilarious; cobras for hair, a dragon mouth for a tail, and enough saliva to flood a river. The bastard son of the two ugliest gods in existence—what did he expect? Draken was laughing so hard tears poured from his eyes.

The paw took another swing. Even in his convulsing state, Draken saw this one with time to spare. Everything moved slower now, he saw ripples in the air as it parted for the giant claw. Draken jumped behind the blow, he landed on Cerberus's right foot, he sunk his fingers into the thick fur of the leg, and quickly worked his way up the side of its body. The dog barked riotously, trying to shake him. Draken held fast. When he reached the mountainous spine, he shimmied up the middle neck until he could grip both sides of the jugular between his knees.

The adjoining heads looked at the middle one in confusion, as if he were responsible for the man straddling their spine. The identical expressions of bemusement set Draken off again. Laughing, and struggling to keep his seat, Draken grabbed a fistful of cobras sprouting from each head. Cerberus barked and howled simultaneously. Draken yanked his arms toward his chest, causing the side heads to crash into the center one with skull crushing force.

Cerberus howled in pain, clawing at the ground, desperate to get the offender off his back. Draken tightened his hold on Cerberus's neck and held on. A few cobras still hissed, the majority, however, coiled into themselves, licking their wounds. Cerberus made a final, desperate bid for freedom. He dropped his center head, and the huge dog shook from side to side, making the rocks tremble, along with Draken's teeth. Draken tightened his hold around the neck, Cerberus began to wheeze amidst desperate, gulping sounds.

"Yield!" commanded Draken. Cerberus bucked and shook. "Yield!" he shouted.

Losing air and consciousness, Cerberus yielded. His front knees buckled, and in unison three heads bowed low to the ground. Draken slid down from his perch, wiping globs of saliva from his skin, shaking off the final aftershocks of his unexpected laughter, and the reverberations of Cerberus's thrashing. Behind him the three heads mewled in unison. A wet nose nudged his leg, Draken turned. Cerberus put both paws over the eyes of the middle head and whined pitifully. Draken knelt and scratched behind the nearest ear. The cobras twined over his arms, licking his skin with their tiny, forked tongues. Cerberus lifted his eyes and kicked his back leg. His tongues lolled out and he sneezed happily on a gulp of air.

"Good dog…" said Draken, patting the middle head, Cerberus licked his arm. "Good boy, you're a good boy! My Pluto would hate you," he laughed some more. "I mean really hate you."

Cerberus wagged his dragon tail—as if other creatures hating on him was part of life—licking any skin he could find, still sneezing happily Cerberus lumbered to his feet. Draken hoisted himself onto the center neck and grabbed a handful of scruff beneath the twitching left ear. "We go to Hades," he told Cerberus. The monster obeyed.

■ ■ ■

Roses, orchids, honeysuckles and hydras, painted Hades chamber. The ground was cool blue glass filled with dozens of silver bubbles. Hundreds of rare blossoms bloomed beneath the surface of the glass, swaying in their crystal cage, screaming with the voices of the unheard dead. Above me the leafy sky glowed like it held a hidden sun. Pearlescent strands of layered snowflakes hung from the stars. Two beautiful nymphs sat in a corner by a violet fountain, devouring a large cluster of grapes and tinkering about on a harp. The sound of their sing-song laughter was just another layer of beauty in this place.

I lifted my head from Hermes's shoulder, surprised I could. Cerberus skidded to a halt in front of his master. Hades threw something into the air that looked like a skinned tiger. Draken jumped down from Cerberus's neck when the dog made a lunge for the meat. The jarring drop ratted his teeth, quickly he rolled to his feet, his pose alert, and hands flexed for danger.

Draken felt a gaze rove over his back, spine tensed he spun on his heels to face the god who stood three feet away, staring at him from eyes identical to his own. I heard Draken's intake of breath over the crackle of Hades's flames. If Cerberus had been a shock, Hades was a revelation. Aqua flames dripped from the ends of his shoulder length hair and poured from the tips of his fingers. A cloak stitched with a piece of the night sky hung from his shoulders, flowing over the golden braces adorning his arms and neck. His bare feet were engulfed in the same green flames, which had not long ago, flowed through a quiet Fairhaven night, in a graveyard of witches.

Hades held out his arms. Galaxies spun and thrashed in the palm of his hands. "Come my son!" he boomed in a voice of a thousand oceans. He flung his starry cloak over his shoulders and smiled at Draken's thunderstruck expression.

Draken said nothing. He looked away from his father, his yearning eyes roved over my limp soul resting in Hermes's arms, my face pressed again to the young god's chest. Hades followed his son's glare. I could not fully read the expression in the god of death's eyes, but I thought I saw pain bracketing the corners.

"They're always more beautiful in death, don't you think?" asked Hades softly. "An enchantment exists in the state, a purity, perchance. I did not intend to be god of lost souls; it was simply the lot I drew. I thought it would be a kingdom fraught with horror," he spread his arms, motioning to the majesty of his chamber. "However, there is still beauty, greater even for its fragility."

"I don't care about your lot, or your notions of beauty." Draken wiped his hand over his face, attempting to stem the surge of rage he felt at it all. "You are not my father, only my sire. I am here to bargain for her soul, nothing more. Tell me what you want, give her back to me, and I will be gone."

"Just like that?" frowned Hades. "Draken, you have come all this way. Stay and speak awhile."

"There is no time," said Draken. "I must be gone from this place before Aphrodite comes to take Arias's soul to the mists. It is not my desire to kill a goddess tonight."

Hades threw back his long hair and laughed. "It's like peering into a glass framing my younger self." Hades held out his hand, flames surged to the ground, they splashed up in swirls, before fading to haunting aqua shimmers. The flowers beneath the glass floor bloomed, and the stars spun in the sky.

"Come, Dragon," he said. "For that is the meaning of your name, and what you truly are. Let us speak later of life and death."

Draken ignored Hades's outstretched hand, he turned and moved to Hermes with purpose, the young god squeaked, nearly dropping our merged soul in his panic.

"Give her to me!" Draken bit out.

Hermes lifted his pert nose. "No. I won't," he pouted.

"Do it," demanded Hades.

Hermes rolled his eyes. "Fine."

Draken's sigh was audible as he reached out and gathered me in his arms. His hands were hot when they touched my neck, and back. I almost felt something, slowly, my tired eyes traveled to his.

Draken kissed my cheek and brushed his lips over the tip of my nose. "Arias. I have you. Stay with me, just stay with me," he said.

Hades placed his hand on Draken's shoulder, for the first time he turned and looked at his father, something other than confused hate in his eyes. Hades's hand roved to the top of my head, his palm touched my skull. *That* I felt! Flames rushed over my soul; the grey of my form faded to white. I coughed, sneezed, then opened my mouth and breathed in the longest inhale of my life. "I…" I stammered. "I…"

"It will keep for a time," said Hades. He touched my hand. "This one is special," he paused, staring intently at my face. "She is untouched. And she is…" Hades' eyes caught my disoriented gaze, he looked directly through me. I knew it the *moment* he saw me, just me, not the strange soul fusion we had become. "A strange bird you've caught here." Hades tilted his head, intensifying his stare, I bristled under it. "This soul is… split, changed. It is an exceedingly difficult spell, impossible, some might say. It involves altering time in a world held captive by it. This is a god's doing."

Draken was gazing at the color returning to my cheeks, the shine to my hair. He leaned in and kissed my cold lips. "It doesn't matter," he said finally. "I just want her. Whoever she is, whatever pieces I can have. Her soul is my soul in any state. I love her."

"Now *that*," said Hades tremulously. "Is something I understand. Come, you cannot deny me the conversation I desire. I have reunited you with your love, courtesy demands you meet mine."

Draken nodded numbly, not really caring where he went, so long as he did not let me go. I understood the sentiment. My hand touched his cheek, he pressed a hot kiss into my palm, and I shuddered. We rounded a curve in the chamber. Vines filled with heart shaped leaves streamed from the sky, curtaining a portion of it. A strange looking plant—more wild red curling vines springing sparkling flowers and raining gold and orange leaves— stood against a spherical window cut in the glassy rock. Through the window I saw a field of wheat bathed in a golden light. The sun set on the horizon, low and swollen, beside a blue corn moon showing a sliver of its enchanting face.

"This is my Persephone," said Hades proudly, pointing to the restless red vines. The plant moved, turned. I heard my own gasp. She was so beautiful, I thought then, if the gods took all the enchanting glory of spring and autumn, and created a woman, this would be she. The gold light flowed off the sunset backdrop and touched her. I realized the curling vines were silky locks of hair raging in a beautiful disaster around her heart-shaped face, and bare shoulders, trailing behind her like a woodland fairy's wedding veil. A string of green diamonds wrapped her forehead, and her wide eyes were shades of purple and pink. Gold freckles sprinkled her nose, her small cherry-colored lips wore a shy smile.

Draken bowed low to the goddess. My face pressed into his neck. "It's an honor to stand in your presence, my lady," he said respectfully.

"Lovely to meet you, Draken," said Persephone. Her voice was spellbinding as her face, something in her eyes made me think of Lily. A wash of sadness crashed over me. I was so far from home. So far from sanity. Who knew if I would ever return? Who knew if I would ever see her again? I was being forced to live in a time not my own, relive a death I did not earn, and visit a culture that should only be a fairytale. It gave me an odd, empty feeling, like I was forever changed. After this, who I was, who I could have been, would be gone. I would be something else. A child of fractured time.

Hades took the cloak from his shoulders. He threw it over Draken's naked back. The cloth flowed over his skin and I heard the thud of metal slapping against leather, watched the stars in the folds, shift and change. In seconds, the cloak was only one piece to a full set of glowing armor. The white shirt held clusters of stars, looking simultaneously impenetrable and fluid. The material of it all was indescribable, like solidified light. I touched his golden chest.

"One of my gifts to you," said Hades, inspecting what the cloak had done. "It is tradition for the gods to give gifts to their…ah…"

"Bastards?" offered Draken.

"Demi-gods," corrected Hades.

Draken looked down at his glowing self, took a piece of the cloak in his hand and rubbed the texture between his fingers. "It is truly spellbinding," he said with difficulty. "Thank you."

"The cloak, Vestis," proclaimed Hades. "It becomes whatever you need it to be." He walked to his queen and took her offered hand. I watched the world fall away for her. Hades leaned down and kissed her lips, she all but melted in his flames. He kissed her until the vines in her hair thrashed, and she giggled. Smiling and flushed, she faced me, hand outstretched. Draken took a step forward, Persephone shook her brilliant head. "No," she said. "Just the priestess. Put her down, child, I won't harm the girl. Never." She held out both her arms. "Never," she swore.

Draken's jaw locked, but he released me, and for the first time in many hours, I felt my feet stand on solid ground. I stepped away, then glanced back at him. He nodded, slightly. "I trust her," he whispered. So, I obeyed. I went to her, our hands touched. She pulled me into her arms, I resisted for a second, then sagged into the hug, returning it with a squeeze of my own. So much of her reminded me of Lily, and someone else, someone distant, a memory I could not quite put my finger on. I felt my eyes water slightly.

"Arias?" she asked, "Or should I call you, Cara?"

I shrugged. "I suppose at this point, it really doesn't matter."

Persephone shook her head, "I promise you; it matters." Her eyes went to her husband. Her full lips thinned out to a white line. "Chorisméni psychí, a twin soul. She is Arias, and she is Cara Wynter. A part of this girl's soul was given to her in another age. Aphrodite's claim is void, she is a daughter of the earth, as such—her soul is mine. Thus, I may choose what comes of it in the afterlife."

Persephone's breath shuddered; her heartbeat surged. "This is Athena's doing." Persephone pressed her hand to my heart. "Arias is here," she said. "Soft and yielded. Cara is dominant, I feel the powers in her. Aphrodite cannot have this one." Persephone shook her head, leaves coasted through the air. The goddess ignored the occupants of the room, she spun in a slow circle, tapping her long nails against her front teeth. I thought it was a very human gesture. "Athena knew what I would do," she whispered. "The wily owl."

Draken fell to his knees, fingers folded over his heart. Golden metal clashed against glass. "Give her to me." Draken said humbly. "I beg you." He turned and found my eyes. "If she wants to, Arias? Cara? If she chooses, let her come with me."

"Oh," Persephone faced Draken. "I don't think that's ever been the question, her body chose you. A daughter of Gaia can be touched by only one man." She looked at Hades in such love it made me rework the stories I knew of them. "Personal experience tells me it is true."

"So, Hades never stole you?" I asked, wondering as I always did, why so many important things were hidden in lies.

"Persephone is mine," said Hades.

"I am," confirmed Persephone. "From the second I looked into his eyes. For centuries humans will write and sing of love at first sight, a phenomenon experienced by a rare few." She looked at Hades. "We were the first. True sight, first love."

"Last love," said Hades, and leaned down to kiss his queen. "She was mine in the summer," he continued.

"We knew we would love forever," said Persephone. "I ate the pomegranate seeds to stay near him. My mother, Gaia, was furious. The winter she inflicted, a terrible thing. Many died. For a time, every frozen soul that entered this hall was my fault," Persephone touched Hades's face. "Still, I couldn't leave his side."

"Finally, I had to let her go," said Hades, the remembrance of pain lacing his words. "I didn't do it to save the crumbling world. I did it for her. She is a creature of life; I offer only death. In the end we came to an agreement. In summer years she is free to run beneath the sun, when she returns to me, winter comes to freeze the land."

"It's a terrible pain to leave him," said Persephone, her eyes roved back to me. "Yet, there is nothing more I hate than useless death."

"Draken," said Hades seriously. "I can only release a soul from death once. After that they leave too much of it behind them, you would not know her. And I would not do it to this girl. If Aphrodite were to take her again…"

Persephone made an outraged noise, her vines and leaves ignited. The flames ran out behind her and up the walls, they rushed over the glassy ground in fiery waves. The nymphs darted from the chamber in fright, and Hermes was suddenly extremely interested in holding up the wall with his back. Piles of skulls replaced the flowers swimming under the glass. Spinning rocks and bursting black clouds obscured the stars.

Draken looked at his father in askance, Hades shrugged. "This place is structured to suit her mood."

"*Hermes!*" shouted Persephone, her voice scratchy and thin.

Hermes was picking his way across the slimy floor on the very tips of his toes, hands held limply out for balance and knees lifting like a gazelle. A grimace of absolute disgust marred his pretty face. Persephone rolled her violet eyes and snapped her fingers. Instantly, the room returned to the sparkling autumn paradise. Hermes stopped mid-step, one foot hanging in the air. "Yes, my lady?" he asked in a lofty voice. Persephone opened her mouth to speak, her words never came.

Aphrodite blew through the room leaving a trail of blue lights twinkling in her wake. Her eyes did a quick scan, they stopped on me. She looked thirsty, like she would happily guzzle the milky substance of our soul. "Give her to me!" she demanded.

"I think not," said Hades simply.

"We have a contract, Hades!" screamed Aphrodite. "All the daughters of Enisis are *mine!"*

"That you would even dare to think you could take a daughter of Gaia from me," said Persephone, promptly bursting into flames again.

"The Fates gave her to me!" bawled Aphrodite. "And..." she brandished a ratty looking piece of paper in the air. *"I have a contract!"*

"Yes..." said Persephone over a deep sigh. "We've established you think so," she snapped her fingers, and the flames went out. "Why don't you take a look at that contract you wave like a shield?" suggested Persephone sweetly, her eyes were shooting poisoned darts. "It says you may have the soul of any human girl you desire in exchange for what you trade Hades." She looked at me. "She is a daughter of Gaia, placed in this body many centuries from now. Her soul, only half human, therefore, she is mine."

"Hades..." pleaded Aphrodite, turning the full devastation of her blue eyes on him. Hades looked unamused.

"Don't try your tricks on me, child," said Hades coolly. "Persephone is right. Please understand, I mean no personal insult in saying that giving this girl over into your tender hands, would be stupid as leaving a baby fox in the path of a ravenous lion. Now, since you and I have no further business, I request you vacate these chambers immediately, sooner if your strength is up to it."

"You can't do this!" screeched Aphrodite.

"Can't I?" roared Hades. He clenched his fists and every object in the room erupted into black flames. "You are in my world now."

Aphrodite rounded on Draken. "I warn you. I am not an enemy you want."

"Get out, goddess of love," said Draken in a flat tone. "Get out before I show you what kind of enemy I am."

Amidst a cloud of sparkling blue smoke stuffed with enraged screams, Aphrodite vanished.

"Come here, Draken," called Persephone softly. He obeyed. Persephone took my hand. "So, you want him?" she asked me.

Draken came to stand beside me, I looked up into his eyes, and sealed my fate. "Yes. I want him."

Caution lowered Persephone's voice when she said: "In her own time, many millennia from now, in her eighteenth year, Nori will come for her soul. They are bound to the small part of her, still beholden to Aphrodite, and they will not stop, they will do everything in their power to prevent this moment, so will Aphrodite. You must protect her. The soul of Cara must live, learn, and come back to this place, in this exact time, or I cannot save her."

"I will protect her with my life," vowed Draken. I knew he did not lie. I remembered him battling through the fiery pillars to save me, then... I also remembered him begging Andi to reverse the spell, begging me to stay away from time, this time, and I did not understand any of it.

Persephone held my hand out to him. I saw tears flood Draken eyes, watched him blink against their heat. "Thank you," he whispered, and took me in his arms. I went willingly, resting my head on his shoulder. His strong hand tangled in my hair, I sighed in rhythm with his rapidly beating heart. He cupped my face in his warm hands and kissed me. Fire butterflies went crazy in the pit of my stomach. The tips of my toes curled into the living glass.

"Is that all right?" whispered Draken against my mouth, "Arias, Cara? Is this…?"

I wrapped my arms around his neck. I thought I would never hear him say my name at this time, the sound of it almost made me swoon. I felt kinda giddy. "Yes. It's sooo okay."

"I fear this is a poison dream. Any moment I'll wake up on that altar. Is this a dream?" he asked me.

I kissed him again. "If it is, it's finally one I want to live in," I said, and meant it. "I can't believe you did this, Draken, came all the way here to get me. You must really love Arias," I finished on a sad afterthought. An acid douse of jealousy put a damper on my butterflies. His hands sunk deeper into my hair, he tipped my head back, so his scalding breath whispered over the curve of my ear. "I can't think of anything I wouldn't do," he said. "Whoever, whatever strange, magical creature you are, I would die for you."

I did not know what to say, emotion overwhelmed me. I was dead, and alive, in love, yet confused.

"Now for the subject of payment," said Hades. He weaved his fingers through the air, flicked his wrist and pulled a sword out of nowhere. Like a rabbit from the legendary top hat. Absurdly I felt like clapping. My fingers touched my lips to keep back a very Cara-like giggle. The summoned sword's serrated blade was engulfed in leaping blue flames. The hilt was a black gem, onyx, or pearl— I could not be sure. Atop it was a bone skull with hollowed out eyes.

"Legux," breathed Draken in wonder. His hands fell away from me, "I thought it was only legend. The sword powerful enough to kill a god."

"Not kill," said Hades. "Trap."

"How?"

Hades swung the blade. The sword sang out the ability to deliver death at a wrong angle. "The Fates created Legux, a precaution, shall we say…against tyranny."

"The Fates?" repeated Draken, his tone distracted, his eyes fixated on the blade.

"They were not always old, bleeding hags. Once, they were beautiful women. Some would say, the most exquisite in existence. Individually, the strength of their powers neared madness. Together they were unstoppable, even Zeus feared them—and my brother fears no one." Hades laughed. "God of lightning, afraid of his own daughters. To honor them, Zeus gave them the ultimate power. The ability to decide what path each human would take, how they would travel it, and in the end— who would live or die.

The power he gave was real as the trap he cast. Every string of life they cut, bled life from them. Eventually, they were the living dead. Trapped by their own hideousness. Impaired by their dependency on their one remaining eye." Hades took a breath, the flames simmered. "In revenge…"

"They made Legux to trap their father," finished Draken. He held out his hand, Hades passed Legux to him, hilt first. "What kind of trap?"

"Stab it in Ares's heart, Zeus too, if you can, and find out. Do this for me and our debt will be settled."

Draken stopped swinging the sword and looked at his father. "I cannot! Ares is my friend. More than that, if I killed him my sister would maim me," he finished, his eyes returning to the blade. "The design is flawless though." He spun the sword in the air, then nimbly caught the edge on the tip of his forefinger. "Perfectly balanced." Draken studied the hulled-out eyes of the skull capping the hilt. Something shifted in their depths, and he looked deeper… deeper.

A blast of hot air rushed past his face, knocking him to his knees. He heard wind whipping the mountain tops, sharp screams cut the air, and Hades changing chamber of death was no more. The skeleton's eyes transported him to the peak of Themis, he was surrounded by a pitch-black night and wrapped in a muck that sucked the oxygen from the sky.

The Fates stood before him. Slimy, blackened limbs rubbing together like a handful of worms. The single eyeball spun in the center of a bleeding sky. Their voices lifted on the wind.

"Allow harm to come to the one he loves, and the contents of Pandora's Box will seem pale in comparison to the horror he will bring."

Draken dropped the blade. The vision faded. "The fates knew it would be me," he choked. "They warned Menelaus." Draken opened his eyes. His gaze found mine and stayed. "I do not want innocent blood on my hands. I might be the villain in this tale, but I am not a monster."

"You will do what you must. You are what you are," said Hades softly. "I heard it takes a monster to bring another down."

CHAPTER VI

THE MORNING AFTER THE SPELL. FAIRHAVEN WASHINGTON. WYNTER MANOR, 3:00 AM

Something sharp forcefully slapped me back to reality. With a cry of pain, I opened my eyes to a vision of Lily's flushed face. Her piercing blue eyes were pools of liquid terror, and a stain of tears marked her cheeks. I moved my jaw experimentally, my cheek stinging like the devil. There was no time to make sense of anything before Lily raised her hand, I assumed to hit me again.

"Um, ouch!" I said, practically forcing the words through my parched throat. "I'm awake." I lifted my fingers to touch my wounded cheek. "And that really hurt."

"Oh! Crap! Sorry!" said Lily, looking only slightly contrite. "You've been out of it for hours; your choice was the slap or the hospital."

"You thought I would prefer the hit." "I thought you would prefer the hit," we both said simultaneously, our muted voices echoing in utter synchronicity.

"Well," huffed Lily, dropping her hand and fluffing my pillows. "Probably better I don't hit you again. You look awake."

"That's good," I said casually. "Because a few seconds ago I was dead."

"Yes, Drake told me everything while you were babbling in nightmares. It really is the most incredible story. And I can't believe you let Andi put a spell on you, while I was sleeping. The nerve!"

"He told you everything?" I screeched. Sitting up, mildly enraged. Lily pushed me back to the pillows and fluffed them once more.

"Yes. Why?" she asked, looking befuddled.

"Nothing. Just more than he has ever done for me. Getting a straight answer out of that man is an unfinished quest, an undefeatable boss battle."

Lily sighed at me over an eye roll, and one hand made a swishing movement over her head, as if my pop culture comparison had soared far over it. "You know I don't get your game references," she said tiredly.

"Well," I smiled at her. "At least you get that they are game references. That's a *huge* start."

Just then Gary's head popped up over Lily's right shoulder, she smacked him playfully away, and I realized he had been sitting silently on the floor, waiting for us to finish bickering. The scene reminded me so much of our childhood days. The nostalgia of it made me want to cry.

I think Gary had similar thoughts because he came to sit at the foot of my bed, making it bounce and winked at me. "Just like old times," he said, and I looked up to meet his smiling gaze.

"Did you hear the whole story too?" I asked him. It was a moment before he nodded an affirmative.

I threw my hands up. "Well, that's just great. Is there anyone who doesn't know? Ryan? Larry? Maybe the Fairhaven Warlocks?"

"That's silly, Cara," said Lily. "Why on earth would they be here?"

"Oh, who knows," I muttered. "All sorts of people have been stopping by lately."

Lily fluffed the pillows behind my head again, and gave me a long, pointed look which said many things I chose to ignore. I turned back to Gary. "How high do you rate it on the insanity meter? Drake's story, I mean."

Gary smiled. "Pretty high, that's some crazy shit senior. But hey, I've seen the unexplainable, and let's face it—I grew up with you two." He looked around the room while he spoke. "Though I haven't seen the inside of this place for years— it's freakier somehow."

I moaned. "Do you hate me for being weirder than humanly possible?"

"Pa—leese," said Gary. "You're a superhero, it only figures you would have a magical backstory."

"Wow Gary," said Lily. "You really do have the best way of putting things, I should have used those exact words on Drake."

Gary made a sour expression. "Don't take his guilt, he deserves it."

"Gary," chided Lily.

Gary shrugged again. "It was a horrible story; he was the messenger. What can I say? I felt like shooting him."

"What did he tell you?" I asked them, hoping for the best, yet, in true Cara fashion—expecting the worst.

Gary cleared his throat and looked briefly at the ceiling to see if any help would be had from that quadrant. "He said you were the reincarnated soul of a girl he once knew. A girl who died being sacrificed for him."

"He's never forgiven himself for that," Lily told me.

"With good reason," barked Gary. "Rape and poising? I mean what the actual hell?"

"Poising, yes," I said, feeling the need to defend the most beautiful encounter of my life, regardless of it resulting in my consequential death. "But it definitely wasn't rape. I was there, or at least a part of me was. I still don't really understand how it works. All I know is—I practically begged him."

"Who wouldn't?" asked Lily seriously.

"Me," mumbled Gary.

I touched Lily's cheek. "I'm happy you're alright. I was so scared."

She patted my hand. "I feel perfect, actually. Like all of that was just a dream. I really would have believed it was if I hadn't seen the house." She made a face. "You really died?"

"Yes," I said. "It was horrible, just terrible, and the most amazing thing that's ever happened to me." I closed my eyes unable to fight the breathless memories. "Drake was magnificent. No pain and so many gasps." My eyes flew to Gary, I blushed, but continued. "I think the reason it doesn't hurt when I touch him is because—I belong to him; I've always belonged to him."

"Oh Jesus," groaned Gary.

"Arias does then," I quickly corrected myself.

"The other girl?" asked Lily, taking out her fluttering nerves on my pillow again. "The priestess?"

"Yes," I said. "She's me, or I am her. I honestly don't know; I was in the middle of figuring it out before you slapped me. I need to go back." I thought of Andi's final words before her spell knocked me out, 'can you give him back to me'? She had asked, 'can you remove your sword from Ares's heart'? Legux, my mind told me. It seemed Draken had paid his father's dastardly price. The sword of Destiny. "I need more of Andi's spell," I said. "I was literally just getting to the good part."

"Humm," said Lily, by way of reply.

Gary looked at his watch and cursed. He stood up, took his phone out of his coat pocket, flicked it on and cursed again. Muttering a stream of unintelligible words, he set about putting on his boots. "I promised I would help with repairs downstairs, now the station is bugging me."

"Repairs?" I echoed.

Gary nodded. "Yes, Lily already put Drake and Ryan to work."

Lily smiled. "I'll be right there. Cara is going back to sleep."

"I am not. I wasn't even sleeping," I said, though neither of them was listening. "I was dead."

Gary leaned down and kissed Lily's forehead. "Holler if you need anything," he commanded.

Lily smiled up at him but made no promises. Her smile stayed painted on her lips until we heard Gary's chuckle fade down the hall. "Reincarnation...my god, what's next?" we heard him ask. I hoped one of the aunts did not break out of their portraits and answer him.

Lily reached for my pillows. I caught her wrists midair. Her energy jolted through me, choppy and unfocused. "Swear to god, Lily, my pillows are fine."

"What? Oh, yes, I know. I fluffed them myself."

I laughed; it was a weak scratchy sound that felt good. A little while ago, in Dengora forest, I thought I would never laugh again. It was nice to remember, even if the apocalypse were near at hand, or the proverbial sky was falling, Lily would always make me laugh. "Is Drake really cleaning the house?" I asked.

"Yes. Even though I told him not to, I think he feels responsible. He looked miserable when I left him. He talked for three hours, trying to explain where you went and what happened. It was hard to watch him talk about it, a slow death if I ever saw one. Andi said, what's done is done. Told him to put it in the past. He's afraid if you fully remember the life of this priestess, some goddesses curse will kill you, again I guess."

"Lily."

"What?"

"Be careful with Andi. She isn't what she seems. I don't think so, at least. I can't put my finger on it, but…"

"Nonsense, Cara. It was the horrible skeletons and all the fire."

"She took a sword through the chest, and I saw her walking a few hours later."

"She's Helen of Troy's daughter," said Lily softly. "Who knows what her powers are?"

"You really believe that?" I asked, shocked. "You believe he told you the truth?"

"You tell me," she said, sounding perturbed. "I just set fire to a pack of zombies with my bare hands, and you?" The arch in her pretty brows intensified. "Who am I to disbelieve? Andi and Drake believe it, I think Gary believes it," she shrugged. "Well, I don't know what you believe."

"That makes two of us," I wailed.

Lily met my eyes. "There's something really crazy between you and Drake, isn't there?"

"Yes."

"He loves you."

"I think so, yes."

Lily sniffed. "Do you love him?"

"How can I? I barely know him!"

"That's not true, is it? Also, not what I asked."

"No. I don't know! Arias certainly loves him, but what? I'm supposed to love a stranger because some dead girl does. Ugh! This is crazy!" I threw off the covers and swung my bare feet over the side of my bed.

"Where are you going?" demanded Lily. "Get back in bed."

"No! I need to brush my teeth," I swallowed a grimace. "My mouth tastes like I slept with a dirty sock in it."

"Pleasant, Cara," said Lily, following me into the bathroom. She babbled about love and destiny while I splashed my face and rinsed my mouth. "Maybe you should go on a few more dates with him. See how you really feel if you could picture yourself loving him?"

I almost laughed. *If I loved him anymore, I would die of it,* I thought, but said, "oh my gods, Lily. I don't have the time for one on ones. Old powers curse me, and the Nori want to drag me to hell. This isn't an episode of The Bachelor."

Lily put both her hands on my bare shoulders and spun me to face her. "Don't fight destiny."

"Lily…"

She shook me a little. "Andi's spell took you back in time, right?"

"Yes."

"What did you feel for him then?"

I dropped my eyes. So much it terrified me. "Everything," I whispered. "I want to go back. I need to know the rest of it. I actually think I died twice, Drake took my soul the first time, I don't think he was as fortunate the second time."

"Who killed you?" asked Lily.

"So, he didn't tell you everything—shame. Well…I can't say it out loud. It's too crazy."

"Cara, please, this is our life. Constantly saying how unbelievable it is, isn't going to change it. We need to start figuring out *this* reality."

"And learn how to live in it," I muttered, then relented—though I could not meet her eyes. "Fine. Aphrodite killed me. I was a priestess in her temple, I wanted to die for her. At least Arias did, and I wanted to stay with Drake forever," I sighed. "She loves him so much," I pressed my hand to my heart. "It's all I can do, to not run to him, tell him I won't leave him this time." I dropped my voice. "Tell him I know who I am."

"Oh, he knows you know. He thinks you; Cara will hate him. He's also very worried about this curse. Andi, less so. She said they were dark words from another time."

"No weight in the modern world? Yes, she told me the same thing." I buried my head in my hands and groaned, while Lily patted my hair and stroked my back. "Ah! This is so messed up!" I howled. "I have to talk to him, try and make sense out of these feelings. Jesus! This really is like an episode of the Bachelor."

"He certainly is dreamy enough." Lily took my hand and led me back to my room.

"What about you, Lily?"

"You mean the whole firestarter thing?" She smiled brilliantly. "I know right? I'm amazing!"

I smiled back. "You really are."

"You know?" said Lily on an afterthought. "I'm quite angry at Hanna."

"You lie," I laughed. "You've never been angry at anyone in your life. That's not to say I wouldn't be proud of you if you were."

"Humph!" Lily put her hands on her hips. "Can you imagine how powerful I would be right now if that woman had just given me a little heads up? I would be a goddess."

I shuddered. "Please don't be."

"Nonsense." Lily did a pirouette on the way to my closet. "Your conception is tainted. I would be a noble and benevolent goddess."

"A goddess who incinerates her enemies."

Lily flexed her fingers. "Boom! Power move," she said, swaying at the waist with the word. "Invincible." Lily reached into my closet to rustle around for a second, then a blue sweater with a white cat emoji on the sleeve hit me full in the face.

"Bra?" asked Lily from over her shoulder. "Lacy or sports?"

"Sports, and yoga pants. I see physical labor in the cards for me today." I looked at the clock on my wall as it struck four in the morning. I had been out for hours. I shook my head. Crazy. The fire, Wynter haunt, Drake's kiss all felt like they went down a few minutes ago. Time was becoming a very strange thing for me. Always one step ahead of me, never there for me when I needed. A pitfall of traveling in it, I supposed. I yanked on my clothes while braiding my hair. Lily went to sit in front of my vanity, she rubbed some coconut oil on her face and pursed her lips. "Do you think we're in shock?" she asked, picking up my mascara and wielding it skillfully.

I motioned to the painting above my bed, a woman burning at the stake—dying in righteous flames. "I think we've been in shock our whole lives."

"Good point." Lily spun to face me. "Do you believe in this curse? Thirteen days, from the day you remember will be thirteen days till you die?"

"Kinda," I said honestly. "You slapped me before I could relive the part where she cursed me, so I am a bit unclear on that plot line in my tale of terror. The real question is, when does the countdown start? How much do I have to remember? Does living it count as remembering?"

Lily came to stand beside me, she held out her arm. I took it. Her blue eyes flashed in her glowing face, alight with humor and peace, as if the events of the past twenty-four hours never occurred. "You know I'll never let anything happen to you," she said. "That ancient goddess hasn't met any of this world's new ones." Her index finger pointed at her nose, like I could somehow confuse who she was talking about.

"Oh Lily," I said and threw my arms around her shoulders. She hugged me back.

"Don't worry," she whispered. "It's better to understand fire, than live in the dark. Now," she kissed my forehead. "Shall we go inspect the disaster that is our house?"

"We shall," I said. "You know I really don't care how it looks, each body, branch and shard of glass just means we lived through extra."

"*So*, extra," agreed Lily.

"I'm just happy to be alive," I said. It felt good to say—better to mean it with every fiber of my being.

CHAPTER VII

Drake stood at the end of the hall, a silhouette in a beam of rainy light. He and Gary were in the process of lifting the front door off the floor—somehow, impossibly pounded in by monster hands. Drake heard my footsteps, he stopped mid-motion and gave me a romance novel look, like I was the focal point of his universe, the only woman in his world.

To him we are, Arias told me. "You are!" I shot back, under my breath. "He doesn't even know me. I don't even know him."

That's not true is it? She returned, echoing Lily.

No, it was not true at all. I knew so many things about him; the way he slept with one hand under his cheek, how he cleared his throat when he was nervous—what all the varying looks in his dark, expressive eyes meant. Especially the look he gave me right now, like his soul had been gutted, and the remaining pieces reduced to ash.

"Will you please, just shut up!" I told her.

"I beg your pardon?" said Lily, sounding mildly affronted.

"Crap, sorry," I squeaked. "Not you."

"You know," said Gary, in a conversational tone, giving myself, and Drake sidelong glares. "This door is about two hundred years old," he grunted, quickly repositioning his hands, "I think it's also solid oak—not exactly the lightest thing in the world, if we could all rape each other with our eyes later, that would be great."

"Sorry," grunted Drake, dropping his gaze.

Swearing, the men jostled the door into place, then, Drake held it steady while Gary set the hinges. Lily let go of my hand and went to hug

Andi, I busied myself by putting on my gloves and trying to walk in a straight line. Drake let go of the door, brushed his hands down the front of his jeans. I saw him try to smile, the emotion on his face conflicted badly with battle raging in his eyes.

Still, my eyes went to his lips—drawn there by a force beyond my control—consequently my right foot tripped over my left foot and I nearly wiped out. I caught the wall.

Steady Cara, I told myself. *It was nothing, just a kiss—an extraordinarily little thing which frequently happens to normal girls, on a daily basis.* "It is absolutely nothing," I whispered. A memory, however, of his hands on my naked hips in a room of gold brought a wealth of shivers and made a liar out of me. My cheeks went up in flames. How was I ever going to properly face him? Talk to him for god's sake—hell, yell if I wanted to.

Gary dropped a screw and said a word that made me cringe.

"Jesus! Gary!" gasped Lily.

Drake bent down, picked up the screw, then handed it back to him. Gary grunted in lieu of thanks—uncharacteristically glum. If Drake noticed the strange rudeness, he made no sign, just bent down again to retrieve the screwdriver.

I love you! I wanted to shout. *Oh my god! I love you so much, and I missed you so terribly*—but *I* had not, *I* did not, so *I* kept silent.

It is possible he heard me anyway, because he lifted his head and looked right at me, looked at me the same way he had in his father's chamber of eternal death, surrounded by fire and stars, our feet planted on that living floor.

"How are you?" he asked, walking to stand in front of me.

"Physically?"

"Yes."

I shrugged and looked into his said eyes. "I'm—"

"Fine?" he finished cynically.

"Yes." I hated the space between us.

He stepped closer. "I'm sorry. I'm so damn sorry, Cara."

"Not here," I told him. I took off my right glove and held out the same hand. "Come with me."

"Anywhere," he said.

My bare fingers touched his palm. I could feel the deep emotion simmering just beneath the surface of his control. Lord, but he was strong! I wished for one second—even if it meant pain for me—that he would just let go and allow himself to feel.

I led him through the living room, past Lily's felled Ficus plants, and through the shattered back door. In silence we walked the small cobblestone path leading to the forest. I stopped a few feet from the tree line, and spun to face him, holding up my ring-wearing hand. "Did you give me this?" I demanded without preamble. I heard anger in my voice. *Well, why not?!* My mind screamed. *Promise breaker! He owes us a freaking explanation!*

Drake shifted his weight; his eyes were burning. "I thought you found it."

I nodded; my hands made fists at my sides. "Yes, I did, right here actually." I pointed to a spot under my foot. "I know where I found it this time, did you give it to me last time?" I shook my head. "The first time?"

"Cara—" he pleaded.

"What?! Where did you get it?" I demanded.

The ensuing silence stretched for so long—I expected him to end it with a lie, shockingly—he did not deliver. "My mother gave it to me, her mother gave it to her," Drake took a deep, bracing breath. "I gave it to you under a tree in a forest, a very long time ago."

"You mean you gave it to Arias?"

Drake shook his head so dark curls fell over his forehead, impatiently he brushed them away while his eyes continued to burn into mine, making ashes of my soul. "No, Cara. I gave it to you."

"I went back?" I whispered, shocked. I had not expected that answer at all. "Oh," I took a breath. "How long?"

Drake closed his eyes. "I had two years with you."

"How?"

"I don't know, little on—" he stopped himself from dropping the endearment in the last second. "Cara," he corrected. "I'm sorry, I wish I did. Were I to guess, from what I saw yesterday, I would say my sister had a hand in it. I never knew she wrote that story. It's sick, such horror—immortalized forever." He rubbed the back of his neck; his face could have been carved in stone.

"Why didn't you want Andi's spell to take me back? If I hadn't gone back, I would be dead."

"Yes," he said, his eyes pleaded with me to understand. "If you never drank that cursed spell, then you never would have gone back. You would not have been visible to Persephone, and she would not have claimed you. You would have died that night—so many thousands of years ago—I would never have taken my father's evil deal—and the world would once again be, as it was meant to be. It would be done. No more curses, no more loss or fear, for either of us. If you hadn't come back—it would simply be over. I don't want to put you through it all again." His voice broke. "Put us both through it."

"I don't understand," I said. Tears of frustration filled my eyes, I blinked them away. "I don't even know who I am anymore."

I watched as the hard lines of his face softened. His eyes—red-rimmed and wide—were twin pools of misery drowning me. He tugged on my hand and I flowed into his arms, they closed around me and I felt *home*. He kissed my forehead and simply held me. "You are Cara," he said against my temple. "You are Lily's twin, a Scorpio and a dreamer. You share the soul of a girl from a lost time. You swim like a water goddess, and ride a Ducati like a devil." Leaning back, he touched my chin until I met his eyes. The dark gold flecks dancing in the amber hypnotized me. "You're brave, selfless and kind. You would give your life to help a stranger," his voice dropped low. "You are Cara Wynter, a writer, a witch and a beautiful creature."

I swallowed hard, shoving away the intoxicating feeling his words gave me. "When did you give me this ring?" I asked.

"A long time ago," he repeated. I heard the smile in his voice.

I could not help my own slight smile. "You're infuriating, did you know that?"

"I've been told a time or two, by you actually."

"Drake…when?" I repeated. He waited, I looked down at my hand, so I did not see his expression, his voice however sounded muffled.

"The day I married you," he said. I watched his knuckles tighten convulsively. "I don't know how it came into your possession this second time—that's the truth, though I do have my suspicions."

"I almost remember," I told him.

He sighed, deeply. "I know. I am afraid it's inevitable, I feel the waves rushing to the shore, I fear there is no way to stop them."

"It comes back to me in pieces." My fingers sunk into his bicep; I think I shook him a little. "Can you make me remember?"

"No! Cara! Never!" His tone made me look up—I saw his eyes and felt a surge of triumph. I had finally broken through his wall—stripped away his tranquil mask. In that second of weakness, I was overcome by his emotions. Rage, anger and so much pain it almost drove me to my knees. Drake held me up. I found my feet, and he stepped back. His face was blank, the emotion gone, his eyes bleak and exposed. I felt him lock it all away behind that steel wall I was coming to loathe. "Erastís," he breathed. "Never."

"But… could you?" His overly intense reaction sparked a thought in my mind. "Is it in your power? What are your powers? Do you have any?"

I ground my teeth when a full sixty seconds passed without him making a sound. I felt my foot stomp petulantly, I felt like hitting him—it was a strange desire, I am not a violent person by nature—instead, I tightened my grip on his arm. "Drake? Can you? Do you?"

"Yes," said Drake, his voice was raw. His miserable desperation almost gave my interrogation pause—almost.

"Yes what?"

"Yes, I have powers. Yes, I could make you remember."

"You have to do it," I stated, my voice surprisingly calm, compared to the seething heat in my stomach.

He shook his head violently, like the movement had power to repel my words. "You can't ask it of me, it would mean your death."

"Drake, Arias was beautiful, and as you said, her soul is fused with mine, but she is not me. She was weak, a broken product of her environment. I am quite a badass," I shook him again. "Please, make me remember." I heard the sadness in my voice and wondered if he felt it. He stared into the distance, his mouth a hard, unrelenting line.

"I'll do the spell again," I threatened, meaning every word. "I'll make myself remember."

"To what end?" he shot back. "Pain and death?"

"Love," I said.

He shook his dark head. "I won't," he said, finally. "I won't be responsible for your death a third time." He met my eyes. "Touch my skin," he whispered. "Know that I want to—that I can't. I've made too many mistakes, what's the point of it all, if I never learn. Making you remember would be the selfish thing to do." He pulled me close and rested his forehead against mine. I relaxed my death grip on his arm. "I've only ever been selfish when it comes to you," he finished, his voice impassioned.

My anger—like a cruel lover—abandoned me. "I think that's the most incredible thing anyone has ever said to me," I told him.

His eyes closed, and he said nothing. I wanted to kiss him so badly, I was actually shocked it was not currently happening. Light as fairy wings, his calloused fingers brushed my cheeks. He opened his eyes, I saw the unshakeable anguish in their depth, heard it when it spoke. "I will do anything for you, anything," he said. "Not that. Please don't ask me for that."

A chill slid down my spine. "You owe me this," I said, suddenly infuriated again. "You can't just come here, make me feel all these things, and not remember why? I deserve to know!"

"No, Cara," he growled.

"Don't you want me to remember? Remember us? What we had?"

Lily's voice floated from the direction of the house. "Cara?"

Drake's eyes flew over my shoulder.

"Never mind that," I said. "This is important."

He moved, his shoulders stiff, spine straight, and stepped back. This time I did not prevent it. "I can't lose you again," he said. So low I almost missed it. "Even if it means—"

"Even if it means what? That I don't remember loving you?"

"Is it not conceivable that you could love me again?"

"I don't know," I said, wondering inwardly how I could possibly tell such an atrocious lie without falling to pieces right in front of him. "You could have told me. Told me everything instead of showing up on my doorstep, kissing me, bewitching me, lying to me." My body shook, rigid as my voice. "You are Hades's son. Hades, mythological god—*Hades!* Do you know how insane that sounds? You are a god! You could have helped me such a long time ago—told me who I was the day we met." My voice dropped on each word until the sounds they made were nearly inaudible. "You could have told me."

Drake took a step toward me, his nostrils flaring. "Told you what?! What Andi forced me to tell Lily and Gary? Do you know how terrible it felt to tell our story in this century?" His shoulder sagged. "The ritual that killed you is monstrous, Cara. I thought so then, so many years ago as a boy dying to hold you in his arms. I swore I would not do such a thing, Aphrodite and love made a liar of me. The look in Saint's eyes when I told him how you died." Drake visibly shuddered, his fists clenched at his sides. "There is no version of our story where I am not the villain." The desperation in his voice melted something in me. "What did you want me to say? Hi, I'm Drake, I murdered you in mythological times."

"You didn't murder me," I muttered, remembering.

"You were actually…spellbinding." He heard my words and reached out to touch my face, I flinched away— the automatic movement as much a part of me as my own skin. He recoiled like I slapped him.

"I'm sorry," he said. "If I could take it back, do it all again—trust me I would."

My heart felt like it was bleeding. "Would you though? If you knew then what you know now, would you have walked away from us that night?" I had a flash of our bodies on that altar, physically remembered the hard feel of him against me. "*Could* you have walked away?"

He said nothing, but we both knew his answer. I sighed. "I understand what you're saying," I said, trying to do just that. "But this isn't only your choice, this is my life, and I say you have to make me remember." *Not that it matters,* I thought morosely—*I couldn't possibly love you anymore*—the thought was just scary. Out loud I said: "If you refuse to help me remember, then I don't see any reason for this dance." I moved my finger back and forth in the space between us. "I don't want it!" my harsh words burned my throat. When I spoke again my voice was a blank monotone. "I don't even understand what the crap is going on and being near you only confuses me more. I don't appreciate feeling what I feel and not remembering why!"

It seemed my words were barbs, and he winced when they struck him. He reached for me again. This time he did not let me pull away, only gripped my wrist tighter and dragged my hand to his chest. My fingers rested lightly over his heart.

"It's impossible," he finally told me. "There is no scenario where we are both alive in this world and I am not with you. We are under this love spell for eternity."

"That's crap!" I shouted, shocking myself. I bit my lip until I tasted blood. "All spells can be reversed. Besides, real love spells are nothing but myth."

"Based on realities from my time," he shot back. "Our time."

"If it is real then we can break it. Every true spell has an antidote."

Drake's eyes darkened to pitch black as they bored in mine. "Is that what you really want?" he asked in a hollow tone.

"I... I..." I shook my hand free of his grip and turned away.

"Cara?" Lily's voice was closer.

Drake grabbed my shoulders and spun me to face him, hard lines bracketed his shattered eyes. "Is that what you want, Cara? What you really want?"

"I don't know!" I almost screamed. "What if I did? Is that even an option?"

His face paled. This time it was him who turned away from me. His voice drifted over his shoulder. "It's always been an option for us, Cara."

He started to walk away, I wanted to run after him so badly it curled my toes. "Drake," I yelled, before I could stop myself. When he faced me again the look in his eyes lashed me like a whip. "I don't want to forget, or reverse anything," I told him, not caring that I had been reduced to begging. "But it's one or the other, make me remember, or take it all away—it's your choice."

"It's an impossible choice, Cara. You cannot ask it of me."

"I do ask it! Because it's the only one you have."

"Cara!" called Lily. The urgency in her voice made me spin toward the sound. "Here," I said and noticed how broken I sounded. Then to Drake I said, "we leave tomorrow morning. I want your answer before I get on that plane. Lily would happily murder me if I backed out now—she wants to go more than anything! It's gone beyond obsession."

"What do you want?"

"I want to be where you are," I said honestly.

"That's all I want," he said.

"Cara!" demanded Lily as she came to a skidding halt a few feet from the borders of our battle.

"What is it?"

Lily did not respond to my unusual sharpness. "Gary needs you," she said, and sniffed. "Another girl was killed this morning." Lily wiped a tear off her cheek. "They found her burnt body a few miles away."

■　■　■

I rode in the passenger seat of Gary's cruiser, Andi—who had insisted on coming with me for who knows what reason—was sitting in the back. Gary sat beside me, squinting against a piercing stream of early daylight. He held the wheel in his left hand, steering the car on autopilot, his right hand hovered over a pack of Marlboro lights wedged between the gear shift and center console.

"If you light one of those, I am throwing myself from this vehicle," I told him.

Gary's tired, angry smile was a fearsome thing to behold. "Not gonna. I don't smoke."

"Ah," I nodded, smiling a little despite the situation. "So…those are just for the days you do?"

"Something like that," he snorted.

We sped up on the next hard right, and the car fishtailed into oncoming traffic. Tires squealed, horns honked, Gary flicked on his sirens, the car started to holler, and my world became a cacophony of flashing blue and red lights coupled with monstrous, screaming sounds. Gary's dashboard crackled and spat out a word I did not understand.

"I'm coming!" he barked, taking a sharp left. My head hit the window, making a loud rather hollow sound.

"Sorry," he said, not taking his eyes off the road.

"Not to sound insensitive but isn't she already dead?" my voice shook as I rubbed the throbbing point of pain on my head. "Why are we rushing?"

"I need to get you there before the big city cops fuck up my crime scene."

"Big city cops?" I echoed.

"Third killing this week," he said.

I felt my eyes go huge.

Gary cleared his throat, his hand twitched over the pack of cigarettes. "Yeah, there was one I didn't tell you about, we didn't get there in time. The FBI are gonna be all over this one, I got to get you there before—" Gary slammed on the breaks, the car screeched to a deadly, shuddering stop— spraying waves of rock into the brush. He had the door open before the engine fully died. I jumped down from the car and ran to open the back door for Andi, she stepped out, shading her eyes.

"Cara, stay near me," said Gary. "Don't let anyone get in your way, just go do what you do."

I turned to Andi, a question in my eyes.

"Don't worry about me, I will not get lost," she told me. I nodded, pulling on my gloves before running to catch up with Gary. FBI and Police were combing every inch of Samish Lake Park. I had never seen so many girls and boys in blue in real life—not even in the movies. Climbing the hills, beating the brush, scaling trees, and pulling the lake—they were doing their part.

I did not have to see her body to know where it was. I felt her little drifting soul the second I stepped out of the car. I walked straight to her, ignoring a tall blond man who asked me 'what the hell I thought I was doing?' The young girl lay on the dark green grass, hands splayed at her sides, face down, one of her red shoes was missing, but other than that little detail, she could have been taking a nap. The spot was perfect for one, a beautiful view of the new morning and sparkling lake. People were gathering behind me, I heard Gary shout something, an angry male barked out a caustic reply, then I heard a huge laugh. I had no time for any of them. I took off my right glove and reached out my hand.

"Touch Cara," I heard Gary say somewhere over my shoulder. "I will knock you down and worry about the consequences later."

"If you let her touch the body, she will contaminate my crime scene."

"Your crime scene?!" bellowed Gary.

I blocked them all out, took a deep breath, then touched the girl's hand that was burnt down to the bone. Black and white dots danced over my vision, buzzing, and whispering in my ears. Colors seeped into the black, expanded into the white.

"It happened last night," I said. Gary told someone to *shush and* knelt beside me. "They put her on an altar." I saw them tie her down, it was all too familiar. "They don't know about the poison," I continued, wondering why that last part was relevant, and saying it anyway. "They think the girls have to die by a blade in the heart. They don't know the full story." Why would they? I thought, god knows *I* should not.

"Who are *they*, Cara?" asked Gary. I barely heard him through the buzzing.

"Priests," I gasped. "It's a ritual, they dragged her body here. I know where they killed her. I can take you there." I let go of Karen David's hand, because that was her name, Karen, stormy grey eyes and chocolate hair, Karen who was getting her braces off next Friday, Karen who got straight A's in tenth grade. Karen who was not a priestess, who had a huge future ahead of her, Karen who was not born to die. "This is unreal," I choked. I looked up, faces stared down at me in confused horror. "Mason Paul, the Raven—he killed her. He has another girl; they mean to kill her very soon." I told them all, sadness making me brave. I stood up motioning to Karen. "I know where they killed this one, if it helps, I also know what the murder weapon looks like."

"Can you find it?" asked Gary.

"Is this for real?" said someone else, someone in dark sunglasses and a three-piece suit.

"It is," I said. I did not drop my head, blush, or twist my hair. I was starting to draw a large crowd, in it I saw a few familiar faces, they did not mock me, only looked on in hopeful silence. I walked to Karen's head and knelt again, then reached out and closed her eyes, closing mine in time. Wind touched my face, a thin line of chills traced their way down my spine, when I opened my eyes Karen stood in front of me, transparent and fluid as a tuft of smoke.

Blood dripped from the slash in Karen's heart, I pitied her, I had been her. I may be again. "Show me where the murder weapon is," I whispered. Karen turned her head, her dark cheeks pale, her bloody lips trembling. She lifted her hand and pointed to the base of a red oak less than ten feet away. I got up and walked over to the tree, stopping to look over my shoulder, the ghost of Karen nodded, and I went back to my knees. Vines and moss covered the rambling roots, I reached into my pocket, took out my glove, pulled it on, and started digging. Gary was beside me in seconds, Andi close behind him. The group of stunned law enforcement moved as one, formed a semi-circle at my back—I thought of Aphrodite's priests and shuddered.

"Here," grunted Gary as his hand struck something solid. Together we pawed at the earth like ravenous dogs digging for bones. A wooden chest began to emerge.

"Take that side," Gary told me, grabbing hold of his side. "Lift on three. One, two—"

"I can't," I gasped. "It's stuck—wait. There's a latch." I pressed it and heard a click, the lid of the box swung open. I scream-gasped and fell backward. Somewhere to my right Andi made a squelching noise.

Lying inside a plush, red velvet case, was a little bone knife, its curved blade still smeared in Karen's blood. I stood up, my eyes glued to the knife, my feet stumbling, my fists clenching. Karen's ghost began to cry, I looked at her and saw the tiny bugs eating the whites of her eyes, gooey as uncooked egg yolk. I saw the blue lights and Aphrodite's red eyes, then I felt the knife, really felt it, felt it ripping my skin and cutting into my heart. My eyes watered, my throat constricted. I turned, ran to the nearest bush, pitched forward, grabbed my knees, and threw up.

■   ■   ■

Forty minutes later I was in the back seat of Gary's cruiser, my head resting between my knees and a paper cup of water balancing in my shaky hand. Andi sat beside me, huddled near the door—far away from me as possible, I did not take offense, I knew she only tried to avoid causing me any more pain.

I took a gulp of the cool water, and a breath of the crisp air. My stomach was still lodged somewhere in my throat, but the initial dizziness started to ebb.

"This is just the worst," I told no one in particular.

"It really is," confirmed Andi. "I've seen that knife before," she said as I took another sip.

"Me too, felt it actually."

Andi closed her eyes. "Do you remember?"

"I actually don't know what that means. Your spell took me back if that's what you're asking. I saw Drake's journey to hell, watched him beg his father for my soul—our soul. Jeez it's all so confusing."

"Hades," corrected Andi. "Not hell."

"Whatever."

"There are a few distinct differences."

"Did Drake use the sword, Legux? Did he kill Ares? Is that what you meant when you asked him if he could give him back to you? If he could remove the sword from his heart—were you talking about Ares?"

Andi closed her eyes. "Yes."

"For me?"

"No, I guess, yes in a way. It was more revenge than payment."

"What happened?"

Andi shook her head. "Apart from what the spell showed you, I do not know all the deals made between gods and men that night. What I do know is that my brother returned to Dengora forest carrying Legux, and your soul. Two short years later, you and that sword ended it all. We were incredibly happy for those two years. They were magical years, my happy days." Andi stared at her sparkling manicure and sighed audibly. I felt her edges softening at the memory. "The years I lived under three purple moons that bloomed like water lilies against a backdrop of lava-tipped clouds, were the best years of my life. I would meet Ares on the fringes of Centaur land, for those two years the world had no war—because I slept in his arms. You and Drake also found a home in Dengora, there was nothing left for you back in Sparta, so there was nothing left for him." Andi turned and looked directly at me, her eyes misty from memories and unshed tears. "He married you in that forest," she told me. "I held your flowers when he put that band of Centaur gold on your finger." She pointed to my hand; I twisted the diamond ring. "It all happened so fast, your death, your return, your wedding—your death, again."

"I need more of your spell; I want to go back. I want to remember…whatever the hell that means."

"You'll know it when it happens." She waved her hand. "I don't think the spell worked properly, it didn't do what I wanted it to do, at least I don't think it did. You were there, you saw it? Felt it? Right?"

I shuddered. "Yes."

"But you don't remember? If I were to ask you what Arias did the morning before she first met Drake in the garden, what would you say?"

"I have no idea," I said. "I don't even remember the meeting in the garden, only what I read in the book. I know it makes me an idiot, but—when I was reading it—the idea of me, being her…well it never crossed my mind, not till…" My words fell away. When had it actually happened? The night we swam in the lake? The Space Needle? The forest behind Larry's? Or had I known it was him all along?

"That's what I thought," I heard Andi say, and looked up to see disappointment flash in her eyes before she could quickly hide it under a delicate shrug. "It seems a god split your soul, and only a god can fuse it."

I shook my head. "He told me he would never do it. Drake, he…" my eyes widened on a hopeful thought. "Could you do it?"

"I don't know, I've never tried, I am not even sure what such a thing would entail. The spell *was* me trying."

I looked out the window, wishing for more water. "Why did we leave Dengora, if it was so perfect?"

"Because we had to. I used to question it, now I don't—who really has a right to that much beauty? I learned then, when everything is lulled by that peacefully quiet of perfect, it is time to run. That's when something dreadful is about to happen, the scales must always tip back into balance, yin for yang. For us, it was our summons home. It was my mother's voice infused in the mulberry ink used to stain the letter that commanded me home. I obeyed," Andi took a deep, bracing breath. "We all did. We were prince and princess of Sparta, duty to our country was coded in our blood."

I drank the small drop of water I had remaining, leaned my head back and looked at her. "I'm so sorry," I said simply.

Andi shook her head. "It wasn't your fault. You had your own drama. You died that day—again—so did my father."

Lightly I touched the back of her hand, it was getting easier to push the pain away. "Tell me what happened," I said. Andi hesitated, then she finally did.

CHAPTER VIII

ANDI'S STORY

Everyone came to see me traded like a Mongolian spice—treated with care on the transfer, always sold to the highest bidder. The palace was packed all the way to the golden dais where my mother and father sat enshrined on their thrones. Jewels stuck out like misplaced boulders on the pointed face of my father's crown, a vulgar display of wealth—exactly what the people wanted to see. Malkalimos stood at my father's right-hand side, sword sheathed and spear in hand. Igori guards lined the east and west walls, stoically defending the entrance to the hall.

I was standing near Draken, Drake—he had one big arm around Arias, and one around me.

"Has someone died, Androsia?" he asked, not unkindly.

"Yes," I said. "A dear friend of mine named Freedom, I only knew her for a short time—I am afraid to say I became overly fond of her."

Arias smiled at me through the dark, silk veil concealing her face. "Look at the man they're giving you too." I could see her hand twitching at her side like she wanted to push the veil out of her way.

"Don't you dare, woman," said Drake. "Move that veil an inch and—"

"Hush!" said Arias, her tiny hand flashing out to bat his words away. "I didn't do anything. He really is beautiful, Androsia, are you sure you don't want him? Humm, let me rephrase that: are you sure you don't want to trade Ares in for this younger, much less complicated version?"

I felt my lips seam together. "I'm sure I don't want anything to do with prince Darius."

Drake gently took my hand. "Come, at least meet the man."

I lifted my chin. "I am here to do my duty," I said, catching my mother's eyes. I did not need to turn around to see who it was that made her eyes flare and spark. I felt Ares's gaze stitching my spine with a needle of ice and fire.

"Duty before lust," whispered Drake.

"What about love?" I queried.

"You have a chance at real happiness," Drake told me. "Darius could love you. Talk to him, I won't let you marry anyone you don't want to. Give him a chance." He squeezed my hand and made a pathetically pleading face until I gave in.

"You bastard," I smiled reluctantly. "Your blood is hot for anyone who can properly swing a sword."

"He is one of the best warriors in the world—he could protect you."

"I'm safe in Dengora," I shot back. "Or at least I was." I turned and looked at prince Darius. In another life untouched by Ares, this man may have been mine. He was what every princess dreamt of. In that other life, I walk to him and take his hand. I look into his scalding eyes, run my hands through his thick, dark hair, he lifts me in his arms and together we gallop off on a white horse, deep into the sensuous folds of a desert sunset. That other life exists in a place I have no hope of finding. In this life, my feet are silent as they glide across the marble floor. My body is perfumed and wrapped in silks because I hope my lover tonight is not my betrothed. Mirrored glass panels speared up from the ground and slated every surface of the gilded throne room walls. The glass duplicated the eyes watching me to infinitum. Through it my gaze locked to Ares as he watched me walk to another man. I wondered if he cared. If it even mattered to him at all. If I had even the barest thread of hope that he loved me, I would have run to him and begged him to take me from that place. I knew nothing, so I kept walking, walked until I was standing in front of Prince Darius, my hand clasped lightly in his.

He kissed the underside of my wrist, his lips were warm, his eyes the color of cherry candy. His skin had a cool midnight sheen, he was naked from the waist up, his body chiseled as a granite statue. He wore gold chains around his neck and jade braces on his arms. From his sword belt dangled rubies and black onyx from the Nile. In the mirrors Ares's eyes burned holes in my skin, smoldering away my brief fizzle of doubt.

"I will not force anything from you," said Darius, he had a deep pleasant voice, and kind eyes. My brother was right, it would have been a fine match. Might have been...

"An alliance between Egypt and Sparta will save many lives, our union will bring peace. Peace is all I desire," he finished.

"As do I," I told him. "I also, however, want peace for myself. I fear I will not find that with you." My words made him follow the path of my eyes. The traitorous mirrors showed him who my smile was for. Darius saw Ares in the never-ending reflection and the corners of his full mouth clenched.

"It seems the gods are here to decide if this is a fitting union." He moved even closer; his whisper brushed my cheek. "If he has had you, I will not."

I heard the threat in his voice, I was truly offended. "I have never been touched." I wanted to slap him. "I have never been with a man; you will certainly not be the first." I stepped away from him and reclaimed my hands. "Are there others here apart from our overbearing god of war?"

"The lady Aphrodite." Darius pointed his eyes to the spot where she stood decked in gold, to the right of my mother and father's thrones, just slightly behind Malkalimos. As I watched, Aphrodite reached over Malkalimos's shoulder, slowly she ran her hands down his bare arms, her fingers stopping just above his wrist. The mirrors showed me the unfolding scene from every angle. I saw her mouth move. In that humming moment of stillness that precedes every catastrophe, I heard her say a single word. "Nakatal."

The second the word left her painted mouth I watched a dull glaze sweep through the captain's eyes. Malkalimos lifted his arm and threw his spear in a screaming arch that hurtled toward Draken's face. My brother swerved, and the spear missed him by a breath. He shoved Arias behind him and unsheathed the sword his real father gave him the night he went to reclaim Arias's soul. Legux, the god killer.

Malkalimos took a deliberate step forward.

Draken held up his empty right hand, shock stiffened his movements while his voice begged for reason. "Stop, Malkalimos. You are not yourself."

Makalimos unsheathed his sword.

'Malkalimos, stop!' yelled my father, leaping to his feet, nearly toppling his throne. Malkalimos heard nothing save the blood rushing in his ears and the haunting deadly song of a goddess. Malkalimos walked to one Igori standing apart from the others. The warrior regarded his captain in confusion but gave up his spear to the persistence of Malkalimos's grip. When this spear whistled through the air, Darius pushed me behind him, and knocked the spear out of the air with the side of his right hand. Malkalimos grabbed the next Igori in his path by the front of his tunic and threw him to the ground. The stunned Igori held his hands up to his captain in surrender. Malkalimos took the Igori's sword, turned and lunged at Draken like a man possessed. Draken raised his sword in response, and their clashing blades shot blue sparks through the room. The captain's movements were awkward, sluggish even, but fierce. Draken defended himself, pleading with Malkalimos to look in his eyes, remember who he was. His words fell on deaf ears, Malkalimos looked at him and saw nothing but the hazy lines of the spell bewitching him.

Then, Malkalimos stabbed forward, Draken spun from harm's way, and leveled his blade. It would have been easy for him to cut Malkalimos's throat, but there was a flash of pain in Draken's eyes and he hesitated. Malkalimos slammed his fist into Draken's jaw and he went to his knees. Malkalimos lifted his blade over his head, preparing for the final downward stroke.

"Enough!" Draken shouted. The heel of his foot struck Malkalimos in the kneecap, the bone snapped. The captain stood frozen for a second—borrowed sword suspended over his head and eyes bulging behind their white mask—before he crumpled. He lay there panting and Draken kicked the sword out of Malkalimos's hand. It clattered loudly as it spun across the marble floor. Darius thrust me at my father who hauled me against his side. In the never-ending mirrors I saw Aphrodite's eyes. She saw me watching her, smiled, then began to sing. As she sang the remaining Igori drew their swords.

I saw Draken shake his head. "Aphrodite, enough!" he shouted.

"The Morae," said Menelaus, his expression dreadful and frightening. "They warned me…" his whole body jerked. "The woman…where is Draken's woman?!"

I searched the crowd for Arias. She stood next to Ares, his hands were on her shoulders, his lips moved as he said something to her, I watched her shake her head. Beneath her veil I saw her eyes lock on Draken who tried to repel the approaching Igori warriors, intent on his death. He called their names, addressed them as friends, they did not hear him. My lips, like hers parted in terror, every breath shook our bodies. Ares put his arm around her shoulders, protecting her from whatever would come. I loved him for it.

"She is safe," I told my father.

Aphrodite's song increased in volume, and my eyes returned to the center of the room. Draken and Darius stood back-to-back surrounded by Igori warriors. Legux showered both men in piercing blue light. Darius held a weapon I had never seen before. A mace, I think it is called. It had a thick brass handle and a long chain. A ball swung at the base of the chain covered in spikes. One of the Igori threw another spear, Darius caught it mid-air and threw it back. It sunk easily into the warrior naked stomach; his arms flew out behind him as the sword he held cut the chest of the man beside him. Both died, more came."

Andi closed her eyes. "It was horrible. I was used to blood, to death, but…" Her eyes opened, I saw her sharp edges, and now knew why.

"Then what happened?" I asked, barely conscious of Gary opening the door and climbing in the driver's seat.

"Between the deadly chain and Legux the battle was macabre. Broken men were pulling themselves across the marble ground, their bodies sliding against blood. It didn't matter if their limbs were cut away or their heads and spines severed—they would not stop so long as Aphrodite sang her evil little song."

"Shit," I heard Gary mutter. "What the hell did I just walk into?"

"Nothing good," Andi told him.

"Shush!" I demanded and motioned for Andi to continue. The look she gave Gary was almost frightened, but she obeyed me.

"My father squeezed my hand. I saw that my mother's throne was empty, and I looked for her in the crowd. My eyes found her standing in front of the double doors leading to the hanging gardens and our freedom. She looked over her shoulder at me, as our eyes touched the look, she gave me was one of sad resignation, then, she turned and walked out of the bloody chamber. No one stopped her, Aphrodite's song screamed in all our ears, and no one was brave enough to follow.

Someone shouted, I turned toward the sound, gasping. A sword flew at me. In the last second Ares crashed against my body, together we fell, and rolled across the blood-soaked ground. I scrambled to my knees and my father gathered me back in his arms. Horrible cries rose behind me. I felt my father's shoulder jolt as he drew his sword. I fell against the ground when my father pushed me away from him, my cheek landed in a thick smear of blood. I looked up and wiped the blood out of my eyes. My father lifted his sword and died in the same instant as Makalimos—still moving to Aphrodite's song—cut off his head. A geyser of blood sprayed the beams above my head, then rained down on me as my father's head rolled slowly across the ground. Malkalimos stood behind my father's swaying, decapitated body, his sword bleeding royal blood. In front of me, I could see the last fringes of the fight reflected in the white of my father's eyes. Everywhere men screamed and died. Malkalimos advanced on me. His glazed eyes stared into the endless space of the mirrors behind, and his lips stretched in Aphrodite's smile as he lifted his blade to stick it through me. Legux busted through his naked back and its tip pushed his heart through his chest, and Malkalimos too, died at my feet.

Draken grabbed my arm, he yanked me to my feet snarling a litany of words I did not understand. Blood covered him from head to foot. Rage twisted his face.

"Are there more Igori?" I squeaked.

"No. They are all dead." His voice was flat and cold as light in his eyes. "Go with Darius now. I will see our father."

Hot tears stung my eyes. "Mother is gone too."

His grip loosened. "I know. I saw her leave. Where is Arias?"

"I don't know. She was with Ares."

His grip on my arm tightened into a vise of agony. "What?" I bawled. "They're standing right there."

I pointed to the spot where I had last seen them. Completely forgetting about the moment Ares had crashed into me and saved my life. Both were gone, in their place was a goddess I knew only by reputation. Athena stood in full armor; her almond eyes stared at her aunt. "Don't do it Dite," she said. I felt Draken follow the path of Athena's eyes. Arias was in Aphrodite's arms, a thin knife held to her pale throat. I heard Draken's low moan. I searched for Ares in the remaining members of the crowd, I found him beside the very doors my mother had disappeared through, arms crossed and a frown on his face."

Andi stopped telling her incredible tale in a long sigh that sounded painful. "It was the worst night of my life," she said. "And, in the span of all my many lifetimes, that is honestly saying something." She shook her head. "I tried to stand up, to say something…but no words came. I sat in a lake of blood while my brother ran to save you. You held out your hand to him, called his name. You told him you loved him. Your fingers touched, then, in a swirl of beautiful blue light, you and Aphrodite were gone."

"Was that the last time you saw me?" I asked, surprised I was not speechless.

"No. Though I wish it was," she said, then said no more. I did not ask.

Gary cleared his throat roughly. "I can't believe we are casually sitting here talking about Mythological gods. I think I would have had an easier time believing tales of sparkling vampires."

I rolled my eyes. "Be serious, Gar."

"I really am."

"Fine. Be that as it may, we don't have sparkling vampires, we have this." I motioned to Andi. "We have Helen of Troy's daughter."

Gary snorted. "And some death god, who can't keep track of you to save your life."

I threw him a look. "Honestly, Gar, you don't know this Aphrodite creature, she is a real…"

"Bitch!" provided Andi helpfully.

I rubbed my temples. "It is all rather impossible to believe, I think if I hadn't seen Andi stabbed and walking a few hours later I would still be a doubter. Speaking of belief," I glanced out the window to the FBI and loitering detectives. "Did they believe me?"

"Well, some didn't for sure. One guy out there says you're a mentalist. Can read people's body language and all that. I told him it was a bit more than a mentalist who could read the language of the dead. He didn't like that much; he was so red in the face I felt like checking his ears for steam. He turned into a freaking cartoon character." Gary smiled. "The reactions you illicit, Cara. God! Never ceases to make my day."

"So happy to be there for you Gar."

"Seriously, Cara are you alright?"

"Right as rain. Never better." I snapped, a little too harshly. I softened my tone. "Of course, I'm not alright Gar, I just touched a dead girl, talked to a ghost and found a murder weapon. All before breakfast." My eyes flicked to the clock on the dashboard. "Fantastic," I sighed. "Seven forty-five, another night of fighting monsters and sleep."

"Draken," Andi started, then cleared her throat. "Drake and I are not taking a commercial flight?"

I turned, wide eyed. "What?"

"Huh?" grunted Gary.

"We are not taking a commercial flight. We flew here on our own plane."

"Oh," I said, stupidly.

Gary whistled through his teeth. "Nice." He waggled his eyebrows at me. "Score."

"I'm happy for you, Andi?" I said, after no one said anything for a long time.

"Thank you, but that is not why I am telling you. I would like you to travel home with us. I think it is what Drake wants, only he is too afraid to ask. And I owe you."

"Why?" I whispered. "I don't think you like me very much, you basically told me so. And you don't owe me anything."

"I do. I owe you for your bravery." She leaned back in her seat and closed her eyes. "You are very brave. You are a beautiful person who has seen only sadness. You don't deserve that. You deserve happiness. We all do."

"Yes." I said. Because that much was true. "We all do."

Gary blew me a kiss instead of squeezing my hand like he wanted to. He started the car and went for the pack of smokes. "Just holding them," he said, when he saw my fresh look of alarm. "Just holding them, a security blanket of sorts." He gave me a scalding glare. "Trust me, you don't want me to put them down. I'll go bat shit crazy on the spot."

■   ■   ■

Drake. Tonight, I would go away with him. To another country, a foreign, enchanted land.

The thought inflamed the butterflies in my stomach—persistent critters and my constant companions all through our packing, which took the rest of the long day. Neither Lily nor I knew how long we intended to stay, and the result of our confused packing was five large suitcases and two trunks of books. Lily had insisted on bringing all the ones I had hidden. I had not even made a fuss. That is how lost I was in my own world.

It was nearly two in the morning when Lily swirled into my room. She wore a white wolf Spirit hood coat, a matching hoodie, and looked like a fairytale creature, it seemed only fitting.

She grabbed my bare hand. "I can't believe we're really going." She was breathless.

"Me neither," I admitted, feeling rather breathless myself as she drenched me in her excitement. "This is crazy."

She stuffed her toothbrush into her toiletry bag and tossed me my wool coat. It was forest green and had a placket of silver buttons in two straight rows down the front. A wide black belt clinched the waist. It dwarfed me, but it was my favorite. I put it on while she stuffed her feet into her boots, tripping and jumping.

"You have your passport?" she asked, a little frantic.

I tapped my purse. "Yes, just checked for the nineteenth million time."

"I'm so excited I might throw up," she gasped.

The doorbell rang and we both froze mid-pose. Our eyes locked.

"It's time," we said. I grabbed her hand as she turned for the door. "Lily?"

"Yes, Cara! I'm sure! We have to do this!"

"I was going to ask you how I look," I said.

She made a face. "Oh."

"Stop feeling guilty, love. I don't want to be anywhere that isn't near him. I know it doesn't make any sense. But I think even if you changed your mind right now, I would still go."

Her eyes sparkled. "You mean it?"

"Yes, I mean it."

Lily kissed my cheek, then dashed out of the room. By the time I made it down the hall, she was already hauling Drake inside and kissing his cheek, he smiled cheerfully.

"Good evening ladies," he said, pulling Lily into a hug. "I am here to carry luggage," as he spoke, his eyes met mine over of Lily's head.

For a breathless second everything was frozen in a strange, dark silence—a silence lit only by the light in his eyes. They were hungry, desperate, and beautiful. Lily stepped back, and the moment shattered, a smile returned to his face.

Lily kicked a broken piece of window out of her way. A shard of glass that escaped our impromptu cleaning crew. I saw my eyes reflected in its mirrored face.

"At least we won't be here when all this gets fixed up. Larry said he would send someone in the morning. I—Cara, did you call the university?"

I smiled. "Yep, all signed up for virtual classroom. I can catch up on any tests when we get home."

"What are you studying?" asked Drake, taking off his coat. His tone was polite, distracted even.

"The Iliad," said Lily. She smiled, brilliantly innocent. "Maybe you could help her."

"I wasn't there," he said.

"Well," she shrugged daintily. "I wasn't there when the Berlin wall fell, but I know how it went down. I have the general gist at least."

I heard the smile in Drake's voice when he said, "so did Homer."

Lily pointed down the hall to my room. "Cara's luggage is through there. Mine is in the library and my room," she sighed. "Some are in the hall, on the stairs…" her voice trailed off.

"I am at your service," Drake told her. Together we led the way back to my room. Vaulted ceilings or not, Drake dwarfed the only room I have ever slept in. I remembered him in my bed and shivered. He leaned forward and lifted one of my larger suitcases. His muscles bulged under his jacket, stretching the leather until it looked in danger of splitting. Lily saw it, her eyes twinkled, and she fanned herself again.

I wondered if I should tell her that leaving with him tonight might be the most dangerous thing we could possibly do, I wondered if it would have any effect on her plans—probably not much. She seemed equally lost in his spell. I grabbed my carry on, my purse and overnight bag. I threw the strap of the latter over my shoulder and sagged under the weight. Suddenly, the weight vanished. I turned to find that my bag had magically teleported into Drake's hands.

"I will start dragging the trunks from the library to the front door," said Lily, she turned to Drake. "You can help me bring the rest of the luggage downstairs. Don't forget your extra coat, Cara," she commanded. Drake gave her bow, she fluttered away, and we were alone.

I stood in silence while his gaze roved over my room. A picture on the wall, near my desk, caught his eye. He walked toward it, paused, then ran the tip of his finger over the wooden frame. The frozen image was of Lily and me on graduation day. Highschool had been a crashing bore, but that day was fun. Gary made me laugh during the boring speeches, Lily had teased my hair, and they both gave me standing ovations when I accepted my diploma. It was all there in my eyes, the laughter, the joy that it was over.

"Strange to finally be in this room," whispered Drake. I made a noise in my throat and he turned to face me. "You told me all about your room, a long time ago. Told me about your purple throw, and the lamp that brightens each time you touch it."

"I did?"

"Yes. You tend to talk when you're nervous. You were nervous often back then."

"Why?" I asked, then wished I had not. His look was so sinful it curled my toes and made blood rush to my cheeks. I closed my eyes and heard him laugh softly. It was a dark, velvety sound.

"You told me a lot about your home. Your sister, your aunt. I feel like I've known Lily my whole life. She was very real to you." He took my hand. "You made her real to me, made it all real. I didn't really believe it at first. But I heard the love in your voice when you talked about her, about this room, your home…the love I heard told me it was all very real. In the end it was easy to believe." His thumb stroked the line running through my palm. "I always knew you were magic."

I was staring at his lips when he said those last words, and before I could think better of it, I locked my hands around his neck, and kissed him. He froze, stunned, then his hands were on my hips, in my hair, and he was kissing me back. Fingers flexed against my neck, he deepened the kiss, tilting my head and lifting me off my feet, I locked my legs around his waist. His burning mouth scalded my senses, I forgot who I was, where I was—there was only him. His intoxicating smell, his skin, like warm steel under my hands. I felt my fingers fly as they undid the buttons on his shirt. His hands coasted over my hip, cupped my breasts. His lips trailed fire down my neck, and my head fell back.

"My bed," I managed to gasp, not caring that this was all kinds of wrong. Not caring if the bloody sky fell. I wanted him now, here in this room where I have dreamed of him so many times. "Take me to my bed."

Drake pulled away and I moaned in protest. "I can't, Cara, not like this," he panted.

"Like what," I murmured, tugging on him, not caring what his reasons were.

"Not with you so confused and angry."

"I'm not angry," I said dreamily. It was true, anger was the last thing I was feeling.

"Lily," he said. "I can hear her footsteps upstairs…and my pilot has the engines running." His nonsensical words calmed the blaze in my veins and signaled the return of my senses.

"Oh." I unwound my legs from his body and stepped out of his arms. "Of course." I brushed my hands over my jeans to keep him from seeing them tremble. I knew nothing about kissing, or how to entice a man I wanted, if he was going to lie to me about his reasons for ending the boiling kiss, who was I to argue?

It was a good thing, I told myself. I needed to figure out what was happening before I let myself go completely. "I understand…I…"

"Don't look at me like that," he commanded.

"Like what?"

"Like I'm rejecting you, like I don't want you."

I shook my head. "I don't think that…I…"

Drake's next words were a desperate growl. "I've never wanted anything more in my life. I want to run away with you, Cara. I want to pick you up and run so far away that no one, not even the sleeping gods will ever find us." He ran his hand through his hair, tousling it perfectly. "It's what I've always wanted. Just not like this."

I took a deep breath and shoved the shaky feelings away. It was hard. I could see his dark skin under his open shirt. It was easy to believe he was an ancient god. One only had to look to know the truth. The evidence was him. He glanced at the door, but took a step in my direction, like it was impossible for him to do anything else.

I breathed through my nose and tried to look casual.

He grabbed my hand. "Cara, look at me."

I shook my head and studied my feet. One look at my blush, at my wild eyes, one look and he would know. My desire to be strong would fly out the shattered window, and he would see, he would know how close I was to falling apart.

He saw anyway and closed the small space between us. "Cara, I want you so much it's madness," he vowed. This time it was him who kissed me. This kiss was nothing like the others. There was heat, but it was the slow, melting kind. His arms engulfed me, and his lips moved in drugging, sensual patterns over mine.

"I missed your mouth, Cara." His hands gripped my hips, unconsciously I arched against him. "The feel of you, your taste." His voice was so reverent, he sounded like he was praying. Warm hands coasted under my sweater; his palms burned my skin. The world swayed, then my pillows were beneath my head, his body pushed mine down into the feathers of my duvet. "You feel so perfect," he panted against my neck. "Flawless. Stronger than I remember." He lifted my sweater, so it bunched under my arms, his eyes dropped to my black sports bra, and I heard him suck in a breath through his teeth. He kissed my bare shoulder, and traced a finger between my breasts, my body shuddered visibly.

Now, I could hear Lily's footsteps in the hall, the look on Drake's face, however, told me he was past hearing. I felt the heat of his breath warm the thin cotton of my bra; my eyes almost rolled back in my head as chills tightened my skin. His mouth came back to mine, and I realized he had dropped his mental wall to let me *feel* him, really feel him. Distantly, I heard waves breaking on rocks, and rushing against a sandy shore. I smelt dry, Spartan air, breathed it in and felt it all. I was not bombarded like last time, but the depth of his emotion was no less powerful. In my life I have touched rage, pain, fear and hate, even deep, sisterly affection, never had I touched passionate love. The way he felt for me was raw and all consuming. It was more than desire, he wanted to possess me eternally. He was a man outside of time, unaccustomed to the modern rules of engagement. He wanted to steal me away from everything I knew, hide me where no one living could find me—make me his alone, forever.

Feeling what he felt, brought Arias to the forefront of my mind, and I was instantly lost in the dazzling colors of her love. It was overwhelming, frightening in its extravagance, yet simultaneously seemed perfectly right, as it should be—like day turning into night, like the river rushing to the sea.

"Drake...I..." My words fell away, there were *no* words.

"I know." His voice was low, and hot in my ear. "Why do you think I hide it from you? The way I feel for you has the power to strip free will. I thought I could come here, to this strange modern place. Date you maybe, make you love me? I knew nothing of your powers...I never expected..." He lifted his body away from mine, distributing his weight to each hand braced on either side of me.

Anger tightened his lips suddenly. "That's my greatest fault," he said. "I have no imagination for the worst-case scenario; thus, I am always surprised by it. I had no idea how it would be for you, not until I saw you walking to that rail...heard you speaking to the wind." He dropped his eyes. "I tried to block away what I suspected you could feel." He touched me between my eyes. "I felt you here," his warm breath wafted over my brow, searing my soul. "I felt your light trying to link with mine." He shook his head; his hair brushed my burning cheeks. "You've always been magic; I don't know why I thought you would be different in this life."

I wanted to deny it, tell him he had no idea what he was talking about, tell him I did not believe in any of that—then I thought about the latest dead girl, and how I had walked straight to the knife that took her life— the knife that looked like the one which had taken mine so exceptionally long ago, and kept my denial of power locked behind my lips where it belonged.

Drake leaned closer; his eyes dropped to my mouth. "Every choice I made to stay away took me straight to you, every moment I lose with you feels like a thousand years. I have always feared time and what I borrow from it, one day it will extract its price." The bed shifted under his weight as he flexed his arms to lean down and kiss me. "I should stay away right now— it's the only thing that makes rational sense." He kissed me again, this time he did not lift his head until I was panting. "I just can't," he swore. "I can't."

I placed my fingers against his lips. "Then don't. Keep me with you, make me remember."

"Anything," he swore. "I will give you anything in the world, but that."

"You are only postponing the inevitable, you said so yourself."

Ice chilled the heat in his eyes. "Then, that is what I will do. I will not be the one that starts the timer on your life."

"I hate to break it to you, but I'm human, there has been a timer on my life since birth."

"Yeah, but I didn't start it." He kissed my forehead.

I pushed him away. "You know…w…hat!?" I stammered. It seemed my temper reacted badly when he was near, around him I went from bliss and burning passion, to insane rage in seconds. "How about trying to help me solve whatever the hell is going on, instead of walking around, looking like someone killed your dog, and telling me how impossible it all is!" I shoved his iron chest again. He let me up, marginally. I leaned back on my elbows and glared at him. "You need to be honest with me. If this is all true, you need to tell me exactly what happened, and how, you need to trust me. Lily is a genius, and I am not without my own set of abilities. I am not a scared little girl in a temple anymore. You need to trust me," I repeated. "We are going to Romania to figure this out. Tell me what I'm fighting so I can win!"

During my rant, the gold in his eyes had darkened to the color of aged whiskey. He was the stone man again, looking at me through the gaze of a breaking heart. "Cara, you don't understand. I want so much to tell it all to you, I want…"

I never got to hear the rest of what he wanted, Lily's heels clicked on the floor just outside my door, and Drake froze. I heard her fake clear her throat. "We'll never make it to Transylvania if the two of you keep tackling each other every time I turn my back," she said, then started to laugh. "A man in that room, in that bed… oh my gods!" Her voice trailed down the hall as she left us with an additional, "oh my gods!"

Drake lifted a single brow and gave me a compelling look.

I ignored him. "We better go before she comes back, and physically hauls you off me. I know it seems impossible, considering your size and the fact that your muscles seem to be made of pure iron, but Lily is a force of nature."

■ ■ ■

I locked the door of Wynter manor perhaps for the first time in its life. I took a step back and looked at the old, imposing structure, mentally saying my goodbyes. I had a strange sense that my life here in Fairhaven had come to a close, at least in all the ways that mattered. I was leaving this place, like mother, like Hanna. Leaving, not knowing when or if I would ever return.

Gary sat on the stairs, two steps down from where I stood, head in his hands. He looked up when the lock clicked.

"Be weird not having you here," he said.

"I know," I sat down beside him. "I can't believe I'm actually leaving this place. I thought I would die here. Hey Gar?"

"Yeah?"

"Look into a Greek mythology ritual called the Aphrodisia, the ritual of Enisis. It might lead to nothing, but…"

"I will. I'll keep in touch, call you if I need help, like I always do."

I smiled and handed him the keys to the manor. "Look in on her for me? I don't think she likes being left alone."

Gary looked behind us and shivered. "Will do. Nothing in there's going to jump out and kill me, will it?"

I shrugged. "Who knows? Come armed."

Gary gave me a hooded look. "I'm not sure if you're joking."

"Me neither. I'm serious about the ritual, though I think it's connected to the Fairhaven Warlocks, and the killings. Oh, and check in on Aunt Jane if you can, and the gardenias in the back..."

Gary smiled at me. "Marsha and I will take care of everything, don't worry, Cara."

"I feel like I'm going to start crying," I laughed.

"I don't blame you. Fairhaven is your home. It's hard to leave home." His gaze hit the pavement. "Though, I think you're doing the right thing, Cara."

I looked in his eyes. "Really?"

"Yeah." He stood up and put his hands in his pockets. "You've gotta understand what's going on. I get it. I would need to know. Even if it were all bullshit and lies, I would need to know." He dropped his gaze. "Do you think your feelings for him are based solely on the fact that he's the first man you can touch?"

"I don't know," I said honestly, glad I did not have to meet his eyes. "I think figuring that out is on the top of my priority list."

"Be careful, Cara. First love, deepest cut. It should have happened to you a few years ago, maybe it should have happened with me, but destiny had other plans." He shook his head. "Destiny, *shit*, thought I didn't believe in that crap." Gary turned and walked down the remaining stairs. I followed him.

"Gar?"

He spun. "Yeah, girl?"

"I want to try something; I'll need you to hold really still though. I just wanna try, it might not work." I felt my front teeth sink into my lower lip, felt a waft of air whistle through the little gap between them. "Don't feel bad if it doesn't work, kay? Please Gary."

Gary backed up a few steps, his eyes tightened as he held his hands out in front of himself in defense or surrender. "What are you doing Cara?"

"Just hold still." I looked down at my hands, I still had not put on my gloves. I took a deep, hesitant breath, then ran the few steps toward him and threw my arms around his neck. Gary froze in shock. Pain rang my eardrums, yet it was almost too easy to push it away. Not into him…not like I had with Trevor…just away.

I was careful not to lay my hands on his body, just used my arms to squeeze his neck. I locked my teeth so I would not make a sound, and quickly kissed his cheek. I stepped away before he had time to recover from his shock and wrap me in his arms.

"I love you Gar," I said, thinking that his dropped jaw was adorable. "I've loved you since the day you knocked Sally Parkinson on her butt for spitting at me. Thank you for everything you've ever done, thank you for being you."

"Jesus, Cara!" gasped Gary, finally regaining speech. "You're not dying. Wait? Fuck, are you?"

"No, I'm not. I just…" I shrugged. "I've just always wanted to do that."

"Did I hurt you?"

"No, you didn't. I focused on your bravery and your dedication to the things you believe in. Your dark side stayed hidden under all the light I threw at it." I laughed, feeling suddenly giddy with personal pride. "I'm sorry. I know that's confusing."

"It isn't," he corrected. "It actually makes perfect sense."

Wheels crunching over cobblestone sounded behind us. Gary turned and scowled at the shining car. It could only be one person. "How is he already back here? Didn't he just leave?"

I smiled at his tone. "He went to change in his bike for a car that could fit all of Lily's luggage."

Gary did not return my smile. "I work with hardened criminals every day. I know the look of a killer." He made a show of sniffing at the air. "I can smell them. See?" he raised a brow. "I have powers too."

"I think I know what he is," I said.

Gary nodded. "I'm a killer too. I have the look; I know I do. I've taken life to save another. I can spot both kinds, evil or righteous—both are killers. That man of yours has something in his eyes that I've never seen— I haven't quite been able to put my finger on it, but it's dangerous—that much I know. Sure, I think he would rather saw off his own head than hurt you, but trouble follows a man like that." Gary zipped his jacket, checked then re-holstered his gun, and took a set of keys from his pocket. "I'm going to take off, after I find Lily and say goodbye. Don't forget what I said, and please take care of yourself."

"I will. I always do."

He said another goodbye and I kissed the air near his cheek, not wanting to risk it.

■   ■   ■

If Lily was not as fully immersed in Drake's spell as I was, the Maybach Zeppelin rumbling in our driveway brought her fully over to his side. Hanna never had a job that I knew of, unless casting spells in the attic qualified, but she always had means. I suppose one could amass a considerable amount of finance if one were immortal. We had never lacked for anything as children, thus—even though she could rough it with the best of them—Lily loved the finer things. She stood purring beside the glistening silver car, purring the way she does when something is just too great to put into words.

"Nice ride, Drake," she finally said, having exhausted her repertoire of tongue noises. She ran fingers down the glowing hood, rain splashed her white gloves and she seemed unphased.

Drake, however, did not hear her muttered stream of compliments because he was busy loading the mountain of awkward luggage in the trunk. Andi opened the door for me, and I folded my body into the butter soft leather seat. A sigh closed my eyes, and I rubbed them until they watered.

Lily climbed onto the seat facing me. Andi sat on the passenger side, then leaned over to push the little red button that would command the car to start. The engine whispered to life, and blessed heat poured through the vents.

Standing in the rain and talking to Gary on the driveway had set my teeth to chatter like a dozen old ladies. Constant shivers rippled my body, and my head was pounding something fierce—yet I had an idea of what Cinderella felt like on her first pumpkin ride. The numerous lights on the dashboard cast everything in an eerie yellow glow, which only enhanced the feel of the magical.

Lily laced her fingers through mine and squeezed. "Not off to a bad start? It's better than a freaking limo back here, there is even champagne and chocolate." She reached into the slim, leather compartment between us, and lifted a small triangular square. "Toblerone, your favorite. He is trying to impress."

"He couldn't have possibly known," I said, then wondered wildly if I told him. I took the piece she offered me and popped it in my mouth. My eyes rolled. "Oh crap! That's good!"

"Try the drinks," offered Andi, pointing to the brimming crystal glasses, sitting pretty in each of our armrests. I lifted mine and drained it, then, gasped as the sweet, honey liquid splashed my tongue. "Wow. I really should have savored that. Amazing. What is it?"

"Mead, called Helen," said Andi. "My mother makes it near our home."

"Drake is taking us to Floathaven airstrip just outside of Bellingham," gushed Lily, taking another sip of the ambrosia. "My first private plane." She leaned back and stared out the rain-streaked window. "I knew I was destined for beautiful things. Why don't we have one of these cars?"

"Because Hanna didn't leave us *that* much money, and you wanted your Infinity. You're crazy."

"I'm happy. I'm drinking ambrosia and I'm about to ride on a private jet with the most handsome man in the world. Even if he is after my sister, I'm okay to sit back and enjoy the perks."

"I thought that same word. Ambrosia. About the drink," I explained at her wide-eyed look. "I thought that very same word, and you said it a few seconds later."

"Humm," mused Lily. "Spooky."

I shivered violently. "It kinda is."

Lily took another sip, then dropped her voice for my ears only. "You're going to sleep with him, aren't you?"

My face went up in flames. "Lily!"

She swirled her eyes. "He was on top of you, in your bed. That's the second time I've seen him there. I went to your room the other night. Just as a precaution, of course, to make sure you had survived the Ducati…he lay beside you, holding your hand. His eyes were closed, though I'm positive he wasn't sleeping. It was like he was breathing you in. He was there most of the night, you know? Left around four in the morning."

"I know. I woke up when he left."

The driver's door opened. Lily and I both jumped like guilty children for no real reason. Drake slid into the seat. Diamonds of water cluttered his hair and jacket; his warmth and heady scent filled the dimly lit car.

Suddenly, I was exhausted again. It was more than just simply being tired. I felt like I was waking up from a morphine induced sleep, all I wanted to do was close my eyes and fall back in it. That was unusual for me. I am not exactly a robust person, but narcolepsy has never been on my list of problems.

Drake reversed down our driveway, and I sunk further into the seat. I barely felt the movement of the car, only listened to the tires gripping the wet stones, the sound strangely comforting in its familiarity. Lily's hand heated in mine. I could hear her breathing deepen as sleep relaxed her. The feelings in her dreams were colorfully peaceful, only small patches of fear lurked in hidden places. She passed over them as easily asleep as she did awake.

Drake's eyes met mine in the rearview, and I marveled at how many unspoken things could live in a single look. No one said a word, not for a long time.

Lily was still wiping sleep out of her eyes when we reached the red tarmac. There were so many lights and people everywhere I felt like we should be wearing gowns and taking bows, while our gloved hands flashed pious waves.

"Good Lord, Drake," squealed Lily, when she stepped out of the car and took it all in. Her blue eyes widening until they were roughly the size of daisies. "See that's what a magic carpet should look like…what with all this, actual carpet stuff?" she said, craning her neck far as dignity would allow. "This is much more the vision; it has a place you can actually park your car." She sounded so relieved that I laughed while she rounded on Drake. "What is it?" she queried.

"It's an Airbus 380," Drake shrugged. "I hear they are all the rage."

"I want one," crooned Lily.

"You can have it," interjected Drake. "Could I borrow it to get us to Vienna?"

Lily gave a long dramatic sigh. "I suppose so."

"Come on then," he smiled down on her and took her pompous, outstretched hand. "Allow me to take you on a tour of your plane, my lady."

I followed mutely behind them while he fulfilled his offer to her, and what a tour it was. The Jet had everything. A home theater, a pool, a stunning, well stocked bar, and the promise of a warm bed. All I cared about was the bed.

Drake had been occupied for the past ten minutes showing Lily how to work the TV remote, and sign into her Netflix account. Now they were sorting through about thirty horror titles. Lily was curled up in a fluffy white chair, surrounded by a couple silky, beige throw-pillows. I looked rather longingly at the chair beside her. I could just sleep right there if it were not for the movie, she planned on watching. Saw, was not my idea of a good evening, to be completely honest, I think I would rather punch out my own eyes.

Drake came and stood beside me, he tried to catch my gaze, but I flicked it to the vibrant scene flashing on the TV. Two minutes in the movie an obese man was already hacking out the fatty contents of his stomach with a rather questionable looking knife, and a young, terrified woman looked like she was considering using a machete to cut off her arm. That was my queue…I threw Lily a disgusted snort and ran out of the room.

Drake followed me as I rounded the corner into what looked like a ballroom. "I can read it, just can't watch it," I said, trying to explain my reaction.

He threw a dubious look over his shoulder. Lily had her face buried in a pillow, only a portion of her eyes peeking above the silk, he shook his head. "Come, I'll show you where you can sleep."

I hardly saw the room he led me to, only the wide, fluffy bed. I crawled up onto it, and curled into myself, like some wounded creature seeking shelter. Drake turned and touched the bedside lamp, a glow spread through the room, encapsulating us in a sphere of gold, and making the champagne bedspread glitter. I smiled. "A touch lamp," I noted, charmed. "Same as the one in my room."

Drake nodded. "I've never bought another kind."

"This is pretty impressive," I said, motioning to the room and giving the devil his due.

"I bought it for Andi," he explained modestly, though I could see from the look on his face, he liked my compliment. "I am constantly trying to make reparations for what I've done."

"What did you do?" I murmured.

Drake briefly closed his eyes. "Too many things."

"Now you want to give it to Lily, dear me, what will Andi say?"

"She'll be all for it, that way she gets the latest model." He sat near my feet. "For a long time, we lived with nothing. I simply didn't care. When Andi left our mother a few years ago, I realized I couldn't keep living in squalor. I had a few battered pieces of my father's armor; each fetched a king's ransom. I wanted to spend it." Light left his eyes. "I never imagined I would see you again." He shook his head. "Never. My father swore to me that such a thing could not happen."

"I remember," I whispered. "He said, he can only release a soul from death once, he said I leave more of myself behind each time, and…that you would not know me." I sat up, holding my tired body on my shaking hands. "But you do know me, don't you?"

"Like my own soul," he said, not pausing to entertain a second thought. He started to stand up. I grabbed his hand. "You're leaving?" I sounded panicked and tried to think of a calm way to beg him to stay.

"No," he said. He shifted his weight and his hand coasted over my ankle. Slowly, he unzipped my boot, first one, then the other. The way he moved his hands on my skin made my mouth go dry, he was sensuality personified. He leaned forward and brushed a strand of hair off my forehead. "I'll stay with you, Cara, and try to keep the dreams away."

I had no idea how he planned to do that, but once again I was too lost in him to ask.

Drake kicked off his own shoes. "Tomorrow," he whispered, answering the unspoken thoughts in my mind. "I will tell you everything tomorrow. I swear it." He stretched out on the huge bed beside me and rolled onto his side. His hand speared through my tangled hair, and he brought my head to his chest. He kept the pressure of his hand light, giving me every chance to pull away— as if I would be unwilling to lie in the arms of a god. My god.

"Tomorrow," he said again, whispering the word like a promise of hope. In the darkness I heard his smile. "You can yell at me then if you want. Tonight, let me fly you to my home, take you to a place no evil can walk. A place where you will be safe." He shook his head, and I heard a layer of self-disgust in his voice. "I told you once before that you were safe with me, for a time I even believed it myself."

"I believe in you," I said, meaning it.

Warm hands coasted over my shoulder, pushed me all the way onto my back. "I wish you wouldn't," he whispered. I felt his breath heat my cool lips.

"Wishes are for nymphs and fairies," I told him, repeating Arias's words. "I am neither, therefore have none."

Strong fingers sunk deeper in my hair; he tipped my head back—there was a strange look in his eyes. Fierce, desperate—and what? Hopeful? Perhaps, though I could not say for sure. "I can't stay away from you," he finally said. "I don't even have the desire to try. Knowing what I know, what does that say of me? I'm the most selfish man alive."

"I don't want you to stay away from me!" I pulled his head down to mine and touched his face. "You've lived so many years…" my fingers moved to his lips. "Have you been this sad for all of them?"

"Yes."

"Did you find no happiness at all?"

"Cara, you exquisite creature, there is no happiness without you. You are, and have always been, the only light in my universe of darkness."

Those beautiful words rendered me speechless. I kissed him, wanting to express what I could not say. He surprised me by returning my kiss so ferociously, it nearly took my senses. The emotion for him welled up so strongly it came spilling out in words. "I want you," I told him desperately when he let me take a gulp of air. "I don't just want these vague images of memories. I want the real thing."

Drake was panting hard; I felt the rise and fall of his chest brush the tips of my breast. "Don't say such things to me. Not now, not 'till you know everything." He took my face between his hands, his golden eyes begged me to understand. "I've done so much wrong, Cara. Please let me do this right."

"When it does happen, between you and I—because it will," I vowed. "I want you to know…though I think it's pretty obvious…I want you to know that you'll be my first. My only. Just you Drake, the only man in all my lives. If we are under a love spell, it's the most powerful spell in the world."

Drake made a broken sound and pressed his forehead to mine. "A spell responsible for your death."

"Some things are worth dying for."

"If you still feel the same way tomorrow, after you know everything, if you still want me, I swear I'll not leave you for as long as we both shall live."

"Okay," I whispered. He rolled off my body, slung his arm around my waist and drew me close. I snuggled against his chest and pressed my lips to his hot neck. Lying in his arms was comfortable as breathing. I had the feeling again, like I had done this a thousand times, lay right here in this exact spot. Only this time the feeling had altered slightly, morphed into a certainty—now I knew I had. Thoughts of dark spells, and murdering goddesses receded like the ground beneath the climbing plane. I fell asleep, the rightness of the moment spilling over all my thoughts. This was where I was meant to be, here in his arms. Witches, heritage, immortality, spells, hell, and gods be damned—this was my place. It seemed every single thing in my life leading up to this exact moment had been nothing more than shadows and parlor tricks. He was my reality. On the glittering trail of that thought came a moment of pure feeling, irrational and possibly volatile, yet altogether enthralling. I wondered if I could keep him with me for always.

Magic freaking carpet, and all.

CHAPTER IX

ROMANIA

Holding your hand, we fall through the skies, I'm screaming your name, terrified by the blood in your eyes.

Who gave you the right to choose which one was Heaven and which was Hell?

"Cara, Cara." Lily's soft voice brought me back from the depths of dreams. "Cara, love, you need to get up and get ready. We're landing in an hour."

I moved the pillow resting atop my face and opened my eyes. Lily sat beside me brushing out her gorgeous hair. She wore knee high boots and sheer black tights. Covering those was a miniscule pink, mini skirt which looked like it had been sprayed on. She had borrowed my loose-necked cashmere sweater; its pastel pink matched the thick gloss on her lips. When I saw that her face was already completely made up, I wanted to throw my pillow at her.

She leaned down and kissed the air beside my cheek. "Get up, you look terrible." She sat back and twisted her mouth in an exaggerated grimace. "And you need to brush your teeth."

I did throw my pillow then, but she dodged it easily. "I borrowed your sweater btw." She tossed a soft towel over me, which I could have easily used as a blanket.

"Sorry I woke you. I wanted to let you sleep, but I knew you would hate me if I didn't let you bathe."

"I can't believe I slept in my clothes," *and, with Drake, my* mind whispered, I ignored her. The voice had been silent for so long, I wished she would stay that way. Right now, I did not need her. Right now, I felt sticky, hot, and a little wonderful.

"There is a shower through those doors," said Lily, nudging her booted toe against my backside.

"Okay…geez." I jumped off the high bed, and my bare feet sunk into the plush carpet. Now that daylight soaked the room, I really saw it for the first time. It looked like it had been decorated by some sultan's wife. There was hardly a surface that was not covered in some sort of silk or velvet. Despite the myriad of colors, everything managed to fit together in harmony. I grabbed my bag, which was right where I had left it, tossed haphazardly at the foot of the bed, and toted the thing behind me as I walked across the long room to the bathroom. The thought of having to go through it for something to wear was rather daunting.

"I don't know what to wear," I mumbled redundantly, stepping into a beautifully lit marble bathroom. In the corner of the room, in its own sunken turquoise grove was a wide Jacuzzi. Thick spirals of steam rose from it, fogging up the mirror. "I can't believe I am going to bathe on a plane."

"I know," said Lily, sauntering up behind me. "I already drew it for you, go get in while I find you something to wear. Don't mope, I don't have exceptionally long to make you pretty."

"Sweet, Lily." I rolled my eyes. "Didn't you sleep at all?"

"For an hour or two, I think. Not much more than that. I am too excited to sleep."

I picked up a brush and looked in the oval mirror that sat atop a wide silver and marble sink. I rubbed the purple bags under my eyes disdainfully. Well, help was near at least…cosmetics covered every countertop. Lily had obviously been here for a while. I battled my hair while shedding my clothes and stepping in the tub.

"Drake came to sit with me about two hours ago. I guess you were finally sleeping deep enough for his satisfaction," said Lily, her tone told me she had a lot more to say on the subject of Drake sleeping with me—

or, more accurately, beside me, but she stopped talking when she began rummaging through my bag.

When I was dressed in tight jeans, a black-turtle neck and heeled black boots, and made up to Lily's satisfaction, she sat me in front of a well-lit circular mirror that looked like it had been stolen from Elizabeth Taylor's dressing room. I winced when she unceremoniously yanked the towel off my mass of wet tangled hair. It sprung out in all directions and I groaned at my reflection, "Give me some twigs and a five-pointed star, I'll be perfect for dancing naked under a full moon."

Lily started giggling because that was right when Drake walked in, his polite knock being merely perfunctory.

"We'll be landing in ten minutes, ladies," he said, leaning up against the door frame and flashing me the sexiest smile. I raised my hand self-consciously to my hair and his smile got wider.

"Adorable," he mouthed, then winked at me. "You two almost ready?"

"Yes, we're ready." Lily fluffed her hands through my hair. "That is about as good as it is ever going to get."

"Good, then…" Drake gave an almost imperceptible nod of his head. A tall youngish man, who wore thin spectacles over watery, light blue eyes that were nearly buried under a crop of red hair exploding out in all directions, appeared at Drake's side as if conjured.

"This is Anderson," Drake told us, we both nodded. I would have felt surprised if his name had been anything less ordinary. His large hands were folded over a briefcase, and he was wrapped in a three-piece, navy Versace suite. He looked like one of those guys who was a genius at everything. Those brainiacs whose idea of a night on the town was round of Dungeons and Dragons while sipping a cup of tea in Hyde Park, or camping out in a parking lot, armed with a thermostat and a book, waiting for the Return of the Jedi. I liked him better for it.

"This is my…" Drake quirked his eyebrow in Anderson's smiling direction. "My…"

Anderson fake-cleared his throat. "I believe it's called an executive secretary, Sir."

Drake snapped his fingers and pulled a face. "Right…bad name."

Anderson's freckled face puckered. "Yes sir." His voice was very somber. I felt like laughing with him. I knew he wanted to. His feelings were pulsating good humor, and devastatingly sweet British charm. I had a feeling I was going to like him immensely.

Drake spoke to the room but looked directly at me. "We land in Bucharest in ten minutes, Anderson will take you to Gara De Nord where I will meet you on the Balau Express in precisely two hours. I'll leave you in his capable hands."

Anderson said something to Lily that made her laugh. Drake reached for my hand. Our fingers touched, his lips moved soundlessly, I read the motion of the words. "Be safe," he said. Then, he was gone.

■　　■　　■

Thus, ensued the longest two hours of my life. The ride to the Gara De Nord train station was almost intolerable. I played that game where you try not to look at the clock for a full fifteen minutes. When I was sure the correct time had passed, I would allow myself to glance discreetly at the braided, gold watch on Lily's wrist only to find roughly fifteen seconds managed to crawl by.

I tried again and again, finally; Lily smacked my bouncing leg. She passed the hit off by pretending to laugh uproariously at something Anderson said. The stinging slap did not seem odd to him, and he carried his story without missing a beat. Lily had basically been laughing and whacking some part of me since we stepped off the tarmac, anyway.

Anderson was telling us about his first carriage ride, I noticed his accent thickened when he was passionate about his subject. I was not really listening to his words, from the faces he was pulling, however, I assumed it had not been a pleasant trip. Apparently, we would be taking the same carriage over the Carpathian mountain range to Corvin Castle.

I sat straight resting my elbow against the limo's leather armrest, staring out the window. The sun was just rising against the endless expanse of glistening white hillside. The glowing orange ball spread its rays against the snowy Alps lining the horizon, the hazy light capped the mountains in gold. The whole world pulsed with life; even the air I breathed seemed purified by the untouched wonder of this place. It was this type of landscape that kept legends alive, anything could happen out here. At the base of those mountains dozens of cave mouths gaped, flaunting ground few human feet have touched. The little chalets and chapels dotting the hillside were built to face the rising sun, more clear gold splashed against their wooden and tile bodies.

"It's so beautiful it's almost haunting," I heard Lily say. I turned to face her. She sat beside me staring out the opposite window, leaning her forehead against the glass, her face rapt and flushed.

"Haunting," I agreed.

She swiveled around. "That's just what I was thinking," she said.

I was confused. "So beautiful it's almost haunting? Lily, you just said that out loud."

"I did? Oh."

"You should have slept more." I rubbed my watering eyes, trying not to smudge my mascara. "How much longer?" I asked, too embarrassed this time to call out anyone's name. Anderson smiled kindly at me, as if it were the first time rather than the hundredth, that I had repeated the annoying question. "Less than twenty minutes now, until we reach the train, that is."

"He said two hours Cara," Lily told me, still staring fixedly out the window. "You might try thinking about something else for a minute."

I can't! My mind hissed. I did not argue. It was true. It appeared I was physically incapable of thinking of anything else besides how badly I wanted to see him. *See him my foot! Be with him…sleep with him…devour him.*

"Please spare me the mental pictures, Cara. Not all of us have candy right now."

Those words rushed through my mind like a thunderclap. My body jolted. My fingers shook and I grabbed Lily's hand—distantly, I realized she was shaking too.

"How are you doing that?" I breathed out loud. Out of the corner of my eye I saw Anderson become conveniently involved in the shiny recesses of his phone. Anderson and the Limo existed in another realm from I—living in a separate layer of the invisible veil—for me there was only Lily, and the sound of her voice ringing in my mind. "Lily!" I demanded when she offered no verbal response.

Lily smiled at me—brilliantly—like I handed her a shiny present instead of my dull expression of shock *"I'm not doing anything,"* she thought calmly.

"You're in my mind!" I shrieked.

"Cool, huh?"

"Lily." I squeezed her hand. "What the hell?"

"I don't know. You just started hearing me…I didn't say anything out loud about the view, Cara."

"This isn't possible."

Her giant mental sigh shrugged my own shoulders. *"You know, Cara, coming from a family like ours you developed a strange defense mechanism to the supernatural…you don't exactly reject it…you straight up deny its existence altogether."* Lily stopped to mull over her last statement, it was strange to feel her thought process.

"You really don't want to believe in any of this do you?" she thought-asked.

"No, Lily I really don't."

"Why not?"

"Because it's never affected you the way it has me. Growing up we lived together, but we didn't live the same life. It was the exact opposite actually…for you it's madly fascinating, for me…it's…"

My mind was whirling; it actually felt like she was inside my head. I could almost picture the bright, open room of my mind, its unpainted walls, and nonexistent floors where we sat having this impossible conversation.

"Terrifying?" she offered.

"Yes…only this…" I thought, "hearing your thoughts, it feels right, like it is something we should have been able to do forever."

"I know." Lily was feeling joyously smug. *"I told you it is worth finding out about our history. Discovering our powers. I feel them growing stronger as we get closer."*

"What do you mean closer? Closer to what?"

"To Transylvania…to this place. Look." Lily closed her eyes. So, did I. She showed me a dark forest, full of tall pines disappearing in the low hanging sky. The damp air smelled like herbs and sap, other smells I could not name. I remembered the forest instantly. Dengora would always live in my mind now.

"Lily." I felt my lungs take a gasping breath. "How are you doing this?"

"I've seen this forest in my mind for days. Sometimes I run through it barefoot. I love the feeling of the moss beneath my toes, the night wind in my hair. Other times I just lie in the thick grass at its borders and watch the stars. I saw you, Cara. Here in this place."

"Lily, why haven't you told me any of this?"

"There was never the right time. I'm telling you now." She paused for so long, I thought the mental dialogue was over until she squeezed my hand. "Show me your dreams."

"No way! Forget it. They're horrible Lily, why would you even want to see them?" I knew the answer before my thought finished.

"Because I want to understand. Share it with you in the only way I can."

I shook my head.

"Please, Cara."

I sighed; she would always get her way with me. It was not hard to recollect my dreams and show them to her, the visions never really left my mind. I showed her everything, the woman…Drake…her…me…I even let her see the knife and hear the spell for whatever that was worth. When I was finished, she opened her eyes slowly, carefully.

"I'm so sorry, Cara. I'm really so sorry. I do understand why you're afraid. Anyone would be after that, and what we fought in the house! Ugh! The Nori? Gross!"

"They are gross, but I'm less scared than I was."

"Good for you! You're going to have a happy ending this time. I know it."

I mentally rolled my eyes. "How can you possibly know that Lily?"

"I just know. How can you feel it when a person stands too close to you and needs to blow their nose? I can't explain it…Hanna told me before she left to watch for the signs." She sounded exasperated. "These stupid dreams are a sign. Drake, is definitely a sign."

"I think I love him, Lily," I thought after a moment. "Not only Arias, me, Cara. I feel like I've loved him forever."

Lily tucked a curl behind my ear. She looked much sadder than she had a short time ago. I wondered if the few seconds in my mind were already getting to her. We were quiet for a time.

"Lily?"

"Yes."

"When you are up here in this crazy mind of mine you, make it peaceful."

"Then I'll stay a while," she said. A petulant frown tugged the corners of her lips, she threw it at Anderson. "Seriously dude, how much longer?"

Yes… I was definitely getting to her.

■   ■   ■

The Balau Express had that timeless look some beautiful relics possess, a look that is simultaneously brand new, and centuries aged.

"Look Cara," said Lily over a wistful sigh. "What do you know? We're going to Narnia." She stood still beside me looking at the decorative train, lightly resting her gloved hand on Anderson's arm. Anderson's orange hair blew about his freckled face, stuck to the fresh Chapstick on his lips. The fumes seemed to be bothering him, and he ushered Lily quickly up the little metal stairs.

I stayed outside to inspect the train, which really did look like it might be able to transport me out of time.

Short smokestacks sat on the roof of the train like pious, little rotund men. There were four on each car, belching swirling clouds in the musky station air. I stepped closer so I could press my hand to the locomotive's cold, metallic body. The vibrations moved under the skin of my fingertips, coasted down my arm as I swept my hand across the smooth surface. There was red piping running through the middle of each car, like a deep knife wound in the thickly polished black frame. Above the crimson slash was a crude representation of a Spartan shield. The circle had three strange points on the top, dragon horns, I realized. In the center of the shield was the phoenix in flight. I recognized it immediately as the one displayed on the back of Drake's leather jacket—the one I had a crush on—except this leaping, scarlet bird was pierced through its heart by an intricate sword. A sword I knew well. Even in illustration Legux was unmistakable. Long streams of cerulean light pumped from the punctured heart of the bird, or perhaps the light came from the sword? I could not be sure. Together the symbol looked like a coat of arms. Beneath each shield was the name: Von Draken.

I ran my hands across the five letters that made up his name, then, ignoring the fresh drizzle continued my perusal. The wind from the large, airy station whipped my coat through my legs, and my hair around my face. It was freezing and smelled like stale boots and sauerkraut. The round face of the front car looked like a pudgy, rebellious child. There was a row of silver bolts going down the train's front, so close together it made the black metal seam look stitched in place. I imagined the train's soft, fleshy pink body beneath the hard shell, sweating under the labor of its simmering fire tube boilers.

Lily was right. It did feel like we were about to go traipsing off to Narnia, the feeling was enthralling. The romance novel feel had always been present in my narrative, but now, I was immersed in steamy Victorian fantasy.

"That is a private train, miss," said an accented voice at my back. I spun around. Three men stood five feet in front of me. Not close enough to be alarming…but still…too close. The man nearest me was younger than the other two, sixteen or seventeen was my guess. Perfect features framed pearly white teeth, and his alabaster skin was shockingly pale against his midnight hair. A pair of bright red Beats hung around his neck; I could hear some faint screams emanating from the speakers. The two behind him looked like concrete bricks come to life. Beanies—decorated by sports logos I recognized yet could not name—nearly covered their eyes. All three wore thick, black clothes and snow gloves.

I took a gulp of freezing air. "I know it is. Thank you. I am traveling on it to Hunedoara."

"This is not a civilian train," the Beat boy told me.

My eyes fell to the family crest near my hand. "I guess that makes me special today," I tried to smile. I prayed it did not look forced as it felt.

Beat boy smiled back, and for a second I thought I saw fangs.

Oh crap! "I'll be going inside now," I said.

"Not just yet surely. My name is Alexei Nikolaevich," Beat boy informed me, he held out his hand. He was beautiful and terrifying. I took a measured step back. I might be mastering my madness—but there was no way in Hades I was touching this guy. His black eyes flashed to my shifting feet, then up to my face. I took another step and grabbed the stair rail.

"My sister is inside already, Anderson is helping her with her luggage," I stated, for no reason. Drake was right, I did babble when I was nervous.

"Will you not shake my hand?" asked Alexei. The concrete statues behind him remained mute and unmoving. "You are American, no?" he looked pointedly at his hand. "Is this not the American way?"

"It is. It's just not my way," I said.

Alexei's eyes drew together, his mouth lifted in a slightly crooked smile, then he moved, faster than I could have imagined. My glove gave me a bare second to brace for the pain—it was more than enough. I shoved the pain at him so fast, it knocked his feet out from under him, then slammed him on his back. His Beats flew off his neck as his head smacked the ground. He looked up at me, shocked and a little hurt.

"Sorry," I said, kneeling beside him, feeling awful. "I shouldn't have done that. You simply scared me."

Alexie lifted his hand and rubbed his neck. He started to sit up, then froze. Nostrils flaring, his eyes flew to my face. As I stared at his befuddled expression, I saw him sniff the air. "Ah," he said finally. "You do know the master of this train. His smell is all over you."

"Excuse me?" I said, wondering if I heard correctly.

Alexie leapt to his feet. The expressions of each concrete statue, cracked. I saw nerves twitch their hands.

"You're her. Are you not?" Alexie shook his head, like he knew the answer to his own question—and hated it. "It would be unfortunate if you were." His crestfallen expression was so precious, it made me relax.

"Why?" I asked. "Why would it be unfortunate if I was her?"

"Because" he said sadly, "I would be forced to cut off my hand for harming you. Or, I will have it cut off for me."

I started laughing. "I think I'm the one who harmed you." I walked over to where his Beats had fallen and picked them up. Absently, I brushed a few specks of dirt away, then handed them back to him. "I think I am *her*. And no one wants you to cut off your hand."

Behind me something growled, a low ripping sound I recognized instantly. I looked over my shoulder to see Drake running down the platform, he was a dark, speeding streak in a sea of people.

"Here comes the hand cutter," said Alexie ominously.

I smiled grimly. "He's not so bad."

Alexie snorted, loudly. "He is dreadful."

I felt Drake come up behind me, chills rose on my skin and the butterflies tickled my throat. I turned to him and looked up to his expressive eyes full of concern. A fierce wind rushed through the station, whistling to rival the trains. I swayed under its violence. "Hi," I breathed.

Drake did not answer, he looked over my shoulder at Alexie and growled again. Literally growled, the sound a dog might make when you grab his tail during suppertime. "I told you," he bit out.

I looked at Alexie who was ignoring my irate god, by putting his Beats over his ears, and turning up their volume. He made a swirling motion with his finger above his head and his concrete buddies spun toward him, both moving clockwise like puppets on a string. Alexie shoved his hands in his pockets and sauntered off, his brick shadows following a few steps behind.

"We are leaving this station in fifteen minutes," Drake called out after him. I cringed at his angry tenor. "Fifteen minutes!" he repeated, when Alexie gave no sign of hearing him. Alexie did not stop walking or turn around, only pulled one hand from his pocket, lifted it above his head, and raised the middle finger.

Drake ignored the gesture, just turned his wild eyes on me. "Where is Lily? Anderson? Why did they leave you alone?!" he barked his questions at me, taking my upper arms and shaking me a little.

"I am perfectly fine," I smiled up at him. "Better than fine, actually. Who was that?"

Drake hesitated, staring after Alexie, an unreadable look in his golden eyes. "Alexie is my…" his words fell away, his eyes locked on the boy's retreating form. "I'll be right back," he told me, quickly kissing my cold lips. I felt a growl of frustration building in my own throat. I shook my head, infuriating man!

I studied the train for another five minutes before the wind finally defeated me, and I shivered up the mechanical stairway leading inside.

The dark corridor of the stairs opened to a sunny dining car. The walls were papered in opal silk. Sakura blossoms bloomed in the silk, clinging to the slim, ebony branches painted near the floorboards. Crystal vases sparked on each of the eight tables, the high morning sun filtering through the windows bounced off a dozen long stemmed glasses, spreading shards of rainbows through the room.

In each vase sat a rose, leaking pink shadows on the white tablecloth like an adaptation of the Beast's enchanted rose.

But when the last petal falls the spell cannot be broken and everyone dies. My mind told me. *Beauty died too, you know, they just don't tell that in the children's stories. Just like life, anything kinder than that would not be reality...It is always the silly girl who gets it, the silly girl in the red cloak thinking she could run with wolves.*

"You're a real cynic, Cara. You know that don't you?" I heard Lily's voice clear as if she stood beside me and shouted.

I rolled my eyes. *"If it bothers you, get out of my head."* I was only half joking. That had felt mighty strange to be interrupted mid-thought. She was not even in the room with me.

"We can hear each other over distances now," she told me, still feeling quite smug, like this new power was all her own making. Maybe it was. I could hear her clearer too. She was right, whatever *this* was, it was getting stronger.

"What are you doing?"

"Looking at the train."

"You have to come see the bedroom! I think I'm going to forget about Corvin Castle and just live here."

"I'll be right there," I told her. This was beyond amazing.

I walked the slender dining car, through a pair of sliding glass doors opening to a bedroom. This room was more opulent than the others combined. It seemed a whole bevy of multicultural concubines had given over to freedom of expression. Resulting in a mix of Asian allure and exotic Arabian flare. The bed was only a continuation of my harem fantasy, its frame filled half the car, dwarfing Lily who lay in the fluffy middle.

"Look at all this," said Lily in pure glee, she tossed a throw in the air, the satin cloth slid sensuously back to the bed. I put my bags down on one of the numerous velvet and gold ottomans. Gold. It was everywhere. On the window frames, the mirrors, the doors, even the etchings on the headboard.

"Who did this man become?" I whispered, overwhelmed by the majesty.

"Maybe he is some kind of king," purred Lily, stretching out against the feather pillows, a dizzy feline drunk on cream. "You know what I was just thinking about?" she asked softly.

I went to sit on the bed. "No love, but I'm sure you'll tell me."

Lily stuck out her tongue at me. "One time, when we were about six years old playing in that willow near the haunt—the one you were convinced could speak? You sat on the branch above my head and told me how you were actually a queen, that one day your king would come to take you away. I think I laughed, but you were very obstinate. Do you remember?"

I did remember. It was a silly memory. Those embarrassing ones only few people know, yet ninety percent of all women in the world have. Memories of the young days, where we placed veils on our heads, stood by windows waiting for Lancelot, or closed our eyes and let the sun wash over our faces as prince Eric rescued us from the sea. Of course, there was the day we pretended to stab ourselves in our broken hearts when we found our fictional Romeo dead. *"It was just a silly child's dream."*

"In your case, a silly child's premonition," was Lily's quick response to my unspoken thought. "It looks like he lives here, sometimes at least," she said out loud. "Go through the next door, there is a library full of books that rival ours in rarity."

A small statue sat on the bedside table near Lily's head. The bust of a Spartan warrior in full regalia. I took off my gloves, and gently touched the small, stone helmet. The buzzing started in my ears, I gasped and let go quickly.

Lily grabbed my hand. "Do it again."

I looked at her. I would not say no. "You sure?"

"Yes. I want to know what you have been seeing. Show me."

"There's pain, you feel... everything."

Lily locked her jaw. "I'm ready."

I judged her face swiftly. "Alright." I yanked off my other glove, linked my fingers through hers, took a breath and lifted the statue. The vision came instantly, sensory, and vivid. The difference this time Lily was in my head, sharing it with me.

I can smell blood on my hands. The train is gone, and I am engulfed in the blackest night I have ever seen. Cold is everywhere, burning me. My hands and feet are numb. The white world stretches in front of me, every inch blanketed in glittering snow. I see a stone altar; it is a five-pointed star. I walk, dragging my freezing feet, feet that want to run—run and run for my life. I cannot listen to my desperate mind. I must fulfil my destiny. No matter who I love…no matter. This was it then. The pain was coming. I touch the cold stone of the altar, close my eyes, and climb atop it. I lie down and wait. Wait for her to come. Wait for the knife to fall.

It is Drake, not Aphrodite who appears in front of me. I lift my hand and touch his face. I look in his eyes, feel tears gathering in my own. His beautiful, golden eyes are changed, gone all bloody like a drunken vampire. Emotion threatens to explode the heart in my chest. I love him. I would die for him. I am dying for him. I feel it then. The knife. Only this time the blade does not go for my heart… this time it sinks into my stomach. The pain is more than anything I could imagine. I open my blood rimmed eyes, and see Aphrodite, her red lips and white skin spattered in my blood. This time she is not smiling, not like last time. This time she throws back her head at an unnatural angle and howls her mirth to the moon. Her black pupils are a burst of darkness against her blood red eyes. "Poor lost girl…poor lost, dying little girl!" she screams the words at me as her image fades into the boiling sky.

While Aphrodite's horrible laughter disappeared, and I slowly came back to the present, I thought about Lily telling me it was *'just a dream'*. I sighed. Just a dream that started with a stranger the way all the good ones do but be sure at no point of this story to smile, because it is something more than a fairy tale now, Ariel lost her feet, and her beautiful voice, and sleeping beauty never woke—fairy tales are just for children—in the adult version everyone dies. I put my hand over my eyes and felt my fingers tremble.

Lily's eyes popped open. "Well," she huffed. "That was just about the worst thing ever!"

"Right? I'm telling you." I rubbed my eyes, hardly able to feel anything besides the pain.

"I am going to punch Hanna right in the face when we find her!" exploded Lily. "Crap, now I'm scared. And you don't remember living that life? Dying that death?"

"No, I only see what I'm shown. Then I remember the feeling."

"Like you could forget it," said Lily, still grabbing her stomach. "Maybe this magical train can make a stop in Oz and I can petition the wizard for courage, you know," she shrugged. "If he has any going spare."

Shockingly, I started to laugh. "Oh Lily, you're the most courageous person in the world."

"I see how you feel about him, it's crazy!" she rolled her eyes. "Gods! I feel it."

"Uh huh, like I said earlier, I think I would go anywhere with him. It's not just this heart that loves him; it is the very inner workings of my soul…" I closed my eyes and realized the truth of the words as I said them. "He is a part of my soul."

Lily sat back. "Yes. I think that is one of the only things we know for sure. Lord, Cara that was horrible. I think I might throw up."

I curled up beside her, and she rested her head on my shoulder.

"You were right about the trip," I said, after a minute of silence. "It was a good idea. Come what may, I'm glad we are here."

Lily made a satisfied sound. "I have a whole slew of 'I told you so' dances up my sleeve right now. Would you like to see one?"

"You're too tired to get up and dance, show me later."

She yawned hugely. "Okay. Wake me up when we get there."

"I will," I told her, and kissed her forehead. "I'm going to find food," I finished, there was no response from her glossed lips. Lily was sound asleep.

CHAPTER X

TRUTH

I heard the music blaring from his Beats, seconds before I saw his face. I had a mouthful of croissant when he burst into the dining car. The slight, dark man serving me, dropped a cup and spilled coffee on the white tablecloth in front of me.

"Pardon madame," my waiter soothed, whipping a cloth from his spotless apron, and dabbing strenuously at the rapidly spreading stain.

"Don't give it another thought," I told him, glaring at Alexie. That one sat on the chair across from me and propped his feet up on the table. "Hello again." I smiled over another bite of croissant.

"Hi," he said. So glum I wondered if it was sarcasm of some kind. He looked at the croissant in my hand and pulled a face. "I hope you know what you're doing," he said.

I hoisted the croissant. "Eating?" I asked innocently.

He winked at me. "Cute."

"Thanks," I smiled. "Where's Drake?"

"You don't want to know," he said mysteriously. "Trust me."

"Well, great, now you made me want to know even more."

Alexie shook his head. I thought I heard him mutter, "humans."

"So, you're traveling with us," I said, blithely stating the obvious, when neither of us said anything for too long.

He lifted his perfectly sculpted brows at me, then smiled a flash of pearly white. "I am part of the family. I go where Drake goes."

"Oh." I took another bite of my croissant, then my gulp of incredibly strong coffee washed it down. "Are you related?"

"Umm, by blood."

"I see," I said, completely in the dark. "I didn't know Drake had a…brother?"

Alexie growled, yet I noticed he did not deny my assumption.

I studied his mulish expression. "You don't look very pleased about this trip."

"I'm not." His smile lacked joy. "You're going to get us all killed," he said bluntly. "I would like to run far, save myself from the approaching apocalypse. Drake is of a different opinion, he believes misery loves company, and has demanded I never leave his side."

"I don't want to get anyone killed," I muttered.

Alexie touched his finger to the side of his Beats, the soft screaming music cut off abruptly. "Well," he said, catching my gaze and staring hard, "that's something, at least."

"Did you know me?" I blurted, then dropped my voice. "I mean before…"

Alexie shook his head making sunlight dance through his hair. "No." He frowned darkly. "I wish I had. Perhaps I would be more inclined to fight for you."

"I don't want anyone to fight for me!" My voice rose on each word.

"It's too late now," he told me. "Drake is ready to die for you, I suppose that means I am too. I owe him everything. My life, even."

I heard a mechanical whirr, and the sound of glass sliding against metal. "Speak of the devil," said Alexie, his smile was darker, slightly twisted. He unlocked his heels and jumped to his feet, each separate movement fluid as a ballerina in flight.

I turned to the sound of footsteps I knew well. Light bathed away Drake's shadows. He stood in a bright patch of sun, staring at me. Motionless as a portrait. Only his eyes moved. Traveled slowly between Alexie and myself.

I swallowed the lump in my throat and tensed for his reaction. Drake did not disappoint. He was by my side before I could blink, snarling at Alexie.

"I was just leaving," said Alexie, touching the side of his Beats and restarting the screams.

"I don't want you to leave," I said truthfully. Then, I looked up at my growling god, felt his anger radiating in a twenty-foot diameter around him.

"Get back to your car, Alexie," said Drake between his teeth, spacing each word.

"So powerful," said Alexie, shaking his head. "Such a damn coward."

I look warily at Drake, honestly wondering how he would react to such an accusation. He only nodded, like he couldn't agree more.

Alexie gave me one last wink, then spun on his heel and headed for the door. He walked quickly, bashing Drake's shoulder he passed. Drake's body swung from the hit, but he made no other sign of feeling or noticing the physical insult. I took a sip of my coffee, waiting for Drake to move, or better yet, say something.

"Please sit," I told him when he did none of those things. "I've barely eaten, and already I'm in danger of indigestion."

My silly comment seemed to break his reverie. Two steps brought him in front of me, he sat down in the chair Alexie had recently vacated.

"Have you come to tell me everything?" I asked, putting extra happy layers of hope in my tone.

His jaw strained. "I'll keep my word," he said seriously, looking like he would rather do anything else.

Beneath the table I nudged his leg with my foot. "Come on Drake," I teased. "Quickly, before it's too late, and all hell breaks loose."

Drake leaned his elbows on the table and linked his fingers in front of him. He did not pick up on my cheery mood. His voice was serious when he said: "you might not want to know. Have you thought about that? Contemplated the fact, maybe some things are not worth remembering."

"Anything with you would be worth remembering," I said honestly, and placed my hand over his. I stared at the way we looked skin to skin, his dark night against my pale, so I did not see his expression. "People I love lie to me, they abandon me, please don't be one of those people, Drake."

"Lying and abandonment may be the least of the evils," he declared.

I finished my coffee, the waiter appeared at my side, in seconds my cup was magically full. I gripped Drake's hand. It felt like I had never wanted anything badly as this. Never.

"Cara," he breathed. "I wanted you to know me first before you demanded this of me. If you knew me better..." he shrugged, then laughed in a self-deprecating fashion. "Perhaps the result would be the same." He watched me take the last bite of my croissant, then lifted his hand.

"How do you like your eggs?" he asked.

"I'm fine," I said.

Drake rolled his eyes. "Cara, you need to eat, otherwise spells, dragons and gods will be the least of your worries. You will simply fade away."

I looked down at myself. "So, the dreams made me lose weight," I said defensively. "Getting stabbed repeatedly in the heart doesn't exactly give one a healthy appetite."

Drake ignored me. "Eggs benedict, two," he said. The waiter bowed and vanished.

"People bow to you?" I whispered.

Drake shrugged. "He does."

"Do you ever answer a question?"

Drake raised a sardonic brow. "Constantly. You have many."

"I should!" I said, yet there was no heat in my voice. The pink shadows of the table rose painted our hands, and I found myself fascinated by the tiny white scars crisscrossing his knuckles. "How old are you, Drake?"

"Twenty," he said distantly.

My eyes flew to his. He shrugged. "What? Are you surprised? How old do I look?"

"Immortal," I said, then, "what happened at twenty? Why not twenty-one? If what Andi wrote, and told me is all true, you have to be over three thousand years old. Are you a vampire?"

His eyes returned to mine, sharp and focused. "No. Of course not. I am older than the vampire."

"Oh, wow." I said. "So…?"

"I honestly don't know. I have tried to find the answer to your question for many centuries. It happened after I used the sword my father gave me."

"On whom?"

"Aphrodite first, then Ares, when he attacked me for what I had done—I deserved it. You were gone, and I was—" his mouth thinned into a white line, "I was enraged," he gritted out. "Ares, he lay beside her, sleeping in the snow, blue light spraying from the wound I put in his chest, and I was frozen in time. We all were. Each soul on the mountain, daring to stand beside me that wretched day."

"Won't you show me," I whispered, squeezing his hand.

Drake closed his eyes and nodded.

The waiter chose that moment to reappear behind me, both hands balancing plates of steaming breakfast. The hollandaise sauce was perfect, and we ate our food in relative silence. I hardly tasted a bite. Being this close to him did something to my stomach, frayed my nerves.

Andi strolled in wearing all black and sat beside Drake. She ordered a coffee, then tapped her nails on the tabletop until it arrived. I had not seen her for hours, she looked worn and I felt her elevated levels of stress. She kept glancing at Drake from the corner of her eye, and I suspected she needed to say something rather urgent to him and did not want me around for it. That was fine. I wanted to wash my face and get the smell of food off my hands before it made me sick. I stood up and whispered that I would be right back. I felt Drake's eyes follow every second of my exit. I walked through the adjoining car, and the following, past the master cabin where Lily slept.

Outside the windows blue mountains flew by, and the sunset hung low on the shifting ground. No light sparkled in this car, and each door lining the hall was firmly shut. A sharp thing in my chest urged me to turn around, a sense of lurking danger raised the hairs on the back of my neck. I looked through the glass door connecting me to the conductor's car.

Alexie stood in the space between, outside, under the moon, his hair blowing in the evening wind. He held a woman in his arms. Her long fingers were in his hair, one of her legs wrapped his hips. Her eyes were closed, her head thrown back. Alexie's mouth was fastened to her neck. I saw his white teeth sink in her skin; a single trickle of blood flowed from the punctured spot. I watched, frozen in horror. He drank her greedily, his big hands twining through her long hair. She sighed in his arms, stroked his face. I backed up a few steps, if she was willing, who was I to interfere. I left silently and walked back to Lily instead of Drake.

In my cabin, the world had fallen to darkness beneath a vanishing sun. Romania, Transylvania, and Vampires—honestly with my life and luck, what did I expect?

■ ■ ■

We reached the city of Hunedoara in a little under five hours. I stayed away from Drake the entire time. I needed to think, and it was impossible to do it around his smoky, golden eyes. The train stopped, I put on my down coat, and warm, cotton gloves. I picked a wool hat and tucked my hair under it. I reached for the door handle of my cabin, intending to escape the train, and see the city before Lily or Drake noticed my absence, and smothered me in unnecessary concern. The second my fingers touched the metal knob, a knock sounded on the door. I cringed, expecting Drake. Slowly, I opened the door. Alexie met my eyes, arms crossed over his chest, shoulder leaning against the golden door frame.

"You're not going to kill me, are you?" I asked, only two percent joking.

White teeth flashed in a stunning smile. "Not right now," he said. "I thought I would take you for a drink. You've looked like you could use one from the moment I met you. I know I could."

I glanced behind me; I could still hear Lily's even breathing. For a second I watched her eyelids flutter while she dreamed. She would freak but… "Yes, I would love to have a drink."

"Perfect," Alexie nodded at me, but did not reach for my hand. I wondered if Drake told him I was not to be touched. I searched my head for any commentary, Arias, however, was silent as she had been of late. Perhaps my growing powers subdued her, the thought made me sad.

Alexie glanced both ways down the hall, then put his gloved fingers against his lips.

I rolled my eyes. "Please," I whispered. "I want to escape as much as you do."

He gave me a strange look. "I like you very much," he whispered. "I wanted so badly to hate you."

"Sorry to disappoint," I whispered back. He gave me his crooked smile and motioned for me to follow. Together, we escaped the busy station and jumped in a rickety cab, which had been white once upon a time. Alexie spat some words at our driver and tossed him a colorful bill.

"I only have dollars," I said, reaching in my purse to take a fifty from my wallet. "Can you exchange some for me?"

Alexie laughed. "Put your money away, doll. Tonight's on me. Drake will probably kill me for it," said Alexie cheerfully. "I suspect it will be completely worth it." He reached out a gloved hand and lightly touched my jacket. Quickly he removed his hand.

"How are you related to Drake?" I asked.

"He saved my life, took me in when I was a boy, cared for me, when all others only showed fear. My name is Alexei Nikolaevich Romanov, on July seventeenth, nineteen eighteen, I was shot and stabbed multiple times. As I lay dying, a man wearing the wings of a bat, spirited me away from my dead parents and siblings, he gave me his blood, and turned me into a split."

"A split?" I interrupted.

Alexie nodded. City lights splashed his pale face, and under them, his skin seemed to glow. "Half vampire, half human."

"Wow," I said, I heard the shock in my voice, even though I had seen him feeding I still doubted it.

"I can see from the look on your face, that you completely believe me," said Alexie, sarcasm drenching his tone. He took off his glove. "Drake told me you can touch people. See their truths. He wanted me to stay away from you for this very reason. He never wants you to know the full extent of what he has become, what he's done."

"What has he done?" I asked. Honestly not caring. I took off my own glove. My fingers were shaking.

"You can give me the pain. Drake says you are learning to control it. Psychometry is a powerful gift; it can hurt the user more than it ever helps."

I closed my eyes, easily remembering past agony. "Tell me about it."

He held out his hand. "Don't you want to know?"

I shuddered. "I believe you."

He frowned, then shrugged and started to put his glove back on.

I sighed and held out my hand. "Gimme," I commanded.

"I've killed," he warned. "In the beginning when I was starving and alone. I killed, I hunted."

"That's okay," I whispered, wondering if it would be. "I've touched bad guys before."

Alexie's smile was brilliant. "None like me," he promised.

"Now, that I believe," I told him, and he chuckled.

I closed my eyes and touched his hand. Pain hovered at the edges of my senses, pounding on the invisible walls that kept it from attacking my nerves. I heard Alexie gasp, his only show of pain. Mists instantly engulfed me, transported me from the speeding cab and straight to another time. I saw a little boy, eyes hidden under a mop of filthy, dark hair. He hid in the shadows of a squat building, watching a man in his shop, cleaning his rifle. I felt the child's burning thirst in my own throat as we watched the man scratching his chin, he blew out his lamp and locked the door of his shop. He set off down the street and we followed him closely, almost hugging his shadow. The man looked over his shoulder several times, feeling our presence. We did not want to kill him, but the thirst was just too terrible.

We wanted to be home, cuddled beside our dead mother, or playing in the village with our decapitated sister. We shuddered, not wanting to think of their broken, dead bodies, not able to do anything else. The man stopped in his tracks, grabbed at his bladder, looked down the street—seeming to contemplate the remaining distance to home—then, turned and faced the nearest wall. He undid the buckle on his trousers, and they dropped to his spread knees. Slowly he began to urinate against the stones. The smell sickened us, but the thirst wiped the sickness away. Under his smells was the sweet scent of his blood, and we needed it. We ran to him. Jumped on his back and sunk our fangs in his neck. The taste of the blood was incredible, beyond anything. It quenched the burning thirst, so sweet, intoxicating.

Suddenly, a fist grabbed a handful of our hair, and our little body rocketed through the air. We hit an iron fence; I felt a blow in the chest. We hung in the air from the metal spike that impaled us. The man who had been our supper, was now feeding three others. Their eyes were red and their skin glistening. They clawed open the flesh on his stomach and stuffed their hands in his gut. One hand ripped the liver free and sucked the blood from it, until it was white and dry. Another fed on the heart. We hung there, dying. Wanting to die, waiting impatiently for it all to be over. We could join our mother, our father, and our sisters.

A black streak rushed in front of our fading vision. I knew who it was before I saw his face. In Drake's left hand, Legux blazed blue light. His movements blurred as he rushed the group of vampires, attacking each in turn, coldly precise. Deadly. When there was nothing left of them, save chunks of bleeding flesh, Drake struck a match and set their remains ablaze.

A cry of fear escaped our blood smeared lips. Drake spun to face us. I felt the air leave my lungs, he was not the Drake I knew, not in any time. His eyes were black holes, shedding darkness on a rage twisted face. His hair was long and matted in blood, his clothes looked stitched from night itself. He lifted his sword and walked to where we hung, a premonition of death. He paused when he saw our face. Something in his expression cracked and changed. I watched him sheath his sword. Carefully, he lifted our limp body off the iron spike, and laid us gently on the ground. His broad shoulders twitched as he sunk his teeth into the flesh of his wrist and ripped it enough to let the blood flow. Then, he let us drink, and drink, and drink and drink.

I opened my eyes and stared at Alexie, speechless. I was shaking badly, but I had survived. There had been little to no rending agony, Alexie on the other hand looked much worse for the wear. Green tinted his pale face, and his lips were drawn tight, white from pain.

"I'm so sorry," I muttered. "Are you alright?"

Alexie nodded. "Yes, it was more the pain of the memory than anything else."

"I have so many questions," I said.

"I'm sure you do," he told me, visibly recovering his composure, rubbing the hand I had touched. "You can grill me while we walk. Drake has warned me not to say a single word to you, which of course means I will tell you everything." He opened the door for me, said a kinder word to the cab driver for waiting, and handed him a nice-looking bill.

"Hey Alexie," I said, shivering in the wind as I placed my booted foot on the snowy curb.

"Yeah," he answered.

"I like you too."

■   ■   ■

The city of Hunedoara was a fairytale realized for me. Every romantic book I have ever read, every secret fantasy my mind ever created, has taken place in a city just like this. The enchanting architecture and icy air took my breath away. The streets were close and well-lit by electric lamps, yet I imagined they looked quite the same as they had two thousand years ago when the Romans walked them.

Giant snowflakes fell from the sky and landed lightly on my coat and hair, I felt them flutter against my lashes. Each touch was magic. Even Alexie smiling down on me was part of the spell.

"You know," he said, reaching past me and pushing open a small, wooden door. "I didn't actually expect you to come with me."

I stepped inside a dark room, lit by a single candle, sitting under a large, silver mirror. The deep, purple paper on the walls was old and torn in numerous places, showing the grey wall beneath, like the stones were leaking brain. Cobwebs huddled in the dimly lit corners of the small space. I gave Alexie an accusing glare. "I thought you weren't going to kill me?"

"Don't worry," he said, a twinkle lighting his eyes. "I only drink women who beg me, and I never, ever kill any of them. They all come back for more," he promised.

I continued my glare at his tall, princely perfection. "Oh, I'll just bet they do."

"You ready?" he asked.

"For what?" My voice and poise were suddenly wary.

"To finally see the world, you were born to be a part of," he said, then passed a single finger through the candle's small, violet flame. The mirror elongated instantly, much the same way my teacup had done in Aunt Jane's messy kitchen. As I watched, the glass changed to smoke, and together we walked through the haze into another world.

Spinning lights danced dizzily over every sparkling surface, and spun across the high, cathedral ceilings, a collage of mirrored glass. On every wall there was a door, each leading to a place I could not see. The diamond shaped room pointed toward a spectacular stage, where two DJ's spun out sets of low, intoxicating beats. I noticed the DJ on the right had huge, curled horns protruding from his pointed, hairless head. The other had a swinging, forked tail. The base reverberated the marble under my feet, and hundreds of creatures danced to the echoing rhythm.

Alexie made me follow him through the writhing throng. I kept my purse tight against my side, and my head down. We stopped in front of a bar, far from the main stage. It was a strange form of aquarium. Behind blue tinted glass, glowing fish swam in tight circles. Shells floated in the bubbling water, and of course—the bartenders were mermaids. I almost started crying when I saw their silver tails swish. The water washed around the first beauty queen's waist when she floated toward us and made hungry eyes at Alexie.

"Hey baby," she crooned, her voice enchanting as a siren's song. "You having the usual?"

"Hi, Trina, yeah, and the lady will have…?" Alexie let the question hang, then raised a brow in my direction.

"Whisky," I said, looking at the unrecognizable assortment of bottles floating above moving shelves. "Or its equivalent," I finished. Trina pursed her lips at me, then swam off to do as she was told.

"I wish Lily could see this," I said, hardly knowing where to look. Everything was new, and my mind reacted to it all, like I had never seen color or heard music properly before this moment—I felt drunk on unfiltered wonder. "What is this place?"

"This is Limbo," Alexie told me. "A haven for all creatures hunted by humans. Each door lining this room leads somewhere, where it leads is up to you."

"Can you explain to me about splits? I thought if a vampire were to bite a human…"

"Yes, that is what all humans think. In a way I suppose it is correct. The truth is, you may only be born a vampire, in which case your pure blood and able to make a split. A split cannot make another, their bite can only kill, not change. Like vampires, if a split is made as a child, they will grow to maturity, then never age again for all eternity. Splits are easier to kill, we can burn in sunlight when purebloods cannot."

"Do you know who made you?"

Alexie nodded. "It was Rasputin who bit me. He was pure blood, one of the first born."

"What do you mean, 'first born'? How did it happen?"

"That is a very long story, and for another time."

I frowned. "I thought you were going to tell me everything."

"We are short on time, darling."

Trina returned, our drinks in hand. Her pink streaked hair billowed around her, she swished it from side to side, slowly, letting Alexie see it move. He ignored her outrageous flirting, took both drinks from her ringed fingers, and handed one to me. I took a sip, it was sharp, bitter, and tasted nothing like whiskey. It was, however, incredibly strong. "Why are you showing me all of this?"

"Drake warned me you were full of questions. Can't just sit and take it all in, can you?"

"Alexie, tell me."

"Because I care about him. If you are walking around like a blind idiot, you're more likely to get us all killed. It's better that you know everything, it's better if you prepare. Get stronger."

"Stronger how?"

"You have so much power, Cara. You need to understand how to use it."

"Showing me all this?" I motioned to mermaids and the room. "This will help me understand how to use my power?"

"It's a damn good start in helping you acknowledge you *have* powers." Alexie turned and pointed to what could only be a dancing minotaur, in his early teens. "Now you can't tell yourself it isn't real." Alexie drained his drink in a single gulp, he turned to me, a thumb resting on the buckle of his dark jeans. "I'm going to leave for a few minutes, I need to feed. Will you be here when I get back?"

I shrugged. "I sure hope so," I said. He nodded, and I watched him disappear in the throbbing crowd.

Trina came back, a frown of disappointment painting her pretty mouth. "That is the witch's section over there," she snapped, pointing across the room. "They never sit at this bar."

I followed her finger, meaning to tell her I planned to stay where I was, thank you very much, but my eyes fell on a group of women and I froze. On the armrest of a lush, velvet couch, past the pointy hats and idling broomsticks, sat an all too familiar snow-white owl. I had seen this owl in my time, and in the past. Her big black eyes swiveled in my direction, then she spread her pearly wings and soared into the colorful air. I knew she wanted me to follow.

I forgot Trina, forgot the water bar and all the impossible creatures. I clutched my purse tightly and chased the flying bird through the room. She landed on a brass knocker affixed to an ivory door just to the left of where I stood on shaking legs. I flexed my cold fingers and reached for her snow-white wings. She vanished the second I touched her, and the door swung open. I stepped inside an empty white room. The brightness dazzled me, and I threw up my arm to shield my stinging eyes. It took a moment for the stinging to subside, when it did, I lowered my arm. A single chair rocked in the center of the room. In it, sat an old woman, she moved back and forth, and the chair creaked under her swaying weight. In her wrinkled hands she held two long knitting needles, they clicked in time to the uneven squeaks of the rickety chair. The blanket she knitted was black wool and, on its face, stitched into the very fibers of the thread, was a snow-white owl. For a moment I smelled lilacs and Fairhaven rain.

"Come closer, Cara," she said, in an old, withered voice, not looking up from her endless knitting. Click, click went the needles, creak, creak went the chair. I remained frozen, hands in the air, like a wind-up toy who lost their batteries. "Don't be afraid of me dear. I rarely mean harm." She lifted her gaze to my face, her own was a study in wrinkles, her watery eyes lost in endless crinkles of flesh. Her red mouth looked like a gash against skin grey as her hair. I looked at her gnarled hands and saw that the tips of each needle dripped huge drops of red blood. Drops that faded instantly when they landed on the black wool. Drip…drip…drip. Her eyes locked with mine. She smiled at my fear, I only saw her blistered gums, and green, squishy teeth. Her black tongue shot out and licked her cracked lips. "I said come!" she told me, and I felt compelled. My feet moving against my command took me to her side. "I've made a blanket for you. To keep you warm when the storm comes."

"Thank you?" I said. I felt my teeth sinking into my lower lip. "How do you know my name?"

"I know everything about you, Cara," said the old crone, smiling her nearly toothless smile. "I've been waiting for you." She rose to her feet, the chair rocked once, then fell still. A ringing, loud enough to rival the DJs resonated in my ears. On the floor, near my feet, I saw a single white feather. Not thinking, I bent down, and picked it up. The instant wash of visions was so astoundingly strong, I had no chance of pushing them away…no time to build up my wall. My knees buckled, pain shot through my temples when my body went limp and my head hit the ground. I heard lightning crackle, and thunder rocked me. Then, all at once, it was Hanna's voice coming at me from every corner of my world. *'I need you to be strong, Cara'*, she said, in that peaceful time before the dreams. *'I am sorry, because strange things are coming for you and there is nothing, I can do to change them. I'm sorry because I am powerless to give you any more help than I already have. Powerless to give you any more help…powerless. You're so strong. Powerless, so strong…strange things'.*

Seconds before my eyes closed, I saw red rubber boots, and smelled lilacs.

▪ ▪ ▪

I am lost in the vision, once again a creature of mists and shadow. I watch through my endless tunnel, understand it in that place where I see and know all.

My feet moved over the sand of their own volition, and my eyes rose to the spectacular view that blocked out all else. In front of me I saw Mount Olympus, it towered over Sparta as if to show the kings of the world who held true power. Its white rock shouted domination. On the east side—atop wind bitten rocks of ice—stood a statue of the great god himself. Zeus, in silver and gold, the first thing on earth to greet Apollo's rising face. Under the statue's golden, sandaled feet stood the most scared of temples.

In it, a brunette goddess lounged on a bed of air eating a fist sized grape. "Why do you always kill them in a gold room, Dite?" she asked. "Is there some vital symbolism I am unaware of?"

"What are you even doing here, Athena?" flared Aphrodite. I watched her stomp past Athena and grab a silver set of chain link cuffs off the floor.

"I'm here, my dear, because you are in trouble."

"I can handle it," spat Aphrodite.

"Oh yes, I can see that. I can see how well you've been *handling* it these past two years."

"I have a plan. It's just taken a little longer than I originally anticipated."

"What do you want?" Athena asked seriously.

Aphrodite stepped out of her gossamer red gown; I watched the material fly when she kicked it across the floor. "Power," she said simply. "That's what every woman wants, isn't it? You have your power in wisdom and battle, and I have…"

"Nice breasts?" Athena suggested.

"Go suck a cock," snapped Aphrodite.

Athena laughed. "Never have, never will." She tossed her hair back over her shoulders, to me her silver irises looked like snake eyes in the dimming light "Does everyone really want beauty so badly?"

Aphrodite gave Athena a cold look. "Of course, they do. It is the one thing a human will trade their soul for."

"Ah," Athena mused, "so Hades owns the soul, and what? Allows you to borrow it?"

"The women who worship me in the mists are willing and grateful, though yes—in a sense. I give beauty, they give their soul. Ultimately it belongs to Hades, though our deal is simple. All the priestesses of the Aphrodisia are mine. I bring Hades many others. Everyone alive wishes for beauty and wealth. It is common as breathing."

"Don't do it, Dite," Athena cautioned. "Hades said Arias is not for you, and Drake will kill you if you take her again!"

"He can't kill me!" Aphrodite rested her hands on her hips. "What do you want, Athena? You only care about a thing if you have a vested interest in it. Why do you obsess over my priestess? What do you want?!" she repeated.

Athena smiled a secret smile; she turned her head so Aphrodite would not see it. "I want revenge," she whispered. "Only revenge."

Aphrodite did not see the smile, but I did. There was something in the lines bracketing her mouth that made me think of Hanna. "You expect me to help you with this revenge?!" asked Aphrodite warily.

Athena laughed. "Of course not. I mean to help you with yours." Her hand flew through the air and pulled a crystal goblet from the nothing. "Make Ares drink this."

Aphrodite eyed the crystal dubiously, one golden brow raised high. "What is it?"

Athena lips curved. "Submission, in a fashion, for an hour, maybe two, he will be your slave. You will need him if you wish your plan to succeed. He will not go against Draken otherwise."

"I don't trust you, Athena," swore Aphrodite.

"That is the beauty of my deal, trust is not required. Only action."

Olympus and the goddesses dissolved to a puff of smoke, then drifted away like the memories they were. I stood alone in the white room, same, yet drastically changed. The creaking chair and old woman were gone. Four green doors faced me. In horror movies, I always wondered why the silly girl did not run? Why she walked in the room leaking monster sounds, or followed a noise through the butcher's factory, chased a shadow through curtains of swinging knives—now I knew. It was because your mind and heart will let you do nothing less. The more afraid you are, the more you it seems you have to know just what exactly goes bump in the night.

I walked to the first door, wrapped my fingers around the brass handle, and threw it open. Sea wind struck me in the face. Through flying particles of red sand, I saw the armies of Greece, standing strong against the Trojan hordes. Men shouted, swords and shields crashed, men died. At the edges of the earth-shaking battle, Athena and Ares circled each other, weapons drawn, teeth bared.

"Traitor!" screamed Athena. "I will kill you!" she vowed.

"Shrew!" shouted Ares. "I have done nothing! I am your brother. I carry the core of light! Kill me, you kill yourself. We both know you are far too selfish for that."

Athena had no response; she planted her feet more firmly in the sand and lifted her right hand toward a tall mountain at Ares's back. She flexed her fingers, and the side of the mountain shook.

"What are you doing?" Ares took a step back, he held out a hand in defense. "Athena, I am your brother... brother."

"Half-brother," breathed Athena. Her fingers flexed again, a chunk of rock—the size of a small house—ripped free of the mountainside and hurtled at Ares. The speed of the projectile gave him no time to react. The rock slammed into his torso, then lifted him off his feet. When he fell, the boulder landed atop him, flattening him to the earth. Ares put his hands against the rock and heaved, it shuddered, but did not move.

I heard screaming in the wind that beat my hair, it took my breath when I turned my head toward the sound. I saw Aphrodite running through the killing fields. A wave of her slender hand threw men from her path. They shouted in fear and ran from the rage in her eyes.

"Athena, please!" she cried, her voice a sound only made when torn directly from a breaking heart. "Athena, leave him!" she commanded, and fell to her knees. I watched her lift Ares's head to her lap. Blood soaked her sparkling, white robes. The robes blew in the wind like a confusing flag on this battlefield. Attack and surrender. "You will live," whispered Aphrodite. "I will take you to my rock, I will heal you, love. Athena please, please, let me heal him, please..."

I slammed that door. There was nothing there for me. Only more pain and dying. I knew the end of that horror story; it was time to understand mine. A single step took me to the next door. I touched the handle, this door swung open of its own accord.

This room showed me a world of burning night. Fire ate across the lands, it devoured everything in its path. I saw a white horse rushing toward the flames at a terrible speed. His rider, Athena, flew fast as the blaze. I saw what she rushed toward, understood what she already knew, she was a million embers too late. She threw herself from the screaming horse and landed on her knees in the ashes. *"No! No!"* she clutched at her heart, tore at her hair, then screamed and screamed while she watched her library of Alexandria burn. Ancient texts and priceless knowledge, taken by the fire gods.

I sucked in a hot breath and slammed the third door. A final step took me to the fourth green door. I knew I did not need to reach for the knob anymore, something ancient, and powerful was breaking apart inside of me. Instead of pain, I felt divine. I pointed a single finger toward the door, it opened at my command. The world behind this final door was a place I knew well. Wynter haunt, its headstones and mists facing an altar of flame and stone. A pentagram spun on the ground, a candle burning at each of its points. Athena sat near a fawn-colored goddess, who held a bow and arrow made of fire.

"You must climb atop the altar, Lillianna," said Athena.

"You sure this will not harm my girls?"

Athena touched Lillianna's hand, and I saw her face. It was changed from the day when she watched her precious library burn, but it was the same. When I saw it, I wondered how I only noticed it now. Athena and Hanna wore the same face, in this time—in all times.

"It will not harm them, I swear it," said Athena—Hanna.

I felt my hand as it flew up to cover my mouth. "My gods!" I whispered. "Oh, my gods, Hanna!" All along, all this time. Hanna—Athena, they wanted revenge. I was the revenge. I felt sick. Saying soothing words to her sister—words I knew were lies—Hanna lifted a sparkling vial, uncorked it, and poured the wispy contents over her sister's very pregnant stomach. It slid over Lillianna's starched dress, fluid as liquid light. Twin lights began to glow under Lillianna's skin. Mine and Lily's soul, I realized. The liquid light moved through the womb and fused to a single soul—mine.

"I must place this soul inside of Cara's body, or she will die, and it will all be for naught," said Hanna. Her revenge—she meant—would all be for naught. I meant nothing. The knowledge was hollow, and deep. I slammed the door. If Hanna were actually Athena, that would mean, the fawn-colored girl—the goddess with the flaming bow and arrow—was my mother. I had just witnessed the night of my birth—my mother, the goddess Artemis—my mind told me. I wished I could slam the door again. Daughter of a goddess. *Great,* I thought. *Just freaking great.*

CHAPTER XI

LIMBO

I did not know who you were.
So, I told you a terrible lie,
I did not know the thing you needed,
Was the thing that would make you die.

A set of powerful knocks sounded against the door. I turned, slowly. Confused. Alive. Lost.

"Cara?" shouted Drake. The strength of the knocks increased. "Cara!"

Did he know? Had he known all along? If he had, had he told me? In another place, a distant time? I marched to the door, used my newfound power, and pointed at the knob, it obeyed instantly. The door flew open. I had no time to say anything, Drake grabbed me, then squeezed my body to his chest, nearly knocking the wind from me. I gasped and tried to slide my hands between our straining bodies.

"Goddamn it!" he said, and pressed his lips to my temple, his breath was hot on my cheek. "Goddamn it!" he heaved.

I stayed silent; my words locked behind one of those green doors. He stared down at me, the devil in his flashing eyes. His face was hot and flushed.

"Cara?" He touched my lips with the tips of his trembling fingers. "Are you alright?"

"Fine," I said.

"What happened?!" he demanded.

"I saw…" I looked behind me, meaning to point to the green doors, try and explain. They were gone. The room was white and empty. The rocking chair sat where it had, still creaking, swaying back and forth. I shuddered. *'I made you a blanket'*, Athena had told me, *'to keep you warm when the storm comes'*. Her storm.

"Cara!" Drake's harsh voice snapped my face back to his. His eyes widened when he took in my expression, and I wondered how I looked to him? The witness to a murder, maybe? The look of someone who had seen too much, too fast.

"What?" I muttered.

"What happened!?" he demanded, looking like he could rip metal with his teeth, then before I could think of something else to say, he leaned down and put his mouth against my neck, groaning my name. I turned my face and found his lips.

Suddenly, the green doors, and the secrets they told me were extremely far away. His kiss was hard and wild. The taste of his mouth made me see stars and I was the brilliance in a digital sky…burning. There was no other kiss in the world like his. We were both breathing heavily when his hands came up to frame my face. "No matter what you remember, just know that I never stopped loving you," he said.

His eyes bored into mine, they told the whole truth. He moved his hand from my face and touched a space just beneath my breast where my heartbeat was the strongest. "Arias, Cara, it doesn't matter," he said, not breaking our burning stare. "This girl in here is mine, and I am hers. I have lived three thousand years in the shadow of her death." Tingles attacked the center of my forehead, I felt something there—tightly closed—struggling to open.

"No, Cara." He kissed the spot. "Not yet, let me take you to my home. It's not safe for you here."

It's not safe for me anywhere, I thought, but said, "how? How will you do it? How will you make me remember?? I want the truth Drake; I'll know if you lie?"

He nodded. "I need to touch your light." He pressed a finger to the tingling spot between my eyes that felt as if it was starting to glow.

"How?" I whispered. Then I knew. "Ah, power found in the highest pinnacle of pleasure. Oh," I said stupidly. "Sex. You need to have sex with me. That's why you won't do that either, why you…if you have sex with me, I'll remember? If I remember, you think I will die?"

"Yes," he rasped. "And" his voice deepened, "it has never been *just sex*—not for you and I."

"I don't think we have any choice then, it's a matter of time. I don't think we can be in the same world, and not have that between us It will happen, and I will remember. You know it, don't you?"

"I can…" his voice broke. "I don't have to…"

"What Drake? You don't have to what?!"

He sighed deeply. "Fuse with you," he whispered, and pressed his fingers again to the ever-warming spot between my eyes. "Here, connect my light to yours, touch our souls."

"Oh," I said, and rolled my eyes. The eloquence of my vocabulary tonight was staggering. "Can you do that with any woman? Fuse?"

He shook his head. "No, Cara. You are my priestess; it could only ever be you. Always, forever. Just you."

I swallowed a gulp of what felt like pure, shimmering light. No matter if I ever remembered, it would only be him for me. Always, forever.

I smiled, then felt his body stiffen in my arms. "Cara!" he breathed, sounding shaken. I looked up. "Oh, Cara, my love. Look at yourself, you're glowing."

"What…?" I lifted my hands and stared at them in shock. My fingers wore thick gloves of luminous light, light that seemed to emanate from my very pores. "Glowing!" I whispered. I stepped out of his arms and twirled. Streams of shimmering light spiraled around me. "Drake… oh crap, this is incredible. You did this to me!" I blamed it brightly.

"No love, this magic is all yours. Zeus, Cara! You are so beautiful," he breathed, and his husky words brightened the glow. I faced the only door left in the room, small and white it blocked my exit to the strange, outside world. I flicked my glowing fingers through the air. The door splintered, then flew from its hinges, and crashed into the dancing crowd of magical creatures. A few jumped out of the way. The silver doorknob struck a tall blond man in the back of his head, and he went down like a ten pin. Power rushed through my arm. The light spreading from my skin was nearly blinding.

Drake lifted me then, one hand cradling my head, the other beneath my bent knees. Alexie stood on the other side of the door I had just annihilated and worry carved strange lines in his perfect face.

"Is she alright?" asked Alexie, he looked uncertain, even afraid.

"She is fine," said Drake. He kept me cradled in his arms until we were back at the bar. Gently he set me on the plush barstool, handed me a glass of water which seemed summoned from thin air, and lightly touched the back of my hand while I drank it all. When I had placed the glass on the bar, Drake rounded on Alexie. He grabbed the boy's dark shirtfront and slammed him into the glass bar. Alexie's body bowed over the countertop, and I saw his hair fall in the water.

"What the hell were you thinking?" roared Drake, scaring Trina badly. She screamed and dunked her head. Bubbles rose to the surface as she sought shelter in deeper places, and I realized the water bar was far larger than it appeared.

"I was thinking that you are an idiot!" said Alexie, quite calmly for the situation. "Now, you are proving me right."

"Let him go, Drake," I commanded, putting steel in my tone. "*You should have taken me here. Alexie did the right thing. Drake!*" I hollered when he ignored me and pushed Alexie's head further in the swirling water. I made a fist and struck his shoulder. It was like punching steel. "Oh, ouch!" I flexed my hand, it felt broken. "Jesus! Ouch! Let him go! Oh, crap that hurt!" I held out the hand that hit him, it was already swelling, and the fingers seemed a little tilted.

Drake let go of Alexie, his low growl said the fight was far from over, but his eyes were for me. I stomped my foot and shook my hand.

"Are you okay, love?"

"No! Honestly, I'm really not, and I'm rapidly losing my temper. Alexie did the right thing. I needed to see this. I am part of this world, same as you are."

Drake held my hand, watching my face.

"You made me stop glowing," I accused.

"A truly great crime," he agreed solemnly. He lifted my hands to his lips and kissed my palm. Chills wrapped my wrists like tingling manacles.

He drew me close when he spoke his breath heated my temple. "I think I can do it again," he rasped.

Neither of us said a word as my hand started to glow between us. Colorful grids of strobe lights painted our bodies, and I moved unconsciously to the music. I took my hand gently from his grip and wrapped it with my other, around his neck.

"Do you want to dance with me?" I asked, leaning up to press my lips to his ear so he could hear my whispered words.

"I want to do anything with you," he vowed. I smiled. His words made me think of water, and a full, blue moon—a memory in this time—and another. It flitted away before I could catch it. Drake's hands went to my waist and he pushed me into the crowd. Over Drake's shoulder I saw Alexie watching us, a huge smile on his face. I winked at him and gave him a thumbs up behind Drake's back.

We stepped on the dance floor, the beat dropped, then the music soared to a flaring crescendo. I had never danced in a club, too much danger of being touched. Now I was unafraid, and it felt amazing. I imagined my glow was a beautiful sphere of light encapsulating us and shielding me from all harm. My bubble of protection, my ward of dawn. The warmth between us grew more powerful by the second.

The glow I shed was brilliant, lighting our space on the floor, no one seemed to notice or care. Deep, throbbing music pounded to the beat of my heart, and my breaths ripped out of my lungs. Drake spun us, our bodies never breaking contact, his hands fell to my back, and I crushed my hips to his. We told a story with our bodies. Our movements a worshipful communication. Music flowing through my bones, my body did what he told it to do. He needed no words; the music was the third character in our story bringing us together.

Drake danced like he did everything else, sensuously, completely, godly. We danced until my feet hurt and my ears rang, we danced until I was dizzy and laughing breathlessly. Sometime in the night Alexie joined us, and Drake was too lost in *us* for anger, so we all danced some more. We danced until the sun came up, and when Drake finally carried me from the club, he whispered in my ear that I was the most beautiful thing he had ever seen. I fell asleep in his arms. Still glowing.

CHAPTER XII

CORVIN CASTLE

I drew back the velvet curtains and looked out the window of the bouncing carriage. The Iron cliffs of Poiana Ruscāi in the Carpathian mountain range were wild and rugged as the black sea rushing against their base. Rainbows speared through the white froth kicked up by high waterfalls, and springing fountains hidden in the moss-soaked rocks. Light green touched with hints of autumn and gold painted the trees and swaying blades of grass. There was magic here in this land, deep and old. I closed my eyes. It seemed magic was everywhere. Last night, Drake had taken me back to his train, and laid me in his bed, we slept till noon. I held his hand all the while and had no dreams that were not of dancing in his arms. When I woke, he was gone, I quickly showered and changed to a clean pair of jeans and a rosy turtleneck. Before I had my boots zipped, Drake burst in and literally whisked me away to a large stretch limo, which took us to an idling carriage, strapped to a team of four, black stallions. Anderson looked at the carriage and groaned loudly, Lily squealed, and clapped her hands. Now we were in it, harshly jolting over a high bridge that overlooked this lush countryside, and I was enthralled.

Drake rode a spotted silver mare alongside Alexie, and I watched them through the window. Alexie wore a wide hat pulled low over his eyes, giving the fierce impression of an old-time bandit. Evening was fast approaching, and the sun hid behind a thick cloak of grey clouds, still, he sheltered himself against it.

Lily took my hand and looked at me. I had spent the last hour showing her everything. Drake, the dancing, Limbo, and each memory the green doors showed me.

Lily looked fresh and lovely, her glowing eyes brightening her flushed cheeks. "What upsets me most are the Hanna revelations," she said. "The rest is of no consequence; I always knew I was the daughter of a goddess. Cara!" she stuck her nose out the window. "Do you see that? Galloping just behind those trees, I think it's a…it's a, Hecate save us! I can't think of the word! I just went blank."

I followed her bouncing finger, instantly spotting what had her in a tizzy. "A centaur," I whispered.

Lily turned on me, eyes popping. "Then, it's true," she said, throwing herself back against the velvet cushions, and sighing loudly, "we really are in a fairy tale." Her fingers came up and rubbed at her eyes. "That's unfortunate, the true fairy tales never end well for the secondary character."

"Lily," I started to laugh. "You could never be a secondary character."

"That's sweet of you to say so, things don't usually go that well for the hero and heroine either," she said, sad for a terrible second.

"It's going to be alright, Lily," I said, loudly in her head. *"You were right about the power; we are getting much stronger. I feel like I could flex my fingers and make the earth move. We always knew there was more… we can't freak now that we are seeing it, for real."*

"Look at you being the strong one." Lily leaned forward and kissed my cheek, good mood restored. "Oh! That view, though! Do you see those towers?" She stuck her pink nose further out the open window. "It has a freaking drawbridge."

"Thank god," muttered Anderson seriously, pressing on a spot at the base of his neck and wincing. I smiled at him, feeling his discomfort, then returned my eyes to the sprawling castle covering the green earth before us like a blanket of stone. Its gothic towers speared up from wide bastions, standing high above the steel walls stretching around the face of Corvin. Past the drawbridge, and cavernous moat were gates of iron and steel, standing alone and haunted.

We stayed silent as the carriage clattered down a cobblestone road, to the edge of the black gates, and the sounds of crunching chain and grinding metal reverberated through the stillness of approaching twilight. When the great chains released, and the metal cogs fell into a mechanical rhythm, the wide, iron studded gates sprang open. Our carriage passed under two rows of hanging metal spikes, wrapped by a network of thick, crisscrossing ropes.

I held my breath as the team of horses came to a stop and watched Drake dismount. He opened the carriage door, before holding out his gloved hand. Lily took it, and he helped her step down. I hooked my purse over my shoulder and ducked my head. I had no time to take a breath, Drake swept me into his arms, and placed me gently on my feet.

"Welcome home," he breathed. I smiled brilliantly. I felt drunk on the fresh mountain air, and him. Lily had Alexie's hand clutched between both of her own, and she was speaking a mile a minute.

"It feels like home," I whispered back, wondering why that was so.

A small break in the clouds let a shaft of setting sunlight spill through. It pooled around our feet, highlighting my god in gold. He touched his forehead briefly to mine, and I threw a covert glance at my hand, wondering if I was glowing again. Holding hands and watching our breaths puff around our faces, we walked through a double set of cathedral arches, framing the edge of the courtyard. Broad, red brick pillars sat between twisted staircases leading to lush green gardens full of roses. Waterfalls that flowed from the shoulders of stone nymphs poured into a sparkling stream that cut through the furthest parts of the vast property.

"When was this majestic place built?" asked Lily, hand firmly clasped to Alexie's sleeve.

"The structure was originally laid by the Romans, or so it is said," Alexie began. "Legend tells us that long ago; a prince came to these lands with priceless treasure to bury. He laid claim to Corvin castle, repaired the crumbling walls, and made this place his kingdom. The people called him Basarab. Basarb fought many battles to keep this land. He was challenged each time a new king came to power. In thirteen thirty, it was Charles Robert of Hungary who wanted his blood. It was called the battle of Posada. Robert's army was thirty thousand strong, and Basarab had less than a thousand men, yet he annihilated them." Alexie gave Drake a pointed look. "Corvin, however, has been many things. Swords and spears were manufactured here during the fourteenth, and fifteenth century."

"They were renowned across Europe," concluded Drake.

Alexie nodded. "In eighteen fifty-four, a rather hefty brawl," he cleared his throat, and tossed Drake another sidelong glare, "started a nasty fire, which burned nearly all the wood in the castle, ceilings, doors, wooden beams—whose destruction caused most of the upstairs floor to collapse—in fact, all save the dungeon doors went up in flames." Alexie rolled his dark eyes. "It took us years to restore the place."

"Sounds like quite the brawl," laughed Lily. "What was it over?"

"Past angers," said Drake, his tone told us that was the end of it. Lily did not listen.

"What past angers? Who were you fighting?" she demanded, letting go of Alexie and rounding on Drake, her eyes wide with leaping curiosity. Drake said nothing, and Alexie threw his hands in the air.

"Where is Andi?" I asked, changing the subject. It was apparently a bad change. Drake's eyes darkened, pain ghosting through centers, howling like an approaching storm.

"She went to visit her mother," said Lily, stretching her arms above her head and letting out a monstrous yawn. "She'll be here in two days, then we are going to Deva. She thought we would want to settle in first."

Drake turned away, lifted several bags, and silently led us into his home.

I moved through the main door, and down the long halls in silent awe, captivated by the high ceilings in what Alexie told us was the Room of Knights. Paintings on the walls and hanging tapestries depicted brave men in shining armor, challenging the gods in the sky. Goddesses cluttered the breaks in the clouds, looking dispassionately down on their mortal prey.

"It would take me a year to properly see this place," said Lily, and ran her hands over a tall, silver candelabra which sat beneath a stained-glass window of the Madonna. "Will you take me to the library, Alexie? I've been dreaming of it since you told me about Galileo's diary. Anderson, will you come? Perhaps we can scare up a cup of coffee."

"Fran Anjou will be in the kitchens. No one can help you better than her," explained Anderson.

"She's been steward of this establishment for many years," said Alexie.

"Humm," mused Lily. "How many years? Years like yours, Alexie?" she asked. I wondered when he had told her, or if she had—in simple Lily fashion—just figured it out. The three of them flitted off, talking, and laughing. I stood in front of Drake in a patch of dying sun. When the final sparkle faded away, Drake took my hand and led me into his home.

■　■　■

Lily and I were given adjoining suites. In my luscious room, blue silk canopies, and shiny mirrors faced arched windows that overlooked a dark forest.

I was fully in my fairy tale now. Yet for some reason, I did not sleep at all well that night. I tossed and turned. Dreamed of running, endlessly running. I had no idea what I chased. My phone rang at four in the morning, already awake I answered it on the second ring.

"Cara?" Gary's voice crackled down the line.

"Hey, Gar what time is it there?"

"Two in the afternoon, why?"

"Nothing, what's up?"

"Found… headquarters…murder weapon was… analyzed."

"Gar, you're breaking up." I stood and put my fluffy slippers on, glad I had thought to unpack them. The castle was freezing, outside the widows I could see the falling flakes of pure white snow. I threw a blanket over my shoulders and stepped into the hall. I shivered, and started to walk, no destination in mind, just service. "Sorry, what were you saying?"

"We found the headquarters of the Fairhaven Warlocks. I had the murder weapon analyzed. More crazy shit, apparently the piece is some kind of artifact, over two thousand years old."

Three thousand, I thought, but said nothing. What difference would it make? "Have there been any more kidnappings?"

"No, shit I hope not, not that we know of…it's just…" Gary's voice cracked. "I read something similar to the story Drake told me…" his voice dropped. "About you."

Ice slid down my spine. "What about me?"

"The lore attached to the knife, it's the story of a girl under a love spell who was cursed to die, be reborn and die again. There's some writing on the blade of the knife, don't ask me to say it in Latin cause you know I can barely speak English, but it's something to the tune of, 'power is in the blood, life in the blade'."

"What the hell does that mean?" I asked.

"I was hoping you would know; you were right about it being a ritual. Ryan says it's an ancient love spell. Told me that his Grandmother on the reservation sells them with lavender oil for five ninety-nine."

"Where is the knife?"

"The Smithsonian has it," grunted Gary. "Artifact appraisals, or some shit."

Neither of us said anything for a moment. I walked down a long hall, feeling ghosts in every shadow. Two empty sets of metal armor guarded the door, I touched a shiny spear. "You sound tired Gar," I sighed.

"In my bones," he said. "Can't sleep until I know this is over, 'till I have all the bastards involved locked up for life."

"Look for a temple Gar, or a place with something that can serve as an altar. I don't know why they burn the girls, that's not part of the ritual."

Gary grunted. "Things get twisted over time, if they were nasty to start with…" he let his sentence hang, I could almost hear his shrug. "Where are you?" he asked.

I looked around. "Well, right now it appears I am in a candlelit chapel. I honestly have no idea how I am going to find my way back to my room."

"You have a room in a chapel?" Gary sounded confused.

"Castle," I explained. "Replete with dungeons, chapel, and golden crucifixes studded in rubies." I pulled the blanket tighter around my shaking shoulders, the icy wind sliced straight through my thin, black nightgown.

"You homesick yet," he asked, hopeful.

"A little," I said honestly, wishing I could tell him everything.

"Go back to sleep, be careful. I'll call in a few days."

"You be careful," I said. "You're the one chasing murders."

"And you're not?" he asked. I swallowed hard and said goodnight.

Candles glowed in every corner of the old, dark chapel, moving varied hues of soft light. Flickering wicks dancing in pools of melted wax reflected in stained glass windows behind my head. Huge rubies in the cross winked and flashed at me. I touched the cross. The gold was so pure, my fingernail left a dent. "Hail Mary, pray for us sinners in the hour of our death," I whispered. The golden cross sat on a high stone table beside a silver sword. A dark, velvet cloth wrapped the blade. I knew the weapon instantly.

"Legux," I breathed. At my words, twined writing etched on the underside of the blade, began to glow. Blue light swirled up from the stone table and wreathed me in smokey ribbons. I moved closer to the glow, mesmerized. My phone fell to the ground, and clattered at my feet, forgotten.

I reached for the blade. It was a metal I had never seen and could not name. Tingles attacked the tips of my fingers as I brushed them over the glowing words, listened to the crying wind banging at the stained glass. I fell to my knees, not removing my touch from the glowing blade. Breath started to wheeze out of my lungs. I bowed my head, submitting to the ringing in my ears, keeping my eyes on the streamers of blue light wrapping my arm, my neck, flowing into my heart. I knew what was happening, I knew the visions were on their way to sap the life from my reality. For the first time, I wanted them to come. I closed my eyes and mentally grabbed hold of the swirling vortex of memories beckoning me. It happened then; in a splintering thunder crash of invisible sound, I flew backwards in time.

The sky is pale blue, blue as the lights transporting me. I am flying, flying away from Drake, Androsia and prince Darius. I am flying in Aphrodite's arms, for a time the blue lights are all I see. Eventually, I see a snowcapped mountain, a lightening scar marring its face. Aphrodite swoops down until I am a mere ten feet from the ground, then, she lets me go, and my body crumples to the snow. I feel cold flakes seep through the silk of my nightgown, freeze my bare hands.

I lift myself on shaking arms. In front of me is a stone altar situated atop a five-pointed star. A candle burns at each of its points.

"It's the symbol of the Olympians," a soft voice tells me. I turn and stare into my own face, nearly unchanged by time.

"Two sides of the same coin," says Arias, reading our mind. Her hair is slightly darker than mine, curling beautifully, and blowing in the icy wind.

"Your slippers," she says.

I nod, understanding. I bend down to untie the silk laces, then slip the shoes off my feet. I know I am about to be murdered, yet the value of ceremony has been imprinted on me since childhood. If I am going to die, I am going to die well. The way a priestess of Enisis should die—willingly and without regret. When I stand, Arias and I move toward each other. Arias holds out her arms, and I rush to her. Throw my own arms around her waist and squeeze. Seamlessly we fuse as before in Hades's chamber of stars.

"We have to be strong," she says. "This is our destiny."

Something in my mind screams it is not *mine— or not all that is mine.*

It seems the walk to the altar takes a thousand years, the cold I had experienced in the chapel had nothing on this deserted mountain. I feel Aphrodite's eyes on me while I sludge through the snow. I am terrified, shaking, but I do not feel like struggling anymore—everyone has a time, and mine is up. I knew it then, I know it now—it was time to die—for real, *this time.*

Finally, I reach the altar. The cold of the stone is a shock, like dry ice. Thankfully, the jarring pain is over quickly. I lie down without hesitation, command my shivers to be silent.

Aphrodite moves toward me; I see the bone knife in her hand.

"It did not have to be like this," she says, almost sweetly. "This time I will not make it quick for you. It will be painful." Her fingers coast over my cheeks, lightly brush away the falling snow. "Hades will give you to me. He can do nothing else. There are no more swords to trade for your soul—it is mine."

Tears sting my eyes, and I understand them. Arias had loved her for so long—this goddess of lust and fire. Aphrodite had been the magical sun in her sky for eighteen years. Even as she moves to kill us, Arias forgives her—having always known in her heart, she someday would. We are humans and they are gods, it feels only right they should be allowed to take our lives, if they need our souls.

"Hades will not give me back to you in any fashion," I say honestly. "I will go to the mists, where I mean to watch over Draken for always, if you are kind to him, I will give you my prayers."

My soft words ignite the banked flames in Aphrodite's eyes. Her hand flashes out, she grabs my left hand and rips my golden ring off my finger. The ring Drake gave me the day we were married. The ring I had found on a forest path in another place, and a distant time. My skin and nail go with the ring, I do not scream, just watch the pattern my blood makes when it splashes on the fresh snow.

"You should not have defied me, little human girl!" hisses Aphrodite. "You should not defy me now. Yours will be a cursed life, condemned to endless misery, always wanting, never having." She leans forward until her red lips brush my ear. "If ever your death god brings you back, if ever you think a day may come when you will have him again, I will be there. Thirteen turns of the sun," her voice rises. "Thirteen turns of the sun for my thirteen priestesses, thirteen turns for our thirteen months, thirteen turns for my thirteen sisters, thirteen turns for the thirteen powers I implore, thirteen turns until you die. This is my will!" she shouts. "This is MY will! So, mote it be." Aphrodite raises her arms, I look at the tip of the knife, the bone blade reflects the discolored sunlight. *Pray for us in the hour of our death*, I think, if I could have crossed myself in that moment I would have, but that religion, and the chapel I knelt in, were centuries away.

She lifts the knife, I close my eyes and think of the way Drake looks when he kisses me, I think about his hands in my hair, how his arms seem to wrap my entire body when he holds me. My shoulders tense at the last second, I hear an owl scream, and flinch away from the blade. The knife cuts into my stomach, pierces upward into my heart. White, hot stars explode in my eyes. That is when my tears finally escape, because I hear Drake's battle cry running through the wild wind, and Pluto's high-pitched wail. Even though I knew what was going to happen, I still felt the agony—they are mere seconds too late.

Drake is running, shouting my name. His eyes are full of blood, red tears pour down his cheeks. I see green flames leaping in his palms. His bronze skin is covered in the blood of the fallen Igori, and of the king, his father, who fulfilled a prophecy this night.

"You can't harm me!" says Aphrodite, squaring her shoulders. I see real fear flash in her eyes. "I am the daughter of Ouranos, god of the sky. I am divinity personified."

Drake's eyes move to the knife sticking out from between my broken ribs, the cut, still spraying endless vials of blood. A low, horrible noise tears free of his throat. The sound ricochets off the icy mountain cliffs. Still moving toward, me at a breakneck speed, Drake wipes his fiery hand over his eyes. Not ten feet separate him from Aphrodite. He lifts his left hand above his head, his shoulders flex—then, he lets Legux fly. Aphrodite holds out her white hands, and screams. The eerie blue lights begin to dissolve her golden image—not fast enough. Legux cuts through the space between them, and violently buries itself in her chest. The impact lifts Aphrodite off her feet, and she is thrown through the air.

Drake crashes to his knees beside me. "Arias, Cara, no!" he cries, every tone of his voice drenched in denial, and shock. We both hear him. His hands fall to my stomach, they come away soaked in my blood. "Hera save us! Cara, love!"

"Drake… I'm sorry. I didn't listen… I should have…"

"Shush, darling," he breathes, touching his lips to mine. "Don't talk. Zeus! *No!*" he rages. Fresh blood tears trace red lines down his jaw. His shoulders shake, and he looks like he is burning from the inside. He lifts my body off the altar, I curl willing against his chest. "Ares had you. I saw…I trusted…"

My feet tumble off his lap and sink to the snow, it does not matter much, I hardly feel the cold anymore.

"I… I love you, Drake," I gasp. It is easy to say those words in this time, words I could not say in my own. I look up to find Arias standing behind him, one pale, ghostly hand rests on his shoulder. She meets my gaze. "It is almost time," she tells me, and I knew it was. Misery fills all the empty places in the silence.

Drake's bloody lips touch mine. "Stay near Hades, I will join you soon."

"Live…" I cough, spattering his cheek in more of my blood.

"I will not live without you," he swears. "My love, I cannot."

"Please. Live for me, be…be… happy."

"You mad, beautiful girl," his voice is hoarse, rasping over each word. I can hardly hear past the heartbreaking anguish. "Do you not know by now? There is no happiness without you."

"I never leave you," says Arias.

"I never leave you," I gasp. I can feel myself dying—actually feel my soul escaping the gash in my skin. My breaths speed up, my back arches strenuously.

"No! No!"

"I…love…" I say and take my last breath. In reality I do not scream his name—I only whisper it in my mind as I die.

I float up out of my body, again. A body lying limp and finished in Drake's arms. The misty light touches the red locks in my hair as it fans across the white snow. I watch Drake kiss my lips; grief shakes his whole body.

I move gracefully to Aphrodite's prone form. She looks like a single figurine in a snow globe, forever encased in a world of glass and swirling ice. Legux still protrudes from her body, and her eyes are frozen, forever wide in horrified shock.

Drake sets my back body on the altar, removes the blade carefully from my stomach, and tosses it—forgotten—to the snow. His legs shake like wind battered branches as he walks to where my ghost stands, and Aphrodite lies. He spits on the ground beside her head, then rips the sword free of her chest. Gold blood rolls down the luminous blade like oil.

Blue light pulses around us all. I reach out to Drake, who stands beside me still cursing at the sky. My hand brushes over his chest. His skin is hot and textured, I shake when I feel him take a shuddering breath—it is the same as when I touched him in life. The feeling, more beautiful and ghastlier than any that had come before. I feel him completely, the warmth of the hot blood rushing under his bronze skin, the touch of his breath on my face. I know instinctively, then, no matter how many centuries I haunt the mists, this phenomenon will not change. When he turns his head to look in my direction, I know his eyes see only snow soaked air. It is a one-way connection. I do not know which one of us has it worse. Him, destined to yearn for eternity, or me, locked in love to a reality, which could never love me in return.

■   ■   ■

Drake lay beside me, his head on my stopped chest, until snow swallowed the sun and painted the silvery moon before the waking stars. I lift my head; my eyes fly to the sound in the wind. It sounds like a hurricane whipping the air, or a sonic blast signaling the end of the world. Overhead, black clouds sculpt an arrow, the wind howls again as it rushes to the ground. Wiping tears off his face, Drake struggles to stand.

"Who is it?!" he shouts. His hoarse voice deadened from crying. "Who challenges me?! I am not afraid. Come. I do not regret what I did!"

When the arrow of clouds touches the fresh snow, Hades steps out of the swirling blackness. "Neither do I, my son. Aphrodite deserves this fate." Hades looks down his long nose at the goddess frozen in a sphere of glass.

"You have freed me from a very tiresome agreement, and some beautiful women may live a few days longer."

"Not my woman," Drake's whisper is toneless, frozen the ice with Aphrodite. "Not my woman…she is gone."

"I know." Hades rests his hand on Drake's shoulder. "I am so sorry my son. I am here to take her. I will let no other touch her."

Drake's eyes flinch. "She's still here?"

"Yes!" I shout, knowing it is useless. "I'm touching you." I crawl onto his lap and press my palms against his cheek. "I'm with you."

"This is a travesty," says Hades, watching me melt in a puddle of dramatic sobs. "I wish this piece of destiny were mine to change. Alas, death is all I was given. I can do nothing more for you now. Ares, however, is coming to avenge his goddess, and there is something you can do for me."

Drake gulps at the cold air. I hold him tighter. "I will kill him, I vow it, or die in the attempt," murmurs Drake. "I have no other purpose now."

Hades nods and reaches for my ghost. I crush myself to Drake, lock my fingers behind his back. I shake my head wildly. "Please don't make me leave him. I'll stay in the mists. I am where I want to be, leave me here." I stroke his hair and kiss his lips while he stares blankly into the distance. "I can't leave him," I say honestly.

"Are you speaking to her?" groans Drake, the cold dead voice gone. He is a man stretched on a rack of torture. "Can you see her?!"

Hades nods and kneels beside his son. "Yes, Draken. She's in your arms."

Drake's broken sound makes more tears stream. Hades reaches out and touches my head, the same way he had in his chamber two years ago, a different place. Another death. Just like before, at his touch my wispy soul solidifies. Drake's fingertips brush my face, and another sound is ripped from him as my skin comes to life under his hands. First, my broken heart, my shoulders, and finally my face. He throws his arms around me, cradles my head against his shoulder.

"I can't believe I'm seeing you like this, again," he chokes.

"It's okay," I sob. "It's going to be alright."

"Never," he swears. "Never, my love."

"I come back to you," I tell him. His head shakes out a broken denial, as if that particular concept is just too terrible. "I do. Trust me. I swear, I will come back. Just wait for me, alright? Live for me."

"No Cara, I am already a dead man."

"Live for me Drake," I demand. "Stay alive and find me. I will go to the mists as I was meant to. I will never leave you for a second."

"I heard Aphrodite's curse over the wind," he says in torment. "Thirteen days from the day you remember, she will come back. She will kill you." his voice chokes off. "I can't do this again. See you like this again. I can't keep losing you."

"I will forget who I am," I state miserably, suddenly thinking of the long, lonely years in Fairhaven. The years void of touch and passion, the life of a girl who never imagined she would fall in love. "The mists make me forget, Arias and I… we are not joined. I must remember. You must promise to make me remember! You have to swear to me that you will find me and tell me who I am."

"Why?" he sounds furious. "So, we can live in torture for thirteen days?"

"Better, than being apart forever." I run my hands over his face trying to memorize every line of it. "Better to touch you, hold you…"

Drake shakes his head; his tears drip on my cheeks and coast over my lips. "I cannot swear such a thing. You cannot ask me to live. Losing you, living without you, is the worst torture I know. My mind will not survive it. Do not force me to exist in such pain."

"I do force you! You must swear it! If you love me…swear it. Don't leave me broken in half. It's unbearable."

"I love you more than my own life." He shakes his head and lets out a long breath. "I swear."

I kiss him then, and it is hot and beautiful. Hades says it is time, tells us Ares will come. He makes Drake swear, once again, to fulfil his vow. I try to listen to their conversation, yet I am fading away. Everything is so beautiful. It went through my mind then, that not the purest form of ecstasy in the world could make me feel like this. I am weightless, I am everywhere, and for a long time I am nowhere, save lost in that loop, that endless zone of repeating time, that oxygen rush which never ends. *Hail Mary, full of grace,* I think, before I cannot think at all, *pray for us sinners in the hour of our death.*

CHAPTER XIII

VOW

His mouth made me see stars, his hands replaced reality.

When I am a ghost, I see everything simultaneously, I am outside of time. The glimmering threads constructing it move like a hula hoop around me, I can turn and see it, I move my body and it spins. I saw Drake standing beside his father, my dead body in his arms. My ghost in his shadow. I saw Corvin Castle, and the chapel where I knelt, still touching the glowing sword. In the chapel, Cara is shaking, on the mountain Arias is fading. In the chapel Drake is bursting through the door, running to my side. On the mountain he is silent, holding me close. In the chapel, I turned to face him.

"What are you doing in here?" he barked in a low, growling voice, making me flinch. "It's freezing. Come, let me take you back to your bed."

"No!" I resisted when he pulled me to my frozen feet, then swayed disorientated—a foot in each time. In the chapel, the stained-glass windows were replaced by the storm raging on the mountain. "You need to do it now," I whispered.

He knew instantly what I meant. "No. Not yet." His eyes were bright and pleading. Please, one more day. I have a plan."

"Screw your plan," I twined my arms around his neck. "I touched the sword. I remember your promise."

Drake closed his eyes, I thought in denial of it all. "Aphrodite told me it would be like this. In mind she whispered of your return. She always knew what I would do, it was her love spell after all— she knows the strength of it. She knew I would always love you too much to say no. She knew I would be the one who kills you every time."

"I don't care if I die. I am not afraid of dying. Just don't leave me living like this."

On the mountain the howl of the wind rose, and the color of my soul bends with the untouched snow. In the chapel I brought his face down to mine. "Please," I begged, letting him see the desire of my heart in my eyes. "Please, Drake, let me be with you… let me be with you, even if it's only for thirteen more days."

"I can't do it," he groaned, but I felt it in my bones, and knew it in my heart the second he caved. On the mountain I saw Arias gasp, then sigh as if she knew what was coming. In the chapel Drake went to his knees and pulled me with him. Suddenly, it felt like he pushed a giant shard of glass in my brain. I shook in his arms. Our foreheads were pressed together, and light started to gather in between us, blue streamers of effervescence, that made a music I could never describe.

On the mountain, Drake holds my dead body, his cheek against mine. I hear a wheezing pop and feel Drake flinch. He turns, frowns when he sees the arrowhead buried in his shoulder. He rips it out of his flesh, blood splashes my cold, grey body. He kisses my forehead, then turns to face Ares, who rushes toward us. No peasant garb for this god now—his armor blazes like supernova.

"What have you done?" shouts Ares. Crimson light shoots from the sword in his hand, and his ringing voice quakes the banks of ice. He looks at Aphrodite in astonishment, then a dull, dawning horror darkens his eyes. Ares leaps from Atheon's flaming back. Where he lands, the ground splits, jets of water break free of the shifting cracks, and spray the sky.

"It is not what I have done!" shouts Drake.

In the chapel Drake knocked Legux to the floor and laid me on the stone table. I tugged at the hem of his black, cotton t-shirt, he whipped the material over his head, and threw it to the ground. Blue light spilling from the sword touched his skin and made him a creature of fantasy. My fantasy—my world. I felt his hand hot on my naked thigh. The glow growing between us intensified.

On the mountain, rage twists Ares's handsome face. He walks to his goddess on shaking legs. The second he reaches out his hand to touch her lips, I realize boy-Draken had been dead right. Androsia never had a chance at this god's heart. "You have killed her," whispers Ares. On his cheeks I see the silver sheen of tears.

"I have not killed her," Drake spits out each word. "She is sleeping. I pray she never wakes."

Ares moves to my dead body. He reaches out a hand to touch a lock of my hair, deep sorrow in his eyes, sorrow I think for both of us. Drake screams the scream of a man gone mad. Blindly he swings Legux, I see the tip of the blade nick Ares's on his neck—this cut is deeper than the last, and the cut does not close. It bleeds like a severed vein. Ares stares down at his blood, eyes wide, jaw dropped. I wonder if he is fascinated by the blood, or just that someone would dare to draw it.

"You cannot mean to fight me, Draken?" I hear the pain and shock in Ares's voice. "We are brothers," he gasps. "I don't want to fight you, I won't. I never meant for it to come to this. Walk away. You are stepping in the middle of an endless war."

"You took her! I saw you give her to Aphrodite," spat Drake, and I saw death in his eyes. *"You killed her!"*

"I was not under my own power," pleads Ares. I know he is not lying. I remember Limbo and all it told me.

In the chapel we breathed to the rhythm of the throbbing lights. Drake's mouth was on my waist, I gasped when I felt his teeth graze my hip bone. Shivers tightened my skin. My pesky nightgown was in the way, I sighed when he lifted it over my head. The blue lights wrapping us in ribbons of moving particles were warm, and glistening. I looked down at my naked body, my hands flew up to cover my breast—a sudden wash of shyness taking control of my limbs. When he kissed my fingers, and said my name again, I knew it was the sound of all his prayers.

"You're so beautiful," he breathed. "My ivory goddess with emerald eyes." The stone under my back was cold, but his body was fire between my legs. I heard my shredding breaths, felt his fingers slide over my waist, down my hip, to curl under the lace edge of my panties. "If you want me to stop, you have to say it now," he told me.

"Never," I said. "Never stop… never…!" He kissed me and the light between us grew out of control, it speared through the stained-glass windows, and glowed under the chapel's closed door. It exploded through the red brick roofs and found crevices in the walls to spill from. Drake's hand moved, and the slip of lace slid down my thighs. He dragged his fingers up my body, and I heard myself make a low, wild sound.

On the mountain I see Darius running flat out across the icy ground, Androsia stumbles behind him.

"NO! Draken don't fight him!" she yells and throws herself to the ground at her brother's feet. The snow splashes up around her. "Please…enough…please," Androsia pleads again.

"Get up, Androsia!" says Drake, his voice harsh as I have ever heard it. "He cares nothing for you! Nothing! Why are you tearing yourself over him? Can't you see he is maddened by grief for another woman?"

Androsia starts to cry. "Draken…how can you speak to me so? How can you…?"

"Look at what this night has cost me!" he raves, throwing a finger toward my shell. "She's dead, Androsia. Again."

"He will not fight me, Androsia," says Ares, as he reaches for her.

Drake throws him a disbelieving look. "Today is your last for many years, my lord."

Ares hollers in frustration. "I didn't wish for this, but if you come at me, I will not play the same games I played in the arena. I will kill you!"

A stream of snarls tear from Drake's battered throat. "Come. Try!" he commands.

In the chapel, we have disappeared in the brilliance of the light. A fine mist covered my straining body, my fingernails dug into his hips, and he froze.

"Look at me," he demanded. I obeyed, blinking, dizzy from pleasure. He moved his hips, and I gasped, held my breath, and gasped again—I tried to brace myself, his eyes burned over me, and he whispered my name. Then, he flexed his hips and I screamed. Even though I had been expecting it, the intensity of the sharp pain took me by surprise. His lips locked to mine, muffling my howl. Sure, another scream would follow, I hitched in a breath. Drake held his body completely still, his heart slammed against my chest, and I could feel the muscles trembling in his back. I shuddered and sighed. Then he kissed me, kissed me until the pain slowly dissolved, like a fading burn, it became another memory.

Drake's teeth sucked lightly on the skin of my neck, then he dragged them across my chest. "I pray to all the gods of earth and sky, that I never have to do that to you again," he growled, and I started to laugh.

I locked my fingers in his sweat damp hair and pulled his lips back to mine. "It will only ever be you who does that, if I die and come to life a million times, it will only ever be you."

He continued to hold himself incredibly still, and I saw sweat mist his beautiful face like flecks of gold. "Should I stop?" he rasped.

I rolled my eyes. "Not if you value your life."

On the mountain Drake runs at Ares. Androsia screams. Ares swings his sword like a lumberjack, Drake parries, and stumbles. Ares moves forward, confident. He does not know Drake like I do; he does not see the cold killer in his eyes, the dark part of himself he tries so hard to hide. In the end, Ares's greatest confidence is his only flaw. Drake stabs violently, Ares leaps out of the way, and the glowing tip of Legux misses him by a breath. Ares swings. This time, I am the one who screams as Ares's blade sinks into Drake's forearm. I see the sharp edge of the steel slice deep. The flesh folds back and shows me the bone. Drake barely reacts, he rushes Ares, swinging Legux in a high arc. Blood paints the snow.

In the chapel Drake moved powerfully, and every inch of my body came alive under his hands, hands that knew me so well. On the mountain something flashes past the corner of my eye, gone in an instant like the tail of a déjà-vu.

"No! Dauris! Do not!" screams Androsia, sobs make her voice choppy. Darius does not hear her. He swings his arm, the whistle of his ball and chain sound deadly, even admits the raging battle of gods. The metal ball hits Ares in the back of the head. The sound of metal striking skull-bone makes me sick. Ares stumbles and it is all the distraction Drake needs. He whirls, I watch snowflakes fly from his hair. I watch Legux as it does what it was born to do. Drake's wounded arm completes the strike. In the instant before the storm, I see the horror in Drake's eyes, the absolute disgust at what he is doing. A final cry falls from his rage twisted lips, then Drake sinks Legux smoothly into Ares's heart.

Shock registers on Ares's face. He clasps both hands around the blue blade and rips it out of his chest. Blood runs down the sword. "Not possible," grunts Ares, falling to his knees. "You do not know what you have done. You will never have her back now, Hades is a liar, Aphrodite, Athena… you do not know." Ares presses his hand to his heart, shards of light slice through the gaps in his fingers.

In the chapel everything inside me built, strove toward some ethereal pinnacle I had to touch. Drake's panting breaths heated my neck, sent quakes through my bones. He crashed into me again and again, I only arched up for more, as my nails scored the skin of his back. He sucked in his breath through clenched teeth and threw his head back, I saw the tendons strain in his neck. Then, my body tensed, and I screamed. Each piece of me coming apart in his arms glowed with a brilliance to rival the brightest star. Light spilled from my very pores, and the feeling was beyond anything. "Oh, my gods!" I breathed, watching galaxies spin behind my closed eyes. He lifted me higher and moved powerfully once more. My spine bowed, and I screamed again. *Oh, my gods! Oh, my freaking gods!*

On the mountain Androsia crawls toward Ares, silver tears pour down her wind chapped cheeks. Drake kneels beside Ares, the wound on his forearm still spraying blood. Glassy ice is creeping up Ares's legs, Androsia holds his face in her hands, she weeps garbled versions of his name, kissing him between words. His eyes are not for her, Ares looks over her head at Drake. "Your father used you," grunts Ares, fighting the encroaching ice. "You do not know the full story; you have given him the world."

Hot white light leaks from Ares's pours, streams from his eyes and mouth in long, mercurial streams that make me think of a bloodhound. Androsia starts to pull at her hair, screaming all the while. She flies at Drake, meaning to scratch out his eyes. *"How could you?"* she wails. *"I love him! Bastard son of a whore!"* she shrieks. "I love him!"

Drake says nothing, and she continues to rage. The dead look in his eyes is all I see.

Ares lifts his face to glare at the sky. "Pluto and Mars impossibly aligned," he says. "Yours and mine, cousin; our destiny written in the very fabric of the Universe." The ice is creeping into his heart, climbing up his chest. The way it slips, and slides makes me feel like I am in a cartoon dream. Ares begins to choke; his final gasps are blood filled and terrible. I think then how strange it is, in the end, god or mortal, we all die the same. Except he was not dying, only fading, more of his essence absorbed every second by the ice encasing him.

In the chapel I am finally calm. I felt my dazed breaths and my soul glow. The blaze between our touching foreheads eclipsed all other light. Drake's words barely registered through the serotonin tsunami that drowned my mind. "Now my darling, it's going to happen now," he whispered. "Stay with me, Cara," his lips brushed mine. "Stay," he begged.

On the mountain it is almost over. The icy glass covers Ares's mouth and nose, slides slowly over his wide eyes. Androsia's wind matted hair slaps her in the face, blue veins burst in her eyes. A second before the crawling ice closes Ares's eyes forever, Drake reaches out his hand, stopping short of Ares's shoulder.

"I had no choice," he says darkly. "I did what I was born to do. Arias was right all along." He looks down at my dead body, and the tense muscles in his face spasm. "She always told me I could not run from destiny."

There is no response from Ares. The trap has done its work, the ice covers his eyes, freezing them in their last sight.

"Nooo!" Androsia's scream is long and wretched, it spins slowly, endlessly, finally dying out on the wind. The world seems to hold its breath, and everything is still. Too still. I am in the eye of the tornado, I know it.

Suddenly, the ground starts to shake, I hear monstrous avalanches breaking loose in the distance. The thunder rumbles, and a lightning rain of stars shoots across the night sky. Zeus rages, yet he does not dare come to his son's aid, not when Legux lies so close at hand. Underneath Poseidon's waters the ground splits apart, the earth's center lets out its fire.

Light explodes from the Ares's sculpture, knives out in all directions, striking the stunned faces of Drake, Androsia and prince Darius. The light goes up Drake's nose. The sharp beam throws his head back before it lifts him off his feet. I watch Androsia and Darius take to the air in a similar fashion. Drake grinds his teeth, Dauris lets out a shout of pain, while Androsia wails in agony. The light seeps further into their veins, it looks as if it means to lift skin from bone. The three royal youths spasm in the air, yell like they are being flayed alive. Beneath my feet the mountain splits down its center, at that moment I think it is the loudest sound I have ever heard. In the sky I see stars falling, and hear the volcanoes erupting beneath the waves.

Then, the light is gone, and Drake, Androsia and Darius crumple boneless, to the snow. Darius knocked senseless, Androsia twitching just slightly. Drake struggles to his knees, and crawls to my dead body. "I'm sorry, my love," he whispers, "sorry to break my promise so soon." He kisses the cold lips of my corpse. Once, twice. His tears fall on my face. Slowly he brushes away the flakes of snow clinging to his bloody blade. He takes a deep breath, and I see nothing left of the boy Arias, and I once knew. He lifts the Legux—eyes locked on my face—he stabs it into his heart, and I scream in silence. In the same motion he rips it out and tosses it, forgotten to the snow. Blood gushes from his heart as he pulls my body into his arms. "Stay with me love," he whispers into my hair. "Stay with me. I'm here, nothing can touch us…stay, my beautiful girl." He strokes my face while the ground under us shatters, and we plummet into an ancient cave beneath the earth. The cave where he held me in his arms until my bones turned to dust. The cave where Androsia wrote the first draft of Blood and Shadows on the stones.

■ ■ ■

In the cave beneath the shattered earth, I float to my knees beside him. I kind of merge in the ground, soak in the pool of blood that surrounds him. There is so much blood. Arias kneels across from me, and this time, I see more of myself in her. I touch Drake's chest, run my fingers over the place on his heart where Legux stabbed him. The skin has seemed back together, there is only a faint pink line left for memory.

"He is full god now," I whisper.

Arias nods her head. "The mists are calling. It is time, this is the space where you and I exist as one. Now is when we merge, now is when you remember. The night will come, there is no stopping it. We must face the dark."

I take her hand. The cave is gone, and I am in a forest. The moon is brighter than our modern sun, the night air clean and balmy, as if the day left spots of warmth in the darkness. I am following someone. The blue-black steel of his sword reflects the moon and throws out javelins of light.

"I'm in the mists!" I whisper, as realization strikes, and I know who I follow. Drake had let his hair grow, it hung far past his shoulders, and his face has changed. A soul killing rage has carved lines where there were none. I stay close, listening to the beats of his heart. I feel different, Arias is me, and I feel complete. I know it was always that way for me in the mists. In this soul-soaked world, I am Cara Wynter, and Princess Arias. In this living graveyard I call an existence, I love this man I follow with every piece of my torn soul. I know him better than any other living thing. I know about his sleep in the cave beneath the earth where Androsia wrote her story. I know he lay until my body dissolved in his arms; I know he took my dust back to the garden where we first met.

"Don't follow me anymore, Arias," he had whispered as he tossed my dust on the ground. "I have only one purpose now."

I never left. I kept my promises and stayed by his side through countless centuries. I know his darkness, his agony, his thirst for vengeance, his fear that I will one day return, his breathtaking hope that I will. I know all his secrets like they are my own. I even know about the gods he has buried under the dungeons of Corvin Castle. I remember the day he buried them.

For one thousand years I stayed beside him, Androsia and Darius. I watched them while they slept for centuries, I tried to comfort them when they raged. For a thousand years, Ares and Aphrodite slept beside the three immortals. No Olympian came to search for them, and in time, only a few knew of their location, or existence. Time passed as it does, and the power of the sleeping Olympians could not remain forever dormant. It seeped down to the dark places in the earth, crawled toward the newly populated cities. It was a living, breathing power, that danced to its own drumbeat of fate. The power began to touch people. Some good, brave souls discovered hidden abilities. They received steel crushing strength, speed, the power to travel by thought, even some—immortality. Others who it touched became heroes, queens, and kings, still others simply found a remote spot to live out their eternities. Every Yin, however, must have its Yang, and the power also found the evil souls, those who harbor hate and murder in their hearts—and turned woman and man, to monster. They were born craving the taste of human blood, needed it to survive, some became wolves under moonlight, then ate the stomach, and hearts of their families. Drake would kill them by ripping out their hearts with his bare hands. He would make them watch it burn. Drake left his tomb; he took the gods to a place he believed humanity would never touch. He buried them in Transylvania—deep in the bowels of the castle he had built with his bare hands—hid them well in the dungeons he dug under the earth. There they lie. There they wait.

■   ■   ■

I continued to move beside him, and I was me again. All the parts that made me, me—all the lost pieces that loved him. We moved, and the blades of grass, and hanging tree branches coasted through my transparent body. I watched the muscles in his back ripple as he ran, saw the tendons in his corded arms stretch and flex. I know every line on Drake's face, had memorized every shade of gold in his eyes. Most nights his eyes were dull and cold, as he lay listless and alone, hidden behind the iron walls of his castle—not when he hunted, when he hunted, he came alive. When he killed, I would catch a rare glimpse of his beautiful smile.

Three strange clouds—like bright slices of a blood orange—lay over the face of the moon, and the stars were thick and traveling. In front of me I saw a man and a woman, locked in a fierce embrace. The woman wore a flour sack gown, her body was small, her fair hair brushed her hips. The man's lips moved against the woman's neck; his white fangs sunk deep. She kicked and fought, her fingers dug in his shoulders, her nails clawed at his eyes. The man hardly seemed to register her struggles as he sucked up her life, desperately greedy to taste the last beats of her heart.

"Icochivich," shouted Drake.

The vampire's spine visibly tensed, his head snapped up. Ruby red blood shone on the vampire's lips, a single stream of it dripped down his chin.

"You are too late, Von Draken, ah! Do you hear? Her heart is already stopping." Laughing, Icochivich threw the woman to the earth, her dress spun as she fell like a pillowcase in a storm.

"They all die. I cannot stop it. All I can do is crave your death in return."

Drake had done this too many times, but the adrenaline rush never failed. I looked down at the dead woman, I liked to look at the dead he meant to avenge before watching him kill, it gave a sad sense of purpose to it all.

The vampire lifted his head and tilted it due east to judge the pace of the wind. I knew he was thinking about running. He knew he was fast, yet he had heard stories about this 'supposed god', this 'death bringer'. The stories said it was useless to run, said it only went worse for those who tried.

"Go ahead," said Drake pleasantly, reading the intent in the vampire's blood red eyes. "A stretch of my legs would be invigorating."

The vampire turned and ran for his life. When Drake caught him, as he always did, I tried not to listen to the scream. It was fine with me that the creature was dying, still, I looked away when Drake torched the throbbing heart.

In the darkness of the night, pictures appeared again in front of my eyes, and blasted past me, pulling me into them. I could see everything at once and understood each thing individually. In all my worlds, in all my long wandering years, hanging in the middle of no place at all—I found the missing pieces of my soul. Feelings. Thoughts. Pictures. Memories. Anything I had ever been, anything I ever was, flew before my eyes. I was in the center of the whirl and time showed it all to me.

Beyond the stained glass of the chapel windows, the view of stormy mountain had changed to dark forest. I sat up shivering again, the room and stone table gone suddenly cold. The hundreds of tiny candle flames dotting the small space burned low in their wax. The light around us flickered and bent. I pulled my nightgown down my legs, very aware that

I had lost my panties—and drew my knees to my chest. Drake was standing beside me, his shirt was still gone, but his belt buckle was back in place. When I finally looked away from his body and saw his face, my blush was so hot it made moisture tingle in my eyes. He was watching me, watching him, my mouth suddenly felt very dry.

"Do you hate me?" he asked. For a second, he was the boy I first met in the garden, young, innocent, hopeful.

"Hate you?" I smiled. "I could never, it is not possible."

His mouth twisted in a disgusted grimace. "The things I've done." He shook his head. "I've always been afraid that you were with me and prayed everyday it was true. I never wanted you to see the true monster I am."

I felt my smile getting wider. He was so perfect, standing half naked in front of me, an actual Greek god. "You held me until my body was dust," I whispered, and he nodded. "I don't care if it's morbid, for some reason I think that is the most romantic thing in the world." I laughed at his disbelieving look. "You know what?" I said. "Maybe that's why we are made for each other. I am a girl who is used to dark corners and haunted souls. I am a girl who knows all about lost parents, abandonments, terror, and death. I am a girl who glows, and time walks, and well… if all those things are true—then I am also a girl who can love the monster as much as the man. Now, if only I can adjust to my new mind."

"It's painful and disorienting at first, the memories are going to come at you fiercely for a while." His hand ran across my cheek. "It gets better with time." His fingers shook. "Time, we don't have anymore." I saw the last of the forest trees—and whatever remained of the mountain and snow—float back to where they came from.

"We're not dead yet," I told him. "We can deal with this together. Who knows?" I took his hand, kissed his warm, scarred palm. "We might even be able to win."

His hand cupped my cheek. "I love your optimism," he said cynically, then his eyes blistered the air touching them. "I love…"

I hooked my finger in his belt and yanked him toward me. I laid my cheek on his heart, and took a deep breath, full of him. We were together again, for right now—in this time and place, that was enough for me.

"I want to see where you buried them," I whispered. "Aphrodite, Ares. I want to see where you have kept them all these years."

I felt his lips on the top of my head. "Tomorrow," he said. I lifted myself to my knees and locked my arms around his neck.

"Tomorrow," I agreed. "Tonight…" my teeth sunk into my lower lip and I took a bracing breath, "Do you want to go to bed with me?"

Drake's eyes glowed down into mine, he did not have to say it—the words floated between us as he carried me to the master bedroom, loud as if he had shouted at them. *Yes, Cara. I want to go to bed with you. I want to do anything with you.*

CHAPTER XIV

ENCASED IN A SPHERE OF ICE AND GLASS. DAY ONE OF THIRTEEN

I woke up naked in his bed. It was strangely disorienting, like I had woken up in the life of another girl. A lucky girl. I locked my hands over my bare breasts and sat up, worlds beyond hazy. Dusty sunlight full of motes fought its way through a small break in the thick velvet curtains, and the black alarm clock on the bedside table told me it was eight AM. I swung my feet over the edge of the bed wincing. I was horribly sore, and very aware of my skin and its continued tingles. I touched the indent his head had left in the pillow, wondering why he always let me wake up alone. After the chapel, the mountain, and the dark forest, he had carried me in here where we spent the remaining hours of the night in each other's arms, as if we could somehow make up for the last three thousand years in a single night. If it were not for the dark bruises running up the underside of my arm, and the fingerprints on my hip, I would have believed I dreamed it all. It seemed a far more plausible explanation for what had been the most wonderful night of my life.

    I stood up slowly, testing my ability to do so. It was touch and go. I swayed unsteadily, before I dragged myself across the room to the mirror. When I saw my reflection, I gasped so hard, it made me choke. My hair had apparently abandoned the plot hours ago, and it flew out around me, sticking up in all directions, alive and crackling. My lips were bright red and swollen. I touched them gently. How many times had he kissed me? Touched me? Done things to my body I had only read about in novels. The memories swimming in my head whispered I had done it all with him before, but those were memories, this was life, and it was all new. The memories were confusing, I pushed them to the back of my mind, wondering—now that we had *'fused'* — how badly I would miss Arias's voice in my head.

I walked to the window and threw open the curtains. The view of the castle gardens and forest beyond took my breath. I stared in wonder. I was feeling so many things—but most of all I was feeling happy to be alive— even if it *was* only for thirteen more days. "The countdown has begun," I told the mirror— trying for a lighthearted tone—I failed. My voice sounded ominous—the combination of words alarmed me—like I had unwittingly just cursed myself. What if I really did have only twelve more days? Excluding the one I lived in of course. Did I feel any different? I touched my face in the mirror. I looked the same, maybe a bit stronger— something in the eyes was older. I moved closer to my reflection. Was my hair darker? Or was it just the change in my mind playing tricks on me. No answer to my questions would come from this silent, empty room. I stomped to the massive bathroom, conveniently located through the closest set of double, quilted doors.

The bathroom was bright, the early sunlight splashing against the marble, made everything look brand new. I tried to ignore my ever-rising fury at Drake's random abandonment of me—in his bedroom no less— while I took a shower and brushed my teeth with a toothbrush, I found freshly packed in the left drawer of the well-lit bathroom vanity. I fought my hair—endlessly searching the room for a brush and failing. In the middle of it all, I realized I had come to his room wearing nothing save a slightly torn nightgown—which currently lay in a ruined heap beside the foot of his bed.

"Perfect," I said, rolling my eyes and clasping my hands over my naked chest. "Walk of shame it is!" I was getting more furious by the second. How could he? Leave me here, naked, alone in his room, sore and confused? I heard a rather loud growl rip through the room, I was shocked to realize it was mine. I grabbed a dry towel from a rack of them, twisted my wet hair into a top knot, walked to the door and pointed my finger at the knob. I kept pointing until the knob started to shake, then turn. "Come on, Cara," I urged, disappointed at myself. The knob shook again, harder this time. I dropped my hand and exhaled, suddenly exhausted. The little shake was nothing compared to my furniture obliteration the night of Limbo, but I supposed it was better than nothing. I moved to open the door, the regular way—before I could touch it, it swung outward. I stood face to face with an elderly woman, who took in my state of undress, and raised a wispy brow. Her eyes were silver as the rest of her. She reminded me of a sharpened blade, her muscled arms, strong looking fingers and pointed chin. She kept her eyes on my towel and said nothing, my feet shuffled nervously so I cleared my throat.

"Silly me," I cough-laughed. "I needed a shower. This one looked amazing, then I realized I left my clothes in my room. You wouldn't be able to tell me how to get there, would you?" I knew I was babbling and had no power to stop. She said nothing, her eyes continued to rove over my towel, finally—when I thought I would just take my chances, and run—she looked at my face, caught my gaze, and patted her throat.

"Oh, you are... nonverbal?" I asked, cautiously. Hoping I had the right term, praying I did not offend.

I was relieved when I saw the corners up her mouth twitch in the barest hint of a smile. She nodded.

"Do you know who I am?" I asked, thinking we should probably start there.

She nodded. Sunlight touched the pure silver in her hair.

"Are you... Fran Anjou?"

She nodded again, then she pointed left down the long hall, and motioned for me to follow. I peeked my head through the door, praying to all the gods that Alexie was not wandering about. I did not know him that well, but I knew him well enough to know—if he caught me like this, I would never hear the end of it. Two spiral staircases, and one ridiculously long hall later, I was in my room shivering in relief. The best night of my life had not equaled a good morning. I was in a mood when I dressed. The second I was finally safe behind a shield of blue jeans, and light cashmere sweater, my thoughts started to settle. It was possible Drake had left me alone, naked in his bed for a reason. Perhaps he thought when the glow faded, my anger would rise. It had not. I had all the memories of my past life stored away in my head, sure, but it was nothing too spectacular. The memories existed like any memory, quiet and hazy, only present when called on. They could have all been a dream, glittering images which were interesting—sometimes breathtaking, or chilling, yet still just images that fade with dawn, and have no place in modern reality. All this confusion really left me only one option. I had to see them. Aphrodite. Aries. I had to see where they were buried. I had to look into her eyes. I knew then, it would be real. Any lingering doubt would fizzle away under the power of such proof. I would be able to tell myself that I was not lying comatose on the kitchen floor of Wynter manor, lost and muttering in an enchantment—I would know without a shadow of a doubt that it was real. If I was really Arias, if all this really was true—I should be able to walk right to them.

I sighed, wondering what Arias would say, and found I was missing the chatter in my head. I thought about laying down in bed, and going back to sleep, but I was so hungry. Starving actually. I decided to find food and figure out the rest later.

I got lost in a sunny conservatory, full of lilies and hydrangea blooms, then heard Lily's laughter and followed it down the wrong hall. This hall was older than the others, the walls and floor were red brick—probably one of the only places not damaged by the fire. Portraits filled all the spaces on the walls, stern faces set in golden frames. I took my wool gloves from the back pocket of my jeans and put them on. Hesitantly, I touched the first original. The oil paint was roughly textured, through my gloves I felt the ridges and bumps where it had unevenly dried. The first image meant nothing to me—a roman, somewhere between fifteen and a man. Next, was a woman, dark skinned and green eyed. Familiar, but unplaceable. Then, I froze, 'emerald eyes', Drake had whispered last night, hot lips tracing fire down my neck. Emerald eyes, exactly like mine stared down at me from the next portrait. I did not even need to look twice to know who it was. Sure, she was in a Victorian gown, and the artist had broadened her forehead slightly, there was however, no mistaking it.

"Athena, I presume," I said, snarling the last word. The portrait stayed mute, I knew the look in the eyes though, it had always said more than any words. *My aunt, the goddess Athena!* My mind scoffed, and my eyes rolled.

"Where are you?" asked Lily, popping in my mind suddenly, like Jack springing out of his box.

"Lost," was my dejected response. *"I am in a hall full of portraits,"* I told her, then showed her the one I was currently glaring at.

"What fresh hell!? Is that Hanna?" she spluttered. *"Oh, of course it is. I am going to punch that woman in the face,"* she thought cheerfully.

"It's still so strange. I suppose Drake would know Athena, in Andi's book, she came and warned him." I shuddered. *"She scares me, Athena, so strange that Hanna never did."*

"Maybe, she really did love us," mused Lily.

I snorted. *"Pish! Maybe."* I walked away from the portrait. *"I need to talk to you, there is something in this castle I need you to see."*

"The buried gods?" she asked, I could hear her mental smile.

"Figures you would already know; you probably knew before me."

"Alexie told me, we stayed up talking most of the night," I heard the humming excitement of her thoughts.

Her words in my mind were getting stronger, louder. *"Are you trying to find me?"* I asked.

"Yup," she said. *"Don't move."*

I stopped walking, keeping my eyes trained on the plush Persian rug beneath my feet. I took a deep breath and pictured Lily in my mind, wondering what she was wearing. A sudden rush of pins and needles attacked my fingers, and toes, while a wave of intense dizziness nearly took my balance. I stretched out my hand, meaning to grab the wall for support, then—there was no wall. Everything went blinding white, and I was spinning, like a coin in a dryer. I did not have time to scream, think or even take another breath—before my feet were on the ground, and I was standing directly in front of a flabbergasted Lily.

She stumbled back, her foot tripped on the hem of her flower dress, while her hand flew to cradle her heart. "Cara! What the hell!?" she shouted; cheeks blood red.

"I don't know," I stuttered, blinking my eyes, trying to comprehend my fresh surroundings. They were very strange; the hall and its knowing portraits were gone as if they had never been. I was in a sunlit dining room, highlighted by tall glass windows. Long tables braced the edges of the huge space, each filled with trays of food, all of which let off mouthwatering smells. My stomach growled audibly. Slowly, my eyes slid back to her face. "I was just thinking about you. I pictured your face, and then…" my words dropped away, I had none to describe what just happened.

"You just appeared out of thin air!" shrieked Lily, her blue eyes wide and glistening.

I flexed my tingling fingers. "Yeah, I guess…weird?"

"You teleported," I heard Alexie say. I realized he was leaning, arms crossed, on the wall behind Lily. He casually pushed out of his stance and walked toward me. "Some witches, the rare ones, can do it. I've never seen it." He shrugged. "It's pretty cool."

"Amazing," gasped Lily. "How do you feel?"

"A little nauseous, starving hungry," I said honestly.

Lily recovered herself and took my arm, linking her fingers through mine. Alexie turned toward the dining room and motioned for us to follow. I started to, but Lily held me back.

"Did you sleep with him?" she asked mentally, I could feel her trying not to pry around in my mind—even though she wanted to.

"Not really," I thought flippantly. *"We hardly slept at all."*

Lily giggled, then she hauled me toward the luscious buffet, her eyes glittering like a thousand falling stars. "Was it good?"

"Is what good?" asked Alexie. "Just dig in, everything is delicious. "

Lily let out a peal of sharp laughter. "Delicious," she said, and bit her bottom lip, shaking her head. She turned back to the array of delicacies, still laughing. I blushed and faced Alexie, trying to change the subject. "Can vampires eat?"

"No, vampires cannot." He put a huge spoon of fluffy yellow, scrambled eggs on his plate, and forked a square cut of steak. Blood dripped from the fork. "Splits can, some things…sometimes…" he made a face. "We do not enjoy it." He shuddered and let out a put-upon sigh. "Alas, I endeavor to bear it, keeps me from other, more dangerous appetites." He waggled his slanted brows at Lily. "Which I exercise on unsuspecting maidens."

"Oh, I'm expecting it," said Lily.

Alexie's eyes stayed on Lily's beatific profile, I saw them travel to her lips, then fly up to get tangled in the golden strands of her hair. When he saw me watching him, he cleared his throat, and shuffled his feet while his eyes rushed back to her. "Where is Drake?" he asked, deflecting the question he saw in my look.

I shrugged, seeing the way his lithe body moved past the breakfast tables, as if his feet never did quite touch the ground. "How should I know? I woke up alone in a strange place, well I suppose it's not strange at all is it? Now that I think about it— I suppose I've woken up there a thousand times. "

Alexie looked at me intently from smoky eyes. "I can't believe he left you."

If you only knew how, and where he left me," I sighed in my mind.

"How? Where?" demanded Lily, then waved her hand. "Never mind, I think I have put the pieces together," she finished, though, her eyes told me she would grill me later. "We have other things to talk about. I thought we could all start in the library today and move our way through this place. I've found books stuffed in nearly every corner."

"What are we looking for?" I asked.

Lily put a grape in her mouth and chewed thoughtfully. "I don't know. I know it's here though—I think we'll know it when we find it. I dreamed about a book last night, when I opened it symbols flowed off the page, a lot like our magic map, only more 3D, in a way. They spun around my head like a halo. In my dream the patterns they made were important, now I can't remember why." The faraway look in her eyes disappeared, her attention flickered back to my face. "I also want to explore." She looked up through her black lashes, the light in her eyes meaningful. "I want to see *them*."

Alexie groaned through a mouthful of bloody steak. "If I take you to *them*, Drake will kill me. *Not* figuratively—he will *literally* kill me." He yawned and raised his arms above his head. His bright white t-shirt stretched tight over the muscles in his stomach. "I've managed to survive a century, against many odds, I might add—I don't feel like dying today."

"He is not going to kill you," I said. I found a croissant, some melon slices wrapped in spiced grape leaves, and placed both on my plate. "He is not going to kill you, because you won't be the one to show me."

"I really don't think anyone else in this place would take us?" said Lily, looking around at the army of servants moving silently through the room. "They scare me—the lot of them." Lily faked shivered. "They look like ninjas in Halloween costumes."

"Maybe vampires playing dress up," I suggested.

Lily spun so fast it made the little cluster of grapes she had just lifted, fly off her plate. "Are they vampires?" she cooed in fascination. "I read Galileo's diary last night, he talked about Vampires. I read for six hours and made it through about ten pages. My old Latin sucks, you might have more luck with it, Cara. You always did better than me, now I guess we know why," she smiled. "So old, so much history," Lily shivered, for real this time. "I would love to meet one, an old one, just to pick their brain."

"Drake said he is older than the vampire, so I guess, you have—in a way."

"Drake, and his family are older than most, save the creatures of Dengora, and those that sleep beneath the ground," Alexie confirmed. He kept talking but his words faded away.

I looked through the door and down a cathedral hall that seemed almost familiar. I had a memory of flames and laughing, for a brief second, I felt strangling smoke in my throat. "Library later," I said, speaking to no one in particular. "First, I have to find them. I have to prove something to myself."

"Prove what?" asked Lily, taking a handful of small, candied truffles.

"Prove that I can walk directly to them. Prove that I've walked these halls a thousand times."

Lily looked doubtful. "Cara, you couldn't even find our room this morning—you think you can find *them*?"

"How do you know I couldn't find the room?" I was aghast, I had been so careful.

"Alexie saw you streaking down the west hall in your towel, hiding in Fran Anjou's shadow."

My cheeks ignited. "Great." The depth of my embarrassment gave me violent thoughts toward Drake. "I was upset, disoriented. Even though we are connected, it's just memories. I have to search through three thousand years—rather daunting actually."

"Goddess, Cara!" the hand over Lily's mouth did nothing to shelter her gasp.

"What?" I squeaked, alarmed. I tossed a quick glance over my shoulder waiting for the shadows to jump—waiting for monsters. I felt a ripple of unease go up my back, I had been smiling, but now my smile faltered when I saw the unspoken revelation in her eyes.

Lily calmed her expression and shrugged. "Nothing, I guess it just occurred to me—that—well—it seems you are older than the vampire too."

"Oh," I said, then said no more.

∙ ∙ ∙

It took an hour of retracing my steps, closing my eyes, and pounding my fist between them, as if I could rattle something loose up there, something that had gotten stuck in the mists. Alexie remained mute during my adventure, and Lily—Lily fired questions at me about my night in the chapel. It was Lily, so I had to tell her everything, yet the truth was—I wanted to keep it just my secret for a while longer. It was all so new, I was so enthralled—I feared her blue searching eyes would make me gush uncontrollably, then it would be worse for her when it all fell apart—if it did.

Finally, my mind clicked into focus as my feet traveled a previously traversed path. I remembered the torches on the walls, reflections dancing in the puddles on the ground. We had taken three flights of stairs, gone through two secret doors—which operated like merry-go-rounds, spinning us from one staircase to another—and one trap door that slammed down on my finger when I tried to close it behind me. After that, Alexie spoke only to reiterate in great detail the death that would befall him were Drake to discover his participation.

Lily held my hand while we walked, she knew there were many questions to be asked, but somehow, she knew I needed to do this first, and decided to stand as my second—I loved her so much for it. When I told her my thoughts, she leaned in to kiss the tip of my cold nose. "I can't believe you lost your virginity before me!" she whispered. "Literally, I can't believe it."

"Lily!" I rolled my eyes dramatically. "You're not a virgin. And who says I did?"

Lily snorted. Loudly. "Your glowing eyes, and twitchy walk say you did. And Carlton Bowman certainly doesn't count, he had no idea what he was doing and it lasted three seconds—I honestly went further with Ashley Seton," Lily pursed her lips and batted her lashes. "You remember Ashley, right, wasn't she hot? Still, we were tipsy fumble one and fumble two, Drake knew what he was doing, didn't he?" she sighed. "You don't have to answer. I'm sure he was perfect."

"It was… he was… I never imagined it could be like that." I paused, then decided to try and explain, completely unaware that we were speaking aloud. "Do you remember that one time we got pneumonia, we were five and mother let us fall asleep in the rain."

She nodded, the corners of her lips kicking up. "Hanna was so mad, she yelled and screamed."

"Yes, she really did. It was glorious."

Lily giggled. "Yeah, I remember, what about it?"

"When we were in our beds that night, Hanna came and put her hands on our chests. They were so warm, so…hot, but never burned. Luminous, like your fire." I whispered. "We were completely better the next morning, do you remember?"

"Of course, I remember, it was like magic," said Lily.

"Yes. Pure magic."

"Did it hurt?"

"Yes…" I smiled, suddenly gushing as memories flowed through me. "Yes, it hurt like hell. Only for a second, and then… oh my gods, and then…"

"I think I am going to puke right here, all over my new shoes," I heard Alexie say.

"Sorry," Lily smiled at him, while my cheeks burned to cinders. "No more. I promise, girl talk later," she finished, and the 'later' word was more command than statement.

Alexie made a great show of shuddering in disgust before he reached out and rattled the iron wrought gate impeding further progress. "I do not have a key for this, Drake has the only copy. I haven't seen him use it in decades."

I reached out and grabbed a cold, metal bar. I, too, shook it. The padlock rattled rebelliously; the old metal winked cheekily. "Hold my hand," I reached out to Lily. I looked up at Alexie, hesitant. "I don't know if I can do this with two people, I don't really even know how I did it in the first place."

"Did what?" Alexie looked worried. "What are you going to do?"

"Probably better you don't know that way you can plead the fifth," I said, and turned to Lily. "Breath through your nose and close your eyes."

Lily's chilly hand shook in mine. "Do it," she said.

"I don't know if I…"

She cut me off. "I know you can. Do it."

"Okay." I closed my eyes, and took my own advice, breathing through my nose, once, twice. On the second breath I imagined Lily and myself passing through the metal, our bodies liquid light, yielding as air. I imagined myself on the other side of the barrier, I imagined the iron wrought gate did not exist at all. At the last second, before the world spun and I pulled Lily into my colorful, endless tunnel, my mind remembered Aphrodite's face.

Lily screamed, then we were spinning. The coin in the dryer, the plastic bag in a cyclone. I saw the purple flowers on Lily's dress, her wide eyes, and the scream on her lips. Quickly as it started, it was done. We were standing between four walls, painted in long streams of muddy rain, and earth water. Lily put a hand to her head, and I felt her body hitch as she tried to hold back a gag.

"Wow," she coughed. "That was…wow…"

I agreed with her stuttered sentiment, though I could not say anything. It appeared I brought my body yet left my words behind the iron wrought gate.

Holding hands, we walked down a long flight of wet steps, careful not to bump or jostle ourselves into the dirty walls. I smelt something then, something that made a wave of powerful memory crash over me. I blinked my eyes and breathed again. It was the ocean, salty and pure, rushing against the hot, spartan sand, then, I smelled pomegranate wine, tied up with a hint of lavender oil, and I knew we were close.

The staircase ended; I took a bracing breath before we rounded the next corner. The darkness, the dirt and the dripping stones above our heads disappeared. The huge room we stepped inside was impeccably clean, and electronically lit, the fluorescent lights glittered busily on each pink-marble surface—perfectly polished. In the center of the octagonal room, two sarcophagi faced each other, both elaborately painted in fresco. Deep carvings telling a story forgotten by time.

"These are Limestone," breathed Lily in reverent tones. "The Greeks called this rock sarax-phagein, it means flesh eating stone. These are so old. Eventually the acid in the rock would dissolve the skin and muscle, then time would take the bones. Snow, this here," Lily fell to her knees, her hands ran over the stone carvings, I saw her fingers tremble. "This snow is so intricate, it's made with pieces of broken pottery, look here! These chiseled edges, this has to be over two thousand years old."

"That sounds about right," I whispered. "Drake laid them here, nearly a thousand years after he trapped them."

Lily looked over her shoulder, peering at me through her fan of lashes, her crystal eyes were grave. "It must have been so terrible for you," her glossed lips turned down. "Do you remember it all?"

"Yes, it's coming back to me in bits and pieces. I am starting to decipher vision from memory. It's hard. I've touched so many things in my life, my mind is full of visions—most of them aren't even my own." I placed my hands on the limestone, just next to Lily's pale fingers. "On the count of *push?*" I asked.

"Yes," she said, already leaning her weight against the stone. I applied pressure, then shoved with all my strength. The stone released a small, white tuft of acid smelling powder, but did not budge an inch.

"Bugger!" declared Lily, shoving again, to no avail.

I stood up. "Here, wait. I want to try something."

Lily stepped back, dusting her hands. "That lid hasn't been moved in centuries."

No, it had not. I knew in that instant I could make it move. I was strong as Drake, only I did not need a host of rippling pectorals, I just needed my mind. I closed my eyes and took off the glove on my right hand. I had a brief flash of the door knob this morning, the way I had only been able to make it shiver. I kicked it firmly out of my mind. "I can do this," I told my hand, I told my hesitant brain. I imagined the heavy stone moving, shifting, not flying, and breaking apart like the door in Limbo, only sliding steadily away. Jolts of heat shivered through my arm, and sparks of light glittered on the tips of my fingers. There was another puff of powder, larger this time.

Lily coughed and waved her hand in front of her face to bat the particles away. I felt my back teeth grind when I flexed my fingers, shoving at the pressure in my mind. The lid started to move, slowly, one nearly imperceptible inch at a time. My hand shook, and I heard my teeth crunching bits of enamel between them.

"Cara, it's moving!" Lily was breathless. I heard a growl building in my throat as it moved again, stone screeching over stone. I shivered, a long shiver, one that traveled from the nape of my neck to the tips of my curled toes. I heard myself make a sound, something betwixt a snarl and a moan. White powder ballooned through the room, spraying outward like a jet of hot steam. Lily and I skittered out of its way. I never took the pressure off my fingertips, never stopped pressing against the stone with my pounding mind.

"There are more things in heaven and earth, Horatio, than are dreamt of in your philosophy," quoted Lily, as the stone moved some more. "Though I don't think Shakespeare ever dreamt of something like this."

"No, never," I panted. The thing inside the sarcophagus began to leak its glow. Blue pulsing lights emanated through the room, illuminating all the dark places in my memory. Touching, highlighting so many millions of stories. I realized then, we know, what we know of the world, of life, from the stories that came before—stories, are all that become of us when we die. I never did die, not really, so my story untold, continues. Then that was it, really it, the quest of a soul—choice—an ability to control the ending of your narrative. Tell a good story, you can control the world. Have stories written of you after you die, have your name spoken in tales that span the test of time—then you are immortal. If that is true, many of us have been gods. Galileo, Aristotle, Einstein, Tolkien, Elvis, and in all likelihood—Taylor Swift, who currently has more followers than any of the gods ever did—combined. People who are remembered for the inspiration they brought, in whatever capacity. I know our modern gods, but these others? These gods from another millennia—who knew what they truly craved. Now, the world begs to be entertained and enlightened—we worship those who can give us satisfaction. I dropped my hand and stepped into the expanding sphere of powder and light. What did we crave in the days when these gods had ruled?

Shivers contracted the base of my spine. My footsteps fell soundlessly against the ground. I heard Lily's shallow breaths, in and out—keeping time with my feet. She held back, just slightly behind me, a little to my left. I smelled smoke and heard hiss and crackle of small, exploding flames. I took another step, then another. My toes touched the base of the sarcophagus, and my body came to a stop. Slowly, dreadfully I looked down. My heart stuttered once, like a child trying to force a word past the steel wall in their mind, staunchly preventing passage. Then, I saw her beautiful face—trapped behind that swirling vortex of ice and glass—blue eyes wide, mouth locked in a forever scream—and it stopped dead in my chest. They were real—and I was not insane. Not insane at all. Rather, it appeared I was immortal.

CHAPTER XV

THE TALE OF THE PRINCESS, AND THE SUN.

Pages I found in Lily's things…after…

I stared at my sister's back. I could see her shaking, and I hated it. Cara was on her knees, where she spent most of the time. Either crying or screaming in pain. It really broke me. Hurt me in so many indefinable ways to see her like this. Physically hurt, every time she felt something, I took it like a punch in the gut, even if I was miles away. It is a twin thing. I never said anything. I really could not. Seeing her scream and fall to her knees, watching the blood vessels pop in her eyes—it helped me not make a sound. What did I have to complain about? A punch in the gut, big deal. I would take a million of them if I could stop her screaming.

In the days after Hanna's departure, I had to be there for her, she was a walking, open wound. I needed to be her band-aid. There was no one else. Besides, the twin consciousness was strong in us. If I were ever to walk away, go and live my own life—I knew I would still feel it. Born sixty seconds before her, it was like I emerged to be her protector. Darling, Cara. Cara, who never cried, never wanted anyone to see, but I did not have to see, I did not even have to be told—I always knew. I always knew.

My feet took a step. Flames erupted in my hands the moment blue light had begun to trickle into this strange room. Now, the flames rushed up my arms, fluttered over my chest. I figured out on the night of the Nori, that danger brought my fire. The more the blue seeped into the room, the more I felt an impending sense of doom. I wondered for a split, mad second if maybe I had been wrong to come here? I always knew what we were. I came to this place so I could understand why, and what we could do about it. I do not believe in coincidence, I knew I would have been drawn here eventually, even if Drake had never darkened our door. Now, I could see what had called me. Drake was smart, he had entombed them in limestone, he had tried to contain their magic in nature's fiercest cage—but they were too strong—as if he had buried a set of charged magnets in the earth. I had followed the call, willingly. Looking at Aphrodite's face, frozen in terror, blue eyes the exact shape of mine, I wondered if perhaps I had led my sister and I into a trap—it was as if each move, I made had only helped to fulfil an ancient curse.

Cara stood up and skittered away. "Enough," she said, waving her hand through the glowing air. The limestone she had moved with her mind scooted back into place. She looked at the flames in my hands, fire balls rotating on my palms. I saw her swallow hard.

"Are you okay?" I asked. Hand to her throat, she nodded. Eyes wide in fresh horror. "Let's get out of here. You've seen them, you have nothing more to prove."

She looked at me, her mouth opened like she wanted to say something. I saw a single trail of drying tears on her cheek. It came, sudden and unwanted—a fury enough to blind me. It made jets of flames shoot in the air. I shook my hands, then clenched my fists. The flames went out like I had dunked my hands in water. I felt duped in a way. I had thought myself to be so intelligent, deciphering the map, figuring out the timeline, leading us here—only to realize, it had been them calling me all along.

I shook my head. Cara needed me now, it would help no one if I went to pieces. I said the first thing that jumped into my head. "Is Drake a good kisser," I asked, my voice only shaking a little. Cara did not seem to notice. She relaxed her clenched teeth, and a softness entered her terrified eyes, her hands trembled as she dropped them to her sides.

"I have nothing to compare it to," she said, and I almost saw a smile. "But I'll never kiss another man 'till the day I die, pray to the moon, not even after that. I could kiss him forever; I go crazy the second his lips touch mine."

I watched her shoulders climb down from their tense perch beneath her ears. I saw her take a full breath. That was better. I kept my eyes on her hands, she had almost stopped shaking, the pressure in my gut relaxed by the second. She wrapped her arms around my waist, and together we stumbled from the modern, shining tomb. We carried each other up the wet stairs, then walked to her room, and I helped to lie her in bed. I had used the walls of Wynter manor, I had used our strange powers—I had used anything I could to build a fortress around us. I felt that fortress crumbling now. As our powers grew, the walls came down. Love is the relinquishment of logic, and I would happily throw it all aside to protect my sister.

Cara's eyes closed the moment her head hit the pillow. I moved a wild lock of hair off her clammy forehead and kissed between her eyes. She always said I was a warrior for the bright side—it was hard to believe that statement today. I stood up and brushed my hands down the front of my dress.

"Okay," I whispered, and tiptoed to the door. "Okay," I said again, and my determination grew, if there was a bright side in this abysmal situation—I was going to find it. Perhaps Drake was the bright side, this love they had could be worth it all, it really could. I almost suspected it would save everything. I was smiling again, when I gently closed the door behind me—just before the latch clicked into place, I heard her whisper his name.

I found Alexie hiding in a den of sorts, a man cave, or game room if you will. Three huge TVs lined the wall, each playing some various, colorful insanity. He was curled in a red bean bag, an Xbox controller in one hand, and a can of beer in the other.

"Is this what vampire's do on their day off?"

"I am not a vampire," he said stoically, not looking away from his game.

I took the beer from his hand and sipped it. "Do you drink blood?" I asked.

He looked at me then. "Yes, sometimes. When I must."

"Then you are a vampire," I told him.

"I am not," he said stubbornly. "Garlic does nothing to me, it's rather good, actually, and I can see my reflection in the mirror."

"For which you are most grateful for, I'm sure," I retorted, and he laughed.

I found a matching green bean bag leaning up against the wall. I dragged it beside him and sat down. White light flashed on all TV's at the same time, something crashed, and Alexie cursed.

"Aww, did you die?" I asked, unable to keep the false pity out of my voice.

He cursed again and put the controller down. "You should sleep," he told me. "You look tired."

"Thanks," I said. "It's the middle of the day."

"Not for you," he said reasonably. "Jet lag is a bitch."

I made a face. "I find that statement offensive to all bitches."

He shouted out a bark of laughter. "You are the most stunning thing I have seen in a century, all I meant was— you look like you have a lot on your mind."

"I really do," I yawned. "I know he is her long-lost love; I know they are meant for each other. I figured that out before I even heard the whole story—what I don't know is... is he really dangerous as he thinks he is? Will she really die because she loves him so?" I heard myself sigh. "I believed Andi in Fairhaven, 'words from another time, no place in our modern reality'. Only this reality is not that modern. Looking at those frozen gods, they look so ancient..." I searched for the right word. "Mythological," I finally said. "The dreams didn't make me afraid, only concerned. I always knew Cara was immensely powerful, so all these new abilities are no real shock... it's just that..." my words dropped away.

"It's just what?" asked Alexie kindly.

"I wasn't even that afraid of the Nori, angrier than anything, but those two..." I shuddered. "They really scared me."

"I wouldn't give that fear one more thought," said Alexie. "Those two scare the stones they lie in."

"I can't let Cara see it. I can't let her know," I heard myself say.

"That's unfair," he chided. There was something frank and sensual about his mouth, and I found myself watching him intently. He misunderstood my wide-eyed look and started to explain. "You are like

Drake, both of you—always trying to protect her," he said. "She needs to know, Lily, let her be strong for you." He shrugged his broad shoulders. "I've seen how the two of you are together, she'll know anyway."

I thought about it for a moment, then shook my head. "No," I said, then found a real smile in my heart and put it on my lips. "No! She will only know if it's real. I won't feel it, I refuse to give fear a reality. I believe and we win. I had a momentary slip into the vile quagmire of doubt, I have climbed out, and it will not happen again. Hanna always told me words had true power, had caused many things to be mistakenly spoken into being. I believe it," I told him, and I decided then and there I would speak my desired outcome into being—I would *will* Cara safe, I would will her happiness, love and life. It was my will. So, mote it be.

Alexie moved quickly, so his face was only an inch from mine. "What's going on in that witchy head," he said, and his grey eyes smoldered. "What strange spells are you casting?"

I laughed, a sound that came out high and giggly every time and winked at him. "Oh Alexie," I said. "I never hex and tell."

"Humm," he rumbled.

I shifted in the bean bag uncomfortably, and my dress rucked up around my knees. I kicked my feet and tugged at the hem, then stood. "I am going back to the library," I declared. "I saw a study on the second floor as well, might check there, too."

"Still have no idea what you're looking for?" asked Alexie, returning his attention to a loading screen.

"Nope," I said cheerfully. "I am determined to find it though—and, for me," I yawned. "Determination always equals success."

He shook his head at me, and I left the room with a bounce in my step.

The study offered me nothing useful, it was filled with ledgers, and scripts demanding currencies from a dead time. "What the hell *am* I looking for?" I asked the wide space of books, stacked high—all the way to the domed ceiling. I closed my mind, tried to search the proverbial haystack for the elusive needle—only I had no idea what a needle looked like. Outside the sky was a bright, crisp blue. Inside the yellow lights were low. I walked to the table where I had left our Book of Shadows. I loved the way things moved on the pages, I laughed when they growled—I never know why. My fingers touched images, words, the pages turned. I stopped on a gold leaf page; the word 'Divination' was scrolled in handwriting across the top. Beneath it read: *'The practice of seeking knowledge, by strange or supernatural means'*. That sounded right. We were nothing if not strange and supernatural—even though I placed a ban on the words—truth was truth. I read the text scrolled beneath, written in the script of someone who shared my blood, a goddess maybe—definitely not dead, regardless of the headstones. I folded both hands over my heart, and quickly memorized the words, then repeated them out loud.

"Help me find what I cannot see, bring the thing I seek directly to me." I shrugged. "Not bad," I told the book. "Straight to the point, modern." I touched the words. "I like it." I said it again. "Help me find what I cannot see, bring the thing I seek directly to me." I took a deep breath. "Help me find what I cannot see, bring the thing I seek directly to me." In the middle of my fourth recital, a book—on a shelf over twenty feet above my head—broke free of its companions and hurtled at my face. I grabbed it out of the air, before it hit me, then stared at it— dumbfounded. I threw the Book of Shadows a grateful look. "Thanks dude," I told it, and sat on the nearest chair—fell really. My knees shook a little. I touched the cover, ran my fingers over the image painted on the front, a small girl lying in the fetal position, her golden hair streaming around her like a living shroud. I opened it, a tuft of dust flew up my nose, and I sneezed a couple of times, then finished the fit off with a cough for good measure. I cleared my throat and started to read.

"Once a princess slept with the sun. In a chamber under the earth and told no one it was the sun who touched her. Her father, the king, god of storms, was the sun's greatest rival. They met at night, the princess and sun. Tried to hide their love in the shadows which could not contain it. In time the glow of the princess grew too bright, and the father knew what she had done. Enraged at his daughter's betrayal, he stuck a golden stake through her heart, tethering her to the thirsty ground. Her sisters found her body in the morning, skin picked at by vultures, heart pierced through, dead in her chest. They gathered the body of their sister in their arms and carried her to the temple of the sun. There they begged him to return her life, told him the fault was his. The sun god could do nothing he wished to do yet despised seeing her dead.

'Give me her eyes', the sun god said. 'Take them from her face and put them in my hands. Life for sight', he said, his voice a broken song. 'It is the only magic I have.'

The sisters hated to do such a thing— but the choice had been taken from them, when their father pierced her heart. They plucked her eyes from her face and gave them to the sun god. He touched the princess's head, and fire burnt all the edges of the hollow, black gaps where her blue eyes had once been. The princess sat up, yet the fire reached her heart. Wings of flame burst from her back, and spears of light shot from her empty eyes. Her body burnt to ashes, while magic flames replaced her bones, and the princess flew into the sky. No longer goddess, longer human— she was known forever as Phoenix—the reborn."

"Yesh!" I shuddered. "What a pleasant bedtime story," chicken skin tickled my neck. "I'll be sure *not* to read that to my future children." I turned the page, the story continued. The sisters were pissed obviously, so they ran off to kill their storm-god father. They were of course met with unmitigated disaster as they tried to murder an unkillable god. The story droned on for five additional pages, detailing the violent death of each sister as they miserably failed. I felt a sudden twinge of pity for the poor humans fighting— then I felt some pity for myself, when I realized that might be my lot. On the final page, the eldest, and sole surviving sister faces her father, in her hands is a weapon of water. Seconds before she is defeated, the blind, fiery phoenix flies up her father's nose, and burns him to ash. Ash from, ash which he did not rise.

'Only god-fire,' the book said, 'only god-fire can kill a god'. I looked down, breathed deep and slow. Only god-fire could kill a god. I stared at my sandals on the pale carpet, the polish on my right big toe was chipped alerting me to my need for a Spa day. I stood up meaning to go back to the Book of Shadows, standing proudly in square one—and start again, but I heard a noise behind me and spun. My hands heated instantly as the hairs on the back of my neck rose higher.

When I saw who it was my breath rushed from my lungs. "Oh, you," I muttered when Drake's eyes locked on mine.

"Hi," he said. The tone in his voice reminded of the tempered music which proceeds any good Hollywood death. Low, scintillating, raw— ominous. "Didn't mean to startle you," he stated, hands dug deep in his pockets. "Are you well?" he looked somewhat nervous, it was cute for a man his size, a man who looked like a natural born killer. "Is your sister… is she…?" his voice broke, I saw him cringe, then he pressed his lips together and waited for me to answer. Damn he was handsome.

"She's fine," I said, using Cara's word. "She's sleeping."

The muscles tensing his spine relaxed somewhat. I slammed the book closed, and the girl on the cover seemed to curl further into herself. I placed it on the table beside the Book of Shadows, sighed so he heard it, and faced him. "Have you ever heard of a text message?" I asked, hearing the censure in my voice. His brows rose and he looked confused.

He nodded absently, obviously distracted. "I have," he said, seriously missing the point.

"You could have left one," I informed him, and my hands went to my hips. I knew I was steaming, but… honestly? "In twenty nineteen it is rude to leave a woman naked in your bed, *very rude* to do so textlessly."

"Textlessly?" he echoed.

"Umm hum," my eyes locked to his. "It hurts," I said, my voice soft. "We are self-conscious creatures, who— when left alone—instantly believe we must have grown four eyes overnight, and just can't see them."

He flinched, and something in his golden eyes crackled. It appeared I could also set fire with my words. He looked like I just torched his skin in a kerosene flame. "I had to," he choked out.

I sighed and dropped my hand. "I thought so," I said. "I knew you wouldn't leave her unless it was important." I rubbed my eyes. "Not now."

"No," he agreed, stepping into the library, and closing the door quietly. His movements were so smooth they flowed together like a dance. "No," he said again. "Not now."

"What are we going to do?" I asked, not bothering to expound, his eyes told me he was well aware of all the dangers.

"I'm going to do what I should have done two thousand years ago," he breathed, and the dark light in his eyes made me cold.

"And that is…?" I prompted.

"I'm going to kill them, Aphrodite and Ares. I'm going to kill them and burn their hearts." He ran his hands through his hair. His jaw clenched tight making his next words come out muffled. "That's why I was gone. I went to my father. I asked him what the repercussions of such a choice would be. He said Ares carried the core of light in his heart. He said if I killed him, my family would die, Persephone told me it could not be done, she told me the results would be catastrophic." Drake threw his body into the nearest chair. "It was great news all around," he said darkly, and buried his face in his hands. "Did she go and see them?" he asked through his fingers.

"Yes," I told him. "I went with her. Not gonna lie, those two sleeping monsters scared Jesus out of me." A thought hit me. "Is your whole family still alive? Everyone? Hera, Hestia, Demeter, Tyche?"

Drake looked at me from between his fingers, not lifting his head. "Tyche? Goddess of Fame and Fortune? She's more alive than any of us. Us! Fuck!" Drake shook his head, his hair tumbled to his wrists. "If it's the only way… then it's the only way."

"Wait!" Surprise constricted my throat as an unpleasant thought attacked, when I voiced it, it made my hands heat up again. "Will it kill you too?"

He looked at me, his eyes in cinders, and I knew then, it was not my words that had torched him, he had walked in here already aflame. "I don't know. Maybe. I don't care. She will live."

My stumbling legs took me to the seat beside him and I fell limply into it. "You were right," I said.

"About what," the tone of his voice told me he did not care.

"It is great news all around," I said, each word dripping sarcasm. I reached out to take his hand.

"It's not all," he grated out. "There is someone here to see you. To see both of you," his words sounded distracted, perfunctory. "I don't know how they came to be here, or why. They are unknowable."

"Oh," I said thoughtfully. "Well, I think that would be my doing, I did a spell before you stormed in. I called something, something I needed. Well, to be honest, I don't know what I was even trying to call, but I am glad whoever it is—is here. A book tried to hit me on the head after I did the spell, so I assumed…" I shrugged. "I guess I must have needed it too…we shall see." I stood up. "Off with you then," I told him, trying to lift the blanket of misery in the air. "I will stay right here and remind myself to be careful what I wish for, while you go fetch the latest boogie man."

Drake stood up. "Brace yourself," he said.

I smiled, a real smile. One that was sparkly and felt like it belonged. "Always," I said.

Two minutes later, my resolve to punch her in the face flew out the window when Hanna walked in.

Her eyes were wide in her heart shaped face, a film of tears magnified them. Her lips fell apart and she sucked in a long breath. "Oh Lily," she gasped, and held out her arms. My heart stopped dead in my chest, as every muscle in my body froze. I wanted to rage, maybe throw something at her, but suddenly—I was ten years old again, watching her old Jaguar coast down the driveway. My heart raced faster than my feet as I ran to her.

"Oh, little Lily love, how beautiful you are." Her arms closed around me, and I was engulfed in the scents of home. I linked my fingers behind her neck, and she held me. We went down on our knees and rocked until she leaned back to look at my face. "Prettier than all the stars dancing in the sky," she whispered.

"I'm rather upset at you," I sniffed. Laughing and crying.

"I know," she said. "I'm upset with myself too." She wiped a teary green eye on her silk glove. "You called?"

"You heard me?" I asked.

"I always told you, I would come if you really needed me."

"You did, didn't you? And here you are, Cara is going to freak," I finished, and glanced over my shoulder. Drake stood behind me looking uncomfortable in his own skin.

Hanna followed my gaze. "Thank you, Draken," she said, after a moment of simply staring at him.

"That is not my name," he nearly barked. His eyes darkened by degrees. "Cara doesn't like it," he explained.

"Oh?" said Hanna. "How do you know that?"

"She told me a long time ago, said it sounded like the lead character in a Greek tragedy. She told me, in twenty nineteen my name is Drake, and that's what she would call me." He shrugged. "I am a Greek tragedy, so I acquiesced."

"Your story is not finished," said Hanna. Arms still around me, we stood. I stepped back and met her sharp green gaze.

"Why are you here?" spat Drake.

"Because Cara needs me, and Lily called me."

"You and your kind are the last thing she needs!" Drake brows drew together as his voice rose. Hot splashes of color painted his cheeks, and his fingers shook when they balled into fists. "This was all started and ordained by you!" His voice broke. "Must she really die again before your need for revenge is slated? You have punished and humiliated them for three thousand years! Killed an innocent girl and destroyed my life in the process. When is it enough?" he asked. His words hoarse and defeated. He sounded as if his throat had been lined with concrete.

"I killed no one," said Hanna. "I saved Arias, I gave her some form of life, Cara is the daughter of gods, last living of the Elemental bloodline. I saved them both. I gave her Lily, a fire goddess and first-rate enchantress. I protected her in my own home." Hanna took a step forward, her voice impassioned. "I took care of her. I stayed until I had to leave, leave or die."

"What do you mean?" I demanded. "What do you mean, leave or die? Honestly, what do you mean by it all! But that last part in particular?!" I gulped in a breath, shocked by my tone, one I had never used on her in my life. Hanna's lips tightened into a thin line, the same line I remember from my childhood, it always appeared when Cara or myself had done something to displease. I looked at my hands, saw the lines crossing my palm start to glow. I took a step toward Drake, automatically it seemed, while I tried to get my mind ready for whatever answer was coming, even if that answer was no answer at all.

Hanna stayed silent for another moment. I felt myself gearing up for a shout when she inhaled through her nose and said, "I cared too much. I would have come here and killed the sleeping gods. Ripped their heads from their bodies and eaten their hearts." Her eyes fell closed. "I do that, I die, your mother dies, and Draken—Drake will die, I cannot destroy my entire bloodline over mere vengeance."

The hinges of the study door creaked, and I felt Drake stiffen beside me. I spun toward the sound and saw Cara standing still in a small sliver of golden light, spilling from the window hidden behind the open door. Her hands flew to her cheeks and she clutched them as her eyes filled with swollen tears. The shattered expression of agony on her face told me she had heard everything that mattered. "What… what?" she lowered her hands and cried out in a shrill, furious voice. "So, you have a limit, do you?"

CHAPTER XVI

TRUTH OR DARE

I woke alone in my borrowed bed, it felt strange to not wake in his. I sat up, heart pounding and breaths ripping out of my lungs like I had run for miles. Lily left me here after we saw them. I remember lying down, I remember her kissing my forehead, and hearing her sad, almost frightened sigh. Then I was running through the forest again, watching Drake kill the creatures his own blood had created. I saw the faded smear of blood on his hands, the thick coating on his sword. I smelled burning flesh and wondered how many years we would live in this horrible way, because it was a hell of the worst kind to not hold him when he thrashed in dark dreams of death. There was a trail of dried tears on my cheeks that I could not recall crying. I wiped them away and stood up. Trying to battle through a wave of black dizziness, I walked to the door, focusing on the voices I heard coming from downstairs. Lily, Drake… and…Hanna. Unmistakable. Well, why not? I touched the god of war today, why should I not touch its goddess? I walked down the spiral staircase, hand sliding slowly along the polished banister.

Drake's voice rose to a shout, and I quickened my pace. Already blushing with thoughts of facing him. Wondering how on earth I would speak if my teeth did not stop worrying at my lower lip.

"What do you mean?" I heard Lily say. "What do you mean, leave or die?!" I walked faster, my feet fairly flying now. I turned a sharp corner, my unbound hair sailing behind me. The partially closed study door barred my path, I reached out my hand and pushed it open.

"If I do that," said Hanna, her voice was exactly as I remembered. "Then, I die, your mother dies, and Draken—Drake will die, I cannot destroy my entire bloodline over mere vengeance."

Rage bubbled inside me like I was the cauldron and it, the liquid spell. I shoved the door wider, then felt my hands fly to my cheeks, as her words registered on my spinning mind. She could kill some, but not all? Good gods, what a pile of crap. "You have a limit, do you?" I heard myself say. In the middle of wanting to take the words back, I was glad I said them. The look in Hanna's eyes was my reward. It was a broken look, raw and bleeding intensity. Lily's face was sad, she held her hand out to me, but I could not relent. "It's okay to kill me a couple of times, and who knows how many others? But none of you? Why? How are you special? Unfeeling immortals, numb to human death and suffering, unable to feel real love."

"That's not true," whispered Hanna.

"Which part?" I snapped.

"I always loved you," she explained, sounding choked and sincere. "You and Lily, I love you. I would have ended it all a long time ago if that weren't true. I knew you would remember one day— Aphrodite's curses always play out— I knew you would remember loving him," she motioned to Drake. "Remember loving a dead man, I couldn't do that. The choice is yours. I never should have interfered."

"Well, there's some real truth," said Lily.

Hanna shook her head. "What's done is done, I cannot undo it. Believe me I have tried. A time traveler, unable to change time. I am the greatest contradictive irony."

I saw fascination widen Lily's eyes, though she said nothing. I almost heard the million questions racing through her mind, but I tried not to listen. My own thoughts were more than enough to contend with. "This seems like a stupid question in light of everything," I said. "But how are you here? How did you know we were here?"

"You sister called me," said Hanna.

"I didn't mean to," muttered Lily, she faced Hanna, and her hands went to her hips. "What are we going to do now, you said that Aphrodite always follows through, so…how do we stop this?"

Hanna looked at the muddy hem of her long, black dress. "We do what Drake said," she told her feet. "We kill them, and pray the old legends are false."

"Pray to whom," I snapped.

"Whoever you want," said Hanna in a tired voice. "They all listen, those who can answer, will."

"Lily and I, you said we are the daughters of a goddess," I thought of the flaming bow and arrow, and shook off a sudden host of forgotten images. "Will destroying this core of light kill us?"

"No. You have elemental blood," said Drake, speaking for the first time, since I stepped into the room. "You and your sister will live."

"But you will die?" I asked. The explosion of shrapnel I felt in my heart at that thought must have shown on my face, because he flinched. I took a gasping breath. "You always say you can't live without me…" I whispered.

"That's my point Cara, I would not be living. You would."

My heart thudded in my ears. Lily and Hanna flitted in my peripheral, my consciousness saw only him. "What makes you think I could possibly live without you!?" I shouted. Drake froze, his teeth locked in that unbreakable vise, then he started toward me.

I held up my hand to keep him away, if he touched me, I would come apart. "Stop making all my choices," I demanded, somewhat bitterly.

He dug his hands in his pockets, his feet nearly tripping in his attempt to obey me and halt his stride. "There is only one choice," he said in a hollow voice.

"That isn't true, Drake," said Lily in earnest, stepping up and lightly placing her hand on his tense forearm. "Maybe before, not now. This is the century of choices, we just must find it, I am close. Perhaps I can figure out how to capture the core of light, no don't roll your eyes at me. It was done once; it can be done again."

"I have tried," said Hanna's miserable voice. I turned toward the sound. She had eyes only for Lily.

"Well, posh!" Lily waved her hand through the air, as if she could physically bat away the negative energy coasting through the room. "You didn't have me helping you, did you?" she asked in a tart tone.

"No," said Hanna, sounding sincere. "No, I certainly did not."

"Well then," said Lily, a smile returning to her lips. "Enough of this, they aren't waking up tonight. Let's play a game, if we are all going to die soon, we may as well live a little."

"And games are the way to do that?" I said, sarcasm in every angle of my face.

Lily nodded. "Games and wine," she sighed. "'Tis the way of the gods, you know?"

■ ■ ■

Drake's black t-shirt and jeans made him blend with the shadows, he was breathtaking, and I stared, shamelessly rapt. We sat in front of a fire, on the floor of what had once been the grandest of ballrooms. Drake and Alexie sat across from each other, Hanna from me, and Lily between us. Andi, who had breezed in less than an hour ago, had—of course—fallen in love with the game idea and suggested spin the bottle, a giggling Lily acquiesced. Now, a wine bottle spun in the center of our circle. I had spun the damn bottle. The magic of our souls made the spinning stop on Drake, suddenly, no slowing down—it just stopped, almost swinging from the inertia of the halt.

He looked at me sharply, eyes narrowed. "Truth or dare," I whispered. All my breaths tangled in my throat.

"Truth," he said instantly.

"Have you ever slept with another woman besides Cara?" asked Lily, raising her glass of Merlot, and taking a sip.

"Lily!" I was horrified, desperate to know the answer. I tried to search my library of memories yet saw no face. "I'm supposed to ask the questions."

Lily looked incredibly innocent. "Sorry, but yours would've been lame."

Drake's shoulders relaxed, and the smallest curve of a smile touched his lips. "Yes," he breathed, not taking his eyes from my face. "Arias," he finished.

Lily dramatically rolled her eyes. "Oh," she gasped. "Is anyone else choking on the suddenly sappy quality to the air?"

Androsia and Alexie laughed. "That doesn't count, Draken," said Andi. She gave me a sidelong look, when I caught her gaze, she quickly dropped it.

"What about before?" giggled Lily.

"That is a second truth," said Drake.

"Not really," Lily snapped back. "Same topic."

"Fine," he smiled. "A few, though I couldn't recall their names or faces if it meant my life." His eyes drifted to me; his voice dropped low. "Not since her." Something burned in the air between us. "You," he breathed.

I felt myself tremble, if we were alone, I would have reached for him, and I found myself momentarily and ridiculously furious that we two were not the only people in the world. Alexie pinched the bridge of his straight nose between thumb and forefinger and groaned.

"We get it, you two are the modern Romeo and Juliet, Lancelot and Guinevere —saints spare us," he groaned again. "I believe it is my turn."

"No," said Lily, and reached for the bottle. "It is mine, now, sit back or it won't land on you."

Alexie clutched his heart. "How will I survive in the face of such tragedy?"

"You'll be fine," snapped Lily. "Only the good ones die young." That pronouncement hanging in the air, Lily reached for the bottle, flipped her fingers, and spun it. It spun forever, round, and round. Finally, it landed on Alexie.

"Truth or dare," whispered Lily, sounding like Eve in the garden, speaking to the enticing serpent.

"Dare," said Alexie. "I am not afraid of any machinations you may devise."

"You should be," said Hanna. I threw her a look but kept my silence. We had not spoken two words since I shouted at her in the library. One part of me felt justified, the other—small and childish part, the part who missed her terribly—felt a knot of awfulness stir in the pit of her stomach.

"Fine," said Lily, stretching her fingers in front of her, and twitching her neck from side to side. "Very well, you asked for it," she taunted.

Alexie wiggled his brows. "Bring it."

"Alexei Nikolai Romanov," said Lily, pronouncing his name perfectly. "I dare you…" she paused effectively; we all held our collective breath. "I dare you to bite me."

Alexie drew back, appalled. "I will do no such thing," he said, turning his face away, I saw his cheeks flush. Lily smiled from beneath her thick lashes, and crawled to him, her rings clicked against the ground as she moved. Alexie jumped to his feet and skittered back like she was a stake pointed at his heart.

"Lily, no," I heard Hanna gasp. "Don't give that creature a single drop of your royal blood."

Alexie snarled at Hanna. "Blue blood is also mine, great queen," he said, in an accented voice holding hints of mockery. "The god of war locked beneath this very earth is actually my great God sire. We have the same blood disease. Hemophilia, I believe it is called— well *had*."

"So…" crooned Lily, tilting her neck. "Royal boy, what are you waiting for?" she asked.

Alexie took another stumbling step away from her advancing figure. "Fuck, Lily—" he choked out, eyes locked to the exposed white skin on her neck, and the vein throbbing beneath it.

"Do you forfeit?" she asked, her voice sensual enough to enchant stone. "What happened to all that masculine bravery? We are playing a child's game in an ancient castle. I'm shaking it up."

"What if I hurt you," he said. Lily flowed into his arms, and pressed herself to his chest, his hands went to her waist. Even as he spoke, he pulled her closer.

"Hurt me," she breathed. "I want to feel it."

I shook my head. "Oh, my gods, Lily!" I put my hands over my eyes. "You are going to be the death of you," I said.

She glanced at me over her shoulder, her body still in Alexie's shaking arms. "Now isn't that just the best way to go?"

I gaped open mouthed; her actions took all my words. She swiveled back to Alexie and smiled brilliantly up into his dazed face. "Just bite me, goddamn it," she said.

Alexie spun her, so his back was to us, a swirl of her blonde hair fell over his arm. His broad shoulders tensed fiercely, I heard Lily's tremulous gasp. Three seconds, no more and she stepped out of his arms, her right fingers pressed to her neck, her eyes wide and glittering. Alexie looked shaken.

"Well," I asked when they both sat back down. "Did it hurt?"

Lily smiled at me. "Yes. Brilliantly." She moved her hand, and I saw two bright puncture marks on her neck.

I rolled my eyes. "Oh brother."

"It's your turn, Alexie," said Lily. She handed him the end of the bottle, smiling. He glared at her.

"Fine," he grumbled, I watched his tongue swipe at his lower lip, dark color seeped into his eyes. He spun the bottle with such strength, it seemed to twirl endlessly.

It came to a final stop on Andi, she smiled. "My very first time," she tittered.

Alexie rose a dark brow. "Truth or dare," he challenged.

Andi stuck her pert nose in the air. "Truth, I won't have you making me jump from the castle ramparts, or something else equally atrocious."

"Fine…" Alexie took a breath. "Who do you love most in all the world?" he asked. When Andi immediately opened her mouth to speak, he held up a hand. "Answer carefully, I'll know it if you lie."

Andi closed her lips, her eyes grew cold, and at Alexie's continued glare, her edges emerged. "This is a stupid game," she said. "Nothing like the movies. Can't you ask an interesting question?"

"What is more interesting than love?" challenged Alexie.

"What is your favorite city on earth?" asked Lily. Alexie opened his mouth, and I saw Lily gently squeeze his leg. His mouth closed with a solid click.

Andi calmed. "Santorini," she said, and reached for the bottle. No one spoke when she spun it. After three quick spins, it landed squarely on Hanna.

Andi jerked back like a snake bit her. "Goddess," she bowed her head in a short nod, that looked automatic. "Truth or dare?" she questioned.

Hanna smiled, an old mystical smile, and her face looked ghostly pale hovering above the collar of her midnight dress. "Dare," she pronounced, and looked me straight in the eyes. Flexing her fingers so we all saw each move her slender knuckles made. "Enough truths for one night."

"Let's see," Andi lightly touched her lower lip as her eyes turned dramatically thoughtful. "What shall I have you do?"

"It's a rare chance," said Hanna. "One few have, I find my self-locked to it because I agreed to play this ridiculous game."

"It is ridiculous," muttered Alexie.

"In the past," started Andi, sounding mildly nervous—a strange condition for her— and twisting her hair through her long fingers. "I have heard you can change yourself into anything. That you have the power of transfiguration, my brother swears he's seen it, so…I dare you to show me?"

"Any particular animal you want to see?" asked Hanna, standing up slowly, the soul of casual.

"The owl," I said. "I want to see the owl; I want to see if it really was you all these years."

Lily squealed. "You were the owl?! At the Wynter manor? This whole time!?? So, you never really left?!"

"That's a truth, dear," said Hanna.

Lily, true to form, did not relent. "Hanna!?" she demanded.

Hanna smiled, a slow smile that touched her almond eyes, then she lifted her hands and started to spin. Her black dress flared around her ankles like a bell, and her head twisted on her delicate neck. Glittering silver light—like Christmas bulbs seen through thick smoke—gushed from her pores, white feathers appeared amidst the darkness. Lily reached for my hand and our fingers locked. We exchanged one, searching look, then turned our attention to Hanna's breaking back. Wings shot from her shoulder blades as she began to levitate…no that was wrong…as she began to fly. Fly and fly until she was spinning high above our heads in an ever-increasing cloud of twinkling silver lights.

■   ■   ■

I left the game, and the drinking girls. Lily held Hanna's hand and drilled her with questions—I did not want to hear the answers. Not right now. I missed home and Drake's arms, not at all in that order. The castle was so huge, it would be easy to get lost. Each doorway opened to another wonder, each hall leading to strange, hidden rooms stuffed with priceless, historical memorabilia, abandoned chests of jewels, and more books than even I could read in a dozen lifetimes.

Finally, I was outside. I had been too long indoors. Breathing deep I stared at the late afternoon sun, wondering at the thousand variations of green surrounding me. Everything was touched by it, even the low hanging sky held a warning shade. I started to walk toward a huge oak to the north, its trunk almost hidden in a vale of wild forget-me-nots. My plan was to lie beneath it and wait out the day, think, sleep, and maybe have a good yell about Hanna. Get it out of my system before I saw her again. Sure, she had her reasons, she would have killed them, and she did not want to die herself. It made sense. Selfish sense, but sense, nonetheless. Besides, I was glad she had decided not to kill the sleeping gods, if he died… I shuddered. The thought was unthinkable.

I felt him come up behind me—as if my mere musings had summoned him—before I heard his footsteps. I stopped walking, though I did not turn around.

"I'm sorry about leaving you this morning," he breathed. Not touching me, from the corner of my eye, I saw his hand curl into a fist, as if sheer willpower alone stopped him. "If it makes it any better—it killed me to do so."

"Was it this morning?" I asked, sounding rather wistful. "I can't even remember what day it is any more." I spun to face him. "It was strange waking up in your bed, I never slept in the mists…" I said, remembering as I spoke. "I always just watched you," I smiled. "You really do love your sleep."

"Because I see only you when I dream," he stated simply, like such a profound, insanely romantic statement was the most normal thing in the world. His black clothes against the backdrop of weird green sky, made it look like he was the storm bringer. He took another step, then stopped. I caught his right hand before he stuffed it in his pocket. His lean, handsome face was solemn when it looked down at me. "When all you want to do is die, sleep is the next best thing."

I nodded unwillingly. "I know the feeling."

"I'm sorry," he said, suddenly impassioned. "I know those are the among the most useless words in language, but they're all I have. I am sorry for coming to find you, I am sorry for not coming sooner, I am sorry for not telling you right away, I am sorry I had to tell you at all."

"I know," I told him.

"Last night was…"

"I know," I said again. "I don't want to go back inside right now; I'm not feeling quite myself. I want to walk."

He looked up at the sky, then back to me. "You sure? A storm is coming."

I stared deep into the moving gold of his eyes. "It is," I said with assurance.

"You're very beautiful when you get angry," he said. At my befuddled look he shrugged. "What? No one's ever told you that before?"

"I don't get angry at people very often. It seems I save it all up for you," I finished. He laughed, and it was an intoxicating sound. "Come then." Hand in mine, he started to walk. His pace increased until he was half pulling, half dragging me down a steep, grassy incline. Snowcapped mountains showed through the closely knit trees and bordered all the edges of my vision.

"Do you remember where we're going?" he asked. Curls blew across his face, and boyish mischief twinkled in his eyes.

"No, not really," I said, and then it came to me. My ghost had followed him on this path many times. "Why are people always dragging me to graveyards?"

Drake stopped. "The hot springs are past the graveyard. Do you not want to go?" there was a note of disappointment in his voice, and I did not want it there.

"Never mind," I said. "Come on." This time I was the one dragging him. I remembered the rocks, and their curves. I remember the path like I had walked it yesterday, not eighteen years ago. Twilight now held the earth in its muted hands, and streamers of mists roamed the ground. We walked in silence, too many words between us to say just one.

Birds harmonized in the trees, knocking freezing leaves to the snow spattered ground. "How is everything so green," I finally asked, more to break the thick quiet. "Shouldn't the grass be dead under all this snow?"

"Nothing dies here," he said, leaning down to press his palm against a stone. "This ground breeds immortality, even in the smallest things." I watched him shake off a dark thought. "Come," he said. "We're nearly there."

I followed him until I smelt the bubbling springs. He stopped in the last rays of sun and took my hands.

"Cara," he looked in my eyes. "I can't keep apologizing for what I cannot change. I need you to let me make this right. I should be dead. By the gods just for the sheer number of times I have wished it— Fates! I should be dead. I will kill them and take whatever comes. My life has been blood soaked; a violent end is no more than I deserve."

"No, Drake, you killed to save lives, that is no crime. No one else could have done what you did, you fought creatures believed to be fantasy. You saved people. So, don't go getting all noble on me, I'm not letting you die for me."

"Why?" he asked bitterly. "Are you the only one who can do that? You're a human girl, despite your god blood, chances are, if I kill them you will live a long, immortal life. You will find another man, in time. Lightning can strike twice."

My ears burned. It was the most ridiculous thing I had ever heard. "How can you say that?" I asked violently. "How can you even think it?"

"Because it is the only way," he said.

"Would everyone just stop saying that!" I yelled, realizing I was stomping my foot. "God damn it Drake, in the choice between you and me, it will always be me." I said my last words to hurt him, and saw that I hit my mark, then felt sick at myself.

"If you die again, I will become the darkness I hunt. Worse. I won't let that happen to the world. You will find someone else."

"Impossible," I shouted, shocked, and stung. My temples pounded louder than my heart, but there was nothing to say, like the wine bottle we just went round and round. I sat down near the stone lip of the spring, its contents steaming and bubbling like one of Aunt Jane's cauldrons. He paced in front of me, and silence ruled our lives for a few moments more. "If I had never died, do you think we would still feel the same way about each other?" I finally wondered aloud. "Romances often flourish under the impending threat of death. If there were no crisis, would there still be… this?" I motioned to the moving air between us.

"I loved you the first day I saw you, standing beside Aphrodite, screaming my name. I loved you thirteen days before Aphrodite fed me her venomous love spell." He stopped and his eyes burned into mine. "Perhaps it was different for you—I can't say how you would feel, or what her magic did to you. I only know my own soul."

"Drake, you were the epitome of a fairy tale prince, every girl in Sparta loved you," I stopped to remember. "Every girl in the known world, most likely."

He caught my shoulders. "You know that's not what I mean," he said, his voice dark again. I could not twist away, only feel.

"How could I find anyone else, even if I wanted to?" I softly asked. "No one but you can touch me, love spell or not, I'm yours… yours, or no ones. You have to know that?!"

Light flared in his eyes, then he sighed. "I know—besides, let's face it— despite my best intentions, I would most likely kill anyone who tried."

"So…we either live together, try to fight, and die if we must, or you kill them, and I live forever in lonely misery. Don't be a coward Drake, our only choice is to fight."

"I'm only cowardly when it comes to you. I would take you through dimensions and hide you in another world if you would let me." His hand moved down to caress my hip.

"Drake," I protested on a broken whisper.

He pulled me closer. "Do you even remember what my life is, now?" he asked, the corded muscles in his forearms straining. "I can tell you about it if you want—the bad in me—if it will somehow make this better." The whole of his body gave a massive shudder, and I listened to his heart. "Look at me," he said. His broken voice made me want to look everywhere else, but I obeyed. His eyes narrowed when he saw the defiance in mine. "I have nothing to give you, as long as they live, long as they sleep under the ground, I must kill what their spilling magic creates, and it never ends, Cara. Evil is like a hydra. Each head I cut, another ten spring up. I have been cutting for two thousand years." He breathed out a ragged breath. "I really am the modern death god, like father like son," bitterness laced his tone like poison. "What am I going to do? Move to America? Live with you and your sister in your haunted mansion? Wait for the creatures to find us, try to kill who I can? Wait for a curse to fulfil itself? No Cara, it is enough that I got to see you again, after all these long, horrible years."

"Drake, I am not going to let you die, any more than you would let me die. If you go and do it behind my back, I will never forgive you—I'll find a way to curse you in death."

His brow rose, his lips curved into a slight smile. "I could take it."

I touched his face. "Sometimes you remind me so much of the boy I first met," I whispered. "You're more serious, scarier, but the same."

"Do I scare you, love?" he asked, his low voice full of gravelly sincerity.

"Yes," I said honestly. "In so many indefinable ways. But that's me, your run of the mill scaredy cat. I'm afraid of loving you, of losing you. I'm afraid of lies and secrets. I'm afraid of dying," I threw up my hands. "I'm afraid of not fighting. Hell, most of the time I'm afraid of my own shadow."

"Says the bravest person I've ever met," he muttered. "I swear I will never lie to you again," he said, then shrugged. "I did it so badly the first time it hardly counted." Light spilled between us as he rested his forehead against mine. "Can you feel me, love?"

Warmth suffused my veins. "Yes," I gasped.

"Then look into my mind, see I'm telling you the truth. I've told you what I want, what I will do if all else fails."

"Drake," I started.

His fingers touched my lips. "We will try it your way first. I swear, I will fight with you. I'll even hit the books with Lily if that's what you want."

"Yes, it's what I want," I whispered. His breath fell against my face and he smelled like peppermint and red wine. I met his eyes. "Last night felt like a fantasy, it hardly seems real. Everything is so confused in my head, so many broken memories."

"That's how it is." His voice was a low shred of sound. "My memories jumble together into one endless image of darkness. You have always been my only point of light," he vowed.

My eyes fell closed, and I listened to my shaky exhale. Palms resting against his chest, I felt the surging beats of his heart. My fingers moved to the hem of his tight black shirt, and I tugged it up his narrow waist, it pulled on the chiseled ridges of his stomach. My hands slid beneath, and I shivered when I touched his warm skin. Drake's reaction was fierce and immediate. His fingers gripped my upper thighs, and lifted me, I locked my legs around his waist.

"I want new memories," I told him, helping him rip off his shirt and throw it to the ground, our skin touched and mine began to glow. "These memories." One of his hands locked beneath my hips, the other tangled in my hair, he carried me to the edge of the boiling pool, and pressed my back against a cold, rocky shelf. I hoisted myself higher, struggling with my own shirt. His hot, shredding breath rasping in my ear intensified as I unclasped my bra. He grabbed the strap between his teeth and ripped it from my body. I did not cover myself like last night, only left my hands on his shoulder and shook while he looked at me, his eyes hazy and starving. "Mine," I heard him breathe, then he lowered his head and our lips touched. The reaction was flame and oil. There in the forest, under the light of the setting sun we ignited, and burned until the purple moon danced high in the star-soaked sky.

CHAPTER XVII

BLOOD CURRENCY IS TO DIE FOR.
DAY TWO OF THIRTEEN

I woke to the thunder of my own heart. The room was dark, the silence broken only by the sounds of Drake's soft, breaking breaths. Against his dark skin the sheet covering his hips was a slash of stark white, it glowed under the eerie light cast by the stormy sky. Lightning crackled beyond the window, and objects in the room shimmered, and faded in the same second, I saw the shadows shift when thunder boomed in the west. I sat up, careful not to wake him. He looked so peaceful when he slept, so young and innocent. I stroked a lock of hair off his forehead, and he sighed, his lips slightly parted, his iron jaw relaxed. My heart calmed, slowly I started to lie back down, when I heard the distinct creak of a floorboard. I held my breath and waited for another. It did not come. I swung my legs over the edge of the high king bed and tiptoed toward the door.

"*Lily?*" I called out to her in my mind. "*Lily, is that you?*"

"*Wha... what? Cara...?*" her thoughts were groggy and disoriented. I knew then, I had woken her. "*Are you alright?*" she was suddenly alert. "*What's happening?*"

"*There is someone outside my door,*" I told her, trying not to freak out.

"*Aren't you in Drake's room?*"

"*Yes?*"

"Well, wake him up for freak's sake!" The floorboard creaked again, louder. *"I'm coming,"* she said.

"No don't!" my mind blasted the words into hers. Something was incredibly wrong; I could feel it. On the other side of his huge bedroom door was no one I knew. I had never felt such strong, smothering energy. I spun back toward the bed. "Drake," I called. He sat up instantly. His eyes found mine, it took him less than a second to read my face. Briefly his gaze flicked to a spot behind my head. "Don't move, baby," he said, in a voice too quiet and calm. Behind me the floorboards creaked again. I clenched my hands 'till I felt my nails bore little half-moons into my palms. "Just look at me," he said. "Don't look away."

My chin lifted slightly in assent; I did not think I could have moved if I wanted to. Fear was ice in the air, and it froze all my muscles. I counted down the next five, endless seconds, then, three things happened in the space of one. Drake's hand blurred beneath his pillow, I saw a flash of silver, and a knife was flying directly toward my face. The need to duck, to throw myself to the floor and cover my head was strong. Yet he had told me not to move, so I grit my teeth and watched it hurtle toward my right eye. I shook as it flew past my temple cleanly slicing a long curl from its perch above my ear. I heard a squishy thud when the knife connected with its intended target, just inches behind my head. I spun around. A tall creature in a black overcoat swayed in front of me, the knife buried deep in his left eye. I stood in stunned silence and watched him fall. Before I could speak or scream, Drake was beside me, grabbing my hand, pulling me from the room, and down the hall.

"I'm going to kill them all!" I heard him mutter. "Each last bloody one of them...*Alexie!*" he shouted.

"I'm here!" said Alexie, running up a flight of stairs I had not known existed. He had a silver gun in his right hand, in his left, Legux glowed like a fallen star. Alexie tossed the huge sword in the air, Drake's left hand flashed out and he caught the hilt. Alexie handed me the gun.

"Silver bullets," he said. "Aim for the heart."

I took it while we rounded a corner, Alexie drew a dagger from his boot. We made a sharp left, and nearly crashed into a flustered Lily and Hanna.

"Did you wake Andi?" I asked.

"Yes," said Lily. "She told me to go back to sleep, said Drake would take care of it."

"I believe that's true," said Hanna. I almost growled at her. Instead, I tested the weight of the gun in my hand and flicked the safety off.

"You alright?" asked Lily, turning to give me a searching look.

"I'm great, for once, no one is trying to kill me."

"Alexie," hollered Drake, peering over the banister and casting his gold eyes to the shadows. "Take them to the dungeons."

"You sure we won't need the goddess of war, and this fire-starter over here?" asked Alexie motioning to Lily. "Who knows what Cara can do," he finished.

"Not Cara," I said. "That's for sure. What the hell is going on, Drake?!"

"He's in the middle of a war," said Alexie, the very soul casual.

"Oh Drake," sighed Lily, "did you start it?"

Drake turned and pointed his sword at Hanna. The blue glow sapped the light, his face was a network of writhing shadows. "No," he rasped. "She did."

A panel of glass shattered overhead, it rained colorful shards on all of us. I threw my body against Lily's, and dragged us both to the floor, trying to use my hands to shield her from the worst of it. I looked through my fingers to see Hanna, her hands raised toward the painful rain. She breathed once, and it all turned to dust. When it cleared the room was full of a thousand screaming bats. Thick, black smoke trailed from their flapping wings, and pumped a bitter odor through the air.

"Don't breathe the smoke," shouted Drake. My eyes followed the sound of his voice, the black fog rendered him invisible, all I could see was the glowing sword. Holding Lily's hand, I crawled in the direction of the light. I held my breath for long as I was able, then wheezed in a choking rasp of charred air. The black smoke rushed down my lungs. It was like inhaling hot ash, I coughed wildly, and my eyes started to stream. I heard Lily's gasping cough and felt her body tremble. Then, Drake's hands were hot on my arms, and he was dragging us from the room. I heard another glass pane shatter, and we were falling. It took me a second to realize he had jumped out of a window, holding Lily and I in his arms. He set us gently on the frozen grass, stroked my hair, touched my chin, and tilted my face to his. "Stay here," he commanded. "Breathe and shoot anyone you don't recognize on sight."

I had no time to say anything. He drew back and leapt into the air. Rising quickly, back to the window more than eighty feet above our heads, from where we had just fallen.

Lily looked longingly at the window. "You want to go back up there, don't you?" I accused.

"I want to see them," she breathed.

"Me too," I whispered.

Lily stood, still gasping, then turned quickly, and walked in the direction of the courtyard. A few bats trailed from the open window and flitted around my head. I pointed the gun at one who got too close. When I had the skittish bat in my sights, the black smoke streaming from its wings ballooned for a second, then swirled like a water cyclone, filling the space between Lily and me. When the spinning stopped, a tall man stepped from the warping cloud.

"Good evening, princess," he said, and bowed.

I looked over my shoulder, there was only darkness. "Who are you talking to?" I asked warily.

"Are you not a blood niece to the goddess Minerva?" he asked, raising a needle thin brow.

I lifted the gun. Crap that woman had a lot of names. "Yes, I am *Hanna's* niece. I don't know if that makes me a princess."

The man laughed and raised a slender white hand. "Semantics, it is lovely to meet you, regardless of your exact bloodline," he said. His eyes were close together and laughing, his nose overly large, his mouth small. His black over coat and strange top hat of the same shade, dwarfed him.

"Shoot him!" Lily's terrified voice jolted through my mind, as it did, I watched the vampire smile.

"Telepathy," he mused. "How fascinating. Don't shoot me yet dear. I might be of some help. We have not come to kill tonight," he paused and looked up at the window we had jumped from moments ago. "Though I am sure a few of us are already dead." A crash punctuated his words, and he shivered.

"What do you want," I asked, and heard Lily's flames ignite.

"Only to speak to your prince," he said.

I lowered the gun, feeling honesty in his powerful aura, seeing it in his eyes. "If this is a trick, I'll shoot you myself," I said.

He lowered his eyes. A slight smile playing on his lips. "I will offer no resistance if that be the case. I come armed only with a proposition of peace."

"And your teeth," said Lily, coming to stand beside me. Her hands engulfed in gloves of leaping flame. For the first time the vampire's expression registered a slight alarm. "A fire witch," he whispered in awe. "Daughter of Artemis." His lips parted. "Tell him quickly princess," he said, his eyes roving back to me. "Not all of us are in agreement on this truce I propose," he finished, then he bowed and vanished in another rush of thrashing smoke. Lily's hands instantly cooled.

I looked at her, brushing wild skeins of hair out of my eyes. "So, you can pretty much just turn that off and on whenever you want, then?"

"Yep," she pointed a smoking finger at her small nose. "Fire goddess am I," she said in a perfect imitation of Yoda's iconic voice. I laughed all the way until the castle doors closed behind us. Inside the grand entrance, chaos ruled supreme. Alexie and Drake stood back-to-back in the center of the throng. Vampires outnumbered them fifty to one. They fell fast as they charged. I watched Drake cut down two in a single stroke. Blood sprayed the walls like graffiti gone wrong. Another breath, another two dead. At the battle's edge I saw Hanna, teeth bared, a knife in each hand. Movement caught the corner of my eye and I swung toward it. A dark vampire—wild red hair spilling like a bloody fountain from the top of his otherwise shaved head— rushed at me. I did not plan my attack so much as fell into it. His claws speared at my throat. My arms flared out and my bare fingers touched his cold, dead hand. I gave the pain of touch no time to take hold. I made a low, grinding sound and shoved the pain back into him, every ounce of my strength set to the task. The vampire's scream was instant and terrifying, and he fell—like my hands were tasers—senseless at my feet.

"Burn them, Lily," I panted.

"But you just told Dracula out there that…"

I cut her off. "I know what I said. We can talk about peace later; they're trying to kill him! Burn them! I would do it in a heartbeat if I could."

"All of them?" she squealed. I saw a dark-haired girl take a slash at Drake's face with her clawed nails.

"All of them," I repeated.

"Jesus," said Lily, and lifted her hands. Fire exploded up her arms.

"He's not here," I said, looking at the host of fangs and slashing knives.

"So much history," sighed Lily.

Watching Drake perform his perfectly choreographed dance of death, we stepped toward the throng. Drake struck a man's head from his shoulders. It flew over the bloody eyes of his attackers, and thumped at my feet, landing squarely on the broken nose. Slowly the head rolled, I jumped out of its path too late, the hair brushed my feet. I looked down in horror at the gushing neck. The pale, marble face still as a statue. Then, the eyes flew open, the lips parted, and the severed head screamed.

Shock stopped my heart, and a wild blast of fear shattered rational thought. I opened my mouth and screamed back. The sound that came from my throat was long and keening. I had never made such a sound in my life, not even in the throes of the very worst sort of pain. My hand flew to my chest, but the screaming did not stop. It rose high enough to shatter glass, ever increasing in volume and intensity. Beside me I saw Lily drop to her knees, hands pressed against her ears, teeth clenched in pain. I clapped my hands over my mouth, it did nothing to stop the sound. It rose, and rose until each Vampire was on their knees, crying out, tearing at their ears and hair. At my feet, the vampire's eyes rolled back in his swelling sockets, his face bulged until it seemed his very veins rode the surface of his skin. My scream reached a deafening crescendo and the head blew apart in a red explosion of bone, soggy tissue, and soft grey brain. Blood sloshed over every inch of my face; I was too dizzy to care. I turned, reached for Lily, and fainted dead away.

■ ■ ■

Pages I found in Lily's things...the day I tried to put the pieces together...

I lifted Cara's head off the bloody ground. My own head still rang like I had just survived the second coming of Christ, replete with angels, and freaking trumpets.

"What in the name of every holy thing was that?" asked Alexie. His voice dazed.

"A siren scream," said Drake. I thought he sounded proud. He knelt beside me and held out his arms. The coat of blood he wore highlighted the savage in him. I scooted back, and he pulled Cara against his chest, cradled her cheek with such exquisite tenderness, it made my throat tighten and my eyes tear. "She's okay," he whispered, and kissed her nose. "You're alright, baby, wake up now," he rocked her, crooning more nothings into her wild hair—if her ears felt anything like mine, she did not hear a thing.

Cara's eyes fluttered open and her lips parted. I clapped my hand over her mouth.

"Don't even think about it," I warned. She shook her head; above my hand her emerald eyes were wide and hazy. "The headache from that scream will linger for the rest of my life," I told her.

Cara raised a shaking hand to her head. I dropped my hand. She licked her dry lips. "Me too, that was the worst sound I've ever heard, I can't believe it came out of me." Her eyes moved to Drake, she reached up to wipe a streak of blood off his cheek, and only succeeded in smearing it across his jaw. "Where are the vampires?" she asked him.

He smiled down at her, his eyes glowing. "You scared them all away."

Cara looked confused by his stunning smile; her hand came up to touch her throat. "I hope I never do that again," she said sincerely.

"It was glorious," breathed Drake, looking starstruck. "Who knew I loved a siren."

"I'm not a siren," she whispered. Her eyes closed and she shook her head, reaching for my hand. "Are you okay?" she croaked.

"Of course," I told her, patting her hand.

"I couldn't stop...it just," her voice dropped to a whisper. "It just kept going and going."

"It was beautiful," Drake told her, and I heard Alexie groan.

"That was the most un-beautiful thing I've ever heard," he said piously. "No offense Cara, but you will feature in my nightmares tonight. My life flashed before my eyes," Alexie sighed in dramatic longing. "It was an exquisite tale."

I stood up and held my finger to my temples as they both throbbed.

"Sorry, Lily," whispered Cara. I stuck a pinkie in my ear and twisted it. "Drake's right, in a terribly painful way it was beautiful."

Cara scowled. "It obviously messed with your head," she said, surprisingly tart for her pallor.

"Sleep if you can," Drake told me, barely tearing his gaze from my sister's face. "They won't come back tonight. Too many of their own have died. Alexie, see to the bodies, please?"

"Why not?" asked Alexie. "Sleep is for the living, I for one prefer to spend the remainder of my night bathing in the blood of the fallen."

"Leave them then," said Drake. He stood, lifting Cara, crushing her closer to his chest. She did not seem to mind the blood at all, just linked her fingers together behind his head, and pressed her cheek to his neck. "If they're still here in the morning," he growled. "I'll deal with it. Let the dead bury their dead tonight." He left us then, and carried my sister up the spiral staircase, I listened to his footsteps recede.

I inhaled, filling my lungs until it hurt, then exhaled in a gush, slowly my eyes searched the dark room for Hanna's slight figure. I found her across the blood sea of broken bodies. She stomped a small, booted foot and shook muck from the hem of her dress.

"You can make glass turn to dust," I said. "But you can't shake guts from your clothes?"

"I don't use my power for little things," she told me. "It takes from me every time. I have taken far more than my share, each time I call my magic, I further upset the balance."

"From my perspective," I said, thinking of tonight, and the world at large. "The balance is pretty fucked as is."

Hanna laughed. "Yes, I suppose it is."

"When I use my fire, do I take from magic?" I asked.

Hanna shook her long, dark hair, the streaks of red hiding in it glittered like strings of polished rubies. "No, the power is elemental, that fire is yours alone."

"Why are you really here, Hanna?" I blurted. Too tired to be diplomatic. "I've called you lots of times over the years, you never came. Why today?"

"Because you needed me," she said simply. "Regardless of what you girls think, I genuinely love you. If Cara is to die again—and trust me I will do everything in my power to prevent that outcome—yet, if it does happen, then I want to be here for you. You will need me."

"I've always needed you Hanna," my voice rose. I could hear other sounds in the house, mutterings on the wind. I tuned them out. "We've always needed you. Aunt Jane, seriously the world's worst custodian."

"Hecate?" asked Hanna. "No, she would have protected you from any real harm."

"Oh, my gods, Hanna. Hecate? Seriously? Did you ever stop to think that *she* might have been the harm?"

"I did what I thought was best," said Hanna. She looked on the verge of tears. "It's all anyone can ever do. It's true in the beginning this was all about revenge. I was young, powerful, rich, and stupid. Ares and Aphrodite hurt my soul, I wanted to wound them in return. That need died years ago, the day you and your sister came into this world, since that day I have tried to undo my actions. I never really left. I always watched you," her lips trembled. "I've always been so proud of you."

We picked our way across the bodies, met somewhere in the middle, and she folded her arms around me, my head rested against her small shoulder. "Where do I come from?" I asked, not lifting my head. "Who is my father, who am I?"

"Who you are is up to you," she said, stroking my hair and kissing the top of my head. "You father is an elemental, a true power of the old world. He fell in love with your mother the summer before you were born. She wanted nothing from him, he scared her. She came to me for help, I was living deep in the rainforest at the time, a hidden witch surviving on haunted lands, I can't imagine what it took her to find me. Your father, however, was not finished with her. He borrowed power from the only god with any left to spare and transformed himself into a human. He seduced my sister in two days, she was carrying his child in the week." Hanna sighed. "His children," she kissed the top of my head. "You and Cara, my beautiful girls."

I stepped away and took her hand. Together we made our way up the stairs. "I didn't love you girls when your mother was pregnant. If anything, I hated you," she sadly confessed. "I didn't care if Aphrodite came back and killed Cara, I didn't care if it saved her. I needed a body to carry a soul, and I chose her." Hanna paused on the top step, she wiped her hand over her face, her shoulders slumped. "I didn't love anything, not once. Not till you were born. You were screaming in my hands, Cara was unborn. Your little hand was reaching toward Artemis's heaving womb, but I knew you didn't want your mother. You were reaching for your sister." Hanna did not move her eyes from my face. "You were perfect, Lily. I loved you immediately, like a golden cord linked through my heart and yours, it was the strongest magic I had ever felt, and I bowed to it. Everything changed from that day. Three thousand years of planning destroyed in a single second of glowing love."

I had no response for her, to any of that, so I kissed her cheek, and we left that stunning pronouncement in hovering in the air between us. I walked quietly to my room. Andi sat on my bed in a white nightgown, her long legs folded to her chest, her chin resting on her knees.

"Hey," I said softly. Stepping inside and closing the door. "You missed all the action," I told her.

Andi raised her eyes heavenward. "And, for these small things, we truly give thanks," she vowed, and gave me a weary smile. "Can I stay in here tonight?" she asked, sounding timid.

"Of course," I said. "You'll have to forgive me if I get up and jump around on one foot occasionally, I'm still trying to get Cara's scream out of my ears."

"Yes, I heard that. Siren, it's a rare, beautiful sound."

"I don't think we're talking about the same thing," I said, crawling beneath the chilly blankets, cradling the pillow under my cheek."

"We don't hear the same sound," explained Andi. "It must have been quite terrible for you."

"Yes, it was, what does it sound like to you?" I wanted to know.

"It's the most beautiful music in the world. Enormously powerful sound, incredibly old. Many men lost their lives to that song. It has a strange effect on vampires, and werewolves—humans hate it."

"But I'm not really human, am I?"

"You are in all the ways that matter," she said. "You can feel, you can love."

"Can you feel?" I asked her, sad at the pain in her eyes.

Andi nodded, not lifting her head from her drawn up knees. "Once, a long time ago."

"Now?" I wondered.

"I want to," she said intently. "I feel with you." She closed her silver eyes. "It's been three millennia since I've had a real friend." Andi sighed suddenly and unlocked her white-knuckled hands from around her slim calves. Slowly, almost hesitant, she scooted under the covers.

"Do vampires often attack this castle?" I asked while she thumped around and got settled.

"Yes," she yawned, her eyes widening slightly. "Why? You don't want to leave do you?"

"No," I said immediately. "No, I don't want to leave at all." My eyelids fluttered closed. I struggled them open, her presence was soothing, and I was an avid participant in the duel between consciousness and sleep. "Did you ever publish Blood and Shadows?" I murmured.

"Yes," I heard the smile in her voice. "I'm a bestseller in twenty countries, Greek tragedies are all the rage, you know?"

"Are they?" I asked, my tone drifting.

"Yes," she snuggled against my chest, and threw her arms around my waist. "No one really wants a happy ending; they just think they do."

"Nonsense," I said. "I want one. I demand one."

"Yes," she agreed. "You could never be no one, Lily."

I fell asleep to the sound of the clock ticking over the hearth. That was the first night I dreamed of fire. I dreamed flames covered my whole body, burning my clothes to ash. I was naked in an empty field. Golden wheat swished under my feet; it did not burn. I spread my arms and saw that I had wings.

Andi rose from the golden stalks, like a mummy springing from its coffin. Her face was deathly white, her hair a halo of silver spikes. She lifted a slender hand, her eyes glazed and sightless. "Give him to me," she said. Her voice was old, and scratchy. I saw dirt in her hair, piles of it sat on her naked shoulders, making her look like someone who had just clawed their way from the ground, after being buried alive. She appeared younger, somehow, barely more than a child. She was perfect, sitting still as stone, a slightly messed up porcelain doll.

My feet glided through the wheat; flames dripped from my hands. Andi's eyes flickered, slowly she turned her head, and looked at me, seeing nothing. "Give him back to me," she said. The wooden movement of her lips shook her tense jaw. "I love him," she said. "I'll do anything, give him back to me." Her eyeballs rolled, and she started to cry.

"I'm dreaming," I said.

"No!" she screamed. "It's a fire dream."

I looked down at myself, glowing like the sun. "A fire dream," I whispered. When next I looked, my hands were black, burnt to a crisp, white blisters in place of all my nails. Skin flaked away as charred pieces flew around me. Hot embers landed on Andi, she ignited in an explosion of blistering heat. I smelled ash and cooked flesh. I watched my bones catch fire, then go the way of my skin. I watched each piece of me burn, until there was nothing left but fire and freedom.

CHAPTER XVIII

TODAY WE BATTLE GODS... TOMORROW? MONSTERS. DAY SIX OF THIRTEEN

Corvin Castle was busy and familiar. Four days ago, my scream exploded a severed head, today the sun was shining, and death was extremely far away. Drake had kept his word, he did it my way, and we all hit the books with Lily. We knew what we looked for this time—the core of light, and anything that referred to it. Drake loved books almost as much as I did. He was a crazy collector, and the proud owner of unimaginable things. Last night, in front of the fire roaring in the master bedroom, he read to me from Guinevere's diary. He made me laugh at the little things, and teased Lily mercilessly, until she punched him.

For days now, I saw no darkness in his eyes. I kept my memories in the back of my mind where they belonged—determined to focus on the now—and the days flowed away. Drake stayed at my side, always. We rode horses at sunset, argued philosophy, and shared stories. We swam in the hot springs and fell asleep under the oak tree. Every night, he carried me to his bed and replaced every second of touch I had ever missed. I found myself not caring what happened when my deadly countdown concluded, it was enough to be with him, and Lily, even Hanna—safe under one roof, currently alive.

Two things of importance happened on that sixth day and looking back now I see that they were forerunners to the greatest horror of all. Looking back is too painful, I can never let myself imagine the *what if*.

I woke that morning—to the sound of singing birds, my body wrapped in Drake's iron arms. I jumped up to brush my teeth, forever terrified of morning breath, but he caught me around the waist and tackled me back to the sheets. He did not let me up 'till past noon, and only because I insisted. Lily and Hanna had decided today was the day to take out a frozen god's heart. Drake forbade me to participate in their witchery, but of course I would—I had to help, no matter how badly I never wanted to see either Aphrodite, or Ares again. Drake stared at me while I showered, and I threw water in his face, hugging the shower curtain to my body. His brow rose at my actions, though he said nothing. Later, in the rose stuffed conservatory, we ate corn flakes and chocolate chip muffins—Drake's breakfast of choice. Lily gave me an adorable mean-girl look when we finally made it to the library. Sunlight poured through the high cathedral ceiling, slipping silently through the glass panels, highlighting the motes of dust scattered across endless tiers of books. In the center of the circular room, five tables formed a pentagram. A cauldron bubbled over an open fire, and the Book of Shadows lay in a chair by the crispy hearth.

Lily walked to me and kissed my cheek. "I thought you were going to obey him and stay away."

I looked at Drake. "Never," I teased.

Drake looked unamused. "I still hate this idea."

"You don't have to come," said Lily, her prim voice firm.

"Very funny," he said.

"I thought so," Lily wiped the back of her hand over her perspiring brow. "You haven't even heard our plan yet."

"Do I want to?" he asked.

Lily tossed him a dainty shrug. "I don't know, let's see. Hanna will hold their snow globes around them while I use my fire to make a small hole in the ice, just above the heart. We have spent the last four days concocting a spell that will draw the light from the heart. It should do so without damage to the organ."

"Have you ever tried something like this, Hanna?" I asked, still hardly able to meet her eyes.

"No, I've not been able to penetrate the shell, yet it was built to trap my blood so…" she shrugged. "I tried once, a long time ago. The light should have been mine—Zeus only gave it to Ares because he was a man. I was the better choice; Ares was a killer—I only want to protect life."

"Besides," said Lily. "I'm the one wielding goddess fire, regular fire is useless, we already tried. Watch this," she said, and pointed her finger at the fireplace. A thin, spear of flame shot from her forefinger, it smashed into a fire swathed log, which blew apart, making a fantastic bang.

"Holy Crap!" I crowed.

Lily's eyes twinkled. "Pretty cool, huh? Sure, it's no mind shattering scream, but…"

"Lily! You can shoot fire from your finger. You're an actual superhero."

Lily twirled and bowed. "I know right, maybe Shield will come and spirit me away."

"Oh Lily," I exhaled. "I love you for knowing that."

Her brow arched. "What? Samuel L. Jackson? He rules." She walked over to lift the cauldron off its metal hinge, and set it on the ground, the handle clanged and bounced. "Come let's away to the dungeons," she said. "And count us lucky that we get to say sentences like that."

"Our definition of luck is different," said Drake.

"You and me both," I agreed.

Lily turned to Hanna. "Shall we?"

"Come what may," whispered Hanna.

"Come what may," repeated my sister, and I thought I caught a small, calculated flash briefly spark her glittering eyes.

Lily made me carry the book of shadows, and I walked down the slimy stairs to the dungeon, holding it at arm's length. Drake stayed in front, always touching some part of me, a reassurance of my mortality, I think. Lily went on about baking soda, wondering if they had added enough to the potion.

Baking soda? I thought but did not ask. Were they trying to pull the light from his heart like poison from a wound?

"Just a quick question," I wondered aloud. "What do you plan to do with the light after you capture it?"

"That's where Drake comes in," said Lily.

"I do?" growled Drake.

"Yes, though we just need to borrow Legux. Hanna thinks if we stab the core of light, the essence of Legux itself will preserve the overall structural integrity, and hopefully keep your family alive." Lily's voice dropped as some of the humor in the tone seeped away. "My family too," she finished.

Drake touched his back, his fingers rested against the hilt pressed to his neck, I knew the glowing blade ran down his spine. I could almost see the shimmer, leaking blue light onto his bronze skin. "I have it," he said.

"Figures," said Lily. "I've not seen you without it since the night of the vampire attack, even though I know Cara told you about the proposed truce."

"They have offered such things before," said Drake shrugging. "It is still the hazing method of all new covens. Who can kill the prince of death? It's a grand game," he smiled. "Sometimes, Alexie participates."

"He does not," I gasped.

"Sadly, he really does," Drake told me. He stopped in front of the gate—the one I had phased through only days ago—then, reached under the cotton collar of his black t-shirt. He lifted a silver chain holding a single key.

"I've never seen that before," I said. "I would have remembered."

"It's enchanted," he explained. "It only becomes visible when I'm close to this gate. You, love, are the only one who—besides me—made it through these bars in two thousand years."

"Amazing," breathed Lily. "Sounds like one of your spells… Hanna?"

"Yes," whispered the culprit. "Drake asked me for my help, I could not refuse."

"Redemption?" I asked cynically.

"Fear," said Hanna.

"Of the sleeping gods? Or yourself?" I concluded, unable to resist. Hanna said nothing, only gave me a look chock full of displeasure. I took one more step, and the watery passage opened once again into the bright, marble room. The long, halogen bulbs on the ceiling seemed to point toward the two sarcophagi—our dastardly goal. Lily came to stand beside me; I felt her fingers link through my own. I squeezed reassuringly, though I felt no such calm. Hanna set the still steaming cauldron near the left sarcophagi, then moved her hand and mind, the way I moved mine, just a few days ago. The limestone lid inched away from the base. Hanna pointed her fingers, and I saw a muscle in her wrist flinch, the lid slowly shifted aside. When the full body of Ares was uncovered, Hanna flipped her hands, so her palms faced the cold blue lights. Inch by nearly imperceptible inch, her hands began to rise—so did the body of the sleeping god.

The look of his spherical, icy cage seemed imagined by science fiction. White light shot through the room, momentarily blinding us all. When my eyes adjusted, Lily let go of my hand and moved to stand beside Hanna.

"If this works…" started Hanna.

"Don't jinx it," hissed Lily.

Drake moved to stand slightly in front of me, blocking me from the hovering god. I looked past his shoulder, I could not stop watching the way Hanna moved, and flexed her hands. I had shoved at the limestone, pushed, and forced, where she coerced, enchanted. The hovering body of Ares swayed as she moved her wrists, her fingers twirling gracefully.

"Hanna?" I asked, calling her name when I did not mean to.

Her bright eyes swayed to me. "Yes, Cara?"

I took a bracing breath. "Can you teach me how to do that?" I pointed to her hands.

"Of course, though it will never work if you refuse to speak to me."

"I have not refused. I've spoken to you, I called, why didn't you answer?"

"I did what I could," sighed Hanna. "I could not further interfere."

Most of me wanted to argue my points, but a small part of me was still the child who had never dared talk back or disobey—so I kept my mouth closed.

"Come," commanded Hanna, returning her attention to the hovering Ares. "Stand beside me. Now, I want you to feel the air, then touch it and understand it. Air is like water— tangible, fluid. Close your eyes and feel it, see it in your mind."

I walked to her almost furtively, lifted my hands, focused on her instruction. Drake stood close, his body radiating waves of heat against my back. I heard his unsteady breaths in my ear, I heard Legux leave its sheath.

"Do you feel it?" asked Hanna.

I moved my fingers. Did I? "What am I trying to feel?"

"The air," said Hanna. "It feels like dry water."

"Like silly putty," I said, and could not help my slight smile. "Yes, I feel it!"

"Good, now make it move. Think about folding a sheet or holding a piece of paper in the air. Keep your fingers strong yet let them be fluid."

I gasped in a breath, my teeth chattered, my mouth felt shot full of Novocain, and something prickly buzzed in my ears, but I was doing it. I was feeling the air, shaping it. Once I felt it, the rest just fell into place. I understood its molecular density without knowing why. It shifted, moved, and I held it steady. Held Ares's body using just my slender fingers, and electrified mind. A few moments later, I realized Hanna had long dropped her hands, she was across the room, leaning over the cooling cauldron, and speaking to Lily, who was smiling—if looking slightly bewildered. Ares was still hanging in the air, body stiff in an exorcist fashion—I was holding him up, easily.

"Lie him on the floor," said Hanna, not looking up from her task. "Lily needs room to work."

I moved my hands and his body swung, lightly—like touching a floating feather, then pushing it to the ground. He landed on the marble floor with a soft thud.

I felt Hanna's eyes fly to my face. "That was surprisingly gentle, considering what he did to you."

My gaze remained on Ares's frozen face, seeing the sadness and shock, the tears forever preserved in the eternal ice. "You mean what you made him do," I said. "He never wanted to hurt me, he loved Drake like a brother. You did this. You did this because he didn't take your side in a freaking argument."

"It was more than that!" said Hanna, her voice rising.

"A burnt library?"

"The history of our worlds!" she cried.

"Can we pick *this* argument up later?" asked Lily, her voice distressed. She cast Ares a disparaging look. "Villain or best guy in the world, Ares scares me. I want to get this done, also my hands are burning, and if the two of you stress me out—I won't be responsible for where the flames go," she said.

"Fine," said Hanna.

"Fine," I said. To regain my cool, I breathed through my nose and stared into Lily's flames. They were a strange color— seen under the electric blue light—dark shades of orange, bleeding into red and gold.

"Now," said Lily, catching my gaze, I knew she saw reflections of her own fire dancing in my eyes. Her arms were covered to the elbow, and the shadows it cast against her face were dark and moving. "I have an idea," she shook her head. "But the two of you have to put this aside. Challenge each other to a duel in the courtyard tonight, or stay silent for another ten years, I don't care—just don't do it now. Hanna you hold him steady. Cara you extract the light. Drake, when she tells you, stab it! Hopefully, the magic of Legux will trap it, Ares and Aphrodite can die, and we can all go back to living happily ever after."

"Why not just kill Aphrodite?" I asked in a thick voice, my words made me sick. Kill a goddess? My goddess. Never. That I would dare to think such a thing, even to save my own life. It just seemed wrong.

"To live a life without her?" said Drake, almost briskly, and shook his head. "I would never do that to Ares, no matter what he has done. It is both or nothing, neither will survive the loss of the other."

"That's not true!" screamed Andi.

Stunned, I spun around. Her silver hair slapped my face as she brushed past me, like I was made of the same air I manipulated. She fell to her knees beside Ares, her horrified grimace cracked, she put her hand to the clear, cold shell protecting his body, then she bowed her head, her eyes fixed on the man she loved, and started to cry. "That's not true at all," she managed in a choked voice. "He loved me, he would forget about her, if she were gone. He would forget! Just kill her! Please, leave him to me! Let me love him!"

"You're wrong Androsia," said Drake using the name of the woman she currently resembled. The one who had screamed on the mountain, the one who would have killed her brother to save the man she loved. "I know him, I know how he feels about her, I would not put you through the pain of figuring it out for yourself, once he woke to realize she was gone. Ares would bring the thunder. He is the most powerful creature I've ever battled. I would not be able to stop his fury. He would decimate everything in his path."

"If you kill him, for real Draken," said Andi, swiping at her silver tears. "I will do everything in my power to kill you. Any of you! All of you!"

Drake closed his eyes, when he opened them, the look he had for his sister consisted only of love. "You will do what you have to do."

"Right now, we are not killing anyone," I told her. "I don't want to kill. Hell, I have a hard time killing mosquitoes, I much prefer to let them bite me. I don't think I could kill either of them, not even to save my own life. I thought I could, but not looking at him like this, not now. I actually feel sorry for them."

"No killing," said Lily. "Just the core."

"This is what you wanted all along, isn't it?" I asked Hanna.

"Not like this," she said. "Ares once mattered to me; he is my brother after all."

"Half-brother," I said, quoting her words.

"Don't hurt him," whispered Andi. Pressing her lips to hairline cracks in the glassy ice.

"No," I said. "I won't. I promise.

Andi sighed, then nodded, she kept her hands braced on either side of his face. I felt another dose of pity, I knew loneliness was a miserable grey, I knew being trapped in it was like drowning in thick mud.

I heard air shatter as Lily inhaled. She pointed her forefingers at Ares's heart, and streamers of fire shot from them. They gushed from her like weaponized flame shooters. Grinding her teeth, she held the flames steady. Triangular shapes formed in the fire, until the end of each stream was tipped by a burning arrowhead. Beneath the pinpoint pressure of the scalding arrow, the ice sheltering Ares's heart began to melt. I had a vivid memory of the consistency as it dripped down his frozen arms. Like Jell-O on the loose, lost in that terrible cartoon dream. I saw his golden armor, and the puncture spot Legux had made near his heart. Fissures in the gold spidered out like cracks in a winter lake.

A fine mist of sweat broke out on Lily's brow, her slender shoulders shook like sheer will power alone staved off a threatening seizure. "I can't hold this much longer," she gasped.

"Has the gold covering his heart melted away?" asked Hanna. "I can't see, there's too much smoke."

Lily breathed deep. "Almost, just a moment longer." She closed her eyes and pressed her lips together. "Now. The spell Hanna, now!"

Hanna hoisted the cauldron up to her small shoulder, then slowly poured it into the smoldering golden cavity made by Lily's flames. The writhing liquid hissed. Ares began to shake. Andi made a small, tormented sound, and turned her face away from the foul green cloud of noxious fumes that spilled everywhere when the acid spell did its work. As the fumes cleared, a white light began to rise, sizzling up from Ares's chest.

"Get it Cara," said Lily, speaking through her grinding teeth, I saw a single drop of moisture clinging to her lash, she blinked it away. "Get the light! There, it's lifting… hold it steady. I can't keep these flames going much longer. I'm so thirsty."

"I've got it," I said. I did. I could feel it. The spell pulled it out of Ares's heart, but the nature of the light battled to return. I fought with it, and it struggled back, like a piece of chewed bubblegum fighting to stick to the bottom of your shoe no matter how hard you tried to pull it off. It seemed to be alive, and writhing, slimy as a worm.

"Cara," gasped Lily. I turned my head in time to see her flames die, while her body went limp, then she fell into a graceful faint. Drake caught her beneath the arms, and she sagged heavily.

"She's just fainted. We need water," he said.

I snapped my eyes back to the light, slowly rising from the smoking mess which once was Ares's golden armor. "A canteen, in my purse, by the stairs," I grunted, jerking slightly as the light spasmed. Bubbling green liquid—the cauldrons previous contents—sloshed Andi's hands and ran over the glass still covering Ares's face.

The light rose by steady degrees. From the corner of my eye, I saw Hanna's smile, it was radiant. She looked at the light the way Alexie had looked at Lily's neck. Something in her look scared me, yet I felt we had come too far to retreat. I had the light completely in my control now, I knew I could throw it at the ceiling, toss it into Hanna, or take a deep breath and suck it up my nose. I turned, moving the light—inch by painful inch—away from the frozen god. Drake came back to my side, Legux in hand.

"Do it," I said, squinting at him through the moving blue lights. "Stab it. Trap it." I held my arms out to him. The twisting light sparked between my fingers. I could see him hesitate even as he raised the sword above his head. Then, he brought the blade down in one smooth stabbing motion. Before the tip of Legux touched the edges of the light I knew something was wrong. The light seemed to harden, as if it sensed the coming danger, I felt it draw a shield around itself.

"Drake! Wait!" I shrieked, but it was already too late. The sword smashed into the light, and the shield detonated. An invisible force punched me in the stomach and spun me through the air. Drake flew in the other direction. We hit the marble ground seconds later, our bodies thudding and cracking against the stone.

"Crap," I gasped, and managed to lumber to my feet. I had—by some miracle—maintained my hold on the light, it thrashed and scratched my skin, hissing while it mimicked an enraged alley cat.

In front of me I saw Drake stand, his hands were reaching for me, his lips were moving wildly, but I could hear nothing save the cacophony of buzzing silence pounding in my ears. He came to me then, touched my arm and the light writhed.

"What?" I screeched, my voice made of cotton and sand.

"I said, you're bleeding," his words were somewhat audible, though he still sounded like he was screaming under water. His fingers touched my forehead.

"I don't feel it. It doesn't matter. That didn't work," I said, trying to ignore the slash of agony in my right side.

"I think you broke something," he said, touching the painful spot. He sounded gutted. "I told you not to do this."

"A broken rib is not a knife in the heart," I said reasonably. I looked back to Ares, Hanna lay on the ground beside him, only now shaking the unconsciousness from her eyes. "What happened?" she asked, touching her head, her hair had fallen free of its bun, and spilled over her shoulders—she looked young and small. Beside her, Andi crouched over Ares's body.

"You have to place the light inside of me, I will carry it," said Hanna, and I saw a spark of triumph in her eyes. This was her plan all along, I knew it, surely as I knew my names. My eyes flew to Drake, a question in them. Hard lines bracketed the corners of his mouth, and I suspected he was considering our options.

"Just hold the slight steady, and walk slowly over here," Hanna told me. A low command in her voice, one I recognized and bowed to. My feet obeyed before my mind acquiesced.

"You're doing beautifully, Cara," said Hanna.

"I don't want to do this," I said, and heard my voice shake. "Drake," I swung toward him. "Take it from me. I don't want it, take it away. Here, you take it," I told Hanna. "Crack open your own chest and stick it inside, I don't want to."

"No," said Hanna. "The light must be given; it cannot be taken. You must put it in my heart."

"And then what?" I gasped. "I make the goddess of war the most powerful being in the universe?" My pounding heart sounded loud as a battle drum. "We need to leave, now. This is so wrong."

"Give it back to Ares," I heard Drake say. "We tried; it didn't work. Let me take you out of here."

"Yes," crooned Andi, still using her arms to shelter her god. "Please just give it back to him."

"No!" Hanna almost screamed. "No, not... not like this," she finished.

That, I knew, had not been what she meant to say. What she meant to say was... 'not when I am so close'. Fear constricted my throat; she saw it and her top lip curled in a snarl.

"You have to do it, Cara! Do it now!" Hanna's eyes went wide, I saw fire leaping in her green irises. "The light is mine," she said.

"Don't listen to her," Drake's voice was a low growl near my right ear. "Let go of the light, baby. Just drop it." His big hands slid against the backs of mine; his fingers brushed my tense wrists. "You don't have to do anything you don't want to do," he whispered. "Not while I'm here."

My hands were shaking so bad I thought the choice of dropping the glowing ball would simply be made for me by my irrepressible nerves.

Hanna took a stumbling step in my direction. "Give it to me!" she hollered.

"I…I…" My eyes rolled in their sockets and burned, and my hands shook so badly it jerked my elbows. "I don't think I can."

"Do it Cara!" wailed Hanna. I saw a thin vein bust in her left eye, the white filled with blood.

The compelling command in her voice was such that I almost gave in, would have—if the light had not been snatched from my hands.

"Don't move!" Lily's sharp voice in my mind further froze my limbs. I blinked my eyes, and she was in front of me, her scowl for Hanna, her hair, and hands aflame, the ball of light which she took from me, was delicately resting on the tips of her painted nails. I could see their edges beginning to melt, scalding nail polish dripped down her fingers.

I heard Hanna make a deep noise, a jumbled combination of fear, rage and denial, the echoing sound was low and broken. Lily squared her shoulders, her face set and intent.

"Gods, Cara I hope this doesn't kill you!" she said, her voice overly loud in my mind, and I knew what she meant to do.

I nodded. "Just do it," I said. She locked her lips, closed her eyes, and shoved the light into my breast. The pain was blinding, and nothing I had not felt before. I braced for it, almost revealed in the excruciating burn. My feet flew out from under me, the impact bowing my body inward like she had just blasted a cannonball into my stomach. Air shot from my lungs. Drake's arms went around my waist, but the force of the magic was too great, the power too much, even for him—it took our balance and together we hurtled—once again—toward the marble wall. The stones shattered when our heads smashed them, my body flopped like a sail in a tornado. My bare skin squeaked as it slid over the broken tiles on my way back to the ground.

My heart felt like it was on fire. My lips pulled back from my teeth, I tried to hold in a scream, while fighting to stay present. I lifted my head, gasping. My hair fell into my eyes. I had no strength to push it away. I rolled onto my back, moaning, fingernails digging into the skin covering my heart. My teeth rattled like crushed glass in an earthquake. I felt Drake's hands touch my shoulders, then move to cradle my head, I strung my aching arms around his neck.

"There," I heard Lily say to Hanna, "now *none* of your kind can kill my sister—so there."

"It was your plan all along," whispered Hanna, sounding breathless with enraged betrayal.

"It was," confirmed Lily. "I don't know you, Athena," she said. "I don't know the finite details of your revenge drama, all I know is—Cara carries the light now, if *you* want to remain immortal, then keeping Cara alive is in your best interest. I want to believe you love us," she sighed, her face hard and beautiful, glowing bright as an avenging angel. "I want to believe it… but it's simply good sense to have insurance. I told you. I will not let my sister die."

■   ■   ■

The second thing of note that happened on the sixth day, after Lily shoved the light in my chest—was when we figured out its name. Aether, it was called. The first light of the universe, and the power source from which stems all things.

"That's why Hades gave Legux to Drake, then demand he use it to stab Ares," Lily told me. "If the light is captured, death will abound. Hades wants all the souls," she finished.

"My father never wanted his kingdom," said Drake, not denying her claim, just stating the facts as he knew them.

Lily's right brow arched. "Well, maybe not in the beginning, but he wants it now. If the core of light is destroyed, humanity will revert to darkness." She slammed the Book of Shadows closed—from where stemmed her endless font of information—and faced the fresh fire, holding out her hands to catch its warmth. The chill of an evening snow hovered in the air. Drake walked to Lily and took her hand, he held it to his chest. "You are truly the best protector Cara could ask for; Hanna underestimated you."

Lily regarded him sadly. "I always knew she wanted the light. Over the past few days, I felt it every time she talked about how her father had chosen Ares over her." She turned away from Drake, her fingers went to cradle her temples. "I wonder if she ever loved us, or if she always knew I would one day use my fire to get her the thing she wanted most? I saw it the night of the vampire attack, when she told me how much she loved us, she laid it on too thick, it sounded like she was telling me one of her fantastical bedtime stories. It's the real and present danger for a person trying to believe their own lies, they are so busy attempting to convince themselves, they don't do at all well convincing others," Lily's voice got husky, and she coughed to hide it.

I went and put my arm around her, Drake rested his hand on my waist—drawing me closer—and the three of us stood together watching the flames, as if our very futures danced in their hot centers.

"It burns," I said, not bothering to rub at the aching spot beneath my left breast—it did nothing to dull the pain anyway. "Do you think it always will?"

"I don't know," he said.

"Lily should have put the light in you," I said.

"No, I am the son of death. The light is life incarnate; your sister made the right choice—I would destroy it. I don't want that."

"I don't want it destroyed either," said Lily. "Life is beautiful…" she finished wistfully.

"I want to get drunk," I said. "That's what I want. Any takers?"

"I'm with you," said Lily. "I need to drink the memory of Hanna away. I know I did the right thing, but holy hell, seeing her look at me the way she did…" Lily shuddered. "It just killed me."

"I'm so sorry, Lily," I said.

"It's not your fault, it had to be done. Hanna was right in one thing—it was my plan the whole time. It was simple really once I thought properly about it. If Aphrodite wants to kill Cara—and she is some all-powerful witch—the only logical solution was to make Cara unkillable. Once I discovered the function of the light, the rest was elementary. I thought we should give trapping it a chance first—but Hanna suspected it wouldn't work, and I agreed. From what I understand, the light changes its carrier on a cellular level—your genetics happen to be capable of handling it. I may incinerate it, Drake could smother it, but you and Hanna, you are so much alike."

"Don't say that," I said.

"It's true Cara, I knew if she could handle the light, then so could you. Sticking in your heart was the only option, I would have done it sooner, if I hadn't passed out from dehydration."

"Is Andi still in the tomb," asked Drake, though his eyes said he knew the answer.

Lily nodded. "She wouldn't leave."

"And Hanna?" Drake hesitated. "Is she gone?"

Lily nodded again.

"Do you think she's going to come back?" I whispered.

"I think so, yes," said Lily. "I pray next time; I am better prepared. Childish sentiment put me off my guard in the beginning, it won't happen again."

"If that was you off your guard —" Drake shook his head. "Cara is right, you are a force of nature."

"It's glorious," I said, then over my next deep breath I asked, "so, am I a goddess, now?"

"Lord, Cara," Lily smiled. "We always have been."

I shook my head. "The world according to Lily Wynter," I said.

We left the library and ate hot bowls of goulash in the kitchen, Fran Anjou staring silently down on us the whole time. No one said much, and the affair was over rather quickly. No fault of the soup—which was delicious—full of soft potatoes and crunchy celery. None of us had an appetite. Drake thanked Fran Anjou when she brought us all steaming cups of coffee, his was topped in a giant helping of whipped cream and smelled like nutmeg.

I warmed my hands on my cup, it had started to snow a few minutes ago, and white flakes swarmed like a seething army of fairies outside the foggy window. It was strange that something so momentous could happen—like the light of life being shoved into my heart—yet everything continued just the same. The sun kept shining, the world kept turning. Was *I* really what kept it turning now? Was it possible for such a disappearing nobody, like myself to become the very force that sheltered life? I felt the light in my chest reminding me it was true. Heat pulsed through my sweater, making tingles run through my fingertips.

A thought hit me, I said it aloud. "If Hades asked Drake to stab Ares in the heart, that would mean he wants to destroy the light, right?" I asked, suspecting I knew the answer.

"If the light is gone, everyone dies," said Lily. "This world becomes his world, nothing left by wandering souls."

"So, let me get this straight, all the gods want to keep me alive, now, but Hades—the most dangerous god of all—Hades wants me dead."

"Or trapped in that snow globe barely containing those two unfortunate souls' downstairs," said Lily."

"Hades won't hurt you," said Drake. "He has some odd, paternal affection for me—" Drake looked sour. "I will never understand it. Besides… he *loves* love. You're safe. He might even help us figure out a way to get that out of you. We don't have to think about that now," he shook his head, and a host of dark curls fell in his eyes. "One ridiculous problem at a time."

"So?" I asked. Sipping the coffee, not taking my eyes off the snow. "What now?"

"Now, we wait for them to wake up," said Lily.

"And do what?" I asked.

Lily smiled and touched her nose to the tip of her nose to mine, nearly spilling her coffee in the process. "Whatever we want, I guess."

CHAPTER XVIV

IS OLD BLOOD ALWAYS PURE BLOOD?
DAY EIGHT OF THIRTEEN

The candle flame danced in the foggy mirror. It lit the small, black cracks running around all four sides. I remembered the mirror and the world it leads to—creatures who glowed like me, mermaids, and minotaur dancing with the unimaginable. Drake had brought us back to Limbo.

This morning, I had stood beside him on the stone steps of the castle bridge as a rider brought him a wax sealed message. He read it quickly—while I felt like I had fallen into the fourteen hundreds—then shoved it crumpled in his pocket, cursing a stream of words in a language I only partially understood. Everything after that point happened in a whirl, he swept through the house like an avenging tornado, nearly grabbing Lily and Alexie and shoving us all into a carriage, then, a white rattling taxi. He pulled us down a long alley, and we went through the small, wooden door. We stepped inside the dark room, badly lit by that single candle, sitting under the large, silver mirror—always burning. The torn purple wallpaper, and grey stones were the same, the corners populated in numerous, intricate webs spun by tired spiders.

Drake waved his hand in front of the flame, and the mirror rippled like water. I heard Lily's sharp intake of breath, squeezed back when she grabbed my hand.

"Are you afraid?" I whispered.

Lily snorted. "Of course not." I felt her hands starting to get hot, she glanced at them, then back at me. "I'm never afraid, anymore."

"You never were," I said. My coat brushed the ground, the cotton material was soft and molded to my skin. The tassel hem was tipped in sparkling beads that shimmered around my ankles. Drake handed the strange, beautiful coat to me before I left the castle, saying it had once been mine. My black gloves protected me from fingertip to elbow, still, touching the coat made me feel like dreaming. The dress I had left the house in was small and black—only bravery and my new devil-may-care life view made me put it on—my heels were unusually high and felt precarious.

"You look gorgeous," said Drake. "Just breathe."

He was the gorgeous one, his leather jacket looked like it wore a moving shader, blue light spilled under his collar igniting the gold in his eyes. "It's difficult," I said. "To breathe, that is. I didn't know what I was getting myself into the first time I came here. Now that I do…"

"Anticipation killing you, is it?" he asked, smiling down at me.

I said nothing, only bounced on my toes and melted a little under his tender gaze.

Lily reached out her fingers and touched the rippling mirror, the glass bounced and writhed. She wore a red dress that swathed her in yards of skintight cloth, and a woolen coat of a matching color, her gloves were a soft blue-gold. Her lipstick was almost black, and I could see flecks of silver in the gloss—she was tantalizing as Lilith, and just as sinful—like Drake and Alexie both, she looked made for this place. If my skin had not been glowing a soft shade of resplendent, I would have been the odd one out, as it was, I shimmered like bottled starlight.

I held my hand out in front of me and stepped through the glass pulling Lily with me. This time we walked through a curtain of beads, and there were no visible doors in the round, humongous room. Torches lit the space, and I saw golden harps, and oil-skin drums instead of strobe lights and DJs. Sparkling moss peppered with blades of red grass covered the floor, the ceiling was a twilight sky painted silver and ivory, purple, and yellow vines swung from the moving tufts of springy clouds. A blue haired girl flew to me on peachy wings and stuck a garland of gardenias on my head like a crown. Another wove three lilies through the long, golden braid hanging over Lily's bare shoulder.

A hundred or so scantily clad people gyrated to the hypnotic, incessant drum beat. All covered in wreaths of flowers, each holding a sparkling goblet of wine.

"They know I hate tonight," I heard Drake grumble under his breath.

"Ah Drake," said Alexie happily. "It's *Bacchanale* tonight, they did this just to irk you, didn't they?"

"A Bacchanale?" cooed Lily, then brushed her hands over her perfect hair, and checked the placement of her teardrop earrings. "So glad I wore the right dress," she said, and turned to Drake. "Where are they? Didn't the note say to meet here at nine? It's fifteen past, is there no time in Limbo?"

"There's time of sorts," said Alexie, and held out his hand to her. "Come, we don't need to participate in whatever mundane, miserable mission Drake has planned with vampire kind. Let's dance."

"We match," said Lily, holding up her draped sleeve against his bright red pea-coat. She turned to me.

"Go," I said, glancing up at Drake, who loomed over me like a dark slice of night. "I want to see how this whole proposition of truce plays out. *"Besides,"* I told her mentally. *"You know I don't want to leave him. Have fun."*

"I will. Cara?"

"Yes?"

"We really are goddess tonight," she told me. Out loud she said: "I would love to, Alexie. Though I want to see a proper vampire. The other night was no good, it was dark and very smoky, here?" she sighed. "I think they would stand out in this ethereal place."

"Not really," said Alexie. "Fantasy blends," he smiled his slightly crooked smile, he had tied his long hair back for the occasion, and the hairdo seemed to sharpen his cheekbones. "I will introduce you to some lovely, shiny modern vampires who have changed and evolved with the times, we will stay away from the old ones, who are more solemn and severe than even Drake, here."

Drake's scowl drew lines between his brows. "I'm not severe."

"He said severely," laughed Lily, mimicking his voice.

"Please babe," I said trying out the word, feeling it melt me a little more. "No one does dark and brooding like you."

Drake was on the verge of saying something when my phone rang. I waved goodbye to Lily while my hands spastically searched my purse for the vibrating contraption. I gave Drake an apologetic look, then answered. "Hello?" I had not bothered to check the screen and I was surprised to hear Ryan's voice.

"Cara, hi," he said.

"Hey Ryan."

"Look, we found Mason Paul, we have him in custody."

"Are you serious?"

"Yes, it was because of something you said, a song. Saint traced it to a website that hosts a private gathering, Wednesdays, and Su…" the line crackled. "Managed to stop them killing another little girl, this one was only nine. I can't talk long, but I just wanted to let you know, Gary is on his way to see you. Said he needs clarity on a piece of evidence."

"Here?" I shrieked. "To Romania?!"

"Yes, his flight lands in Bucharest tomorrow at four in the afternoon. Said he'll call you from the airport, sorry Cara—I gotta go. Be well."

"Wait! Why didn't he call me before he *got* to the airport?" I wailed, but the line was dead.

"Is everything alright," asked Drake, he seemed to only be listening partially for my answer, his eyes were searching the room.

"Yes, I think so…" I meant to expound, but a woman broke from the dancing crowd and walked towards us, her eyes for Drake alone. Face looking like it had been made up by ten skilled professionals, and deep black hair piled high on her head, she sauntered past Drake, her bright red fingernail dragging the black shirt roughly over his chest. She made a full circle around his body, pausing to touch the sword on his back, while I had thoughts of lost Egyptian princesses, and snakes wearing human skin. Behind her lusty smile I could see a hint of sharp incisor teeth, just barely brushing her lower lip.

"My father is waiting," she said, in a tenor overly deep for a woman.

Her fingers wandered up his neck. Drake snapped his head out of her reach. "I am standing here in plain sight," he said. "He may come to me where all can see, I am too mentally exhausted to go through another one of his botched-up ambushes, tonight."

My arm flashed out, I grabbed her wrist—it was like gripping stone—and threw it from him, quickly— before the grinding pain broke through my barrier. "And, I want to dance," I said, giving her back an evil eye that felt piercing.

She dropped her sharp chin, and looked at me, her black eyes blinked like a snake, the iris separating, moving, then coming back together, her tongue swiped at her lower lip, then she touched the tip of it to the edge of a sharp tooth, and smiled. "So, go," she said, only acknowledging my touch by a flick of her wrist. Her slender arms linked around Drake's neck, ignoring his slight efforts to pull away. Every flower, glass and face in the room developed a strange green haze. I had a happy image of myself jumping on her back and screaming in her ear until her head popped like a crushed grape.

"Enough, Navara," said Drake, his tone not unkind. "Go get your father."

"You won't kill him, will you?" she whined.

"Go," he told her.

She sighed, long and loudly, then dropped her hands to her sides. Eyes dark as pitch found my own. "I don't know who you are, but you will never have him. He's in love with a dead girl you see—it's sad really," she sighed again. Two steps back were all it took for the dancing crowd to swallow her.

"Lovely girl," I said.

"Yes," said Drake, catching my tone. "Her whole family is sensational; I've been killing them for centuries."

"Why not her?" I asked.

"Navara was the first child born in the blood, she is a piece of history."

"She said you loved me?" I whispered.

His fingers came up to cradle my neck, he pulled my head back. "Love is such a pale word, and often misused in this time. I treasure every beat of your heart," he said, and moved closer, Limbo and its occupants seemed to disappear in a smoky haze, until he was the only point of focus in my world. "Se agapó," he said. "You are my soul."

"Drake... I..."

Drake's arms tensed suddenly, as a grinding snarl built in his throat. "They're here." Said through his teeth, the words were low and menacing. He moved then, half carried, half dragged me to a broad willow tree decorated in thousands of tiny, flickering lights. Mirrors lined the wall on this portion of the room, and the glow of the tree reflected all the colors of a rainbow. I looked at my reflection, and flinched, barely recognizing the girl I saw standing in front of me. My hair was definitely darker, deep crimson locks that looked designer, and shockingly authentic. The lights, and the glow spreading from my pores made my skin look like Tiffany rose gold.

I heard movement, felt eyes roving down my spine—yet the only reflections in the mirror belonged to myself, and my scowling god. His eyes met mine in the glass, then he sighed and turned, I turned with him. Four vampires hovered less than three feet away—and I knew at least one of the legends were true, they had no reflection at all.

Navara, stood between two women who obviously shared her blood. Their slanted eyes were dark, and wide, their full lips slightly parted by shiny sets of curved fangs, all three had red roses twined through their luxurious black hair. The women—though unreal in their beauty—looked as if they could pass for humans, in the middle of a busy city, on a very dark night. The man flanking them, did not. His fangs were long and folded over his thin, bottom lip.

Nearly transparent skin stretched over his cone shaped head, his eyes were red slits, his ears were long and pointed, cupping inward like a fruit bat—hairless and dominated by purple veins. I concentrated on the constant steady beats of Drake's heart to stave off the fear. The electric light fluttered just under my breast—sensing danger, like it had a consciousness of its own. I wondered what powers crackled in its hot center, and how many I could access.

"Talk," growled Drake. His arm was still wrapped firmly around my waist, and I felt Navara eye his hand, her look an awful blend of shock, pain and hurt.

"Von Draken," the male vampire said. When he spoke his lips parted, behind his teeth his forked tongue looked bloody. "It's so lovely to see you," he bowed. The old body beneath the black robes creaked.

"Lord Methuselah," said Drake. He turned to the women. "Queen Page, queen Tara."

"Oh Drake," said queen Page. "Do listen to us, we have known each other for two thousand years," her voice was velvet soft, cajoling. "Friends? Just for five minutes?"

"Yes," said queen Tara. "Only listen?"

"Five minutes," barked Drake.

Queen Tara took a deep breath when she spoke her voice was low and sincere. "We are like any culture; good and bad personalities make up our whole. You have massacred my children by the thousands. We cannot stop our nature, not all of us can feed without killing."

"Nor do we appreciate being slaughtered when we fail," said Navara. "We cannot live without blood."

"Or, a simulated source," said queen Tara. "Our scientists can create such a thing, a way for our people to move into the future. Our royal family does not want any more death. We acknowledge that life is precious, and no longer wish to take it."

"Stories have reached our ears," breathed queen Page. "Stories of two elemental girls, born in human skin, girls you have under your protection."

"He does," said lord Methuselah, speaking so low I strained to hear him over the beating drums. "He has one standing right beside him." He lifted his finger and pointed it at me. Nevara gasped, queen Page looked suddenly ravenous as crimson flooded the whites of her eyes.

"We need her blood," moaned queen Tara.

"Just a few drops would be enough for a thousand doses," said queen Page.

Drake unsheathed his sword, in that sudden, fluid movement that took me by surprise each time. "You will touch her blood, over my dead body."

"Blood gods below," squeaked Navara, watching Drake's defense of me. I saw the second when realization of who I was flooded her black eyes. "It's her," she said in a horrified whisper. Her hand flew to her throat as she took a stumbling step back.

I did not confirm or deny the accusation. "If it will stop a war, I will happily give you my blood."

"Cara!" Drake looked truly appalled.

I shrugged. "What? If I can help, I want to—it's a curse."

Delight filled queen Tara's eyes. She rushed to me and took my hand. Her skin was icy. It took real effort, yet I succeeded in sticking all the pain from the touch in the corner of my mind. I closed my eyes and looked at the pictures that always came with the pain. I saw dark forests and mountains covered in snow, golden parties, and ruby liquid, I felt the chilly draft of an old castle, and tasted blood in my mouth. She let go of my hand; the enchanting visions receded.

When my eyes opened, she was staring at my face, then she spoke, and her voice was full of wonder. "Prescience," she whispered. "What an exceedingly rare gift. Expensive…"

"Priceless," said Drake, and drew me back to his side. His hand on my hip, and his deep velvet voice saying that word made me start to glow. Nevara's shrewd eyes took in the whole exchange, her ensuing growl was louder than the endless drums.

"Drake," said Queen Page, reaching out a hand to him. "I cared for you in the beginning, I hid you, helped you, I stopped killing for you—" she motioned to her companions. "My whole family has, please Drake."

"It's not up to him," I said. Getting slightly miffed at all the growling and ignoring. "He doesn't speak for me, and my sister *definitely* speaks for herself. I am sure she would help you too."

"Cara," he warned.

"Oh, for crap's sake, Drake!" I breathed, stomping my heel, nearly tripping on it in the process. His eyes drew together, but he relented and sheathed his glistening sword. I sighed and unlocked hands I did not remember clenching in fists. My eyes returned to the four vampires still ominously looming. I noted each wore an identical expression of hilarious shock. Nevara recovered first, her mouth closed as something cold filtered into her piercing eyes, she looked on the verge of rageful tears. I felt a moment of irrational shame and pity. I wanted to run to her, throw my arms around her small shoulders, tell her I was so sorry for the pain my presence obviously caused. I wanted to make her understand I was here through no fault of my own, assure her we were both just as confused. I knew the hurt in her eyes, I felt it. My feet made an involuntary step in her direction, but she moved behind queen Page, Methuselah bowed, then, as one they disappeared in the crowd of the hanging vines and dancing creatures.

Drake rounded on me. I lifted my chin, ready to meet his fury with my own. I heard the grind of his clenching teeth, saw the red slash of color on the sharp bones of his cheeks. Suddenly, his head moved, and his lips—defying all—were achingly gentle on mine. I felt my hands and feet start to tingle. "Why are you so good?" he asked against my mouth.

"It's not goodness," I whispered. "I hate death. I always wished I could conquer it."

He shook his head. "It's impossible for me to think when you yell at me, you know?"

"Nonsense," I scoffed. "You think just fine."

"No, you're too pretty when your eyes catch fire," he said, his face glowing with warmth.

I blushed and rolled my eyes. No one—besides Lily—had ever called me pretty like he did, it was rather intoxicating.

"Cara," his mouth came back to mine. "You have, you know?"

"What?" I whispered, dazed, and lost.

"Conquered death," he said. I felt the light sizzling in my heart—and it knew it was true.

■ ■ ■

The sun was rising when we finally stopped dancing. I lay in a soft patch of moss, my head resting on Lily's lap, listening to the glittering music of the harps while her fingers braided flowers in my hair.

"Could you ever have imagined a world like this?" I asked.

"Not in all my wildest fantasies," she sighed. "I never want to leave. I belong here, I belonged at Wynter manor too, but I finally understand it. This place is the center of magic, other places may be home, but where we are, right now?" she motioned her slender hand towards the partying throng of fairytale creatures. "This will always be where we truly belong."

"I think so," I said.

"We can be part of this world and ours as well," she said. "You wouldn't really have to give up anything. Hanna and our histories don't really matter anymore. Drake can tell us who our father is if we even want to know. We could also just keep discovering powers for ourselves, it's pretty fun actually."

"For you," I mumbled.

"Oh, please, you know you love it."

I smiled. "Most of it."

In front of me, two nymphs were dancing for a tall, horned creature, with a face like a denim model. Red, and yellow flowers hanging around his broad, muscled neck, wrapping all the way up his curled horns made him seem the god of summer. His hands were on a woman's waist, his dance sensual and pagan. Wine poured down his naked chest, a young man—who had a unicorn horn protruding from between his hazel eyes—kissed it away.

Lily purred. "Don't you dare treat him to the heat of your witchy gaze," I warned. "We don't want that kind of trouble."

"You don't!" she shivered.

"Great, now you've done it... he's coming over here." I sat up, unconsciously straightening my hair. He moved incredibly fast, a mere moment flashed by, and his feet came to a stop inches from Lily's legs.

"By Hera! What luscious beauties have wondered in my hall tonight," he crowed. "Sisters, I see… no twins! Ah, I love nothing more than a set of lovely twins." A glass of wine, literally appeared in his hand, he drained it in one gulp and threw it to the ground. It shattered into tiny motes of dust that floated harmlessly away. He pulled another from the air, plucked a flower from the chain of them around his neck, and placed it in the glass. The flower dissolved into a violet smoke that swirled restlessly. He bowed at his trick and handed the crystal cup to Lily. She smiled into his eyes and took it from him.

"If I drink this, will I transform to something horned?" she asked.

"Only if you wanted to," he said, and bowed again, lower this time. "A drink created in your honor fire queen."

Lily laughed prettily. "And to whom might I give my thanks?"

"I am Bacchus, son of Zeus, god of wine and lush delights, welcome to my party."

"Thank you, I think I could dance here forever," said Lily, and took a sip of the drink. "Oh Jeez," she gasped, and closed her eyes in ecstasy.

"That's like liquid moonlight," she turned to me, pressed the crystal into my hand. "You have to try it."

"If I drink it, will I ever be able to leave?" I asked.

"Do you want to?" he queried.

"You know, your family really loves answering a question with a question," I told him, then took a sip. It was beyond divine.

"And where, may I ask, is your brave protector?" Bacchus pulled another goblet from a space between the waving, swaying vines.

I pointed at Lily, who was gulping her drink. "Right here," I said.

Bacchus flashed me a row of straight, white teeth, and inclined his head. "Touché," he said. "Though I am sure you know I meant our handsome son of death."

"He's with a bunch of vampires talking about giving them our blood," I said honestly.

"How appalling," he said, making a sour face. "That one was born for violence, and your blood is truly sacred."

"How do you know?" asked Lily.

He knelt beside her, resting his arms on the knees of his shredded jeans. "I know everything about you darling," he said. "I watched the stars on the night you were born. I saw the fire phoenix light up the very darkest part of the sky. I often prayed for you to escape your fate." His eyes grew distant as he focused on a spot just above her head, sadness flowed from him, like a river finally broken free of the dam binding it. He smacked his knees and stood. "Come! Hear me sing," he held out his hand to her. "It's a pleasure only the rare few experience."

Lily helped me to stand, for a nauseating second, the spherical room spun like a disco ball as the violet drink sloshed in my empty stomach. Scattered all around me were flowers, their petals turned to the impossible sky. I tried to watch the placement of my feet, careful not to crush the velvet blooms. Holding hands, Lily and I followed him across the room, weaving through a host of flapping limbs and wings.

Bacchus prowled, there was no other word for his walk. He only had to lift a brunet brow, or fake-clear his throat to make the inebriated dancers skitter out of his path. Despite its circular frame, the room seemed to come to a point at his huge, horned, golden throne—our destination. In front of it, Bacchus twirled, hand outstretched toward the golden chair. "For you, fire goddess," he told Lily, then his eyes fell on my face. "You," his voice dropped. "There is no name for what you are."

"Cara," I said.

"Very well, Cara, Cara the reborn, goddess of prescience, and mind bender divine—sit in your sister's lap," he commanded. I rolled my eyes but obeyed.

Bacchus *tisked* at me. "No, not like that, yes there. Ah!" he held up both sets of thumb and forefinger, making a picture frame with his hands, and centered it on our faces. Two clicking noises came out of his mouth, then he dropped his air camera, and sighed. "There," he said in satisfaction. "Perfect."

"Mind bender divine," giggled Lily. "That's what I am going to call you—forever," she threatened. She was having way too much fun with this—and why not? We were lost in a midsummer night's dream.

I took another sip of my drink, when it slid down my throat, everything in the room went slightly blurry. Bacchus stood right in front of us, he moved his hands and the music slowly morphed its tempo, the drums increased, and the plucking sounds of harp strings rose. Bacchus cleared his throat with dramatic fanfare, then he began. I did not breathe, or even—it felt like—blink my eyes until his song was done.

I never heard anything like Bacchus's voice, before or since. It was strong and pulsing like an electronically enhanced tone. Verses seamlessly merged, new sounds beginning, before previous notes died. The music seemed to lift me from my body, erase any pain I had ever felt from my bones, make my blood hum, and my nerves tingle. I heard the hitch in Lily's breathing, felt her heart kicking against my back.

The song he sang was sad, the tale of a fire bird trapped in the sky, she cries because her only desire is to return to the ones she loves, she cries because she loves the sun and sky. Torn, she wishes to flee, yet never to leave. His voice was pure enchantment, each word seemed nearly visible in the torch lit air. The music left a glow every place the sound fell—a primary color—nothing on earth combined could make that hot, glowing shade. It shimmered like gold, like the petals of a pink rose seen through a sunlit, scarlet tinted glass. When his song ended, I felt tears on my cheeks.

As the last note faded into stillness, not a soul in the room moved. We were lost, our eyes seeing the images his music had created. None of us breathed. Then, an earth-quaking roar erupted—more inhuman sound—and I found myself standing next to Lily, bashing my hands together like a maniac, while screaming, whooping, clapping wildly with the rest. Lily bounced on her tiptoes; hand clutched to her heart. "Holy freaking hell!" she shrieked. Her eyes were wide, the black lashes spiked in drops of moisture. Bacchus bowed deeply—drinking in the praise—then straightened his chiseled arms, held out his hands to the crowd and beckoned for more. We gave it to him. When he dropped his hands and walked to us, the room still hollered his name, the applause remained deafening.

"Oh, my gods!" I shouted when he was finally in ear shot. "You were so amazing!"

"I'm dying," gasped Lily, her hand still pressed to her audible heart. "I'm actually dying, that was… that was… everything!"

Bacchus bowed. "Thank you, darlings," he reached out a hand and touched Lily's flushed cheek, the blood beneath it rushed harder, then he smiled down at me and briefly pressed the pad of his thumb to the tip of my nose.

"I sang for my elemental twins," he said. "In four thousand years, I never fathomed in all my wild imaginings that I would see such a marvelous thing. It is your song now, for all eternity. It must have a name, all the great songs have names, perfect ones that bring it to life. Ah! The name is already in my mind, I truly am the first genius—I will call it, the tale of Wynter and flame."

CHAPTER XX

ELEMENTALS UNITE.
DAY NINE OF THIRTEEN

The sultry, freezing air rushing over the old cobblestone streets gushed down my throat. I shivered, and Drake's arms came around my waist, his chest hot against my back. I tried to call Gary when we left Limbo, but got his voice mail, twice. We walked to the cab, Bacchus's song still ringing in my head, turning my vision misty and my bones to liquid. When we were safely bundled inside the murky interior of a well-worn Ford taxi, I saw Drake's eyes watching me warily.

"What?" I asked defiantly, folding my arms across my chest— thinking I knew exactly what.

"You can't just go offering your blood to ancient Vampires," he barked.

Sinking through varying levels of bliss and violet alcohol, I almost did not hear the real edge in his voice. "I have my reasons," I said.

"Please, share," he said, spacing his words for intent.

"So long as it doesn't hurt myself, or anyone else— this will help people, maybe thousands of them," I sighed. "Please let me," I finished meekly. "Besides, I've donated blood before, it's practically the same."

"Hardly," he snapped, exhaling impatiently. "It will be seen as a pact," he bit out. "The king of Lycaon kind will try to kill me for making it—he won't succeed of course, but he will try—most ardently." He made a sound in the back of his throat and shook his head. He looked out the window, I saw his eyes wander over the early morning snow.

"Oh," I said.

"I don't want any more killing…" he breathed.

"I'm sorry, I must have danced past a few important details. There's a king?" asked Lily, making her final word tilt up at the finish.

"King of Lycaon kind," he murmured.

"Yes," she sighed. "You said that. Let me make sure I have this straight, Lycaon kind are…?"

"Werewolves," said Drake.

"Ah, I thought so," said Lily. "And they want to kill you because they hate vampires…? They want humans to die…? They hope vampires starve?"

"Yes." A shadow crossed Drake's expression. "All of the above."

"Cara?" Lily's flashing eyes swiveled in my direction. "You made this deal?"

"Yes."

"Humm," Lily tapped her chin. "Can we just explain it to them? The Lycans?"

Alexie gave Lily a deeply sour look. Half his face was buried in the bright red collar of his coat, his hazy eyes pierced her. "You can't explain anything to rabid dogs," he stated. Then, he sat up straight in his seat, and pounded his fists together. "Let them come."

"No more fighting." Drake sounded disturbed. "Not them."

"Why?" I asked.

Alexie shrugged. "Lycans are strong and old, much older than the vampire. Drake needs actual skill to fight them—he doesn't want to show you his *true* monster."

"Do you catch fire like your father?" I asked. "I remember, from the mountain, green flames," I breathed, seeing them in my mind.

"Can I see?" asked Lily.

Drake stared at her, humor and confusion battling the anguish in his eyes. "I…" he shook his head.

"Don't force him," murmured Alexie. "He'll blow this poor taxi to pieces."

"Would he really!?" Lily sounded thrilled.

"Umm," confirmed Alexie. "He has an unfortunate habit of bursting into flames when enraged." He lifted a dark brow high. "Don't brood, Drake, not after such a fine night, if they attack, we'll kill them," he finished, I saw a hint of a smile play around his lips.

"No," Draken raged. "I want no more killing."

"There will always be more killing," stated Alexie, sinking further into his coat.

Drake said nothing, his gaze remained on the distant, snowy landscape speeding past the window.

"Well, it hasn't happened yet," Lily smacked Drake's knee, making him jump a little, startling him even. I smiled. "No point sitting here moping, let's talk about the gold dust still lingering in the air. Bacchus and his voice," she said, touching her hand lightly to her throat. "No offense Cara, but his voice was probably the only thing in the world that could erase the memory of your awful sound."

"I'm with you," I said. Snuggling deeper into the dirty taxi seat. "It was so incredible."

"I believe sounds like the ones I heard tonight could create life, I think they probably have," mused Lily, then leaned her head on Alexie's shoulder and closed her eyes. Alexie hunkered further down, and his dark lashes fell. I took Drake's hand, he squeezed my fingers, not yet looking at me.

"Drake," I whispered. "What's the matter, besides me giving away my blood, of course?"

His head whipped around, his eyes fastened on mine, I could see him burning. "I would do anything to save you," he said abruptly, and it sounded like a warning. "Anything. I would cross all my lines, break every rule."

I stroked my finger over his knuckles, "I know," I said, and leaned my cheek on his arm, my mind blank, slightly glazed—I understood the emotion breaking his normally composed expression—it was fear. He knew exactly what he was capable of, and it scared him. Drake's eyes stayed on the window, though his hand stroked my hair. I was sleeping when we reached the city limits of Hunedoara and made the switch to the rattling carriage. Drake carried me, Alexie held Lily's arm, and they moved carefully across the frozen ground.

Wind whipped the ice on the mountains, made flurries dance on stones, and snow laden branches. In the distance I heard something howl and cry, yet I felt safe in the carriage, and slept in his arms. His hands on my body saved me from the worst jolts, and his husky voice soothed me back to sleep when I stirred with fitful dreams. I could hear past the thick wall of forest trees to the small village hiding beyond them. I heard songs, high, trilling voices of laughing women, and horses braying impatiently. Sounds too far away to hear—I know—yet they were in my ears just the same, dreams pulled me under.

Huge wolves, taller than men stood on taloned claws. Their snouts were long, drenched in blood. Yellow eyes watched me from all the dark spaces between the snow drenched pine trees. The sticky gaze crawled down my spine. The howling drew closer. So close, I could not tell if I was dreaming anymore.

I had fallen asleep in the bouncing carriage, and now, I lay on the freezing ground, my cloak wrapped between my legs, my deep red hair fanning out behind my shoulders, like a fallen angel's bloody, broken wings.

Soft hints of stormy grey light glinted in the snow clinging to my hand. I saw a streak of blood on my thumb. I felt something hard, and sharp jabbing in the back of my head. I sat up quickly, bracing my palm against the throbbing bridge of my nose. Thirty or so feet in front of me, I could see Drake dragging himself through persistent sheets of swirling snow. Beside me, Lily was on her knees, pressing her fingers to her eyes and shaking her head.

"What happened?" asked Lily, her voice lighting up my mind like a blue firework.

"I don't know." A little to the north, I saw a still spinning carriage wheel. I thought I saw the imprint of a horse, fading out in the endless world of white.

"We crashed," hollered Alexie. I squinted through the snow, trying to see him. His voice seemed to echo off the boundaries of the world, then come back to me from all directions. Struggling against the wind, Drake unsheathed his sword, blue light cut through the white froth.

"Wolves," gasped Lily. Her hands burst into flame; orange light blended with the blue.

"Lycans," snarled Alexie, took the silver dagger from his boot and moved in front of Lily.

"I don't remember," said Lily.

"It's the way of the Lycans," he snorted. "They call it memory fog." The wind and snow took his voice, he raised it. "It's how they trap their prey."

"Not very fair," said Lily.

"Or honorable," I finished.

"Why didn't they kill us?" asked Lily.

"Drake broke the enchantment," said Alexie.

"How?" I wondered.

Alexie shook his head and looked at the devil in question, now moving like a ghost across the snow. "You have to kill the wolf who cast it," he said.

The howls grew closer. "He's going to kill them all, I've never seen him in such a mood. You bring out deep contrasts in him," he told me.

I said nothing. There was a low grumble moving across the ground, and I heard the patter of what sounded like a thousand feet. That was when I saw it—shadows in the light, huge grey shapes prowling the edges of my vision. A jolt went through me when I saw the shadows had fur. The wind whistled, the howling paused—and the silence was profound.

Alexie dropped down on his haunches, his shoulders tensed, his fingers clawed into the snow. A snarl bubbled in his throat; it curled his lips. Lily's flames crackled.

The howling started up again, and I heard my own growl. Then, dozens poured from the trees. Wolves— standing on hind legs, flashing yellow eyes, and gnashing teeth—rushed at us with the crushing speed of a tidal wave. So many I could not properly make out their numbers. Through the shifting snow I saw sharpened talons flash, a huge creature broke free of his pack and lunged at me. Alexie crouched, prepared to spring. Lily's flames grew brighter. The grey wolf flew through the air, his claws aimed at my face. I saw clear, soggy strings of saliva hanging from his extended front teeth.

I lifted my hands, closed my eyes, wind rushed over my freezing cheeks, and I felt the air like Hanna had taught me, felt it bend, obey. I flexed my fingers, and his body froze in flight. He howled and thrashed his arms, but I held him. Held him the way I held Ares in his glassy cage, fought with him the way I had battled the light.

"Put me down!" howled the wolf, he sounded human, it surprised me, and I was not sure what I had been expecting.

"So, you can rip out my throat?" I growled. "I think not."

He raged like a bear with his paw caught in the metal teeth of a hunter's trap. "Witch!" he spat.

"Why does everyone think that's an insult?" I inquired of no one in particular. I heard Drake shout words, but I could not make them out. His hair had come free of its tie, and it fell around his shoulders. The back of his leather coat was caked in snow and ice, and I saw that his black t-shirt was torn at the collar. Legux cut a trail of thin blue light, it orbited his dark figure like a comet. Dust and snow gave the light a thick, sparkling tail. Drake was fighting them five at a time. I saw one leap on his back, as another tried to sink a set of filthy teeth into his stomach—they screamed and whined when he punched and knocked them away.

I looked back at my Lycaon captive, still suspended, dangling in the air. "I have to ask you to stop struggling," I said. "I'm not sure, but I think I could snap your spine quite easily," I told him, raising my voice over the wind. "Please don't make me want to."

"I think we should really talk about this," said Lily, and came to stand beside me, raising her hands so the tips of her flames danced dangerously close to his underbelly. I flinched as another dying scream tore the air.

"Where's your king?" barked Alexie. Stepping up and pressing the flat of his blade to the wolf's throat. "Fine," sang Alexie's melodic voice when the wolf said nothing. "Don't tell me what I want to know—I dare you," he hissed.

"He will kill your prince tonight," the wolf moaned.

Alexie chuckled darkly. "He may try. This here," he motioned to me, "this green eyed darling, you see before you, this is his girl, the fire goddess standing behind her is the sister. Then of course, there's me? I think the odds are in our favor."

"There are too many of us this time, he broke the treaty when he decided to help the blood suckers. Your prince will die tonight," the wolf proclaimed.

"If you think that, you obviously don't know my prince," said Alexie imperiously. "He won't die easy, doesn't tire, he never falters," Alexie rolled his eyes, "he is without a doubt the most stubborn soul I know. If you keep up this foolishness, he'll kill you all," he finished quietly.

I turned my head and attempted to peer through the opaque blur. I saw him instantly, he was running to me. Then, the snow parted and showed me the thick blood painting deadly pictures on his blade. His sharp gaze took in our strange scene, there was more blood streaking his jaw, splattered across his chest and neck. His blazing amber eyes found me, then flashed to the wolf I held suspended.

"Tyrell?" asked Drake, wiping the snow and blood from his eyes. The hint of a worn smile touched the corner of his mouth. "Way to be a friend," Drake shook his head. "You still owe me for drinks last week, you said we were brothers forever, now you want to kill me?"

"Surrender," gurgled Tyrell.

"The fuck I will," said Drake. There was a mocking inflection in his voice. "Go and get your king, tell him I'll kill anyone else who tries to speak to me. That includes you Tyrell. You son of a cyclops," he muttered. "I saved your damn life like ten times."

"Orders are orders," said Tyrell.

"Orders? What is this? A gang? Don't you have a mind of your own?" I retorted.

Tyrell cast me a disgusted look. "Stupid human girl," he snarled. "Mind your own business."

"*You* mind your own business…" I muttered.

Alexie rolled his eyes. "Good one, Cara."

"Let him down," said Drake, staring at me, something like pride flickering in his eyes.

"Do you really think…" Lily started. I turned to face her, and saw a dark shadow rushing at her back.

"*Lily, behind you!*" I wailed. Drake spun and threw his sword in the same move, it was an impossible shot, the visibility was zero. Legux flew like a tracking missile, I heard the wet thud when it connected with its hidden target. The smack of a dead body hitting the snow was a silent shout in my head.

Alexie's knife was back in his hand, his rasping snarls ripped through the air. I held Tyrell suspended one handed and used my other to catch the next wolf who lunged for my neck. A flick of my wrist forced the massive creature to his knees. He whined, fought, and kicked, snapped his giant teeth at me, stabbed his claws into the thick air, and howled at the hidden moon—none of it mattered—in the end, he bowed to my power.

More wolves charged, a massive grey one lunged for my ankles, I caught him in the air, not needing another hand, holding him with my mind alone, keeping them, all locked in place, by sheer, grinding will power. I felt my lips pull back as I ground my teeth, heard my own snarl building in my throat.

Lily lifted her fingers and threw two, crackling fire bolts. They smashed into a snowbank, and the patchy ice sizzled, as it incinerated— burning, not melting. The approaching wolves backed away from the magic flames—screamed, hid their eyes, and cowered from the smoky heat. My right hand was starting to prickle, pins and needles stabbed every inch of my skin. I flicked my fingers and Tyrell dropped like a stone, his body thumped against the uneven ground, and he whined like a chastised puppy.

Two more flew at Drake, he caught one by the neck and threw him into a sharp outcropping of rock. I heard the crunch of bones, and the creature howled. The second met with the flat of Drake's sword. The wolf's body bowed where the blade struck him, he stumbled and skidded away, the slippery snow working like a moving conveyor belt. Three more came before the wails of the first two had died.

All the while, fire poured from Lily's hands, making rivers and walls. In time the remaining wolves skittered away howling piteously. I felt the air around me trembling, shivering ripples electrifying the light in my heart. I could feel myself glowing brightly, see the golden aura I cast, shifting over the restless snow.

Beside me, Drake threw a fist, I could not see his target through the blinding white, but I heard a wolf wail.

"Is it not enough?" shouted Drake. He raised his head toward the foggy streams of light trying to break through the snow. "Must I kill them all?" He spun around when he spoke, like he called to the wind and sky,

Legux made hula-hoops of blue light that disintegrated even as they whirled. A huge, black wolf burst from the wall of dizzy snowflakes, as if in response to Drake's words—teeth and claws barred, he dove for us. Knees braced; Drake held his ground. He moved his body in the last second, jerking to the left, then falling in a backward roll, before smoothly gaining his feet.

Lily's next bolts threw up more fire walls. This new wolf did not bother to dodge the blaze as the others had—instead—he walked through it, changing with every step. The flames ignited his fur. Arms held out at his sides, he let the fire burn him—burn away his wolf. When he finally stepped from the flames—he was a man, and I knew him instantly. From his right hand hung the chain and its fixed metal ball, decorated in needle sharp spikes. That ball and chain, which tipped the balance in the fight between Drake and Ares, on that mountain—so long ago.

Lily and I exchanged a glance.

Drake turned and held out his hand. "Darius, brother, is it not enough now?"

■ ■ ■

Closing my eyes, I listened to Drake and Darius argue fiercely for the full duration of the ride back to Corvin. I abandoned them to their bickering when we reached the shadowed courtyard. Occasional bellows of rage shook the castle. I was far too exhausted to be furious with the way they discussed me and my choices, as if I were not there, and had none. I dashed up the twining stairs to my room, stripped out my torn, black dress and broken heels, grimacing when I saw the damage the night had inflicted on my once killer outfit. Miraculously, the coat seemed to have emerged unscathed, it was dry and fluffy as before. I lay it at the foot of my bed, blinked and yawned, taking in the room. Not much had altered since I left, yet it felt everything had changed. Tonight, I had accessed real power, and my nerves still hummed like a struck tuning fork. Tired as I was, I knew sleep would not come to my rescue for hours, I was simply to wound up.

I walked to the tall window to watch the wintery world. Bacchus's song was still stuck in my head, the tale of Wynter and the flame. It was such a sad song, yet so beautiful. I wanted to hear it again. Understand what it meant. "*Gods…vampires, werewolves…* " my mind began.

"And witches oh my!" thought Lily as she burst into the room, she threw her coat on the chase lounge near the door and kicked off her shoes. "My feet, oh my feet," she moaned. "Look at my pinky toe, it looks like a clown nose. You have to give me something to wear," she motioned to her ruined red dress. "I can't stay in this thing one more second, I think it is actually frozen on."

"I know," I shivered. "I haven't even begun to defrost."

Lily took a deep breath, trying to calm her shaking. "They're still yelling at each other downstairs. Alexie said it will go on for hours," she was breathless. "Prince Darius, alive, a werewolf, not just any—the first. I did not see that coming."

"You know who he is?" I asked, and I saw her flash through a series of word pictures in her mind. "You read Blood and Shadows," I accused.

Lily took a long, black wool dress and a gold chain-link belt from the closet and lay it on the bed. "Yes, of course I did," she said, ripping off her dress, and kicking it across the floor. She gave it an evil look. "I read it on the plane while you were sleeping. I had to know. If I weren't so busy chasing rabbit trails, I would have caught on at Wynter manor—I think Andi hoped we would. I remember her betrothal, her description of the day Ares gave you to Aphrodite, but that is where the book ends, with you—disappearing in blue sparkling lights—the lights from the crypts—Aphrodite's lights," she said, figuring it out. Her eyes were thoughtful.

"I don't know," I said. "I never finished the book, I probably should."

"I don't think it matters now," she said. Her words trailed off as she pulled the dress over tangled golden hair, her voice fading into a whisper gave me goosebumps on my arms. I went to my closet for a sweater, and a pair of dark jeans. My skin was still slightly wet from all the clinging ice, and I had to jump to put the jeans on. On the small, circular table near the room's high cathedral windows, someone—probably Fran Anjou—left a pot of coffee and a basket of scones, wrapped in a checkered cloth, near a bowl of fresh strawberries. The coffee was still warm, the scones hot and soft, the strawberries blood red, and sweet. I popped one in my mouth, and I sat down in the nearest chair then pulled the white sweater over my head. Swallowing the strawberry, I picked up a scone and bit down, it squished like a sponge—salty, buttered, and divine. I closed my eyes and chewed, grateful for the cold breeze gusting through the windows, soothing my wind chapped cheeks.

Lily came and sat beside me, she poured herself a cup of coffee, and warmed her hands on the flowered porcelain. "So, you signed us up for the next blood drive, then?" she asked.

"I had to. They want a serum; they say it will stop the killing. They were telling the truth, I felt it. Drake would feel it too if he weren't so overprotective. They love him— one in particular," I muttered, envisioning Navara's beautiful, sultry face.

"Can you really blame him?" asked Lily. "About the whole overprotective thing?"

I shrugged. "No. I guess not."

"He's easy to love," said Lily. "Drake, I mean. He's so honorable, honestly, there is no surface crap you have to wade through with him, it's refreshing. I feel sorry for him—though I know he would never want my pity. It really does seem like he is cursed. Just when everything was finally peaceful—you go and offer up your elemental blood. Maybe you're the curse," she teased.

"Jeeze, thanks, and actually, they asked for it," I muttered. "But you're right. I didn't see this coming at all." I wiped my hand tiredly over my face, accidently rubbed a crumb in my eye and battled to blink it out. "Darius, Lycaon, I can't believe it. I remember him, you know. Tall and dark, so handsome. I thought he was perfect for Andi, powerful, rich as Croesus, wealthier actually—his entourage took three days to enter the city." I pulled on my gloves and went for the coffee. It was warm and strong enough to wake the dead. "They'll come to some kind of terms. I don't think they actually want to kill each other. Drake and Darius are friends, they slept entombed for a thousand years. That's gotta build some kinda relationship." I took another bite of my scone; Lily sipped her coffee.

"Gary's here," I blurted, remembering the fact the second I said it.

Lily's head swiveled as her eyes darted around the room. "Where? Here?"

"No, not here, in Romania, though. I'm kinda worried about him."

"Well, he's a big boy, he can take care of himself. He knows where we are, I talked to him two days ago, or maybe three— time really blends in this place."

"You did?"

"Yes, he thinks he might have solved the case, he is of course, eternally indebted to you, as always." She shook her head. "Cara the detective," she giggled. "Mind bender divine…"

"It's not solved," I said. "It's a four-thousand-year-old cult, there is no way it's over—not just like that."

"You really think it's related to Enisis? To the Aphrodisia?"

"Damn, you did read the book!"

"I told you I did. So, you think they're still killing these girls? Why? Who do they think they worship?"

"Aphrodite, I guess. People worship crazier things. Like crosses and crowns."

"True," she dropped her hands to her lap, I saw her study them while she fiddled with her fingers. "You know," she said hesitantly. "I was thinking of going to Deva with Andi today." She lifted her gaze of sparkling blue. "I would invite you, but I know you don't want to leave him, and no offense to this place, but I want to get out for a while. Shop maybe spend some of the blood money Hanna left," she smiled. "Are you going to be okay without me?"

"No," I told her. "But I'll survive."

"I'll be back before D-day; I would never let you face her alone."

"Don't worry about me, you already saved me, I have the light now, all that's left is to explain it to her, and ask her nicely to lift the curse."

"Then we live happily ever after?" asked Lily.

"Yes, then— happily ever after."

We ate in silence for a while before she asked. "Have you told him; you love him yet?"

"Who, Gar?"

Over another sip of coffee, Lily dramatically rolled her eyes. "No, Cara, Drake, have you told him?"

"Yes, I think so—maybe, no I guess not, not in this life anyway."

Lily reached for a scone, took a bite, and spoke over it. "Why not?"

"He knows how I feel, I mean he has to, doesn't he? It's so obvious. I'm like a moonstruck child."

"I don't know Cara, for someone like him? I think he needs to be told. Drake doesn't have much experience with love, I think. Real love anyway. Loss he knows." She sighed and shrugged her dainty shoulders. "If these few days turn out to be our last—you'll wish you said it."

"*Our* last?" I questioned.

"You die, I die," she vowed. "You know I could never live without you, Cara."

"Me neither! Never, it would be like trying to breathe underwater."

She sighed. "Or trying to live without a heart."

"I would rather die," I said. It was true. I wanted to say more yet, it was so hard for me to talk about my feelings, there was always so much to say. I decided next time I would say it—next time I would tell her exactly how much she meant to me; I would tell her, without her it was all darkness, I would thank her for bringing me here, and saving me, I would thank her for her strength and positive outlook, I would tell her that seeing her face every morning made that day worth living. I would tell her there was no one as kind, as brave, as lovely as her. I would tell her all of that next time—but of course, there was no next time. Now, I wished I had wrapped her in my arms, chained her body to mine, cuffed our limbs together and never let her go. I wish I had done all those things, because the next time I saw Lily was the last time—the next time I saw her, she was dying.

CHAPTER XXI

WYNTER FIRE.
DAY ELEVEN AND TWELVE OF THIRTEEN — PAGES I FOUND IN LILY'S THINGS THE DAY I GOT HOME.

Gary called me about twenty minutes after Andi and I left the castle. He was in Deva and needed to see me immediately. I asked him if he had called Cara, he said he had not, I asked him why, and he hung up on me. I understood everything when we made it to the station, and I saw the ginger woman standing beside him, holding his hand, her stance almost childlike. Her big blue eyes, and adorable freckles peaking at me from under her wide-brimmed hat. The girl had not changed since middle school. Seeing her, both of them made me miss the manor, badly.

"Hi Lily," said Marsha sweetly, holding out her hands to me. I pulled her in a giant hug, she squeezed me tight, and rested her head on my shoulder.

"Oh! I am so happy to see you!" I heard myself gush. "You're just in time for girl's night." I let her go and stepped back. "This is Andi," I said, turning slightly to let Andi step in front of me, and shake Marsha's outstretched hand. As the two were taken up by pleasantries, I rounded on Gary.

"What the hell is going on?" I asked, more with my face than any words.

Gary's eyes narrowed, emphasizing the bags beneath them. "Not now," his look said, and that was the end of it. When he wanted me to know, he would tell me. I turned back to the chattering girls, and forgot about anything sad at all, for the first time, in a long time. Transylvania was such a magical place and Deva was the pinnacle jewel in the center of the crowning brilliance. The three of us girls visited every shop, and I purchased more shoes than I could ever need. It was almost December now, Christmas was in the air, and Deva was decorated spectacularly, like holiday art in a Disney movie. We saw a play at Teatrul de Arta, a beautiful story about two women in love, in a culture where the offense is punishable by death.

I danced and laughed, drank hot glow wine, and ate everything in sight. Marsha made us stop to watch a live air orchestra in the piazza, and it was so beautiful that I cried. During the flood of feeling, it was difficult to keep my hands from catching fire. It seemed not only danger brought my flame, but deep emotion of any kind also set me off. When the concert was finished, Gary made a phone call, and there was an urgency in his tone. I knew he was talking to my sister, his voice always changed with her—dropped by a few degrees, not bad—not the religious devotion Drake bestowed on Cara— but enough to notice, and I knew Marsha was not blind.

"He doesn't want to hurt me," said Marsha, looking up at my face, hers brilliant under the soft lamplight. "I know he needs Cara—she has a real gift." She sighed loudly, and her small body shivered in her down green jacket.

"You have him Marsha," I said, reading the expression on her flushed face, her nose was rosy.

"I know, he loves me—he's the best husband in the world. Like a superhero really. But loves her too."

I shrugged. "Yeah, but he's with you. Cara didn't have dibs, you've known him just as long, you had a crush on Gary in the first grade."

Marsha's intelligent eyes fastened on mine. "And he, on her. Would he be mine, do you think, if he could have touched her?"

I thought about that for a second. "Yes, I think so. Drake and Cara are a force of nature. They were always going to find each other." I rolled my eyes. "If he wasn't so damn handsome the whole thing would be rather nauseating." I smiled. "She's lost in the sauce."

Marsha laughed, and her sparkle returned. That was good. No point breaking over things that cannot be changed.

The first day in Deva felt surreal, endlessly long and way too short. I barely saw the dainty chalet Andi led us to when the lot of us were too tipsy and tried to keep standing. Andi gave Gary and Marsha the guestroom on the ground floor, then led me up a flight of stairs to a blush-colored bedroom, with farm-style curtains and two rocking chairs. I fell asleep in the feather bed, holding Andi's hand and dreamt of fire again—we slept till way past noon.

In the morning, I missed Cara with a persistent, needling ache. I felt it when she stubbed her toe yesterday. The pain was so severe it made my eyes water. She was not eating enough either, my growling stomach told me so—but she was well. Drake would never let anything happen to her, at least I hoped so. To be honest, his track record was not that great—he was famous for getting there seconds too late. Part of his curse, I supposed, and I prayed the light would protect her—prayed to any god who would listen, that I had done enough.

For the most part I ignored the little tingle of fear that told me I should not have left her alone, and Andi did her best to keep my mind on just about any other topic. The chalet's small, chic kitchen—checkered tablecloth, bottles of table wine, and a big basket of steaming, fresh bread—smelled like tequila and lemon. Andi made breakfast margaritas. It was over from there—when Gary stepped into the kitchen three hours later, we were still drinking.

He walked to Marsha and took her face in his hands, the kiss he gave her was overly sweet. Andi caught my eye then, smiled and touched her heart. She seemed brighter today, silver dress, silver hair, silver eyes—all aglow.

Marsha was giggling as Gary stepped back. "I have to see Cara today," he said, not looking at Marsha. Tomorrow at the latest, we can't stay much longer. Mason Paul's hearing is on the sixteenth, we need to be home long before that. No new missing girl's yet, so that's good. Whole city is on high alert, so his cronies might be laying low."

"You don't think he's the head of the snake, do you?" I asked, easily reading his eyes.

"No, I don't. I hate saying that out loud, but it's true. This cult is old and powerful, if I'm right..." his voice dropped off, his expression deeply disturbed. "If I'm right, it goes all the way to the top."

"The top of what?" I asked.

His hectic eyes drilled holes in mine. "Of everything," he said.

"In the morning?" Marsha almost begged. "There is nothing you can do about anything right now. Let's go tomorrow, one more day of fun before it all starts again," she gave him a tired smile. "Pretty... pretty...please."

"Would say yes if I could, mainly because you have so many freckles," said Gary, his eyes seeming to rove over each one of them. Marsha blushed. "But we have to leave tonight," he finished.

"Tonight, is still seven hours away, we can leave at sunset," I suggested.

Andi whooped, and refilled my margarita. We let the drinking commence once again. Andi changed by the hour, the constant tension in her shoulders relaxed, as her hard edges softened—a visual I had pulled straight from Cara's mind—I realized I was rather obsessed with her. I took a nap at sunset, meaning to sleep off the alcohol. The bed was insanely comfortable, and my lashes felt weighted. I was out in moments.

I had a dream that Andi stood at the foot of my bed. There were tears on her pale cheeks, and a crystal cut in the shape of a diamond clasped between her small hands. She told me she was sorry and whispered that it would not hurt. My dreaming eyes did funny things to her face and wild silver hair.

She wiped at a tear, then he placed the diamond against my heart. I felt flames rush out of my chest and go into the sparkling stone. When she moved the stone away, I felt weak and dizzy, then the dream faded and I was glad, I had not liked the desperate look in Andi's eyes.

When I woke in the dark, the chalet felt haunted, yet empty. I stood up, staring at the dark blue night light, and the way it touched the quiet city sprawling beyond the open window. Straightening my black sweater dress around my hips, stuffing my feet into a pair of pumps, and fluffing my hair, I looked for my phone. I found it under the bed and rolled my eyes, resolving to never day drink again. A resolution I had unfortunately made and broken many times in the past. I flicked the screen on, bright pink light made me squint my eyes, digital numbers flashed 10:40pm. "Oh my god!" I screeched. How had I managed to sleep so long? Even now the fuzzy world wanted to take me back to dreamland. Hand to my head I tried to focus, it felt like I had been roofied. I swiped once, then tapped on Cara's name, and I waited. The phone rang for a full minute before it clicked over to her voice. "I can't take your call right now, I like texts," the message said.

"Cara!" I called in my mind. I waited, there was no answer. *"Cara!"* I cried—to no avail. We were either too far away, or something awful had happened. I tried Alexie and got another voicemail—fantastic. I rolled my eyes. "She's fine," I whispered, and felt my lips tremble. "She's safe, Drake's there," my words bouncing around the empty room scared me even more. I grabbed my purse and ran out the door. I called two more times—on the second: 'I can't take your call right now' my heart started to pound. I was shaking when I knocked on the door to Gary and Marsha's borrowed room.

The door flew open. Gary's hair was badly tousled, he was shirtless, and the top button of his jeans was undone. I felt my eyes widen. "I can't get a hold of Cara," I said, my voice a whisper-scream. "We need to leave right now!"

"Okay," he said, already walking to the bed and reaching for his shirt. "Time to go, Marsha, baby? I think Andi would let you stay if you would rather not—"

She cut him off. "I'm coming."

"Why didn't anyone wake me?!" I almost yelled.

"Shit," barked Gary, looking at his watch. "Is that the real time! God damnit, we just woke up ourselves." Gary shook his head, rapidly blinking his eyes. "What the hell was in that margarita?"

"I'm going to go find Andi," I said. Though something in my heart told me it would be useless, something told me the flame-sucking diamond had not been a dream, if it was real, then I knew she was long gone. I ran through the house, calling her name. Fear was melting ice crawling up my spine as I descended a twisting flight of stairs three at a time.

Rounding the next corner, I saw that the back door was partially open, banging in the night wind like a broken shutter. I pushed it wide and stepped outside, barely feeling the chill. My heart was galloping now, I heard my own blood rushing in my ears. I followed a small path around a sharp curb, the stones were covered in bunches of yellow flowers, threaded through by thorny vines.

"Andi?" I called again, trying to peer through the encroaching darkness. "Andi!"

"She's not here," said a voice behind me. I screamed and spun around, nearly jumping out of my skin. A woman in a long white dress stood in front of me. Head held high, chin defiant, she was a ghostly shell of the true beauty that had once been, yet I knew her, even though I had never met her—even though the essence of her soul was muted, shining dully behind her ridiculously long lashes. She was more beautiful than even Andi, her hair seemed to have actual gold hidden in it, and her eyes were brilliant, shining a vivid violet that made her look otherworldly.

"Helen," I said, swallowing hard to recover what remained of my composure. "Where is she?" I asked, hoping the nettling suspicion I had, did not turn out to be fact.

I heard Helen suck in a sharp breath, it whistled between her clenched teeth. "She has gone to him of course, one hour to midnight. It's almost time—three thousand years of nervously waiting, and it is finally, almost time— stupid girl," she said, her voice rising on each word. "Ungrateful, miserable child."

"Gone to whom?" I asked, already knowing. The ice had finished with my spine and moved onto my stomach where it stabbed and writhed.

"It was her plan all along, Draken meant to stay away. Androsia wouldn't have it," whispered Helen, shoving her face deep into my personal space. "She would have gone to the reincarnated princess regardless; we all knew when she was born."

Helen went suddenly silent, her eyes closed, her mouth fell slack, her head went limp and tilted to the side like a broken neck hanging from a noose. She held that pose, still as stone, the wind blowing at her hair and dress.

I leaned closer. "Helen?" I whispered and moved even closer. "Helen?"

Her eyes flew open, her jaw dropped further, then she screamed—a deep rasping sound—like some unseen force was strangling her. I yelled and jumped back, barely managing to stay standing.

"YOUR SISTER!" she wailed. "Your cursed sister! Androsia wrote that book just for her, you know? She thought it would bring him back to her. I told her it was a terrible idea, I told her the god she loves is death incarnate—she would not listen." Helen took a step away from me, as she moved, I could see the outlines of shrubs, and a piece of the porch stairs though her body, I realized a portion of her stomach and thigh were almost completely transparent—just like the aunts in the manor or Wynter haunt. It hit me then, Helen was not a ghost, perhaps none of them were. She was not dead—simply fading—fading into oblivion—which was, I decided more—dreadful than an open casket.

"They are death," whispered Helen, her rose bud mouth soft in her poignant face. Then, she began to twirl in a wide circle, her white dress spun out. She lifted her hands and started to laugh; the pitch so high it was almost a scream. "Run, run, run," she yelled in the voice of a soul utterly lost. "See if you can catch them before the clock strikes twelve. The clock strikes twelve—what will it be? A fire bird falling, falling down, down into the sea." Helen spun some more, and her eyes grew ever hectic in her wild face, I looked at her shaking, vanishing limbs, and knew time and magic had driven her insane. I was gasping, stunned and frightened. It was at least an hour to Corvin Castle from Deva, and I still had to find a cab. I swallowed my need to cry and rage, whirling away from the sad image of Helen of Troy and the love spell gone wrong, all I could see was my sister's face. I knew then that I *had not* done enough—choking back the threat of frightened tears—I started to run. Hoping, praying to any god who would hear me, that I was not already too late.

■ ■ ■

DAY ELEVEN AND TWELVE OF THIRTEEN

I stood at the top of the gothic towers to the east of the castle, facing west toward the hall of knights, and dark forest beyond. Cool wind blew through my hair as I listened to the sounds of evening. I missed Lily terribly, like someone had fired off a round of buckshot into my chest, an hour ago marked the longest time I had ever been away from her in my life. I missed her eternal laugh, and soft voice in my mind. Only an hour or so left until midnight, and each slow, seemingly endless minute that ticked by further stole my breath. Light or not—I had to admit I was afraid—the fear was worse without her here to tell me all would be well. I rested my hands on the cold bricks of the surrounding wall, all that kept me from plummeting down the rocky cliffs to my death. From my vantage, the ground was nothing more than a minuscule dot, disappearing in roving mists. I stepped back as a wave of vertigo hit. Unconsciously, my hand went to my heart, I felt the light burning there, yet the heat was not enough to rid my bones of their eternal chill, the icy feeling of phantom feet marching over my grave.

These last thirteen days had changed everything, I had gone from vanishing girl to goddess. The night of the Lycaon fight I had felt something old and terribly strong running through me. I had been invincible yet knew I had only barely touched the full scope of my power. That truth gave me some hope, perhaps we really had a shot at changing fate tonight.

I turned around before he said my name. Drake was in front of me, his dark skin and clothes blending with the winter night, his loose hair falling around his shoulders, wet and curling. Lowlights touched the underside of his jaw, and the rays of a single moonbeam chiseled his straight nose, and full lips, highlighting his pagan beauty. He reached for me as I reached for him, I fit so perfectly in his arms, like they had been designed to wrap around only me.

"We might just get away with this," I breathed.

"It's hard to even hope," he said, his voice hot on my neck. "To live, fearless—with you? It's more than a dream." He touched my chin, and I met his eyes. "I would build you an iron palace and keep you there, safe from anyone who would harm you, no dark devils, or evil goddess could come."

"She wasn't always dark and evil," I said. "I remember how much I loved her, loved Aphrodite," I whispered. "I wanted to die for her, for you, it was my destiny, my honor. Some part of me will always love her. Now, standing on the precipice of her curse, I can't stop thinking about how I used to feel." I sighed, sad enough to cry. "I know you feel the same about Ares," I finished. His eyes flickered away from my face; I saw him swallow hard. "You love him," I said. It was not a question, but he nodded quickly.

"He's my blood," he said. "If I had not just lost you, I would never have…could never…if Darius had not—" his voice broke. I touched his cheek and turned his face back to me. "The only thing I have ever genuinely wanted, beside you—is a family, yet I am forced to brutalize and kill my own. Ah, Cara," he breathed, pressing his forehead to mine, his voice breaking over my name. "I'm so sick of it all. So tired of death."

"It's a silly thing to be sick of," I said, trying to smile. "It's as common as life, you know?"

"That *is* actually a good one, Cara. Fates," he rasped. "Pretty and witty, what will I do with you?" I thought I saw the hint of a smile before he kissed me. I bowed to the power, and depth of my feelings for him. Three-thousand-year-old love spell or not—come destiny or damnation, this touch, this kiss, this man was everything. I leaned away and searched his face, finding my religion in each line and curve, forever imprinted on my soul.

"Will you wait with me?" I asked. "I can't sleep, I don't even want to try."

He lifted me without warning, I gasped as my feet flew off the ground. "Nothing could take me from you tonight," he told me, settling my body in his arms. "We will not, however, spend it on the edge of this cliff."

"Your bed?" I whispered, hoping.

"In front of my fireplace?" he countered. His frank look made me shiver. I twined my fingers through his hair.

"Your choice," I said, thinking of dark nights, our naked bodies soaked in a fiery orange glow. "Did you and Darius make a deal?" I asked, in an effort to distract my melting senses.

"To give away your blood?" The appalled expression he wore turned his mouth down at the corners. "Please, Cara, how can you honestly ask me such a thing? Once Darius understood that you offered the blood knowing nothing of the pact, he calmed a little. Werewolves have excitable natures— him more than others."

"Because he was the first?" I asked.

Drake shook his head. "No, because he is immortal. Lycaon kind are not. Darius was the true innocent bystander. When the light went into us, it changed us all—eventually it found its way back to Ares, but not before it made him into something unrecognizable. Our Olympian blood saved Andi, and I. Darius was not so fortunate. He had been given immortality but cursed to live it out as a monster. Karma may be vicious, but there is no denying her sense of humor," he said wryly. "I will never forget the first time Darius changed. He tried hard to die that night."

"I hardly remember," I said, trying to stretch the boundaries of my foggy mind. "I only remember fading to dust in your arms—it's like trying to remember a childhood dream," I confessed.

"Thank the fates for small favors," growled Drake, carrying me back inside, and up the spiral stairs. He kicked the door to his room open, it hit the wall with a crashing thud, then bounced back and he kicked it closed. On the mantelpiece, the ornate silver clock told me it was ten forty-five. I had a strange urge to check my phone, but I knew it was dead, and pushed the thought away. A fire roared in the hearth, highlighting the dark auburn in his furniture, touching the fibers of the white rug making them jump with golden light.

He lay me down on it. I kept my arms around his neck. His face was soft as he leaned down to kiss my temple. Settling my legs close to the toasty blaze, he stood up and grabbed the duvet from the bed, then came back to me—dragging the feather quilt behind him—and wrapped it around us.

"Nearly an hour till midnight," I whispered, not really caring at all. I was losing myself in the dark, fiery world he created. I reached up to touch the lines of his stunning face, he took my hand, his kiss was fire in the center of my palm. "I want you, Cara. Gods above and below, I want you," his whisper hoarse, ragged—it crackled like the flames. Desperation was in his touch tonight, his mouth on my body hot and urgent. We ripped at our clothes, both seized by some strange madness. We rose to our knees, his kiss was savage, his scalding hands made me tremble. When he moved to take off his jeans, I saw that his eyes were nearly black, and green fire burned in their hot centers. I stared at him, naked and painted in firelight. As he moved, the hard lines of his body rippled like living stone. His spell over me was complete, I knew—come what may—I would want him, love him for the rest of my life. Not just any love, but a love that transcended time, death, and hate.

My fingers touched his stomach, stroked lower. I heard him suck a hiss of air through his teeth, then, there were no more walls to hide his raw desire—our explosive passion had incinerated them all—and I felt him, really felt him, his need for me a tangible thing in the glowing air. He was both enchanted and enchanter. Wrapped in our cocoon of blankets he held me to his heart, like he could pull me into his own skin. His hands touched me everywhere, his mouth on my breast made me taste liquid fire. When my exhausted body was limp, my soul mindless with simmering sensations, he took me to his bed and started all over again, not stopping until I was screaming, lost in an exploding world of black stars, and golden afterglow.

■ ■ ■

I must have dozed off because when next I opened my eyes it was to the sound of the clock in the ballroom signaling midnight. Twelve long, *gongs* banged out the time like a warning. I climbed out of bed, careful not to wake him, I froze when he stirred. Some absurd notion made me want to kiss him goodbye, but I resisted it. Kissing him goodbye would mean I was planning to die today—and I certainly was not. I picked my clothes off the floor, found my bra hiding dangerously close to the dying fire, then dressed in silence. I grabbed my shoes and tiptoed into the hall, nearly running Andi down. She wore a tight black jacket and jeans; her hair was hidden under a baseball cap of the same nondescript color. I almost did not recognize her.

"Cara!" she whisper-gasped.

"Crap, Andi, you scared me! Is Lily here?"

"Yes," she gushed, and huge tears momentarily obscured her silver eyes, she wrung her hands clearly distressed.

"What is it?" My voice rose in alarm.

"It's Lily," cried Andi, tears gushed, and glistened on her pale cheeks.

I grabbed her arm, I shoved the visions away, embracing the burning pain.

"What?! What happened to her?"

"She, ugh! Cara, I told her not to, but…"

"What?" I was almost shrieking now, blood pounded hard in my ears and red was beginning to blur my sight. I shook her, hard, heard her teeth click. "What the hell happened?!"

"She's in the dungeons, in the crypt," said Andi, verging on hysterical. "I told her not to go, but she wouldn't listen. If they wake to find her there," her eyes rolled back in terror. "I can't imagine…"

"What are you talking about?!"

"She woke up from a dream screaming, said she didn't trust the light—I tried to convince her that all would be well, she was inconsolable."

"I don't understand," I shouted, letting go of her arm and running for the stairs. "How did she even get in?!"

"I don't know," cried Andi. "She must have taken the key from Drake, I don't know, all I know is that she is down there all alone, I'm so afraid."

"Lily!" my mind wailed. *"Lily, where are you?"* Screeching silence greeted my rising panic. Why? My mind spun, why would she go down there without me? What did she possibly think she could do? None of it made any sense. I tucked in my chin and ran faster down the hall, we blasted through the first room in seconds, in the next, a table blocked my path. I lifted my hand, it flew across the room and smashed into a wall. In the third room it was a chair, old and stuffed to the seams, I waved my hand through the air and it went the way of the table. We reached the enchanted dungeon doors in record time; I grabbed the bars and shook them. "Lily!" I shouted, listening to my voice tremble, my heart was shaking in my chest. "Lily!"

Andi grabbed my arm, I shuddered and bit back a cry. "No time! Take my hand. Phase us through."

"No! I can't!" I stumbled away. A flash of confusion almost short circuiting my terrified mind. Andi blinked slowly, her mouth working silently.

"There's no time," she finally exploded. "Do it now, Cara!" she said, her voice straining hard over every word.

"Oh, crap!" I looked down at her bare hand, my mouth filled with liquid acid in anticipation of the pain that came from touching her. I watched her expression change and harden, as I pulled off my glove and held out my quivering fingers. "Fine," I choked out. "I'm going to try. Don't be surprised if I pass out, you're ancient and scary."

"You're wasting time!" she screamed, her strained features so red I thought she may bust a vein.

"Then take my hand," I said reasonably, looking down at my own limb like a foreign, unwanted thing. I saw my reflection glimmer in her distress ridden eyes. She locked her teeth and grabbed my fingers. I gasped in a breath that stayed in my lungs, the touch was light, the visions immediate—In that moment I knew everything she meant to do. I saw her steal the goddess fire from Lily's heart and sneak out of her own home. I saw the spell she concocted to drag Aphrodite from her trance, and how she meant to do it—I tried to stop myself from passing through the iron bars, but it was too late. My body was liquid, and we were flowing through the metal like water. I crumpled into a heap on the other side. The wet stairs cut my knees, and elbows. The pain of touching her was a bell ringing in my ears, the extreme noise took my sight. I lifted my hands out in front of me, waiting for the agony to recede and return my vision. Nothing made sense, why would Andi lie to me? I tried to stand, slowly my surroundings began to blur into focus. A few feet away I saw Andi lifting a torch off the wall, then she walked towards me, her face rigid, her eyes narrowed and set. There was no feeling in my limbs, everything seemed so unreal. I saw her lift the torch above her hair, the flame cast her face in black shadow.

"I'm sorry," she whispered, then swung the torch at my head. I tried to dodge, tried to stop the hit with my mind, but I was too slow, still reeling in pain and confusion. The base of the torch struck the side of my face with a loud bang that popped horribly against my eardrum. I saw a flash of bright white, just before everything went black.

When I regained consciousness, I was back in the electric tomb, my hands and feet wrapped in the same thick chains that clenched my waist. Andi hovered over the sarcophagus of Ares, gently placing a large slab of glowing crystal in the gaping hole previously made by Lily's flames. She flicked her head briefly in my direction when I opened my eyes.

"What are you doing?" I screeched, coming suddenly to my senses. "Are you crazy?"

"I will not let Drake kill him," Andi said in a deceptively gentle voice. Her crocodile tears were dry on her face, her eyes were thoughtful, and calm.

"Did you hurt Lily?" I asked, realizing it was all I really cared about.

"Of course not, I would never hurt her. She is the only precious thing in this mess. I love her."

"If you love her how can you do this? If I die, it will kill her," I said.

"How can you die? You carry the light. Aphrodite will see that, she will leave you alone, leave all of us alone, and Ares will finally be mine."

"What if Drake is right, what if he doesn't choose you?" I asked, trying to stall. Wishing I had woken Drake, before dashing down here like a mad woman.

Andi sighed and released the cut of crystal. She walked towards me, all the while, keeping a wary eye on the staircase, listening for the squeak of the iron gate it led to. I tried to fight the chains, but they rasped against my wrist and cut into my ankles. "This is insane," I gasped. "Andi! Let me go!"

She shook her head. "I'm sorry, Cara. I can't do that." Her hand flew behind her back, I heard the distinct sound of a knife leaving its sheath, when she moved again, I saw a flash of silver. The electric light bounced off the knife and threw a beam in my eyes. I started to struggle in earnest. She knelt beside me and placed her non-blade wielding hand on my head. I nearly blacked out again from the pain, it seemed I could no longer push it away. "I'm not going to kill you, Cara. I just need your blood, don't I?" she said, phrasing her demand as a question, I knew she meant to take it with or without my consent. The chains scraped and scratched the ground as I tried to back away. "I need your blood to let her know it's time to wake up, I need her to taste all your memories."

She placed the blade against my sweater, near my right shoulder, then sliced in a quick painful stroke. I gasped, watched my red blood expand in the sweater's pearly white fibers. I heard my teeth chattering and wondered if I was going into shock. "The chance is slim, of course," said Andi, lifting the knife and inspecting my blood on the blade, then she stretched out her tongue and tasted it.

"Oh gods," I groaned.

"Slim, yes," she said again. "Yet, if I can taste your memories, I just bet she can too." Smiling, she carried the knife to Aphrodite and stabbed her ice casing, the tip of the knife came to a stop a bare centimeter from Aphrodite's lower lip.

"Now what?" I said, listening to the glassy ice creak and crack around the knife's still twitching blade.

"Now we wait," she said.

"Wait for what?"

Andi did not look at me, her eyes were fixated on Ares's face. "We wait for her to taste your dreams and fulfill her curse. Wait for her to wake." Her soft-spoken words made shudders of fear rip through me.

Fire began to pour from the diamond, it ran over the sides of Ares's transparent cage like water, dripped on the tiled floor, then rushed to the feet of Aphrodite. Soon both gods were engulfed in magic fire. Slowly, inch by imperceptible inch, the cage of ice began to melt. The thick, strange liquid evaporating under the persistent flames.

Andi backed away from the fire, locked her fingers around the chains wrapping my feet and dragged me out of harm's way. I looked carefully at her face; she did not appear insane, only desperate. I suspected this night was three thousand years in coming for her. I almost hoped Drake was wrong, I almost hoped Ares loved her as much as she loved him—almost, but I knew in my heart he did not. I hurt for her, she was setting herself up for an incredible heartbreak, there was nothing I could do, save lay here uselessly and watch. When the icy cages had nearly melted under Lily's fire, Andi knelt and rather calmly pressed the blade of her knife to my throat.

I looked deep into her silver eyes. "You can't kill me Andi," I said reasonably.

"No, but I can make you suffer," she said casually. "I never cared whether you lived or died, I only needed you to remember. Aphrodite will not leave Ares in his sleep, she will wake him with old magic, and he will choose me." She pressed the blade tighter, I felt it split my skin, and knew when the stinging cut released another drop of my blood.

"Put the fire out now, or I will slit your throat with a smile," she promised, truth in her touch.

"Fine! I will! You don't have to threaten me, in case you didn't realize," I lifted my hands and shook my chains in her face. "I'm kinda in it to win it here—I just don't know how."

"Figure it out, you have five seconds."

"Then what, really Andi, if you kill me those flames will incinerate your god!"

"Do it!" she shrieked.

I honestly considered not doing it, I was getting ready to tell her so when I heard hard footsteps on the stairs.

"Quickly!" she hissed.

"Androsia!" I heard Drake roar. Somewhere a metal door smashed open. He was across the room in what seemed like no time at all, I barely registered the furious expression on his face before Andi took a handful of my hair and tugged hard, further tightening the stressed skin on my neck. My eyes flew to the ceiling as my head was forced back, the halogen bulbs made them water. I swallowed convulsively and felt the knife shave off a layer of skin.

"You took the love of my life," wailed Andi, swinging my body around so she could meet his eyes. "You took him from me, now I am going to take yours."

"Andi," Drake held out his hand, his voice was wretched.

"Don't! Don't say one word to me! I have had enough of your apologies and lies; Ares did not deserve the fate you dealt him."

"Cara is innocent," he barked.

"So was he," Andi cried. I could feel her body shaking. "Now," she hissed in my ear. "Put the damn fire out before you *are* a killer."

"Technically you would be the one who did the killing." Her grip in my hair tightened. "Fine, I will. Not because you are threatening me either—I hate death, I want no blood on my hands today, even if it bounced off you and hit me."

I closed my eyes, imagined the fire dying, pictured a huge arctic wind blowing through the room. When I opened my eyes, a layer of snow covered the tiles, the fire was gone. All that was left were tufts of grey smoke sucking up the last of pieces of melted cage. Inside their coffins of aged limestone, the gods were free. I could see the edge of Aphrodite's golden gown catching the wind trickling through the high window that overlooked the sea—it blew softly around her feet. My legs and hands felt numb, the chain binding me was suddenly very heavy. The knife fell away from my throat, Andi stepped back, then pressed the tip against my heart. While she held it there, she took a vial of dark liquid from the pocket of her jeans and threw it to the ground. Black smoke swirled—hissing and writhing like a snake, it touched my toes, crawled up my feet. A strange feeling came over me, like all the strength I possessed had been sucked out of me, I blinked my spinning eyes.

Drake unsheathed his sword. Blue light momentarily blinded us all. "Andi," he whispered. "Please don't make me fight you. I've loved you since the day you were born. Please."

Andi pressed the knife; I felt the tip slice through the soft fibers of my sweater. I took a step back, she pressed again, and I took another. "No," she said, not taking her gaze from my face. "I am going to trade her life, for one with Ares. I am not selfish, I will only ask for one lifetime, as that is all I am giving in return, I know how Aphrodite feels about your girl, she will take my deal with a smile—what is a single lifetime to someone like her?"

"Do you really think you can make her stop and listen?" asked Drake. Aqua flames leapt in the iris of his eyes, while more green fire dripped from his hands, I saw that the ends of his hair were also blazing, he looked every bit the son of death, or a younger, more frightening version of the grim reaper.

"I guess we'll have to wait and see," said Andi, her eyes and voice fervent. "It's almost time," she promised, using the point of her knife to walk me across the rest of the huge room, putting greater distance between myself and her brother.

"You don't have to do this," I whispered.

Her eyes flared. "Quiet!" she screamed. "I have been planning this for two thousand years, nothing will stop me this night. It's my turn!" The knife in her hand shook badly, I tried not to breathe. "No one has ever asked me what I want, it has always been about you, you and my brother, and your blood-soaked love. A love that has cursed the rest of us! Enough! You stole my life, and Darius's life. Lives you had no right to!"

"I'm sorry," I said. Meaning it, I could see the deep pain in her eyes, despite everything I did not want it there. Before I could say other apologetic words, I heard a scratching sound behind me, my eyes flashed toward it.

The gold cloth in Aphrodite's sarcophagus shifted, the white hands serenely folded across her stomach, flinched. The fingers, lifting and falling by slow degrees. I started to look for an escape route, this was getting out of hand. I had tried to talk, tried to reason with her, but the girl holding the knife to my heart was too far gone.

I locked my jaw and lifted my arm, my fingers flexed as my mind shoved Andi against the far wall. Nothing happened. I tried again, dropped my hand, and used only my mind. Her feet stayed firmly planted on the ground.

Through her lowered lashes she gave me a furious smile. "Don't try it! What do you think that black smoke was? Your power no longer works here. I told you! I've been planning this for two thousand years, two thousand, I've forgotten nothing. My brother is the only real threat, as he always has been," she finished, her thick voice full of malice. "Though, so long as I am holding this knife to your heart, I don't think he will dare move. Throw his massive sword at me? Well, he risks hitting you, that he will never do. No, you were always the key, this is fate, unchangeable."

A soft series of clicks sounded behind me, I heard long nails scratching over dry stone, and listened to my own shattered gasp. Dread locking my heart in a steel vise, I saw relief and triumph flood Andi's face. My head whipped around, and my shattered gaze saw what Andi had already seen. Drake cursed behind me; I heard his bitter words echo off the walls.

Aphrodite blinked her eyes— slowly, like Snow white waking from her poison dream—she sat up. Shoulders stiff as the dead, her expression enraged, her gaze locked on me—she looked somehow young and innocent, like her long sleep had done her well, and heartbreakingly beautiful. Then, she smiled, a dazzling deadly smile.

CHAPTER XXII

YOU DIE, I DIE.

If I did not remember everything yet, seeing her face—watching life ignite the blue fire in her eyes—brought every detail back with soul crushing clarity. I was her priestess again, innocent of life and all its pain, on my knees, laying my rose at her feet—willing to die for a destiny I craved. She slowly stood, not bending her knees, or moving her body at all, she simply lifted in the air, it seemed Andi's wards had no effects on the powers of this goddess—and I hated myself for not being stronger, I hated Hanna for not preparing me for this moment that was always fated to arrive.

Aphrodite's feet hovered over the ground as she moved to Ares, after smiling her evil smile, she had not spared the three of us a second glance. She knelt and placed her hands on his head. I shook in my chains, struggling in silence.

Drake took a step towards me; Andi tightened her hold on the knife. "Uh, uh, uh," she sang, and twisted the blade. I felt a drop of blood drip down my stomach. I winced; Drake froze. Still kneeling beside the slumbering god of war, Aphrodite leaned down and kissed his cold brow. Ares twitched, his eyelids fell closed, and beneath them his pupils seemed to spasm.

Andi whimpered; Aphrodite's eyes flashed to her face. "That it would be you," she said in a halting whisper, her voice parched, scratching from lack of use. "The thorn in my side is the instrument of my release." Aphrodite shook her head, golden curls tumbled past her waist, her shimmering gown—though torn in places—was perfectly preserved. She moved like a phantom in a dream, the blue light hovering between the floor and her sandaled feet appeared to propel her. "I see you brought me my priestess," she crooned. Moving to stand beside me, she reached out her hand, Andi surrendered the knife to her. "Though you're not Arias, anymore are you? You are also Cara, the daughter of an elemental, and my niece. Oh, this was clever, very clever indeed. And you," her eyes flashed to Drake, standing—sword in hand—tense and watchful by the stairs. There was murder in his eyes when they met hers. "Dragon of death," she sang, her voice was the sound of brilliant, sparkling waves. "Draken, right where I expected to find you, standing guard over your soon to die."

"The light of Aether," said Drake distinctly, through clenched teeth, he pointed the tip of Legux towards my chest. "She holds it in her heart. Kill her and you die."

Aphrodite's face was mere breaths from mine, otherwise I would have missed the slight tightening of her mouth, and the quick way her eyes snapped to Ares. "Athena, she is the only one who knows how to extract the light, well," she smiled in my face, lifting Andi's knife, testing its balance on the edge of her finger. "Athena, and myself of course, I suppose that is what I will have to do." She turned back to me, blue lights twirled and spun. "I will cut it from your living heart," she said, her smile never faltering.

"It was me who brought her to you," said Andi. "Me who touched her deepest memories, me who gave her the dreams that started her on this path, I have done this to wake you, now you must do something for me."

Aphrodite laughed, a high chilling sound, more terrifying than the knife *she* now pressed to my heart. "Must I?" she queried, arching a single brow.

"Yes," said Andi simply. "I poisoned you, before I woke you up. Just a drop on your lips, the dose I used would kill a human in seconds, for you?" she shrugged. "I believe it will put you back to sleep. If you give me what I want, I will give you the antidote. You have about three minutes to decide."

Aphrodite's careful composure snapped like a dry twig, blue flames rushed up her arms, wreathed their way through her hair. Her face and limbs were still for so long, I found myself holding my breath. Eyes wide and glistening as a group of deer caught in headlights, we stared at her.

"Take him then," she finally said. "I know that is what you want."

"A life for a lifetime," said Andi.

"I swear it." The flames in Aphrodite's hair faded to embers, and her serene smile returned. "But will he have you? Ask him, I feel him waking, not much longer now."

"Andi," said Drake brokenly. "Don't do this."

"Draken," she said his name like a curse. "It is already done." Hands pressed against her hot cheeks; Andi knelt beside Ares. "Wake up," she prayed, I saw Ares's hands twitch. "Please my lord, wake up."

"Andi," said Drake again, and there was a deep warning in his voice, she heard him not at all. She kissed Ares's slack lips. Ares opened his mouth, I heard air rush down his lungs.

"He is waking up," murmured Aphrodite, locking her tempestuous gaze to mine. "Let's wait before we start carving," she said. "It will be vastly more satisfying to give Ares back his light, when he is awake to know it," she too twisted the knife. "You must be blood of Athena, otherwise you could not carry it."

"Yes, I am," I said, surprised I could speak at all, the tip of the knife pressed ever deeper—I had to have a sizable cut by now.

"Then you will remember being mine, you will recall the vows you made me. You promised to serve me in life and through death."

I took a shallow breath, careful the rise and fall of my ribs did not jostle the knife. "I remember the promise Arias made to you," I said. "She kept it, she died by your hand in the arms of the man you gave her, she protected him in the mists as is her commission, and I can tell you that she offered many prayers to you in that silence. Her vow is fulfilled—she has been released from it, she is part of me now and we are complete."

"The soul of Arias is mine, consecrated to me before birth, she is from the *house of beauty* and belongs to me, if she is inside of you…" Aphrodite smile grew, and I saw a flash of pearly white teeth. "Well then," she whispered, so close that the blue light she shed, fell on my face, in her eyes I saw the glow dancing on my lips and nose. "If Arias is here," she increased the pressure on the knife. "Then, she is just another thing I will have to cut out."

A dark shadow fell on both of us. I saw Aphrodite stiffen. Squinting through the blue lights, I saw burning amber eyes, the mouth I loved was twisted in rage.

"Enough!" said Drake. "I have never stabbed an enemy in the back—but I fear that the concept of honor is lost on you. Let her go," his voice was a low blast of sound. "Let her go this instant, or I will put you back in your cage, that is Legux you feel tickling your spine."

Fear flashed through Aphrodite's expression. "Do it now," commanded Drake. He took a step forward, Aphrodite arched her back, a small sound escaped her, and she dropped the knife. I shoved past her and threw myself into Drake's waiting arms, sighing deeply as they wrapped me with a tenderness that belied his murderous expression, Legux and his hands created a shield that closed around me—walls constructed of blue flames, and steel flesh.

"I have you now," he breathed, his free, right hand stroking my spine, trying to calm my shaking. Aphrodite stared at us, her expression a jumble of conflicting messages; shock, fear, rage, and dumbfounded astonishment, like she still could not believe any creature would dare harm her yet felt only terror of the man holding me. She recovered herself quickly, and a cold smile slowly wreathed her lips, never reaching her eyes.

"Plot all you wish," said Drake reading her smile, his voice calmer now that he held me. "Scheme until the ages turn to dust, but I am not the boy you faced three thousand years ago, I am the killer you made."

"Oh Draken, do not lay that charge at my door." Aphrodite laughed, and it was a living, colorful sound. "You were always destined to be a killer. Look at those green flames pouring from your hands, and soulless eyes. You are your father's son. Why do you think I gave my most loyal, beautiful priestess? Because I am so fond of you?" She laughed again. "Do remember the first day you saw her? The day she called your name in the arena. Do you think she was there by accident?" Aphrodite spread her arms and motioned to the smoky, blue room. "You think any of this is an accident?"

"You wanted me under your control?" spat Drake. "Your personal henchman."

"A crude description, but yes."

Drake pressed me closer to his chest, I felt his heart beating against mine. "You know what, lady?" he asked sharply. "I simply don't care. I don't care about the curse placed on me at birth—by my own kin, I might add—I don't care about the dark bane, your reasons, plots, and plans. I simply don't care. In my arms is the only thing in the world I want, and she is safe." His lips brushed my temple. "Time has changed many things," he continued. "You will be incredibly surprised, there is much to entertain—I suggest you walk the streets and see what this earth has become. It is a world of many dead gods, and centuries of lost history, the old ways are no more. And if nothing in this wild age is to your liking, perhaps you can track down a butterfly to strip of its wings." Drake released a long-ragged breath. "Do whatever suit your fancy, but please, for the love of all you have ever held dear—leave me and mine alone."

Aphrodite seemed to consider Drake's impassioned words. I was not fooled, her eyes on me were hungry. I took a breath, but the words I meant to speak never came. Andi screamed; my eyes flashed toward the sound. She was on her knees in front of Ares who was sitting up in his coffin like freaking Lazarus. His stiff body twisted, his furious expression the stuff of nightmares. She screamed again when he lifted his head, and turned his arms, his movements wooden and robotic. He grabbed a handful of his dark hair and pulled as if he could somehow rip the grogginess out of his mind.

"Dite?" he rasped, then opened his mouth and tested the ability to use his tongue. "Oh, by the cock of Cronos, I've never had such a hangover!" Shockingly I heard him chuckle. He shook his head, once fiercely, his eyes seemed to rattle in their sockets. "Draken, tell me the party was at least worth it?"

Under my hands, I felt Drake's heart skip a beat. He went very still. "Ares," he rasped, his eyes soaked in sadness. "Give it a moment, it will come back to you." I did not need to be touching him to feel the regret in his voice.

Ares lifted his head, his eyes drifted over me and his grin became a frown. It took some time before I saw it all come rushing back. His eyes widened; his hands twitched at his sides as if he looked for a weapon. "How long?" his broken, tenor voice demanded.

"Three thousand years, my darling," trilled Aphrodite.

Andi leapt to her feet and threw her arms around Ares's waist. "How I've missed you," she sobbed.

Ares barely acknowledged her clinging presence, his eyes were on Draken, in them I saw real remorse. "I didn't mean to," he gasped. "I would not have given her to Aphrodite, that was her war—I would never have betrayed you like that."

"I know," said Drake. "It was Athena."

"Ah!" exclaimed Ares, connecting the puzzle pieces in his mind.

"Stop clinging to him child," said Aphrodite in irritation, her flashing gaze fixed on Andi's adoring face. "The deal is void; I no longer have the priestess."

"What deal?" asked Ares, finally giving the top of Andi's head a brief glance.

"Your spartan princess, offered to trade me a life for a lifetime," she pointed her finger at me. "Her life, for a lifetime with you." Dealing me one last, desperate look, Aphrodite moved the few steps to Andi, then held out her hand. "The antidote please."

"I lied," whispered Androsia, staring only at the face of her god. Aphrodite seemed to consider this, she reached past Andi's head, and stroked her fingers down Ares's jaw. "I missed you my darling, even in my dreams. Get her back for me please," she whispered.

Ares gave her a pained look. "I love you the way the sun loves the moon, the way the earth craves the rain, and I dreamed of you too," sincerity rang in his voice. "Yet, I cannot."

"But you can, my love," Aphrodite leaned closer, her lips caressed the shell of his ear. "She stole your light and carries it in her heart." As each of her words sunk into his mind, I saw the lines his face change. His lips tightened, and black expanded in his eyes, seeping through all the white. *"The light is mine!"* he bellowed. Andi flinched when Ares locked his fingers around her upper arms. She screamed as he threw her away from him. Her silver body sailed through the air, I cringed when she hit the wall. Drake's head swung in the direction of his fallen sister, but he did not run to her, his chest swelled, and his arms tightened around me.

Ares's expression was colder than I have ever seen it. "Give her to me now," he bit out. His knees tensed to spring; his fists clenched tight.

"Never," said Drake. "Never!"

Ares launched himself across the room, hands outstretched like an attacking tiger, black eyes shedding dark light on his barred teeth. His golden armor blazed, the braces on his forearms caught the electric light. I rammed the shock of fear to the back of my mind, and tried to find my way through Andi's enchantment, tried to touch my power. Drake's arms dropped, he swung my body behind his, one hand touching me, he thrust out his sword. Ares used the side of his hand to smash it out of the way. The second his hand connected with the blade, there was a fantastic bang, like bursting dynamite, and the east and west walls of the tomb exploded outward, marble, and solid stone shattered like glass and blew away in the wind. I saw the midnight sky, and the dark water looming at the base of the cliffs we stood on.

Clouds of dust billowed as a giant gust of wind blasted through the room, howling like a banshee, even Aphrodite swayed under its force. The hit was so powerful, the aftershock sent me flying against the wall. My head struck the remaining tiles at my back, and a sound of pain escaped my lips before I could stop it.

Drake heard it, and his eyes flicked to me, only for a second, but it was enough. Ares charged headfirst. Drake caught the blow in his solar plexus, he made a low sound, as his body bowed. Together they crashed to the floor, in a tangle of green fire and thrashing limbs. Drake threw a solid punch, a quick jab that snapped Ares's head back, lifting some of his weight, partially breaking his hold, then his fist returned a second time to smash against Ares's teeth, and a weird moan escaped Ares's lips as the bottom one split. Drake used the war god's moment of shock to wedge his knee between their bodies and shove. Ares faltered, Drake rolled out from beneath him and gained his feet, his body a living shield between me and the enraged Olympian.

"Come on you bastard," bellowed Drake. "No spells or betrayal this time, if you want Cara, you will have to kill me with your bare hands." He threw Legux to the floor and it clattered near my knees. Ares let out a bellow of rage and charged again. With an echoing bang the two men met chest to chest, their arms locked in a battle of sheer power. I saw the veins in Drake's neck bulge.

Andi glared up at her brother fighting her love, with blank incredulity, her expression of horror belonged to one who was caught in a nightmare from which there is no waking. Aphrodite edged slowly away from the gaping hole in the wall, the wind rushing through it tangled her hair. In front of me, Drake's superior force drove Ares to his knees, as he stared down at his opponent, I knew he had never looked more like his father. Green flames obscured the black locks of his hair, flowed from his eyes, pulsed from his punishing hands. Ares kicked his foot, his heel hit Drake's shin, he stumbled, and the hold was broken. As they circled again, I saw a flicker of fear in Ares's eyes, felt it in the whistling air. He could feel it now, the loss of the power I held in my heart—I knew it.

Aphrodite knew it too. Her lips pulled back, blue lights swirled, and she was at my side before I could blink. I dove for Legux, felt my fingers close around the hilt. Her arm flashed out and she caught a fist full of my hair. I kicked blindly and felt the heel of my foot connect with her nose, there was a distinct snapping sound. The hand in my hair tugged until my eyes watered. I fought back, bucking, and screaming, lashing out when I could. Suddenly, I was lifted off the ground and flying towards the visible break between earth and sky. I landed hard, my body skidded over the broken stones, and dashed toward the gaping hole in the wall to the cliff beyond. My hands flailed looking for anything to grab, they came up empty. My feet slid over the edge, then my legs, then my torso. I screamed helplessly as I felt myself starting to fall. My hands made one last ditch attempt to catch hold of anything. My fingers bumped something, and I scrambled madly. I screamed again when I felt a strong hand locked around my wrist, just a second before I went over the edge completely. My body swung in open air. I looked over my shoulder, only to be hit by a wave of intense nausea, the ground seemed miles beneath my kicking, dangling feet.

Slowly, inch by painful inch, my body began to rise. The dragging pressure felt like it would pull my shoulder straight out of its cringing socket, and my eyes watered from the stretching pain. Over the raging wind, I heard Ares howl, the chilling sound was followed by Drake's grunt of pain. The hold on my wrist slipped, my body dropped like an anchor.

Drake roared my name, he caught the tips of my fingers, his short nails dug into my skin and held me up. My head was already over the edge, I could not see the fight I knew he battled, only feel him holding onto me with all his strength. He gave one strong jerk on my arm, my body rose a few inches, and it was enough. I found a foothold in the shattered brick, and swung my other arm up, my finger touched rock and I clung for life. Drake let out another shout of pain. "I'm fine!" I yelled, trying to be heard above the savage, pounding wind. "I've got it!" I finished, praying he would hear me, I knew he did when the iron hold on my wrist slackened, then fell away. I grabbed the stone lip with both hands now, grit my teeth and pulled myself back over the edge. Across the room Drake and Ares were locked together, punching, and shouting like a pair of brawling maniacs.

"Enough," I yelled as the stones scraped over my hip bones. "Take the damn light! I don't want it! I give it willingly."

A wash of blue ghosted over my face. My feet and calves still dangling over the edge, I looked up helplessly to see Aphrodite smiling down on me, the knife in her hands reflecting her glowing red eyes. "Now why would I acquiesce to that? When taking it by force is so much fun," she whispered, then raised the knife above her head.

They say your life flashes before your eyes the moment you die, that all the little things and events which made you, you—come together in culmination of color and pictures in which true understanding is achieved, but in all my times of dying, I only ever saw Drake's face and the horror in his eyes. He threw back his head and roared his fearful rage. Jets of green flame blasted from his pores, and swept through the room like a hurricane, knocking Aphrodite off her feet, and throwing Ares into the remaining wall. Ares recovered quickly, but Drake landed a solid kick to his face and the war god went limp.

On her stomach, Aphrodite lunged for me. I managed to haul myself to my shaking, bleeding knees. I turned my face toward the falling knife. The next three seconds took an eternity to transpire, dumbfounded I watched them happen in the blink of an eye.

I felt a whoosh of air rush past my cheek, my eyes flinched toward the swirl just in time to see Lily hurtling down the stairs, her hands and hair ablaze. The expression of rage on her face was one I had never seen her wear before, and fire spewed from her eyes. The wind pouring through the room and over the cliffs whipped her hair in all directions.

Her eyes met mine, incredibly blue, endlessly piercing, it was clear on her face that she knew what was coming I read the words 'I love you' off her lips, then she went up on her tippy toes in a most dainty fashion and threw herself across the room. I held out my hands to catch her as she collided with my body, trying to brace my knees to keep us from flying backward over the edge. On the moment of contact, I heard Aphrodite's wrathful wail, there was a solid *thunk!* Like a baton meeting flesh—Lily's whole body went rigid. An airy sound of pain gushed from her lips on sigh. I twisted my head in vain to see her face, her head and shoulder blocked my view.

"Lily!?" I tried to shove her hair aside. "Lily?!" she did not answer me, instead covered my body with hers, another sound, a screeching breath escaped her. I heard Aphrodite utter a breathless scream as Lily grabbed her arm and tugged with shocking force. Aphrodite pitched forward, Lily let go of me, her free hand pushed me away. I stumbled, confused. As I recovered my balance, Lily wrapped her arms around Aphrodite's willowy thighs and dragged her ever closer to the edge.

I saw her whole body for the first time since I heard the thud, and my eyes flew instantly to what should not be. In the center of Lily's delicate spine protruded the knife Aphrodite had intended for my heart. My legs turned to water as my vision dimmed to shades of black and white. I know I reached for her when she stood, still holding Aphrodite, and took another step toward the ledge, but I cannot for the life of me remember if I screamed her name. Her eyes met mine, and she blew me a kiss, a second before she and the wildly struggling goddess disappeared behind a flowering burst of Lily's magic fire. I heard her say my name, not a call or demand, simply a goodbye. In each other's arms Lily and Aphrodite fell off the edge into nothing.

Then—I screamed! I threw my body across the remaining distance to the edge; I caught her flaming hand at the last second. Her body swung wildly as mine had, the weight of it dragged me forward, pulled me until my upper body dangled precariously over the cliff. Lily clung to my wrist, one handed as I clung to hers. Her face and eyes now, almost invisible through the roaring flames. Past my burning sister I could see Aphrodite's golden robes, and her hand clutching Lily's ankle. Lily's eyes stared into mine, full of love and goodbyes.

"Don't let go!" my scream tore at my throat. "Don't you dare let go, Lily!"

"Cara," she breathed, her eyes fell closed, then opened in a spinning rush, I could see her consciousness fading, see the river of blood that poured from her back to splash against Aphrodite's thrashing golden head. My body continued its slow screech over the edge, my stomach, hips, and thighs, I knew it was only moments before the restless momentum pulled me over completely, and I did not care. Across the room was a series of low thuds followed by a loud crack. Before the echo of it faded Drake was beside me, his hands on my hips holding me steady. Ares crawled to me on his belly, Legux in his hand, a snarl on his badly bleeding mouth. He placed the tip of the sword against my neck. Drake held me one handed and aimed his fist at Ares's jugular. I heard a loud smack and Ares stumbled back a pace.

Relief surged through me, bringing a renewed blast of strength, and I held onto my sister with all of it. Lily's fingers loosened. "I can't..." I heard her say and screamed back some garbled denial. "Damn it, Drake! Forget about me, I can hold myself. *Let Ares cut me to pieces! Get Lily!*" my voice was raw, ragged. "Let me go! Get Lily, she's falling, I can't hold her." Drake gave Lily a pain filled look, but Ares held a sword to my throat, and he did not move.

"My gods!" I screamed when I saw the decision strike flint in his eyes. "Lily look at me! Don't let go, I can't! I can't. I can't hold her, Drake what are you doing?! HELP HER!" She was sliding, I was barely gripping her fingers now. My heart was locked in vise of pure fear, every inch of me shook, as my muscles tensed and my nerves spasmed. "NO, NO, NO... Lily no, you die I die! You die, I die!"

"I love you, Cara," she said, so very softly, a look of pure peace replaced the flickers of fear remaining in her eyes, and I knew then I would lose her.

"Don't do it Lily! Don't you dare! Don't you dare!"

"It's why I was born," she whispered. "I'm here to save you," she finished.

"You did Lily," I sobbed, choking so hard it was difficult to breathe. "You always save me, please don't go. Please don't!"

Lifting her head, she smiled a beautiful smile, I knew that if I did not tell her everything in my heart right now, I never would.

"I love you so much!" I screamed, my voice no longer resembling human speech, it was the sound of agony rent from a dying soul.

Like I said, it never happened to me, yet in Lily's final moments, her life did flash before my eyes, every golden beautiful inch of it. I tried to hold on, tried so awfully hard, screamed for Drake to save her, kicking at him, knowing she was falling, and I was going mad. I felt every inch of her fingers as they slipped from my grasp. Screaming in helpless denial until my eyes and ears burst and bled, I watched her fall until only the final pulses of her dying fire could be seen against—what had just become—the very blackest of nights.

EPILOGUE

Once upon a place…there were two sisters: daughters of fire and time.

One loved a god, and one loved a past,

Only one of these lives was fated to last.

The girl made of fire found her powers without a try,

The girl of time only ever feared she would die.

And so, the sisters chased destiny's glimmering tale,

One desperate for a forbidden love, and one yearning for what was behind the veil.

When passion and magic found them, for a time they thought all would be peace…

Yet never did they know—in the clutches of black night—one of their beating hearts was fated to cease.

A spell already cast, thirteen days turned the hands of the deadly clock,

'Till finally the sisters came face to face with the ancient gods buried deep in Sulphur rock.

The sister of fire battled the goddess of beauty—ice and flame that night did collide.

And the sister of fire, kissed the sister of time—for it was the time to decide.

To die, to save the sister she loved. For the girl of fire, it was no choice.
So, her life did end on the tip of a cursed knife, and death gave destiny a voice.

Oh, she fell, so far, she fell, her fire wings dying in the air.
Yet, when her body crashed against the waiting rocks,
Her soul was not even there.

Up she flew to the arms of the fire god, from where her magic begun,
And the tale of the phoenix is yet to be told; her song only barely sung.

ABOUT THE AUTHOR

JP Roth is an American Novelist, and owner of Rothic comics, founded in 2012, through which she has produced and published five of her original series. JP Roth lives in California with her husband, son and their adorable Bichon Frise. She spends her days writing fanciful stories, walking on the beach, and attending comic conventions across the globe.

JP Roth was born overseas, and spent her life roaming the world. She still enjoys travelling to exotic locations, but admittedly prefers to stay home, wrapped in a soft fluffy blanket, drinking, tea and penning her next novel.

NOTE FROM THE AUTHOR

Word-of-mouth is crucial for any author to succeed. If you enjoyed *Blood and Shadows*, please leave a review online—anywhere you are able. Even if it's just a sentence or two. It would make all the difference and would be very much appreciated.

    Thanks!
    JP Roth

Thank you so much for reading one of
JP Roth's *Ancient Dreams* novels.
If you enjoyed the experience, please check out our recommended
title for your next great read!

Ancient Dreams

View other Black Rose Writing titles at
www.blackrosewriting.com/books and use promo code
PRINT to receive a **20% discount** when purchasing.

Lightning Source UK Ltd.
Milton Keynes UK
UKHW010712110721
386955UK00001B/15